"COMPLETELY ENGROSSING."

The Boston Globe

"Vivid . . . Enticing . . . [A] passionate multigenerational novel about the endlessly intriguing family of Albert Louis . . . Immensely entertaining."

The New York Times Book Review

"*Tree of Life* is a panoramic novel of twisted lineages, squandering birthrights, family secrets, and the haunting spirits of the dead, densely interwoven with historical details spanning several epochs and political regimes. . . . This is a big book, a grand narrative, an absorbing drama of sweeping and majestic range."

Deborah E. McDowell

"Condé's tree of life is a family tree, with branches spreading from the Caribbean island of Guadeloupe to Panama, San Francisco, Harlem, Paris, London, Haiti and Jamaica. The fruit of this tree is pungent, heady, bittersweet, multicolored, and thick-skinned . . . Condé, acclaimed author of *Segu* and *Children of Segu,* animates her new, potent epic with tremendous emotion, vigor, and vibrancy."

Booklist

"Masterful . . . Condé's vast skills as a storyteller rest in her intensely vivid characterizations, and her gifts for nuance, humor and analysis command the reader's attention and respect."

Publishers W

"Condé's style is spare and elegant. . . . Her story is str and original."

D

"Vivid . . . An impressionistic saga."

Also by Maryse Condé

SEGU

THE CHILDREN OF SEGU

I, TITUBA, BLACK WITCH OF SALEM

TREE
OF LIFE

MARYSE CONDÉ

Translated by
VICTORIA REITER

BALLANTINE BOOKS NEW YORK

For Albert

PART ONE

1

My forebear Albert Louis was not yet the forebear of anyone that day but a handsome Negro of around thirty-two years of age. I say *around*, for, as everyone knows, they paid scant attention to birth certificates in those times. The people of the plantation simply remembered his being born in the year of the terrible hurricane that downed trees and cabins from one end to the other of both Basse- and Grande-Terre and swelled to overflowing the tranquil Sanguine, which usually provided the islanders with just enough water to fill their water jars and wash their clothes nicely white. So that day, Albert Louis, handsome as I said, with his egg-shaped skull, chin marked by a dimple and wide mouth opening onto an infinity of teeth made for devouring the world, looked at the handful of coins he had just received from the overseer, raised his eyes to Heaven as if asking courage of the sun, and thundered:

"It's over! This is the last time I come here to get my pay like a dog!"

Accustomed to his cries, Isidore, the overseer, went on calling out workers' names as if nothing was wrong:

"Louison Fils-Aimé!"

But people sensed that this time Albert was not speaking lightly, merely to make noise as he had often been reproached for doing, that this time there was something firm and definite in his voice they had never heard before. And so their eyes followed him thoughtfully as he circled a pond where lean-flanked donkeys were drinking the muddy water and walked down the path leading to the cabins. Albert's eyes were filled with tears. He would have liked to have ended his service on the Boyer-de-l'Etang plantation with an outburst, to take Isidore by the throat for example and send him rolling in the dust along with his grimy register, his inkpot, and his Sergeant-Major writing pen, to kill him perhaps—and that inner violence frightened him. He could sense that throughout his life he would have no greater enemy. To rid himself of the feeling, he slashed at the grass bordering the path, then bent and picked up three stones, which he sent flying.

People were to remember that day for several reasons. It was the Friday before Palm Sunday. In the cabin where she lived with her eight-year-old son, whose father no one knew and who was seen for the first time one fine morning smiling up from inside a wicker basket, Eudora was entering the passion that would end only with that of Jesus Christ. She would die with Him and be gloriously resurrected with Him, after which the entire village would gather in her hut to celebrate. Thus the departure of my forebear remained linked with the idea that suffering precedes a very great happiness. Several years later, when Albert returned to release his mother, Théodora, from the hell of the plantation, those who had seen him leave were not surprised and loudly declared that they had been expecting him.

Albert did not enter the village. He did not want to bid Théodora good-bye, for he knew he could not bear to see her cry. Once again because of him.

Théodora was always saying that he had made enough tears flow from her eyes to fill the Sanguine and the Bois-Sans-Soif pond, where the cattle were watered.

She was always saying that he had never ceased making her cry since the day he came kicking like a colt from her belly, a viscous caul clasped about his hair and forehead. At the age of four, as a result of tormenting Père Saturnin's donkey, he took a hoof kick full in the chest from the usually sweet-tempered animal that almost left him dead. He would surely have departed this life without opening his eyes again if not for the help of Eudora, who in those days had not yet begun entering into passions but had no equal as a healer. At eight he launched himself from the main limb of a breadfruit tree, for he had taken it into his head to fly. Covered with blood, he was helped to his feet from amid the dry leaves. Only at puberty had he rid himself of that desire to fly, as if he suddenly realized that men's feet are bound to the earth; and then, no doubt to forget, he had wallowed in women's beds to the point of drowning. Young, old, the not-so-young, the not-that-old—he had them all. For a while he was making love at the same time to a mother and her own daughter. For a while to twin sisters. Luckily his seed bore no fruit and his mistresses' bellies remained flat. If not, he might have peopled the region with his bastards. And he was quarrelsome, too, a bad loser, apt to beat his gambling partners with a bottle for the loss of a few sous. Théodora had no other son, although she did have five daughters, already grown and mothers themselves. So she doted on Albert, who was the apple of her eye.

It was four in the afternoon. The sun had not paled since rising. Now it could be felt tiring of its own fury and preparing to withdraw from the sky for a short rest. The trees stood as straight as an I. Not a breath of air. Only the sea toiled, violet and raging at the foot of the gray rocks. A mother hen and her chicks were crossing a path where two dogs made panting love. Which reminded Albert that he had not bid farewell to Létitia, his favorite mistress, she who had abandoned three sons in their father's bare hut for his sake. He considered turning back, since he truly cared for her, then told himself he did not have time. The boat would not wait for him.

Ever since watching his father, Mano, die, his body so emaciated it weighed no more than that of a child, his arms and legs twisted like the branches of a guava tree, Albert had sworn to himself that he would flee the sugarcane.

Ah, he had had a fine funeral, had Mano! People came from as far away as Grosse-Montagne and Belle-Epine to pay their last respects to a man who in spite of everything had left this world with a smile and a song on his lips. It was no small surprise that he left Théodora such a son. God knows where she, who was months in arrears at the local store, had found the money! But the cabin was so lit with candles, it looked like daylight; it was so hot inside that the mourners endlessly sweated and wiped their foreheads. Mano had been laid out on his bed in his black suit. Albert . . . how old was he at the time? . . . around twelve . . . in tears in a corner, stared at his father, and people thought he was feeling sorry for making him angry so often. They did not suspect the boy was making himself a promise. Not to live and die like Mano. To leave the plantation. To settle elsewhere.

For a long while he could not keep the promise he made himself that day and had to hold those desires prisoner in his head and heart. At times he unburdened himself of them in a flood of obscenities, insults, and threats against the villainy of life itself, to the point that people gave him the nickname Hellmouth. The chance to satisfy his yearning had only presented itself several weeks earlier. He had been at a brothel in La Pointe, half drunk on alcohol and lust for a *chabine*, a girl with nearly blond hair, who wanted no part of him. A man named Samuel was there, throwing his money around, paper as well as coins. After a few moments Albert asked: "Say, my man, what're you celebrating?"

Samuel had needed no coaxing, confiding in Albert with drunken good grace. The Americans were afraid of nothing. Now they were tampering with the very structure of the world and cutting continents in two. In Panama they were digging a canal that would allow their ships to sail more quickly from New York to San Francisco on the Pacific coast and were sending out a call to workers from around the world. To this superhuman end they had set up a hiring hall in the very center of La Savane in Fort-de-France. Two thousand seven hundred and eighty men had already left.

"It's a two-year contract, and the pay's ninety cents an hour in their money. Room and board. That gets around, nigger, that gets around!"

Panama, New York, San Francisco—Albert was hearing these words for the first time. At first they floated in his head like a dream. Then the dream wound up solidifying like lava on the flanks of La Soufrière volcano and leaving no room for thought. This Samuel, was he not the finger of destiny pointing in the direction to follow? Albert made inquiries. Once a week the *Mary, Queen of Every Virtue* left La Darse; bedaubed in the Virgin's colors of white and blue with a narrow gold stripe running along her hull and a picture of the Holy Mother on her sails, she made sail for Martinique, reaching it in just a few days. The price of passage was affordable. And besides, what sacrifices must a man not be prepared to make, a man who wants to change his life? From hesitation to cogitation, Albert now found himself on the road to La Pointe, the Boyer-de-l'Etang plantation behind him and a waning sun overhead. A mother's grief followed him, too, for without his being aware of it, Théodora had mysteriously been warned that her boy was about to cross the sea, and long years might pass before she could again clasp his great mahogany-wood trunk of a body close to hers.

It took Albert three days of continuous travel to reach La Pointe, since back then there were no well-kept roads as there are today, and people journeyed on the meat of their feet. He passed through small market towns and villages, through hamlets of hardly more than two or three shacks in the shelter of a *mapou*, a ceiba tree, or a royal poinciana. When they saw this stranger with his face as shut as a prison gate, little boys, naked and with their *kikis* exposed, stopped playing, and in fright rushed behind the tattered skirts of mothers busy combing out their little girls' tousled mops of sun-scorched hair. At night, when Albert allowed himself to rest a while, he bedded down on a pile of leaves, and the nocturnal animals came to sniff him. Dawn was fading when La Pointe appeared, set between land and sea. Bells pealed, then fell into that profound silence from which they would not wake again until Christ was risen. In La Darse men were storming the *Mary, Queen of Every Virtue*, and Albert realized that Samuel had not been the only one spreading the good news. Every Negro on the island who was weary of swinging a machete, driving an oxcart, or sweating in the sugar factories was now hurling himself through that narrow gateway opening onto hope.

"Ninety cents an hour in their money, that gets around!"

No one dared protest as Albert forced his powerful body to the front of the crowd. Thus when the skinny mulatto selling tickets for the crossing decided to stop picking his teeth and do his job, Albert was the first to set foot on the tar- and oil-stained deck. Many men fell into the water that day as they used their fists, elbows, or feet to board the *Mary, Queen of Every Virtue*. A few tried to swim after the ship in hopes that the captain would take pity on their plight and stop to fish them out. One skillful swimmer reached the middle of the Dominique Channel and there, carried off by the heavy swell, disappeared without leaving a trace on the surface of the sea. The most superstitious crossed themselves, seeing it as a bad sign. For his part Albert fell into a leaden sleep that would not end until they were entering the roadstead at Fort-de-France.

The hiring office was made up of four pieces of sheet metal set at right angles to each other under a roof of straw. Two Americans with the flushed faces of well-cared-for children flanked an Indian of some sort, who served as their interpreter. After a quick glance at Albert, they handed him a sheet of paper:

"*Ou sa ékri?* Do you know how to write?"

Albert nodded his head. It was not for nothing that Théodora had bled herself dry to send him to the school in town! He signed proudly with a beautiful paraph, and this is the first document I have of his: his name at the bottom of a two-year contract to dig the Panama Canal. The year was 1904; the month, March; the day, Tuesday. Tuesday, March 14, 1904.

My own existence was still in limbo. That of my mother as well. Even my grandfather Jacob was not yet nesting in his mother's belly.

At the Americans' call, men of every race flocked to dig the Panama Canal, as they had done years earlier to build the thirty-seven miles of railroad that crosses the Isthmus. As they had done at the call of Monsieur de Lesseps's Frenchmen, who had also tried to cut the continents in two, only to become bogged down in mud and failure. Men of every race and every color. White men. Blackmen. Yellow men. Men of mixed race. They died by the tens of thousands, and the *Journal du Canal* coldly enumerates:

"Joshua Steel, of Barbados, identification number 23646, killed in an explosion at Culebra;

"Samuel Thomas, of Montserrat, identification number 456185, killed in an explosion at Satun;

"Joseph Jean-Joseph, of Haiti, identification number 565481, buried alive at Chagres."

Because of his size and strength, my forebear, Albert Louis, was assigned to the explosives team. Over the centuries giant trees had spread with impunity to block the way of sun and moon, and these colassi marked the planned route of the Canal from Colón to Panama City; that is to say, from ocean to ocean. Therefore holes had to be dug into their sides, where the dynamite charge was set. It was covered with mud and the match left exposed. Then, at nightfall, the men launched their attack on those ancient monsters, all the while beseeching God that they, too, might not be swept away with them into death. Man fought tree in a fearsome bodily combat that the latter often won.

In Panama six months of the year were enveloped in the steam of an incessant rain, whereas the other six were inundated with downpours. In that hothouse atmosphere there grew not only the mangrove, the deadly manchineel, and the mahogany tree, but insects carrying virulent fevers, dysentery, and pestilence. Panama is a grave in whose bosom tens of thousands of men have lain themselves down never to rise again.

Colón and Panama City guard the gates of Panama from one ocean to the other. Colón, the youngest, rises on Manzanillo Island, on the northeastern point of Navy Bay. There, through the ages, Atlantic tides shaped organic material, firmly depositing it on a coral bottom to form a rich, spongy soil. Panama City, built several centuries ago to defend Spanish treasure from buccaneer voracity, clings to a rocky point overlooking white-sand beaches and thickets of island growth. No similarity exists between these two guardians. One wallows in the mud. The other holds to the memory of its past splendors.

The one is listless and unwholesome. The other proud and true to its breeding, although fallen, like the Panamanians who are no longer masters of anything after abdicating their suzerainty to the Americans. To the builders of the Canal.

Yes, Panama City is fallen.

Before the railroad route was traced, four to five thousand inhabitants vegetated there. The Creoles and the well-to-do mixed-bloods lived within the ramparts, and the people of color crowded into the outlying district of El Varal, at the edge of the fortified wall. In former convents now beyond repair, palm trees grew deep inside the cloisters, while climbing plants clung to the walls of stone. In the half-abandoned houses, rats, giant spiders, carnivorous ants, and cockroaches led a perpetual dance.

Then California gold and the laying of the railway, even before the digging of the Canal, brought renewed importance and life to that region of the world, without restoring Panama City to its former grandeur.

2

It did not take Albert long to realize that he had changed nothing but the color of his rags.

The Canal Company cared only about its American employees. For them, it was bringing in fortunes from Wall Street. For them, it was draining the coastal area and constructing pleasant bungalows complete with running water. For them, it was planting signs in the ground: RESERVED FOR WHITES, WHITE ONLY.

Like the rest of his countrymen who were putting up mud and straw lean-tos around Gatun, Bohio, Baja Obispo, and Culebra, Albert settled in close by the stagnant waters of the Chagres.

Each morning he went to take the workers' train at Gatun. At night he returned, stretched out on his tomb-cold bed and immediately fell into the salutary death of sleep. No one ever saw him buy anything at the store. He ate the fish he caught himself and the plantains that he grew behind his hut. He spent no more of his time with the men from Guadeloupe or Martinique than he did with Jamaicans or men from Trinidad; it was as if the only language he knew was the one he had forged for himself in the silence of his being. Every Saturday he put aside his work clothes and, donning a Panama hat, left for Colón. There he waited in line outside a Front Street brothel. This was his sole expenditure, and people tried to estimate the amount of his savings.

"Ninety cents an hour! That gets around, nigger!"

This lasted for almost a year.

One day as he was returning from washing his ragged clothing in the Chagres, Albert passed a girl carrying a pail of water balanced on her head. He walked on without stopping or greeting her when splash, splash, the water spilled to the ground and she burst out laughing. Astounded, Albert looked at her, and all that youth and beauty stunned him. He stammered:

"What's your name?"

The girl did not stop laughing: "What about you? You know what they call you? Modonga, like those slaves they tell about who hardly ever say a word, or *Soubarou*, wild man."

"Modonga or *Soubarou*?" Albert repeated, then exploded into laughter in turn. "Modonga or *Soubarou*?"

Accustomed to the graceless whores and strong odors of Front Street, his senses were intoxicated by the girl. No longer laughing, he repeated:

"Tell me, what's your name?"

But the girl ran down the path without answering, her skirt raised to reveal a dancer's tapered legs.

From that day on Albert began losing sleep. He could no longer eat or drink. Saturday found him in his hut, his penis proper between his thighs. At last he could take no more and went to knock at his neighbors' door, neighbors he had not said a word to that entire year.

"Pardon me for bothering you! Whose girl is that, about sixteen or so, black but not black-black. Beauty marks covering her right cheek, and eyes that promise Paradise."

The answer was not long in coming.

"You're talking about Liza, Ambrosius Seewall's daughter. You know, that Jamaican who's always rambling on about gold miners!"

One Sunday morning Albert ironed and donned his best clothes, rubbed his neck with bay rum, and took the path to Ambrosius Seewall's hut.

Liza was in the garden combing out the hair of one of her younger sisters when she saw him suddenly appear beside the calabash tree. Dropping her hairpins and comb, she ran to huddle behind her mother's skirts. All her impudence had fled. She was no longer anything but a little girl, frightened by a man's desire.

Albert was granted permission to return each day after work, and soon he was seen hurrying down the muddy road the moment the train stopped. There was much gossip when Old Seewall gave his daughter to a man from Guadeloupe. Those people don't even speak English, but they still think they're better than everybody else!

However, what was supremely irritating was the new couple's obvious happiness.

Liza sang from morning to night. She started while she was preparing the lunch her man would take to work and went on until the moment she lit the fire for his dinner. When Albert returned, it was all laughter, small cries, two birds happily chirping. No, no one has a right to that much happiness! People were waiting for the split, for the breakup. People were waiting for Albert to find his way again to the brothel in Colón or, better, to cast his eye on another woman of the village. They were waiting for him to fill himself with drink and batter Liza's pretty face. None of that! And Liza was still singing!

After a few months people noticed her belly growing rounder and they understood that the hut would shortly have a third occupant. It was then that Albert himself began to sing! Word of honor!

Before getting off the train and plunging into the

forest's spongy underbelly, as foremen armed with automatic rifles led the way, he sang! Returning at night, a burnt odor floating about him, he sang! Soon he set about clearing a space in the forest. He began to build not another hut but a bungalow modeled on those of the Canal's American workers. Making no effort to help, the people watched him saw planks, plane them, and fit them together. When the bungalow had taken shape, he painted it white and placed a mahogany-wood rocking chair he had purchased in Colón in the center of the veranda. From then on Liza sat there in the unbearably hot hours of the afternoon whenever the desire for a short nap overcame her.

Pregnant, Liza resembled a supple passionflower vine heavy with the promise of fruit. A new awkwardness tempered her customarily lightning-quick gestures. At times she went to meet her man along the path, her small feet sinking clumsily into the mire and leaving a whimsical trail. Oh, yes! Liza was beautiful in those early days of her pregnancy!

The women always gave birth in their huts with the help of some experienced old crone. If they were not carried off by malaria, dysentery, or yaws, their babies came safely. But now wouldn't Albert take it into his head that Liza should give birth in the hospital at Ancon, under the care of American doctors! What did he think his wife was going to bring into the world? A white baby, perhaps? It's not good to forget what color you are. It was like that cradle he bought from a Chinaman in Colón and covered with a square of netting, as the Americans recommended be done. Foolishness! Foolishness and pretension, all of it!

Old Seewall was not so old, but they called him that because he had arrived in the time of France's Compagnie Universelle du Canal Interocéanique. After Monsieur de Lesseps's departure he was unable to find a way of returning home but had managed somehow to support himself until the Americans took over the operation. Old Seewall shifted his pipe to the corner of his mouth and began:

"Yerba Buena, that's what they named it. You know what that mean? Good Grass, that's what it mean! Then the Americans, they come with their rifles and raise their flag, and they're the ones find the gold that the Spanish before them couldn't fucking find. So the ships begin to piling up in the bay, and the riders to roaming the roads. Yankees, Californians, Chileans, Kanakas from the island of Hawaii, Chinese, Malays, hordes of adventurers headed for the foothills of the Sierra Nevada. All you had to do was dig a knife in the ground, mon, and there was gold in your hands."

From time to time Albert broke in:

"Gold? You say, gold?"

Old Seewall nodded his head.

"I'm saying, gold. Gold dust. Or nuggets, some of them big as a fist. You see, after Monsieur de Lesseps's Frenchmen abandoned us here like dogs, I wanted to leave too. I earned my living carrying baggage for Americans embarking at Panama City, and there was more than one time I almost went with them. But . . ."

"But what?"

"I was afraid. It seems they keep Negroes in slavery in America. Of course they don't put them to planting cane, but cotton. Acres and acres of cotton to pick and then load into small baskets you carry on your back. They say it's even worse than the cane."

Albert shrugged his shoulders.

"Come on! Slavery, that's old history. My mother didn't even go through it. You Negroes, you're always chewing over the past. When there's no more juice in the cane, spit it out!"

"Old history, old history! It's not old history to the Americans, and a Negro's still a slave to them. That's why I didn't go, and it wasn't easy, because it was like it was calling me. It . . . !"

He started rambling again: "After Yerba Buena it became San Francisco, and everyone who saw it fell in love with it. It sits deep inside its bay, and the English and Spanish ships sailed past hundreds and hundreds of times before they found the entrance. Like a virgin hiding her little honeypot. Then, like in every story of this kind, some battle-scarred old soldiers wound up lifting her skirt."

In the beginning Albert listened to Old Seewall as to a storyteller. He was inventive, clever at weaving together the comic and the fantastic. Like Pè Théotime, for example, who lived near Théodora's hut:

"One night as Tertulien was heading home, filled with rum and having won his old friend Gernival's pay at dice (he was still laughing about it, alone there in the dark), he saw a calabash tree and under it, a little boy no bigger than three stones piled one atop the other who was crying, crying his heart out:

" 'Lost, lost! I can't find the way to my mother's cabin!'

"Touched, Tertulien drew near: 'Don't cry, little bit o' nigger. Tell me your name.'

" 'My name? Ti-Sapoti!' "

And that was the start of the extraordinary adventure stories the young Albert listened to, excitement stirring sweetly in his heart!

Yes, at first Old Seewall's stories were nothing more than that! Tall tales to ease the harshness of life. Then ideas began sprouting in Albert's head. Was this not, again, the mysterious voice of destiny urging him back onto the road? His son would soon be born (for it was a boy, he knew that with every bit of expectation inside him, and feeling her daughter's belly, Mama Seewall had also confirmed it). Yes, his son was about to be born, and here he was, stranded on this riverbank, risking death at every turn! In vain had he saved cent by cent. Even if he did renew his work contract over and over again, he would never see an end to his troubles. One day he would founder like a broken animal. He would leave behind a young wife with no man, a child with no daddy, and two pairs of eyes to weep. Was it for this he had fled the Boyer-de-l'Etang plantation?

So he began to press Old Seewall with questions:

"You say all you have to do is dig in the ground with your knife?"

"Not dig, nigger! Scratch! You just scratch with the point of your knife. And the gold is there, yellow under the topsoil. . . . "

Liza didn't like Albert wasting his time listening to her father's nonsense. She had heard enough of it, she and her mother and sisters! Whenever they went to bed, stomachs full of wind and gurgling like an air chamber, they could hear their father braying: "Gold, gold!"

And their mother, at the end of her patience, would slap them to make them go to sleep.

So every time Albert headed for Old Seewall's hut

instead of remaining by her side to read and reread the *Journal du Canal* with its obituary notices, she fell into a fury. If he stayed more than a quarter of an hour, she gave him a tongue-lashing, and Albert, no longer Hellmouth, groveled at her feet.

How a woman changes a man!

Albert never dared to stand up to Liza, to make her angry. He feared she might give birth to a son who was deformed, like the one Eugenia Charles had finally pushed from her belly after heavy labor and that had not lasted more than three days in this world, thank God. All of Albert's thoughts revolved around his baby. At times he was surprised to find himself already loving it more than he loved his Liza. Was it possible? Is it natural for the baby to drive the mother from the father's heart?

In the fifth month of pregnancy, however, everything changed! Liza began to waste away. No more winged songs now, but moans, groans. Sweats. Fainting spells. Pushing her huge bale of a belly before her, she soon aroused pity. Her complexion took on the color of an overripe guava. Her eyes grew too big for her face. At night when Albert took her in his arms, she, usually so hungry for love, pushed him away and in a tired little voice begged him to leave her in peace.

Mama Beah, who had seen such things before, offered to treat her with herbs, but Albert lost his temper:

"You niggers, still sticking to your leaves and roots! Your plasters and poultices! That's why the white man walks all over you. Haven't you seen the Americans' doctors?"

Then he asked the foreman for a few days off, which it took him no little trouble to obtain. He borrowed a donkey from his father-in-law, who owned a pair of them, placed his woebegone wife on its back between two baskets of victuals, and in the bluish light of dawn took to the road. Four days and four nights! It takes four days and four nights to go from Gatun to the gates of Panama City, where the Americans' white stone hospital stands. Four days and four nights for a man who is rested and whose legs do what they are told. Four days and four nights during which he must avoid the nocturnal snares of a forest where ferocious animals scream as they hunt each other, and where he must protect himself from the bite of bloodsucking insects attracted by his scent. In places he must follow the rail line running alongside the slow waters of the Chagres; but when it crosses over the river on huge pinewood billets and the train suddenly appears, its mouth agape, he must flatten himself against the parapets in order not to be eaten alive.

How I picture Albert and Liza's agony!

She can barely hold her weary head erect, and it falls forward onto her chest above her jutting belly. She can no longer take food, and Albert squeezes oranges, letting the juice run drop by drop between her ashy lips. At night she whimpers like a baby, and mad with grief, he holds her tightly in his arms!

"Be brave, my sweet girl. Soon we'll be back again, and the sunshine of our child will light our days. . . . "

And one morning they reached the hospital at Ancon.

What happened there? Albert never spoke of it, and one may suppose what one will.

Was she refused entry to the hospital built for the white men working on the Canal?

Was Liza admitted only after endless quibbling, thereby causing irreversible damage to her state of health?

Was she admitted routinely, and did she lose her life despite the doctors' efforts?

The fact remains that Old Seawall, who had watched

every day for the couple to return, three weeks later saw
a zombie, face hidden behind a beard, stagger past his hut
holding against its heart a tiny bundle wrapped in paper
and scraps of jute. The zombie entered its bungalow and
slammed the door shut behind it. Then the small crowd
that had immediately begun following it heard a howl rise
that was enough to shiver the soul and freeze the blood
in one's veins.

Albert moaned for threé days and nights, and the
village knew no sleep.

At the end of the third night Liza's mother took her
husband's ax and came to break down the bungalow
door. She found Albert stretched out on the mahogany-
wood bed he had bought for Liza, the bundle still tied and
resting on his chest. Pulling away the rags in which it lay
wrapped, she found a face no larger than a fist listening
intently to the father's grief. Tears filled her eyes, and she
shook Albert:

"I know what you're feeling. Myself, when I think
my Liza has crossed over to the other side, I want to drop
everything and go after her! But you have to live. For his
sake!"

Albert straightened and sat up on the bed. His hair
had gone completely white and now crowned the
ravaged face of an old man. He burst out weeping:

"She's dead, she's dead."

Liza's mother gathered him in her arms as if he were
another heavier, more heartbroken nursling and whispered:

"She's not dead because he's here. . . . What did you
name him?"

Albert obviously had never considered the matter. He
stammered: "Albert."

The child was fed a gruel made from blue corn his

father bought from the San Blas Indians. No one had ever dreamed that a man could take care of a newborn. People flocked in astonishment to the veranda to watch Albert feed his son with a spoon. That Albert did not go back to work also shocked them. Did he think the Americans were going to wait for him, even as the lines grew longer in front of the hiring halls? And anyway, was Albert the first man to lose a woman? Did he know how many children's mothers lay in the silt of the Chagres? Panama was nothing but a huge graveyard beneath the sun and rain, the sun and moon.

Finally Albert went back to work.

Still like a zombie. He who was in earlier days so daring, the first to hurl himself into battle against the huge trees, now wove through the forest, torch in hand, feet slogging through the mud. No doubt they would have fired him if his team foreman had not himself been a Negro, a man named Jacob. In any case, a black man. A black American! Try figuring that one out! Gigantic, nearly six and a half feet tall, square-shaped, almost two hundred and twenty pounds, but black. Speaking with a nasal twang, his finger on the trigger of an automatic rifle. But black.

On the whole the Jamaicans had never understood how there could be black men among the Americans, and neither could the men from Martinique and Guadeloupe comprehend it.

Albert and Old Seewall laughed at their questions: "What a bunch of ignorant . . . aren't you dumb! The same ships that stopped at the islands where we come from to sell your African ancestors went on to America, where they come from, and other white men bought them.

"So, they're your brothers!"

Unconvinced, the people shook their heads: "Our brothers? Our brothers? You see the machine gun those niggers carry around? They're no brothers!"

And yet this Jacob was a brother to Albert, and became the mysterious voice of destiny pointing out the new road to be traveled.

It was around that year, the year 1906, that the people of the Boyer-de-l'Etang plantation saw Albert return holding a sickly child in his arms, a child exhibiting that fragility caused by a lack of mother's milk.

Albert was wearing a black serge suit and black patent-leather boots, and his tousled white hair foamed forth from under a Panama hat. It was amazing that he had aged so much in so short a time, a man who was barely thirty-four, thirty-five years old. Yet people were too dazzled by his magnificent clothing to pay much attention to his face. Several more observant minds noted the bitter set of his mouth, the dullness of those eyes veiled with the mournful haze of sorrow. But for the most part, the majority of the people were just trying to calculate how much he had saved. In all that time what a pile of money he must have accumulated!

Suspicion turned to certainty when it became known that Théodora was leaving the plantation to settle in La Pointe, in a one-story, four-room house near the refitting dock, with its water supply in the courtyard above a basin of stone.

Stories began to circulate.

It was said that Albert had paid for the house in cash, with green American dollars. That he had given Théodora more money than she had ever seen in the whole of her unlucky life, money she kept stacked in a Caribbean basket she had fearfully hidden beneath her mattress. That he had promised to send her much more on condition that she do nothing but take care of his son.

And so from one day to the next Théodora's world changed from something familiar to something she'd never known before. She left behind the village where she had slaved for forty-six years, where her children were born, where her Mano slept beneath the earth in a small grave whose edges were outlined in the pink and ochre shells of the *carrucho* conch. She wept for a long while. However, no sooner had she arrived at her low, trim house in La Pointe than she imprisoned her heretofore carefree toes in shoes and ordered to be made for her a dozen of the Creole dresses known as *matadors*. Most notably, she set herself to speaking French, a language that had always made her mouth ache. And thus are our bourgeoisie born!

3

Théodora held her own son's first son on her knee, the frail nursling who symbolized her hopes. She barely listened to Albert, who sat stammering on the other side of the oilcloth-covered table that held a bottle of Féneteau Les Grappes Blanches rum and a carefully rinsed glass:

"You never know why you start in loving a woman like you never loved one before. Her skin isn't any lighter, she isn't any slimmer, or any prettier. But even so, when you're with her, you're like an old-time slave before his master. Ready to dance to take her mind off her troubles. Ready to hang your head and beg her pardon. It all started because she made fun of me: 'You know what they call you? Modonga or *Soubarou!*' No woman ever made fun of me. Bitches at my feet, that's what they were. So I disrespected them. Liza, Liza was different. She was, she was . . . "

"Take a drink of rum! It'll do you good."

"I went down to the Chinaman's store in Colón and bought her a bed, a rocking chair, a round pedestal table, trunks to hold her things. And people made fun of me: 'Nigger, where are you going with that?' I wanted to take her far from Gatun. Gatun is mud, mud and affliction, mud and sickness. I heard it said the American white men were digging the Canal—a thing the French white men couldn't do—to show that they're the greatest of all the whites. But let me tell you, it's our hands, our gorilla paws they call them, that're doing the work. Doing the dig-

25

ging. Doing the cutting. Doing the hauling. Putting it together piece by piece. Mama, I met Negroes there who talk English, who talk Portuguese, Spanish, who talk Dutch! But the common language, Mama, is poverty! So, I wanted to take her far from Gatun, here maybe, and give her her own house on the hill. When I said things like that, she'd make fun of me—she'd make fun of me! 'Get those ideas out of your head! Who do you think you are? You forgetting what color you are?' And now it's too late!''

Once again his sobbing interrupted Théodora's smug adoration of her son's first son.

"Take a drink, I said," she repeated impatiently.

It's strange, but Albert's sorrow did not touch her. Its cause was a woman she had not known. It even irritated her to hear her son, always so hard on others, moaning like a weakling!

Albert filled a glass with enough rum to revive three fighting cocks, then pressed his cheek flat against the table.

"Mama, my boy is the apple of my eye. I want him to go to the best school, to have the most beautiful clothes, to wear patent-leather shoes on his feet and speak French-French like a white man—you hear me?"

Théodora nodded, and Albert began snoring, his mouth open.

That night little Albert slept pressed against his grandmother's ample side. And so he did not hear the growling of the great wind as it rushed over the sea. He did not hear the galloping hoofbeats of the Beast at midnight, thirsting to suck children's blood. He who had always slept unprotected from nightmares by his father's encompassing sharp and gloomy odor, now knew his first night of peaceful sleep.

Looking thirty-three years younger, Théodora felt as she had back in the days when she was carrying the fetus that not even four months gone had pummeled the walls of her belly with its head and feet. She had taken that violence as an omen that she was at last to have the son who would avenge her for all the squalor of life. It had not turned out that way. Albert had done nothing but pierce her already aching heart with a thousand knives. But now she was sure of it! The nursling he had brought her would be her redemption.

As for Albert, when the alcohol fumes dissipated, he reached that quiet place where dreams are ageless. He believed himself back in the time of childhood, when he was not yet trying to drown disillusion and rancor in the bodies of women, when he had faith in life as a succession of wondrous marvels.

4

"The whole city has been destroyed by an earthquake and a fire!"

"Who told you that nonsense?"

"It's not nonsense. I read it in black and white in the newspaper, and that's all the tourists talk about. San Francisco is nothing but a pile of ruins."

Albert was speechless. He felt as if he was losing his Liza a second time, since it had seemed to him that both the woman and the city had been sired by Old Seewall. Sperm for the one, creative imagination for the other!

He stammered: "What will we do with our lives?"

Jacob shrugged: "That story of yours doesn't hold water anyway. There's no more gold in California. The bosom of the Mother Lode's as withered and dried up as an old hag's; no way now for a nigger just to bend down and make his fortune."

Eyes clouded by disillusion, Albert repeated: "What do we do with our lives? What do we dream about to forget the mosquitoes sucking our blood, the worms and caterpillars gnawing us down to the bone, and the sun and the rain bleaching us out like cloth?"

Jacob did not answer, for he had nothing to offer instead and in place of the defunct woman-city.

Jacob was born far away from the Boyer-de-l'Etang plantation, in a forest in Massachusetts, three years after Albert's head had slipped down between Théodora's tortured thighs while she prayed to God: "Let it be a boy! A boy!" His first cry had risen from beneath a tree where his mother, Cecilia, heading north to flee Southern persecutions and unable to carry him any farther, had lain herself down on a bed of pine needles. Unlike Albert, Jacob had not been a ruffian and a loudmouth but a good boy who studied hard at school. He was one of the few blacks the Americans employed on the Canal, paying him a salary lower than they gave the whites; but it was a tidy sum nonetheless in the eyes of Albert, who still had to sweat for his ninety cents an hour.

That friendship between Albert and Jacob, between an American and a man from Guadeloupe, between a foreman and a simple worker, was born unexpectedly the day that Albert walked straight into the area of a forest fire, his eyes blinded by the pain of losing his wife. Setting down his machine gun, Jacob had rushed forward to save him:

"Hey, man, you looking to die or what?"

That's how it happened! An American foreman, even if he is black, and a dynamite worker from Guadeloupe are not supposed to become friends. And yet the miracle happened, and the two men grew inseparable.

The workday over, Jacob was as talkative as Old Seewall. A mill, a sackful of words! Never-ending stories of Louisiana, of the bayous, of dogs hunting down fugitive slaves dripping water and terror. He strutted and sang, accompanying himself on a banjo:

"Run, nigger, run, the patter-roller git you.
Run, nigger, run, yuh better git a-way!
Run, nigger, run, don't let 'em take you.
Run, nigger, run, it's al-mos', al-mos' day."

Albert sighed. "Oh, yes, you did have a life as hard as ours at home. Maybe even harder! But that's not all America is. Listen . . . "

And he began to recite Old Seewall's rubbish, which had never stopped running around inside his head:

"After Yerba Buena it became San Francisco, and a prettier city there never was. Sitting deep inside the bay, guarded by the Golden Gate. The Golden Gate! You hear that, man? It seems there's no blacks or whites there. A nigger can get rich just scratching the earth with the point of his knife. He comes there butt-naked in his rags. He leaves drawn by horses!"

Jacob shrugged. "All that's just tall tales! California's no good for the black man. It's the North . . . "

Returning to Panama from Guadeloupe where he had entrusted his son to his mother's care, Albert had rid his life of all the comforts introduced into it in Liza's time. He had sold his furniture back to the Chinaman in Colón and now slept rolled up in an old Indian blanket on the filthy floor. The house had become a paradise for rodents, insects, and parasitic plants. A banana tree that had thrust its way through the pickets of the veranda flaunted its violet flowers and dwarf fruit. When the vegetation grew so thick he could no longer push his way through the garden, Albert cut it, whack, whack, with great sweeps of his machete. Only on weekends did he take time off to have some fun with his friend Jacob. Early on Saturday morning Jacob would show up on the streets of the village and, American though he might be, wallow in the filth with Albert. He would eat *migans* mush straight from a *coui*, a calabash cut in half for use as a kitchen utensil, then get drunk on rum and brandy and covered with vomit settle himself in a tattered hammock to snore. In the beginning, Albert had done the visiting, going down to Cristobal, the tidy, flowered suburb where Jacob was lodged a healthy distance from his countrymen. But the whites quickly made it clear that they would not tolerate the presence of this raggedy individual.

For four years Albert lived in the mud on the outskirts of Gatun, working like an animal, saving cent by cent.

One morning, without saying a word to anyone, he disappeared. For is there any need to say that notwithstanding his interminable conversations with Jacob he had gone back to being the Modonga, the *Soubarou* he had been before meeting Liza? At first people told themselves that he had gone to see his mother and son in Guadeloupe. But the weeks passed, then the months . . . and Albert did not return. Nature took full possession of his bungalow, planting a kapok tree at the entrance and mango trees at the windows, while a giant bougainvillea entwined itself around the columns of the veranda.

Old Seewall and his wife were furious and shouted their anger to anyone who would listen. Really, Albert was a bad nigger, a heartless nigger! Hadn't Mother Seewall been the first to care for his nursling, the fruit of her own daughter's belly! And this is how he repaid them! One Sunday morning a bedraggled man appeared in the center of the village and beat his clenched fists on the Seewalls' door. The night before, in Colón, he had run across Albert and Jacob. Get ready for a shock: The two of them had gone into business and were making money hand over fist! A business? What business? The undertaking business! With the number of dead adding up each day in Colón from work accidents, epidemics, and delirium tremens, nothing could be more profitable! The year before, cholera alone had led to twenty thousand coffins being built. . . .

From then on everyone who went down to Colón

made a side trip to see Albert and Jacob's shop, not far from the railway terminus. To tell the truth, it didn't look like much, a sort of passageway where the coffins were piled, some roughly built, others a bit more ornate with gilded handles. Outside the door a pair of horses, all skin and bone, were hitched to a cart; when they were not transporting a body to its last resting-place, they stood defecating droppings as dark and melancholy as the street. The business had a third partner named Manuel, a Panamanian half-breed with the look of a man capable of murdering both his parents. And there was a woman, too, called Centinela, probably an escapee from some brothel, who kept house one rickety story above the undertaking parlor (if that is not too pretentious a word).

That Albert had turned himself into a transporter of stiffs was profoundly shocking. The job is an unhealthy one. The spirits of the dead cling to those who handle their bodies. Such people sire nothing but monsters, and their business is branded by an acid odor that seeps from rotting flesh.

As if to make Albert and his associates happy and to add to their profits, a new epidemic broke out in Colón. People died in their sleep after emitting nauseating, violet-colored bile from every orifice. Corpses piled up in the morgues, and the Americans hired teams of rubber-gloved cremators. Night and day the long purple smoke rose from the funeral pyres and stormed the sky.

Truly Albert, Jacob, and Manuel were making money!

It was then that a Jamaican named Marcus Garvey came to visit his unhappy countrymen, who were using up their lives digging the Canal. The man had left his own country at an early age and had wandered around Latin America. He had already caused trouble for himself in

Costa Rica, where he violently denounced the state in which his brothers were kept on the plantations. It was said that his words flowed like a torrent of lava rushing down the sides of a volcano. It was rumored that after his lengthy speeches those who had bowed their heads under the sad weight of their lives raised them up and suddenly felt courageous enough for the adventure of a revolt.

Joining a crowd of workers, Albert traveled to Bahia Soldado to hear him.

Black and with the short legs of a fighting bull, Marcus Garvey jumped up on a platform and began to speak. And his words transfigured the present as they built a future.

"One day, one day, the black race will astonish the world. . . . "

Carried away, Albert followed Marcus Garvey to Frijoles, Gorgones, Baja Obispo, Paraiso, to every place where he addressed his brothers—without, however, ever attempting to speak to him. In warehouses or under sheds fiercely guarded by the Canal Zone police with their machine guns from the very first pointed at his seditious belly, Marcus Garvey spoke words no one had ever heard before he came. Justice. Liberty. Albert subscribed to *La Prensa*, the paper Garvey was publishing as well as he could. On Saturdays, declining Jacob's binges, he absorbed himself in his reading. Once, he went to loiter near Garvey's modest office, where wrinkled copies of *Africa Times* and *Orient Review* were sold, and after much hesitation finally went in. Unfortunately Garvey himself was not there, and one of his lieutenants sold Albert a pamphlet for a dollar.

Yet Marcus Garvey could not fail to notice the large black Negro with the white mane, silent and somber, dressed with an elegance in sharp contrast to the Canal

workers' mud-covered appearance. For Albert was beginning to display that dandified air that so struck everyone who came in contact with him. When Garvey asked
about him, his entourage replied that he was a man from
Guadeloupe, the partner of an American exploiter who
was making his fortune from sickness and death. So Marcus Garvey completely lost interest in him, and the conversation that might have changed my forebear's fate
never took place.

Having set out to attract the British consul's attention
to the terrible conditions the West Indians had to work
under, Marcus Garvey was finally expelled from Panama.
Albert followed at a distance in the small sad group that
accompanied him to the ship, after which he stopped at
the Chinaman's, bought a very fine brush, some ink, and
a roll of paper. Then Jacob and Manuel saw him hurry
across to the undertaker's shop and shut himself up in his
room on the second floor. An hour later he called Jacob
upstairs and had him decipher the poster he had just put
up on the wall: "I shall teach the Black Man to see beauty
in himself."

Jacob held his sides with laughter, he who saw nothing but ugliness and degradation around him!

"Go on, man! Why don't you come have a drink
with me. The stiff I just dropped in his last resting-place—
his feet stank!" A frown pressing two lines across his
forehead, Albert went along with him and spent the night
silently emptying glass after glass.

From that day on my forebear, Albert, was a different
man. He stopped drinking and getting drunk, and
brushed off Jacob, who was always ready for a drink. He
improved his English and Spanish to such a point that
people began taking him for a Jamaican or a Panamanian.

He was even known to open up a book on mathematics or the natural sciences. . . .

He tried to learn what had happened to Marcus Garvey. However, as he had broken off all contact with the Jamaican community, he never managed to do so. So at night, when his business with the dead was over, he would cross-examine Jacob:

"Where do you think he could be?"

Someone told Albert that Marcus Garvey was now in Harlem, in the United States, stirring up crowds of blacks. Pursing his lips, Jacob declared that hardly believable:

"A Jamaican? In Harlem?"

From that time on Albert began to display the greatest of hatreds for whites. He who had never paid much attention to Jacob's stories now began prodding him with questions:

"Tell! Tell!"

When Jacob finished, Albert would explain that the whites afflicted not only the black race but the yellow race of Asia and the Indian race as well. He made Jacob gag, inundating him with detailed descriptions of how the Chinese who had come to build the railroad several years earlier took their own lives:

"Some strangled themselves with their pigtails. Others knotted them around their necks and hung themselves from trees. There were some, too, who threw themselves into the Chagres, their pockets filled with stones so they would sink straight down. There were some who split their bellies open with their machetes and others who paid Malays to kill them."

Jacob did not like whites any better than Albert did, but he had learned to live with them, a necessary evil, and he saw all that as sheer madness. When Albert took it into his head to reserve the services of the undertaking parlor for nonwhites, Jacob finally became angry.

"Oh, no. You're ruining the business! And anyway, a stiff's got no color."

Albert had taken to going to brothels again, since the body has its own laws that all the grieving love in the world cannot repeal. The establishment he preferred dated back to the time of Monsieur de Lesseps. There one made love in French, for its moth-eaten red velvet sheltered whores from Brest. While not especially pretty and fairly well past their prime, the women were skilled at giving pleasure; they knew how to bind up the wounds of the heart for all those men who missed a mother's breast, or a wife's.

One of them, Marthe, had never hidden her fondness for Albert. After making him come, she liked to listen to him dream. To dream about his childhood.

"You see, the earth seemed too crude and drab to me. I'd make my eyes water staring up at the sun in the sky, and I'd say to myself: 'It must be so fine up there! No rich white man, no overseer, no drunk of a father.' One day I made myself wings from the leaves of a coconut palm and launched myself from a kapok tree. Bang, down to the ground! Nearly drowned in my own blood."

About his Liza.

"That woman, she was as sweet as a *tourment d'amour*, the coconut pastry they make in my country. Every part of her would melt, from her mouth to the tip of her toes. I couldn't get enough of her. I'd say to her: 'Flower of my life, are you weary?' She'd laugh; she laughed all the time—oh! so pretty. A bird singing in a tree. 'Come on,' she would say, 'Give me everything you got. I'll take it.'"

About San Francisco.

"I know I'll never get there. Where would I find the money? But I have to tell myself it exists, that it lies deep inside its bay guarded by the Golden Gate. Open, but inaccessible, like a princess on a purple velvet couch. It's thanks to that I can stand Colón, Chagres, Gatun . . . all these places of sorrow and perdition. See, I came here to dig gold and found nothing but the mangrove."

But then wouldn't it happen that one night when she invited him upstairs in her usual way, Albert assaulted her, beating the daylights out of her and shouting:

"Devil! You belong to the race of devils! But we'll be rid of you someday!"

A great to-do was made about the matter.

The English-language *Star & Herald* and the Spanish-language *La Estrella de Panamà*, two of the largest newspapers of the time, printed letters about the affair from many of their readers. One correspondent even called upon the American consul to rid Panama of the West Indian Negroes who were infesting it, and protested against the West Indian whores who had gone into competition with honorable European ladies (*sic*).

However, neither the American nor the Panamanian administration appeared to react quickly enough, and one night some men attacked Albert, leaving him unable to move on the dirty bed of empty bottles that clogged the mud streets of Colón. Somehow Albert managed to avoid being taken to the hospital. He was cared for at home by Jacob, Manuel, and Centinela, who wept upon seeing the state he was in. Since he seemed to be on the verge of death, Centinela went to the San Blas Indians at Limon Bay and brought back armloads of leaves, roots, and dried plants from which she concocted potions, unguents, and poultices.

Four months went by, then Albert returned to the shop, where business was prospering again, thanks to an epidemic of smallpox. The force of the blows had broken his right leg in three places. It had healed badly, and he had to lean on a cane. Several scars now crisscrossed his face; yet far from rendering him frightening, they added to his air of vulnerability. Throughout his life Albert would suffer pain from the aftereffects of his wounds and fractures. As the decoctions of passionflower root had done him the greatest good, flushing the bad humors from his blood, he was careful to plant some wherever he lived. The passionflower displays a mauve and lightly perfumed bloom that has little medicinal value. It is the branches and above all the roots that do the healing.

5

Meanwhile in La Pointe, in the low-roofed house at Carenage, the child was growing up amid the dry odor of tar and the sea.

Not too husky, even skinny. But he was as quick and lively as the *mal fini* hawk. He made Théodora happy. The old woman bathed him in water warmed by the sun, first steeping a handful of soursop leaves in it to ensure peaceful naps and long slumbers. She smeared the parched grass of his hair tuft by tuft with palma Christi oil, then rubbed his entire body with bay rum. His small teeth flashing, he would laugh under the liquid's icy kiss, and Théodora would devour him with kisses. She had consecrated him to the Virgin Mary in order to guard him from pleurisies, and he went about clad in white and blue.

In the afternoons, attired like a little prince, he went to play on the Place de la Victoire among the children of the bourgeoisie.

6

Albert's and Jacob's dreams were not of a common color. All Jacob wanted, once he had amassed his hoard of dollars, was to marry a girl from Colón. Mixed-bloods abound there and they aren't too particular about a man's color! For the news he received from home had encouraged him to settle in Panama. In the last few months sixty-nine lynchings had taken place in the South, and the blacks were surging in great frightened waves toward the cities of the North: New York, Detroit, Chicago. . . .

But Old Seewall's city still shimmered in Albert's mind. So the two cronies held interminable discussions:

"In Yerba Buena . . . "

"Stop it, man. There's no more gold, there! Nothin' but some yellow dust under the horses' hooves . . . !"

What finally brought them to an agreement and obliged them to pack their bags was a phenomenon known by the name of "The Blue Hand," which for generations has puzzled historians.

Along the entire length of the Canal, West Indian workers were being murdered. At night their villages were set afire. In the morning, amid smoke and a charred odor, men, their tongue and sex torn away, women who had been raped before being massacred, and children with their bodies cut in half were dug from the mud. Then "The Blue Hand" struck in Colón and Panama City. From his pulpit a Panamanian priest named Gonçalvo Bobo dared rise up against these crimes and recall that all men are brothers. He was struck down at the foot of the main altar. Since few West Indians could pay their way back home, they raised walls of mud and stone around their villages, topping them with shards of glass from broken bottles. Some, remembering the "maroons," their rebel-slave ancestors, dug ditches in which they fixed poisoned spikes covered over with patches of grass.

One night in Colón all the hospital's Jamaican nurses had their throats slashed. After that the terror reached its height.

On a September morning in 1911, Albert and Jacob boarded the S. S. *Oregon*. Standing on the dock, Manuel and Centinela waved their handkerchiefs. Salt and water filled their eyes, especially Centinela, who had gone to bed with each of our three rogues and was feeling doubly widowed.

Although Albert had never met that Mr. Jim Crow of whom Jacob spoke so often, he quickly made his acquaintance when he and his companion were ejected from the cabin they had paid for in good green bank notes. The white passengers would not suffer the presence of those Negroes in beds next to their own. So Albert spent the entire voyage in a corner of the deck, staring out at the leaden walls of the sea. He ate the leftovers that the philosophically resigned Jacob went to get from the kitchen when the passengers and crewmen had finished their meal. He relieved himself in a pail that he emptied over the side, and slept staring up at the calm or turbulent sky with wide-open eyes. Halfway through the voyage the wind freshened, and Jacob brought him some Moroccan blankets a few of the passengers, moved to pity, had offered. Albert refused to use them and remained haughty and stubborn, letting his blood freeze.

The voyage lasted for weeks.

The water. The sky. The water. Wind blowing in gusts and dredging trenches in the furious sea. Or falling with all its weighty silence.

At last some whales and seals were spotted, and they knew that land was not far off.

The fog was thick as they entered San Francisco Bay, thick enough to cut with a knife, trailing low over the water. Impatient, the voyagers crowded on deck, vainly searching the cottony gray shadows about them. Abruptly, as the ship docked, the veils were torn asunder. The sun and the city appeared, and Albert almost fell to his knees. For the beauty of his lost wife had been restored to him.

Yerba Buena. San Francisco.

Those who loved it had repaired the indignities suffered years earlier when land and fire had fiercely leagued against it. Pink, red, and white houses rose up the sides of the hills in tiers to the mauve-tinted sky.

Gasping, without a thought for Jacob, Albert jumped down to the dock and elbowed his way through the crowd onto a swarming thoroughfare that vibrated as a cable car passed over it. Yerba Buena. San Francisco. At last! He had reached the land of beauty that would cleanse him of all his humiliations. That would restore him to life, clean as a new penny. Limping, he climbed higher, ever higher; and suddenly he found himself on a sort of esplanade facing the narrow gateway through which John Frémont had dreamed he saw the riches of the Orient come pouring. The Golden Gate. Old Seewall's words returned to whirl through his memory:

"English and Spanish ships passed by the entrance to the Bay hundreds and hundreds of times. It's like a virgin who hides her fragrant little honeypot."

In the meantime Jacob, frightened by the clanging of

the cable cars, the galloping horses, and the look of the armed patrols, was more prosaically seeking a boarding-house for blacks owned by a certain Macon Dennis. He did not like the look of this city. It was a city of whites. No warm, brotherly black quarter. It was a cold whore selling herself to the highest bidder. It smelled of luxury and ill-gotten gains.

God knows how the two friends found each other again in Portsmouth Square, the one bedazzled, the other disappointed, for his search had been in vain. No trace of Macon Dennis in that maze of streets! Since night was falling black over the bay, barely brightened by the gaslit streetlamps, the two men set out to find a room. Ports-mouth Square bordered on Chinatown, and they entered the Celestial Empire.

There were many Chinese in Panama. So Albert and Jacob did not feel out of their element among those furtive, courteous men, eyes lowered, pate shaved—a glistening, fat serpent nestled between the shoulder blades! On the contrary. And it was quite natural to find themselves engaging in a conversation with a certain Chi Lu Lee. He was a large, mustachioed Chinese in a bro-caded gown who turning and turning his bowl in his hands told them a story that woke more than a few echoes in Albert's mind. Was this not his own tale? And was he not, himself, a Chinese?

One knows only one's own troubles and those of one's kin. One is unaware that other, almost identical troubles lay shriveled: cow dung beneath the harsh sun of unhappy lands. There, too, an ocean away, men's hearts were the same!

"My father, my grandfather, and my grandfather's father before him grew rice in Kwang-Tung Province, whose capital is Guangzhou, which the Americans call

Canton. From this came their bowed backs, calloused hands, and life empty of its best hopes from the moment of birth. I, too, began as they did, in the green hell of the rice fields. And then one day I had enough of it. I lifted my face toward the sun, saying: 'Do you not shine for me, also? Then give me the strength. I want no more of this life.' I borrowed money and took the boat for Kum Shan. . . . ''

"Kum Shan?"

"Yes, it is how San Francisco is called in my country. When I have made my pile of green cash, I will go home. I have a wife waiting for me, and a child too. A boy!"

One thing leading to another, Chi Lu Lee invited Albert and Jacob home to smoke some opium.

The next day, leaving Albert immersed in a blissful torpor and determined to find Macon Dennis's boarding-house, Jacob left the home of Chi Lu Lee in the morning fog. As for Albert, he had already made his decision: He would not leave Chinatown. It was the belly in whose depths he would be reborn. He would stay there. He would take a room looking out over the bay, on the second floor of a wooden house with balconies and a carved railing under a pagoda roof. He would breathe in that odor of ginger, of rotting fish and green onions. He would cradle himself in those high and mysteriously friendly voices. He would never weary of the hieroglyphs on the shop fronts. When Jacob returned with Macon Dennis, a carpenter whose business was not doing badly, Albert refused outright to go with them.

Some time later Albert entered into partnership with Chi Lu Lee, the proprietor of a laundry on Washington Street. The entire trade of washing and ironing laundry was run by the Chinese, who trotted from house to house, their baskets on their backs. But Albert had ideas.

It was not for nothing that he had gotten the hang of such things in Panama! He pushed Chi Lu Lee into buying a horse, all skin and bones, and a cart for delivering the laundry; now they were always ahead of their competitors, and the city's leading citizens took notice of this. Chi Lu Lee employed three "brothers," paying each one no more than a bowl of rice and five bowls of tea. Albert took on three more, and eliminated the rice.

The partners became rich.

Albert was happy in San Francisco. He was forever reveling in the beauty of the city. Each morning, leaning on his cane, he walked along the Embarcadero, letting his mind wander over the forest of masts, filling his nostrils with the odor of sea and tar, of tallow and bourbon from the docks. He stayed out of the numerous taverns on the Coast. He walked on, dignified and proud, and people turned as that imposing, impeccably dressed Negro passed by. Even those who thought that Negroes were far too tolerated in the land of California, who were annoyed that they had come so many miles to find themselves face-to-face with them here, were seized by a sort of fear and never dared to jeer at or insult him. Albert would walk up and down the length of the Embarcadero four times and then, his blood running high, go to quench his thirst with a lemonade at the Palace Hotel. An emperor of Brazil had once slept in that marble palace with its seven thousand windows and its magnificence celebrated as far away as the eastern cities of New York and Washington. There Albert allowed himself the luxury of being served like a lord, since his money had no odor. The black servants, bellmen, messengers, porters, and stableboys who swarmed about the hotel watched with baleful eyes as he sank into a velvet armchair. Had he forgotten that his mother was a Negro woman? Never a smile, a joke to remind people which side he was on! In fact Albert was not the arrogant egoist they thought him to be. He simply did not see them, absorbed as he was in savoring the returning strength that was causing his blood to seethe.

At times Albert extended his walk by climbing Telegraph Hill before returning to the Washington Street laundry. On Sundays he accompanied Jacob to the Black Baptist church situated at the corner of Clay and Hyde, where the Reverend Mr. Kelly led the services and made the vaulted ceiling vibrate as he sang "Swing Low, Sweet Chariot." Until that point Albert had always thought of God as the protector of white exploiters. Now he suddenly learned that He could be black. And so it was quite willingly that he set his two knees upon the ground to ask Him to bless his life. After the service, people gathered at Macon Dennis's house. Like Macon Dennis, Reverend Kelly came from Virginia, and he wept bitter tears as he read aloud letters he received from his relatives.

"The War Between the States did no good. Nothing's changed. . . . "

After consoling him, Harriet Dennis, Macon's wife, served a bountiful meal that invariably ended with sweet potato pie, and no one noticed the glances she cast at Albert.

7

San Francisco
June 15, 19—

To the Honorable Marcus Garvey:

I was one of your followers when you were in Panama and I am one of the innumerable Negroes on the surface of this sad planet Earth who is moved by your words. I carry one of your phrases in my head and in my heart. . . .

"I shall teach the Black Man to see beauty in himself." I have learned that you have founded an association for the Betterment of the black race. Please send me details. I cry out to you from my desert.

This is the second document from my forebear that I have in my possession. The letter he never sent and that I found yellowed and almost crumbling in spots, in a packet of pro forma invoices.

It proves to me that he did not give up his dreams and that, beneath his convalescent appearance, the turmoil lived on inside him.

8

Jacob Armstrong, my forebear Albert's friend, was a quiet man. He had taken it into his head to marry Louise Grasshopper, the youngest daughter of Macon Dennis's wife, who taught at the first school for black children, on Clay Street. Finished were the card games that had been his wont in Colón and where he had often lost a small fortune. Finished were the mistresses so generously kept. Every Monday he hurried to the Wells Fargo Bank and there deposited all his pay.

He had only one remaining weakness: He liked to drink. From time to time he entered one of the innumerable gambling dens on the Barbary Coast and downed one drink after another. The gin made sun bubbles blossom inside his head and the sea turn pink as a child's dream. He could already see himself sliding a wedding band onto Louise's slim finger with its shell-like nail, then slipping into a bed with her to sink like a stone, clinging to her breasts in the middle of the ocean. And then they would have five children, three boys and two girls, whom he would name Sabrina and Fabiana, for he adored Italian first names.

On a day that rose like any other, the sun having sailed forth no more quickly than usual after breaking through the fog, he came hurrying into the Wharf, a bar no more dangerous than the others and where, besides that, he was known.

As soon as he seated himself at a table, however, he

noticed a group of beefy men who wiped their mouths with a sweep of a cowpuncher hand and had the yellow dust of Sacramento clinging to their boots. Having been born and brought up in black America, Jacob did not need to be told that he was facing dangerous racists. How may one be recognized? In the case that interests us here, by the narrowness of the rectangular forehead, by the sickly cap of hair above sly, porcine eyes.

Jacob hunched his back, trying to make himself invisible. He gulped down the throat-burning drink and hurried toward the door. One of the beefy men was already leaning against it, and he addressed the room:

"You-all like seein' evil, hellish faces hangin' 'round here?"

Silence fell like a damp curtain, and no one even thought to go on pawing the bare-breasted barmaids. Jacob's shrill laughter rose:

"Hee, hee, hee! 'Evil,' 'hellish'—that's like what she used to say, my pore mother!"

"Your whorin' mother?"

After a silence Jacob's laugh rose again, perhaps more gratingly. The beefy man touched his arm:

"Say she was a whore, that mother of yours. *Say it, boy!*"

Jacob hesitated. Maybe he did not understand himself what was happening inside him. Swept away was the cautious concern for survival and the advice drummed into him from childhood on the necessity of hiding one's feelings from whites! Swept away by a torrent rising from the deepest part of his being! Leaping, foaming over rocks, spurting right and left in nacreous drops. Bearing away the old fears! Refusal, revolt, and rage! He charged headfirst into the beefy man's fat belly.

His bullet-ridden body was found, his face viciously

kicked in, in the mud of a Kearny Street gutter.

The affair turned into something of a scandal. A branch of the NAACP had just been established in Los Angeles and it asked the governor of California to open an investigation. The small black community of San Francisco sent a delegation to the mayor, who promised that the facts would be brought to light. Ralph Dwinddle, a noted white lawyer, lent his name in the service of this just cause. It all came to nothing. Jacob's murderers were never found.

People feared the worst for Albert.

He had to be tied up to keep him from going down into the street and shooting his rifle at every white who moved. He wrote to Theodore Roosevelt and, receiving no reply, asked how one went about assassinating presidents. Then he tried to starve himself to death. His teeth were so tightly clenched that even the tea poured by a devoted Chi Lu Lee could not manage to find its way between them. He lived on nothing but opium, perhaps making his dear, lost friend rise up again within the clouds of smoke.

One morning Harriet Kelly dropped her children off at school and entered Albert's room.

If truth be told, this was not the first time she had found herself alone there with him. Nor the first time she removed her clothes and slid beneath the heavy counterpane to press her naked body against his. Yet their other meetings had been a matter of sharing pleasure, not of easing pain.

No one, except Jacob, ever suspected what was really going on between the two of them.

At first, faithful to his usual habits, Albert had frequented the brothels. He had chosen the one on Dupont Street, where he spoke French with the whores from

Cherbourg, who had arrived there by way of Lima and Valparaiso. One day after Sunday services, while she was in the kitchen cutting sweet potato pie, Harriet had gazed up at him with dark reproachful eyes.

"Ain't you 'shamed, making love to white women?"

Albert was flabbergasted. Harriet went on: "The white man beats us down and kills us on sight, and you, you're messing with his women!"

Albert managed to stammer: "I pay, I pay . . ."

"Well, I'll do it to you for free!"

From then on, twice a week, while Reverend Kelly initiated the children's choir into the subtleties of gospel music, Harriet initiated Albert, although already something of a rake, into certain purely American caresses. Albert came out of it exhausted:

"God, what a woman!"

When they had caught their breath, her head nestled against his shoulder, Harriet told him of Nat Turner's great rebellion in Southampton County, Virginia.

"He was a saint and a holy man. The Spirit was in him."

However, Harriet had never heard of Marcus Garvey.

When Harriet took Albert to her as though he were a newborn baby, he burst into great sobs, and the tears he had not yet been able to shed came pouring down his cheeks.

"He came into my life when I had just lost everything that made the sun shine on it. 'Hey, man, you trying to die or what?' That's what he said to me, and he didn't know that that was what I was trying to do. Life, life for me was a muddy swamp where I could never quench my thirst. Why is it, every time they kill what's dearest to me?"

"Hush, hush."

The following Sunday at the hour services were due to begin, the faithful in the small Black Baptist church saw Harriet arrive propping up, dragging along a great body wracked with suffering but willing to let its voice join in the psalms.

The Lord trieth the righteous;
Upon the wicked he shall rain
snares, fire, and brimstone,
and a horrible tempest: this shall be
the portion of their cup.

Yet when Albert became convinced that God's holy fire would not burn those who had killed his friend and brother, that this crime would be but a small mote of injustice within a greater whirlpool, he closed out his account at Wells Fargo and went to the offices of the Pacific Steamship Line. There he purchased a first-class ticket for Colón, where he intended to board a ship for Guadeloupe.

Just before his departure, he limped for the last time to the top of Telegraph Hill and bid his farewells to the city. Ah, it had truly deceived him! He had thought to make himself over here, to rediscover the way to happiness as if born anew. It had cheated him, fooled him! May a new earthquake destroy it from top to bottom and erase all memory of it from the mind of man! Meanwhile the firebird sun had at last gained victory over the fog and was soaring sovereign above the bay, and all that beauty tore at his aching heart. Cruel, cruel!

The voyage was uneventful. This time Albert was not ejected from his cabin, which he shared with a group of

French tradesmen, who were returning from a business trip empty-handed.

I have the journal my ancestor kept, seated in the middle of the ocean-sprayed deck, his inkpot filled with violet ink and propped against a pile of rope. It is of no literary value. The syntax is awkward and the spelling errors frequent. Therefore I shall not take the trouble to reprint extracts from it. It simply allowed me to learn what sort of man Albert Louis was.

An intelligence quite superior to the average, but alas unenriched by any reading. An excruciatingly acute sensibility. The susceptibility of an autodidact. No guide. No model—apart from Marcus Garvey, whom he had glimpsed only from afar. In short, the journal is a succession of questions, of reflections that would make an educated man smile.

During his stop in Colón, Albert went to see Manuel, his former business associate. While he had been away, however, the business had failed and no one knew what had become of the Panamanian. So he took the workers' train and once more headed for Gatun.

In the village, where no one remembered him, he learned that Old Seewall was dead and that his wife was living in Baja Obispo with one of her daughters.

He went to look for Liza's grave in the small cemetery that was periodically inundated by the waters of the Chagres, which would carry off the bead crosses, the artificial flowers, and the ceramic candle holders placed there by pious hands. Stretching his stiff leg out before him, he sat down on the bare ground and began describing to the dead woman the taste of the bitter potion that had been his life. Happily, there was the child.

"I'll make a man of him. Solid as a manjack tree, royal

as a sago palm. He'll tower over all the rest and you, you who'll see it, you'll be happy. . . . "

The whistle of the train that dragged itself weary with the fatigue of all those uprooted men split the cottony air. Albert pulled a small leather sack from his pocket and filled it with earth. Then he rose clumsily, even more clumsy now with his pain.

That year the Canal was finished and the whole world marveled at the Americans' Herculean labors.

9

The child had been raised on marvelous tales about that father who lived in a place where no one, not even Ti-Jean hunting for the Beast, had ever been: America. There, men with red skin, oil smeared on their bodies and hair, hung hammocks from trees or floated down the lazy waters of great rivers. At times they shot arrows at animals that had the bodies of men.

One day he was slipped into sparkling-clean underwear that smelled of vetiver, then into short blue velvet pants and a little shirt with a lace jabot and real cuff links at the wrist. After that, and with some difficulty, a part was drawn through his frizzy hair. However, standing before the mirror, he did not laugh to see himself looking so handsome. He was afraid. He knew his father was coming home. . . .

Around four o'clock they headed in the direction of the docks. Théodora walked in front beneath her parasol, and people asked her:

"*Sé jodi la?* Is it today?"

She nodded her head and swaggered, her velvet bag swinging at the end of her arm. In La Darse an enormous black-and-red ship was docked, linked to the land by gangplanks black with men, women, children, porters. . . . And now Théodora was moaning as if in travail.

"*Pitite-mwen! Pitite-mwen!* My little one! My little one!"

The child felt very hot. An acid sweat running down

55

from his forehead flooded his eyes, but he dared not use the back of his sleeve to wipe it away for fear of dirtying himself. In her emotion Théodora had forgotten to seat him on the high earthenware chamberpot she kept behind a flowered Indian curtain, and he was in agony.

Suddenly he saw a man appear dressed entirely in black, except for the shirt with its high white collar that gripped his throat like a garotte. His hair was so closely clipped, one could see the skin of his scalp, and he leaned with what might be deemed considerable weight on a silver-knobbed walking stick. The man began descending the gangplank with a heavy, halting step while his gaze, like a lighthouse beacon, swept endlessly over the ocean of bewildered families. The child shuddered when that beacon fell on him, surrounding him in its glow; he felt it accentuating the details of his face, the scars left on his arms and legs by so many games and scuffles. The man drew near enough to touch him, and at last, looking at Théodora, who at present was weeping into her handkerchief, let drop:

"He's pretty little."

People say that when Albert Louis returned from his ten-year stay overseas, he deposited so many American dollars in the bank that the white manager came out of his office himself to stare at that river of green. They also say that he bought, for almost nothing, a strip of insalubrious land to the west of La Pointe. There he had constructed a gigantic *lakou*, a tenement yard, overseeing the work himself and bullying the workers whenever they stopped to eat a little manioc meal or avocado drenched in oil. In our day one rarely sees this type of dwelling. In those times it offered a refuge to all those leaving the plantation to seek social advancement in the city. Following this,

Albert purchased an import-export store that had belonged to a white from Saint Martin, who was too overcome by his wife's death to worry about the color of his successor. A Negro in the import-export trade! As far back as any one in La Pointe could remember, such a thing had never been seen before; and people flocked to Quai Louis-Philippe to watch Albert and his three employees examine and sign for the cases of salt cod, the sacks of rice, and the barrels of oil that were to ensure the growth of Albert's wealth.

Finally he acquired a piece of seafront property in a still largely undeveloped area of La Pointe. He brought in truckloads of workers and caused to rise from the earth a high-class, low-roofed house with a habitable loft and a balcony on every floor, the very one in which my mother grew up.

On a peaceful September morning the people of La Pointe watched a caravan of porters stretching through the noisy streets, their legs arched and their backs bent beneath the weight of enormous packing crates. It was Albert Louis's furniture, and they were carting it from the belly of a docked ship that had come directly from Bordeaux. Under his watchful eye they arranged it throughout the twelve rooms of the new dwelling. When Albert planted pots of bougainvillea and poinsettia on the balconies, the townspeople's fury rose and overflowed.

Certainly there was no lack of Negroes in La Pointe who belonged to the upper classes and ruled the roost in politics. But they were doctors, lawyers, even teachers— that is to say, people who had risen to where they were by dint of education. Who was Albert Louis? A former sugarcane cutter whose mother, a former cane bundler, still wore the Creole dress called a *matador* and did not know how to read. Poor Théodora! Jokes were being made about her in every drawing room. Again and again, between bursts of laughter they recited her errors in French. She said:

"*Bon dié, je suis faillie m'estromain!* Good God, I almost hu't mah han'!"

"*Les matins, je fais un petit pé té.* Mornins, I make a liddle tea!"

"*Je suis restée mofoise!* I stood there mah mout' open!"

Albert's numerous sisters were trotted out, so that fingers could be pointed at them, from the houses where they leased their labor, from the *lolos*, the small frontroom stalls they kept, as well as from the bars where they polished countertops and from time to time offered more personal services to hurried customers. Gossip had it that the only presentable one was Maroussia, who was married to a master sailmaker from Port-Louis. And one Sunday someone arrived with incredible news. Word of honor, Albert was practicing *kimbwa*, he was casting spells! The messenger had seen him, seen him with his own two eyes, seat himself in a far corner of the graveyard where none of his own dead lay. Then he bathed a clump of tuberose with his tears, kissed the ground around him, and intoned an incantation from behind sealed lips. It was but a step from that tale to attributing the origins of his wealth to obscure and magical practices. . . .

Albert appeared unconscious of it all. He walked straight as a capital I from his dockside store, whose façade he had repainted and decorated with a metal plate reading

ALBERT LOUIS
IMPORT-EXPORT

to his house on the Rue du Faubourg-d'Ennery, with a side trip to the post office, where each day he sent a letter to San Francisco, addressed to Mrs. Harriet Kelly. As for Théodora, she was in seventh heaven. Especially when, in the evening dew, she settled herself on the balcony to rock her grandson and fill his mind with stories the plantation Negroes tell. Yet there was but a single shadow on her happiness! Her son took practically no notice of her. At mealtimes he took his seat across from her on the far side of the oak table and ponderously chewed. Returning from the store, he closeted himself in a room on the second floor that he called his office, and when she timidly knocked at the mahogany doorposts to ask for a little money, she found him surly, sitting entrenched behind *La Voix du Peuple*. Oh, no, this was not the sort of life she had expected!

What Théodora did not know was that her son lived his days in a fog of pain made up of humiliation and regret. For from below his mustache, from behind a rampart of pinched lips, he was addressing a constant plea to the child.

"Avenge me. Avenge me for it all! Is it my fault if their fathers learned to read before mine did? Did we not all come from the same belly, in single file out of the slave ships, before being scattered to populate the hills? Avenge me for their laughter! Why did I come back to this land, without a wife, without a friend? They sleep beneath the earth, the two I loved. . . .

"I lived in Chinatown among the odors of ginger and pepper. My window looked down on shops with celestial names; 'Peace and Plenty,' 'Faith and Charity.' At night I wallowed in the delights of opium, or else went to lose my money in the smoke of the *tong toy* parlors. Here, I measure my solitude!"

10

Slight of build, the child headed toward his fifteenth birthday. One day as he was coming home from school, he saw a line of men tramping along the length of the Vatable Channel. Very young, obviously the same age, dressed in khaki uniforms and led by several whites with suitably red ears. Somewhat surprised, he questioned an onlooker who was loitering nearby:

"What's that?"

The man looked at him. "They're soldiers."

"Soldiers!"

"Yes, you little blockhead, soldiers! Don't you know there's a war back home in France?"

Yes, in his French-history book the child had seen soldiers on the battlefields of the Napoleonic Wars. But, first of all, they were not black and they in no way resembled these youngsters limping along in step.

He ran into his house, shouting:

"Grandmama, I saw some soldiers. There's a war back home in France!"

Unfortunately Albert, who at that hour should have been in his store counting up his holdings, was in conversation with Narcisse, the cabinetmaker, from whom he was ordering an armoire. On hearing the child, he turned as quickly as his bad leg would allow, grabbed him by the back of the neck, and slapped him three times across the face.

"War or no war, all that's white man's business! And don't ever let me hear you calling France 'back home.'"

The child wiped away the blood running from his mouth. For the first time he dared stare back at his father before flinging himself onto the stairway leading up to the third floor. In his room he threw himself on his bed, bit his pillow, and sobbed:

"I hate him! I hate him!"

11

San Francisco,
March 24, 19—

Dearest Albert,

Our small community has just grown larger again. Three new families have arrived from Alabama. They crossed the entire country in a mule cart, traveling by night and holing up by day, so fearful were they for their lives. Last week Reverend Kelly performed almost a dozen baptisms, and the sight of the congregation in their white robes, clapping their hands and singing that gospel song you like so much, "Jesus Is My Lord," was wonderful.

However, outside of that, things are going rather badly for us. All the black employees were dismissed from the Palace Hotel due to a racist decision by the new management. Our men are without means, and our women must work twice as hard. Since it is becoming impossible for us to find a place to live in the city, we have had to cross the bay and settle in Oakland. The area is marshy in some places, very wooded in others, but we do not shrink from toil. A representative of the NAACP came from Los Angeles to encourage us in our efforts. He reminded us that, considering what is happening in the rest of the country, California is still a paradise. Have you heard of the killings in East St. Louis, in which hundreds of our own perished? Perhaps news of such events does not reach your far-off Guadeloupe!

I pray for you every day of my life. If any man
deserves a little happiness, it's you.
    Your affectionate,
    Harriet

This is the only letter from Harriet that I found
among my forebear's papers. However, it appears that
they corresponded until her untimely death in 1936.

12

One March morning, when he had been back in La Pointe for little more than a year, Albert entered Théodora's bedroom as she was sniffing smelling salts to clear the blood from her head and said to her:

"Mama, I'm going to be married."

It's for sure that Théodora found herself mout' open! She stammered:

"How's that?"

Not really answering the question, Albert went on:

"Her name is Elaïse Sophocle. She's a school-teacher."

At four o'clock, when the child returned from school, he found Théodora with her eyes purplish and big as duck eggs. He shuddered:

"What did he do to you?"

"Marry! He wants to marry!"

Elaïse Sophocle arrived the next day at six o'clock sharp to make the acquaintance of her future mother-in-law and her future stepson. She was accompanied by her mother, who wore a headkerchief but was otherwise clothed in European garb. She was scarcely more than twenty years old. At first view she seemed ugly and insignificant, her body imprisoned in a dress of inelegant blue, her thick, well-oiled hair pulled back and rolled into a knot held together by tortoiseshell pins. But when she found the courage to lift her head and show her eyes, which were a lighter brown than her velvety night-dark skin; when her mouth stretched into a smile filled with shadow and sweetness; then they knew that he who acquired her was endowing himself with a jewel.

Since Louise Sophocle, the mother, opened the conversation in Creole, Théodora set her back on the path of French so as to remind her what family her daughter was entering. From that moment on the two women hated each other, and it was a fight to the death between them around the cradle of the children that were to be born.

Elaïse Sophocle was the illegitimate daughter of one of our country's premiere political figures, the one whom Légitimus beat so soundly when he was elected deputy and who turned so bitter about it that he retired to Capesterre to raise chickens. Her father had never given a thought to her, and Louise, that worthy, had raised her by selling sweet potato and marble cakes behind the Cathedral of Saint Pierre and Saint Paul. It is amazing how those businesses bring in enough to make a girl into a schoolteacher! In any case Elaïse Sophocle was one of the first of her generation to obtain the primary license that in those days gave entry to the teaching profession.

Seated in her rocking chair in the small drawing room of her house on the Rue Rouget-de-Lisle, Louise, the mother, had watched many men file through to ask her for her daughter's hand. She had listened to them politely before conducting her own investigation into their bank accounts and future prospects. Then she had given them her answer. Invariably negative. This little game had lasted for two years, and people were beginning to laugh, prophesying that Elaïse would wind up bringing her mother a paying-for-her-sins belly, when Albert came to seat himself in the narrow, cluttered living room. Elaïse was not consulted. One Thursday, as she was allowing herself a long, lazy morning in bed, Louise, bringing in her bowl of coffee, said to her:

"Albert Louis is coming to talk to you at four o'clock."

And she had understood what that meant.

Albert's courtship lasted exactly three months. After sweating through the day in his black suit, he went home to Faubourg Frébault to change, then hobbled back toward Rue Rouget-de-Lisle, stopping at Melanie's shop to buy candied pomelo rind or the fine roasted peanuts Louise, the mother, liked so well.

He said not a word to Elaïse, knowing that there would be years of months, of weeks, of days, of hours, of minutes, and of seconds to be spent beside her that would have to be filled with words. And she dared not think of the terrible moment when she would have to show herself naked before this forbidding stranger and allow him to rip the frightened flesh of her loins.

The announcement of Elaïse and Albert Louis's engagement filled the newspapers. So dubious was Albert's reputation that the Reverend Father Altmayer left his presbytery to warn Louise, the mother, against the temptation to sell her child; it was he who had instructed Elaïse for her First Communion and, week after week, on Thursdays, had heard her girlish confessions. Victor Achille, the income tax collector, dropped in his tracks, felled by a stroke; mad with love for the girl he despaired of offering the mother a bank account that would satisfy her, and his paralysis was attributed to Albert's *kimbwa*.

The week preceding the wedding it rained without stop, the Herbes River, which cuts through La Pointe as a sullen trickle, swelled and poured torrents of muddy water into the sea.

Then, the Sunday of the wedding, the sky stretched cloudless above the houses while the reborn infant sun appeared, laughing, with its toothless, dribbling mouth.

On one of the sitting-room walls in the house on the Rue du Faubourg-d'Ennery, the very one where my mother grew up, hangs a photograph of that wedding. I think she must have looked at it without seeing it, like those too-familiar objects to which we pay little attention. Albert so large next to Elaïse so small. Albert so somber beside her so radiant, she so imbued with that beauty that was nevermore to leave her. Albert trapped in his memories of humiliation and suffering. She hoping in spite of everything to see the joyous dawn of children's babbling.

At afternoon's end, while demijohns of Féneteau Les Grappes Blanches rum were being emptied, Albert climbed into a gig with Elaïse and took the road to Port-Louis, where his sister Maroussia and her master sailmaker owned a house.

Now, it so happened that the house across the street was in mourning, a telegram from the Ministry of War having announced the death of the eldest son.

Gaston Philibert, age twenty-three.

One of the 1,637 men from Guadeloupe buried in the muddy trenches of World War I without knowing why.

When Albert learned why that house was draped in black and the women in tears while the men were melancholically drinking themselves blind, he ran like a madman in the direction of the sea. He returned only as midnight struck, stinking of fermented rum, to take the fragile and instinctively rebellious body of Elaïse by assault. A fine red blood spotted the center of the bed, and at that same moment my grandfather Jacob was conceived. Jacob! Jacob! A Lebanese first name: one had to be a singular creature such as Albert Louis to so baptize his firstborn! Jacob, the eldest of the boys Elaïse was to bear, boys who, after him, were successively named Serge, René, Jean!

Dead Liza raged and wept much that night, she who had never feared a thing. For she sensed it, love was being born between this ill-matched couple, a love that would never betray itself by words nor by any untoward display of emotion. But love still, strong as life!

13

Until then the child had been slight and small in size. Suddenly he began to put on weight and grow. He was two heads taller than Théodora, one head taller than Elaïse, and now stood straight as an Iroko tree beside Albert and no longer needed to look up at him. Paradoxically it is at this exact moment that everyone began using the nickname Elaïse in her affection had invented for him: Bert.

Bert was brought up according to strict principles that had the particularity of never being stated but nonetheless were to guide him like so many invisible signs.

One was to frequent neither whites nor mulattoes, the whites being natural enemies and the mulattoes despicable bastards who had inherited the arrogance of their fathers and forgotten that they came from the bellies of Negro women.

But above all, one was to avoid other Negroes. For from time immemorial Negroes had hated their fellows and sought with all their might to do them harm!

Therefore one was to live alone. Superbly alone.

And so, Bert took refuge in reading. From morning, when he opened his window so as not to miss the first rays of sunlight, until the moment Théodora called to him:

"Doudou, I made some tea!"

Immediately after returning from school, instead of studying the boring declensions *"Rosa, Rosam, Rosae . . . ,"* until the moment Elaïse called:

"Did you finish your homework?"

And after the dinner, during which the boy forced himself to ignore the methodical rhythm of his father's jaws wordlessly grinding the fried fish, the chayote gratin, or the chicken fricassee, and stared at Elaïse's belly, heavy with promise, and at her sunshine smile.

That year there occurred two events following which he was no longer the same and slowly entered into adolescence.

Each week Théodora went to collect the rent from her son's tenement yard and immediately brought the proceeds to him at the store, where he kept a safe. She also conveyed the tenants' complaints to him, which he paid no attention to in any case. One Saturday, on the pretext that her aged legs could not carry her, she sent Bert in her place. Bert did not know that his father owned a tenement yard; and filled with a strange apprehension, he crossed the town deaf to the calls of the shaved-ice "snowball" vendors, stopped at La Darse to look at the sailboats from Marie Galante, and then, skipping a stone across the water, started off again.

The tenement yard opened onto the street by way of a small, malodorous alleyway squeezed between two shanties. Since it had rained the day before, a wood plank had been thrown across the mud, and woe to him whose foot slipped! The plank led in to a two-story-tall rickety quadrangle encircled by a balcony swarming with women busily cooking, children at their breast or running underfoot. They were ferocious, toothless shrews and, at the sight of Bert, called to their men, who huddled inside, clad in their undershirts. Bert choked. Cries and laughter and curses were already raining down on him:

"*Vini pou mwen kasé grin-aw!* C'mere so I can break your balls!"

What occurred next reminded Bert, unreligious as he might be, of the images of Jesus the Son of Man's Stations of the Cross. He was forced to collect the money, when someone was willing to give it to him, count it, and give out the previously prepared receipts under a heavy hail of jeers and insults. Ten times, Bert almost fainted. Ten times, he almost bent over the railing to vomit up his disgust and his hatred of his father. He managed to control himself. When, his mission accomplished, he walked through the passageway leading to the street that glowed like the Promised Land, a rock hit him in the center of his back, causing him to cough up blood. Turning, he saw a huge man moving toward him. He took to his heels.

"I have to kill him. Have to kill him! Only his blood can wash away what he did to me today!"

But can a mere boy kill his father?

Mad with rage and pain, Bert rocketed into his father's house. Climbing up the staircase, he bumped into the midwife, Madame Labasterre, on the second-floor landing and into Théodora, whose poor legs had miraculously healed and who was showing her gold teeth in a wide smile.

"Come see him!"

He let himself be dragged into Albert and Elaïse's bedroom. Having never entered it before, he was unaware that the West Indian locustwood furniture took up the entire space and that the side tables were covered with photographs, one of which showed his father, young and bareheaded, next to a man with an open and smiling face on an unfamiliar street where Asiatic children stood dressed like Jesus Christ the King. In the bed, that was as wide as Rue Frébault, lay Elaïse, weary and beautiful in her very weariness. Clasped tightly against her bosom, bundled in lace, dotted swiss, and fine linen, he saw the

triangular and sulky face of a wet kitten. Elaïse murmured:

"Kiss him!"

He could not; and all his life he was to carry within
himself remorse for that kiss refused his newborn brother.

14

Up until then Liza had left her son in peace. Suddenly she began tormenting him. He would wake in the night to find her sighing and weeping brokenheartedly at the foot of his bed. When he tried to lose himself in a book, she stretched her hand through the page and the letters blurred before his eyes. When he laughed, she would strike him viciously in the pit of his stomach and his laughter would change to sobs. He began to dread the dark. He began to people the silence with voices he alone could hear. And from then he could be seen: rigid, wary, starting at the slightest sound, watching for his unseen tormentor. He lost weight; he grew even taller. His features grew hollow, and everyone blamed it on puberty.

I shall risk an explanation. Liza had not taken umbrage at the love her son bore Théodora. On the contrary. She rejoiced at seeing him cajoled, dressed up, flighty and capricious. In spite of her years Théodora would kneel down on the ground and lift the child onto her back, while with great peals of laughter he whipped at her with his hands. But Liza could not bear her son's affection for the woman who had already taken her man from her.

Bert adored Elaïse. How could he do otherwise? Elaïse's husband was twice as old as she. He made love to her without speaking another word to her the rest of the day. Each week he handed her a paltry sum of money for an endlessly expanding family's needs, and she was forced to spend almost every cent of the salary she received as a ninth-grade schoolteacher. In spite all that, Elaïse exuded tenderness as a flower does perfume. It was enough for her to place her finely veined hands on someone who was ill for all his pain to disappear and peace to descend upon him. Sundays she attended church alone with her children because Albert refused to accompany her. She sang so sweetly there that she was asked to donate her talent to the service of the community and to participate in the artistic associations—The Torch, The Flambeau,—which were being formed among members of the teaching profession.

Elaïse was water from a spring, the small breeze that forms above the sea and lavishes its coolness on sweating foreheads. She was the flute carved from bamboo that grows at the water's edge. Yes, Bert adored her!

As did all the people of La Pointe!

At her death they all exclaimed:

"Ah, yes, Albert Louis's wife, she was an angel of God. . . ."

And the streets filled with white-robed children, their hands full of roses and lilies from the school that today bears her name:

"Ah, yes, she was a child of God! Every devil in Hell has its angel. She was Albert's. . . ."

And so wouldn't it come to pass that out of the perverse jealousy of the dead, Liza came to riddle Bert's love with dreams of flesh and incest. She caused him to cast longing glances at the beautiful breasts Elaïse bared to nurse Jacob, to peek at her body when she took her bath in the courtyard every Thursday as Théodora scrubbed her back and shoulders with a handful of leaves—caused him to wake with his thighs wet following fevered fantasies. Poor Bert, unable to bear it any longer, exhausted by the desires of a body that no longer listened to reason, one day moaned:

"What a shame you're not my mother!"

Misunderstanding him, Elaïse whirled about on her little ankle boots: "Be quiet! Your mother was . . . Your mother was . . . "

"Who was she, really?"

Caught unaware, Elaïse gathered up the few fragments of knowledge she possessed and murmured:

"She was an English Negro woman your father knew in Panama. . . . "

The phrase was magic. From then on the dead woman came into the life of her son, who divided his dreams between two women. Where the live woman was serene, placing her hand on his forehead to ease his terrors, the dead one was violent, forever angry; and the youngster, alternately mild and impassioned, docile and rebellious, no longer knew which way to turn.

When Albert learned from his favorite newspaper that a great congress was to be held in Paris bringing together delegates of all the black people on earth, from Africa to the Americas, he lost all reason. He who had practiced a prideful and prudent reserve now wrote to those political figures who were to attend the congress. He assured them of his support in the stirring mission to rehabilitate their fallen race, and despite his lack of education he humbly offered to accompany them. For two long weeks his letters remained unanswered.

Then, in perfect concert, there appeared articles of a rare violence in *La Vérité*, *Le Libéral*, *Le Citoyen*, and *Le Peuple*, which is to say in the great newspapers of the time, regardless of their political differences. These articles denounced a Shylock who meant to clothe himself in the tawdry finery of a friend of the people, an exploiter who aspired to change camps. Without ever naming Albert, they described the store where three underpaid employees toiled, as well as the dreary promiscuity of the tenement yard whose roofs leaked and whose walls housed wood lice, and compared them to the magnificence of his house on Rue du Faubourg-d'Ennery.

In particular the editorial writer of *Le Peuple* ended with these words: "Who is he trying to fool? An exploiter has no color. He is neither black nor white nor mulatto. Ever since casting off the dark night of slavery, the people of Guadeloupe have many times proved their political maturity; they will not let themselves be deceived by such masquerades. If the shoe fits, wear it!"

As if that weren't enough, in the hours before dawn, when only old maids and churchgoing old women forever hastening to confide their afflictions to the Eternal trotted through the streets, someone's henchmen came and tipped over a full wagonload of night soil in front of the store. Some venomous hand completely befouled the Bakelite sign. When the first employee arrived to raise the metal shutter, he slid through the shit, then hurried to warn Albert, who was still at home drinking his morning coffee, and thus spared him from doing likewise.

As after the death of his friend, Jacob, Albert reached for his rusty carbine and talked of shooting down politicians and journalists. Then his passions ebbed and he went into seclusion. For one whole week Elaïse had to pound his office door and stand there begging him to take a little food. Then he emerged from his lair.

This nasty press campaign completed the change in the personality of my forebear, who once again fully merited the nickname *Soubarou*. The sound of his voice was rarely heard again. His conversations were confined to two, sometimes three, more or less short grunts signifying his satisfaction, his impatience, or his ire. Paradoxically it is around this time that he fell into the habit, once his letter to Harriet Dennis had been mailed, of going into the new flower shop, the Dona Flor, to buy his Elaïse a bouquet of orchids.

Children rarely take part in adult arguments.

At the lycée Bert was left in peace even though he was ostracized. However, when it became known that someone's henchmen had strewn pounds of excrement on the sidewalk in front of his father's store, that truce was broken. When he appeared beneath the mango trees in the school yard, the students all shouted:

"Oh, something stinks!"

Bert faltered, then went over and sat down on a bench, his eyes staring off into the distance. When the bell rang, he rose. As he drew near the area set aside for his class, the brats scattered in every direction, holding their noses and shouting:

"Oh, something stinks!"

Beaten, his shoulders hunched beneath the weight of his father's shame, Bert was heading toward the exit when Gilbert de Saint-Symphorien broke from the pack and thundered:

"He's not the one who stinks! It's you, it's your dirty bunch of parents!"

That was the beginning of a friendship that was to last a lifetime. Gilbert de Saint-Symphorien was a mulatto, son of a lawyer so idolized that the whole country called him Sympho. He was credited with being a liberal because he had kept some poor cattle or yam thieves from jail and had beaten up a rich white man suspected of raping and murdering a servant girl. As it turned out, it was an infatuated suitor paralyzed by fear who had committed the crime, but Sympho's audacity had remained legendary. Contrary to what one might expect, Gilbert, who was left entirely to his own devices, was an incorrigible boy. A rapscallion, sighed she who had named him. On Thursdays when school was closed, he hid his book bag and violin behind a sandbox on the Place de la Victoire, and instead of cooping himself up with Mademoiselle Artémis, took off catty-corner or straight ahead. Now he was master of the sidewalks, his flag flying in the street winds, sailcloth shorts soon stained, socks corkscrewing about his ankles. His beautiful curly hair crowned him like an Arab street urchin's mop while milk-white teeth laughed in his only slightly swarthy face. Bert, until that point, buttoned-down and stiff-necked, began to unwind and went along with him. Yet his stomach quivered at the thought of coming face-to-face with a friend of his father's, or of Elaïse's.

I pick up our two rogues again at Loretta's; she was an older sporting lady but one who liked them young. Ah, how she remembers!

"Bert was so 'shamed he got into bed, head and tail low! It took some doing, getting him squared away! I shamed him, and said to him: 'Good Lord! You forgetting you're a nigger!' "

What Loretta did not know is that Bert made love to her while thinking of Elaïse, despairing of taking his father's place and quenching his thirst at that particular spring.

"Ah, how good it would be, making love with her! Between her sheets, against her skin! Instead of this body that's sagging everywhere, hers so firm in spite of the pregnancies and the overflowing cups of her breasts!"

I also find traces of them at Gosier, from the bars, where fishermen guzzle 100-proof rum and suck on cigarette butts brown as the stumps of their teeth, to the boxing rings. Gilbert, son of a lawyer and grandson of a court clerk, dreamed of making a future for himself as a pugilist. Try figuring that one out! Bert, having put on some weight yet still not too muscular, watches Gilbert—rechristened Sonny for the occasion—being demolished and wipes his friend's bleeding nose with his own handkerchief.

Finally I see them in a dinghy filled with food rowing toward the islet.

Then Monsieur and Madame Saint-Symphorien, wearying of the red ink of their son's failing marks and seeing shame burgeoning about their name, send Gilbert to a lycée in Paris. The two friends write to each other every day:

> Dear Bert,
>   You can't imagine what kind of city Paris is. Our little La Pointe we all love so much would barely make one of its neighborhoods. A river thronged with barges divides it in two, and pigeons from around the world perch on its statues. Night never falls and, near midnight, light flashes across the sky. How I miss you!

Bert slept with the letters under his pillow for fear of their falling into his father's hands. What a situation! He, friend of a mulatto, and which mulatto! For certain, one of those who had loosed the dogs of the local press!

It was around this time that Albert purchased a dozen acres of land at Juston from a planter ruined by the fall of sugar prices following the end of the war. On it stood a cabin built of imported lumber, and from then on he brought his son on Saturdays to hunt the rats who had taken up residence there. It was a matter of luring out the rodents and, once they poked their muzzles out of their dens, smashing their heads with one blow of a club. After that, the bodies were burned on a bonfire. Each time, Bert almost fainted, gritting his teeth so as not to vomit up his stomach and guts. In vain did he flee as far as the Sanguine, which also marauds about Juston; he could not erase that odor of vermin, of blood, and of scorched flesh.

During those moonless and unquiet nights at Juston, surrounded by the squeaking of bats, the croaking of frogs, and the wild song of the sea, Liza and Elaïse clashed in fierce combat. Whenever a feverish Bert laid himself down upon Elaïse and readied himself to become one with her, Liza, beside herself, let fly a vicious blow to the base of his spine and rid him of all notion of pleasure. When he curled himself against the former's shoulder to stammer out the dreariness of his days, the latter bloodied his mouth with her elbow and left him panting in the dark. At times, unable to find sleep, he went out onto the porch. The blackness engulfed him. The plantation tales Théodora had filled him with went around in his head, and he no longer trusted his eyes or his ears. Was that the beating of the *gwoka* drum or of flying wings? That twinkling, was it a lightning bug or a spirit that had lost its way? And what was that, lying in wait in the ylang-ylang? Suddenly three toads scurried past, and he rushed breathlessly back inside, where Albert, after drinking vast quantities of fermented rum, to make the time fly, was snoring like a saw. The racket did nothing to ease his mind, and he waited for the white stars of morning to rise.

15

Unlike twelve of her children who remained unacknowl-
edged by their fathers, Nirva, one of Albert's sisters, had
a daughter, Létitia, who had been sired by the printer Jean
Repentir, himself son of the printer of the same name.
Jean Repentir loved Létitia like the apple of his eye, since
his wife had been unable to make him a legitimate father,
in spite of two pilgrimages to Lourdes and novenas offered at Notre-Dame-du-Grand-Retour, to say nothing
of the various potions and decoctions of plants from her
garden. Besides his name, he had given her everything
and, when she reached sixteen, had made her a student,
a fairly mediocre one at that, at the secondary school for
girls in La Pointe. One day as Létitia was strolling home
from school in no hurry to listen to complaints from
Nirva, whose small shop was failing, she passed a boy who
called out to her:

"Your name, or I'll die!"

She hurried on.

This boy, younger brother of a member of the town
council, was named Camille Désir and he was the head
tutor at the lycée. Like his brother and father, he was a
Mason, a member of the Elect of the Occident Lodge.

With his marriage to Létitia dates the end of the
hostilities against my forebear, Albert.

The wedding was held in the Rue du Faubourg-
d'Ennery house, which on that day took its place among
the notable houses of the city. For the first time, those

acknowledged leading citizens who had a family pew in the cathedral and a family crypt in the cemetery were brought together in the person of friends and relatives of the Repentirs and the Désirs. All of which came too late for Albert, who went up to his office and shut himself in. Having made up his mind about the man based on the calumnies he had heard about him, Camille Désir went to join him there and found Albert with his shirt collar open, drinking from a bottle of rum. A friendship mysteriously sprang up between these two men, apparently so little made for understanding each other and so separated by age. From that day on, Camille Désir took up his duties as confidant and mentor.

"I don't fit in with these smokers of Havana cigars," said Albert, "these embellishers of French-French and marriers of light-skinned women! I am a Grosse Caye yam, black as the earth it comes from. I love my race and I want to carry it on. . . ."

"Nor do I, no matter what you may think. I don't feel like them. I'm a communist. Have you read Marx?"

Albert had never heard the name and incredulously listened to himself being informed that race did not count, only class. He shook his head vigorously:

"No, no, no! They hate me because I'm a Negro!"

That was to be the beginning of endless arguments between the two men.

For the time being, they christened their newborn friendship with fermented rum, and Camille Désir came downstairs dead drunk to take possession of his new wife. Not without having listened to a long speech about Marcus Garvey.

"That man there said things I never heard said by anybody. 'I shall teach the Black Man to see beauty in himself.' Do you know English? Do you know what that means? That the black race is beautiful. That it is great. That it will astound the world."

Camille shrugged his shoulders.

"What are you talking about? It's the proletariat of every color that one day will take their revenge and astound the universe!"

Théodora's old heart could not withstand the pride caused by her granddaughter's marriage to a man equipped with such intellectual baggage. It gave way. Two days after the wedding she fell across her bed and could not rise again. As Elaïse flew into a panic, Théodora whispered, forgetting to torture her mouth with French:

"*Sé Douvan zot kalé à pwezen. Mwen pé pati!* You carry on now. I can go!"

With a smile of happiness, she passed away.

People thought Albert would go mad.

He who since his marriage had not spoken to Théodora, since he stopped giving her money every week, mounted a horse and disappeared at full gallop. In vain did they search for him at Juston. They combed the woods. They followed the Victor-Hughes Trace as far as the foot of La Soufrière volcano, inspecting each hummock of heavy clay soil at the foot of the tree ferns. They set fire to cane fields on the chance that they might drive him out like some vicious animal. They had lost almost all hope when he reappeared in the midst of the properly grieving relatives and friends, his eyes red as cayenne pepper and with breath that could have killed flies.

Knowing her man well, Elaïse had insisted the coffin be left open, and they sealed it in Albert's presence. As they were tightening the last screw and that good-natured old face was about to disappear forever, Albert fell to his knees.

No one paid attention to Bert, standing in a corner,

a mourning band around his right sleeve.

The teenager lived his days in extreme solitude. Elaïse had just given birth to her second son, my great-uncle Serge, and she divided her time between nursing bottles filled with rice water meant to prevent diarrhea and powderings of cassava flour to avoid rash. So she hardly had time anymore except to brush his forehead with absentminded kisses as light as hummingbirds.

Since the teachers rarely called on him at school, Bert went for hours without opening his mouth. Not a single friend. Gilbert was wasting away in his Paris boarding school and his letters to Bert, even though ten pages long, did not make up for his absence.

The only thing left for Bert had been that everadoring, elderly presence. And now she, in her turn, had abandoned him and he was alone.

Alone in the world.

And so he tried to overcome the aversion he felt for his father and grow closer to him. Saturdays he clenched his teeth and killed rats. One night when Liza was tormenting him more than usual, he went outside for a breath of air on the porch beside Albert, whose pipe glowed red in the dark. Albert did not turn his head toward him. Nevertheless after a while he said in a grating voice:

"Seeing me the way I am, you must think I have a heart of stone. It's because you don't know what I've been through! They killed my wife, your mother. They killed my friend, my brother. Who are they? The whites! They're devils—never go near them. Never defile your blood with theirs! Ah, I was like a zombie! It was she, Elaïse, who put a pinch of rock salt on my tongue and I began to act like the living again. Money! Children! Are you studying English at school? Then translate: 'I shall teach the Black Man to see beauty in himself. . . . ' "

Then Albert rose and left an astonished Bert to wonder if it had not been a trick the night had played on him! He hurriedly wrote to Gilbert, who answered by return mail:

> My dear Bert,
>   I don't know where you uncovered that phrase. In any case, it is beautiful and meaningful. Do you want us to make it our motto?
>   Your friend who loves you,
>   Gilbert

The reconciliation between father and son ended abruptly.

A controversy, about which the local papers published a great many articles, rekindled the fire of Albert's hopes, rendering him surly and indifferent to everyone but himself. The black American intellectual Du Bois, the Senegalese deputy Blaise Diagne, and a deputy from Guadeloupe were arguing over how much support should be given to the ideas of Marcus Garvey. Marcus Garvey! It is thus that Albert learned his idol was alive, still alive! All the rest was of little importance; the question of whether the so-called Pan-African Congress should be held in London, Brussels, or Paris; the torrents of flattery being poured on the deputy from Guadeloupe ("leader of black Frenchmen"), and so on and so forth. Only this news counted: Marcus Garvey was alive in New York. Albert pressed Camille Désir to gather more information from his contacts in the world of politics. Désir discovered that Garvey was publishing a newspaper called *The Negro*

World and even procured Albert a copy; he also learned that Garvey was owner of a steamship line that was to take all the Negroes to Africa.

At this point in the conversation Albert blinked:

"To Africa? Why?"

Camille Désir raised his eyes to the heavens:

"Is it not the land from where our ancestors came? Your Mr. Garvey, who I've heard said is a dangerous fanatic, naïvely forgets that three centuries have passed and a lot of water has flowed under the bridge!"

To tell the truth, Albert did not burden himself with these considerations. He was carried away on the tide of his own joy. Frisky as a child. Then and there he wrote a lengthy letter to Marcus Garvey, reminding him that he had been one of his followers in Panama, telling him of his "brother" Jacob's death, for which he could not be consoled, and offering him financial help to carry out his stirring work.

Did that letter reach its destination? It is doubtful.

In any case Albert waited weeks in vain for a reply, his face more frozen, his grunts rarer and even more inaudible as one day followed another. One evening when Bert took his courage in both hands and came to ask if he could accompany his father to Juston, Albert struck him furiously with his cane, cutting open his eyebrow. At that Elaïse became angry. After placing a plaster of pepper leaves on Bert's forehead as it leaked bright-red blood, she dragged a straw pallet into her sons' bedroom. For two weeks she slept there. At the end of the second week Albert returned from the store and handed her, stiffly and silently, a spray of arum. She dissolved in tears and returned to the marital bed. That night my great-uncle René was conceived, whose life was to be so short.

16

In the meantime my grandfather Jacob was heading toward the age of six. He was a fierce and quiet child who scratched the servant girl and trampled on his toys while his mother taught her classes at Dubouchage. People rightly recognized the marks of his father's character and ventured none of those caresses or insipid cooing words reserved for children.

He was unrelievedly ugly. People wondered where that ugliness had come from! Ugly and black. Blue-black like certain icaco plums. No doubt because of that he was Elaïse's favorite, and she would bury the homely little face between her breasts and sing:

> *"Ti-Kongo à manman*
> *Ola Ti-Kongo an mwen?*
> *Little Mama's Kongo*
> *Where's my little Kongo?"*

In return the little boy would prattle a string of tender words while running his fingers over his mother's eyes, nose, and mouth.

"Mama-sweetie-darling-honey-sugar-lovey . . . "

17

Bert passed the first part of the science baccalaureate with honors.

Elaïse wept every tear her body held whenever she thought how Théodora could not be present on that glorious day. Ah, what great strides the cane bundler's descendants had made; how they had left the cane fields far behind! And now there was not even a glimpse of the noisome excrescence of the Negro cabins, so fallen into disrepair through the tribulations of man that the sword-like leaves of the pandanus could not beautify them! And now they were striving upward toward the level of a *habitation,* a family holding, were attaining the top of the hill! A Negro baccalaureate! How many Negro baccalaureates were there in La Pointe, or even in Guadeloupe? Nirva had a thanksgiving Mass said. Albert himself instructed Elaïse to present the young graduate with a gold pocket watch hanging from a chain twenty inches long and bearing the engraved initials "J.H.A." And Camille Désir gave him the *Complete Works* of Marx and Engels, taking care to underline certain passages in red ink.

But Bert did not leaf through those forbidding and hardbound volumes. For Gilbert was home! Gilbert de Saint-Symphorien, that happy dunce who had failed his baccalaureate exams, was spending his vacation in Montebello at his parents' "change of air" house. Braving the prejudices of two families, Gilbert crossed over the threshold into the store that smelled of salt herring and cod to invite Bert to his home—and the daring of this dashing young mulatto in his suit of tussore silk drew a groan from Albert that Gilbert hastened to interpret as acquiescence.

Montebello!

Gilbert de Saint-Symphorien, Gilbert's father, had married Adrienne Crespin, bastard daughter of sugar-factory owner Hyacinthe de Belle-Eau. In doing so, he had received in the Caribbean basket of his wife's dowry twenty-four acres of yam fields and a main house situated on the crossroad to Carrère. By no means did Gilbert intend to remain confined to that mulattoish fiefdom, and he quickly said as much to Bert. That young man was flabbergasted, because each night Madame de Saint-Symphorien would sing while banging on her piano, and because some cousins, virgins with siren hair, slept in the attic loft inside a chaste enclosure of mosquito nets.

The mocking one-eyed moon rises, and the two boys slip out the kitchen door, setting off a German shepherd alarm. Halfway down the hill, Omer runs a rum shop where Gilbert knows everyone by name:

"*Ti-Pol, saòu fe?* Ti-Paul, how's it going?"

At the bottom of the hill, Céluta's bed is wide enough for two to wallow in. In the village of Petit-Bourg is a black Negro woman named Délices, whose volcanic pubis spews not lava but scalding seawater. Bert, who little by little has recovered from Elaïse, discovers that brief, pleasurable death under a low roof beaten by the September rains. Délices remembers!

"It was like a racehorse who is beginning to discover the quality of his gallop, or a gamecock the power of his talons. I'd say to him: 'God's thunder, nigger. You want to kill me or what? Three times already you've crowed like Saint Peter's cock! Let me sleep!' But he wouldn't listen."

Between sessions of drinking and making love, Gilbert, drunkenly serious, lectured his friend:

"Color doesn't count. Mulatto or Negro, it doesn't mean a thing! What you should hate are every level of the middle classes, yours and mine! Both of them, equally, turn their backs on the people! So then, we should go back to that which is wisdom itself. . . . "

Bert paid no attention to this smooth talker. He was discovering his body fully, the sap seething in its center and no longer overflowing in a cold and solitary embrace but in furious, close-quarter combat!

On August 15, the day of the Assumption of the Virgin Mary and a holiday in Petit-Bourg, the two rogues stride through the streets. They toss darts into the bull's-eyes in games of skill, uncork bottles of champagne, and then, from drinking to boasting abruptly find themselves at Grande-Savane, eating *macadam* fish broth out of glossy banana leaves.

Throughout that entire vacation, Liza left her son completely alone. She allowed him to carouse, to sow his seed, to turn the pages of *The Well-Tempered Clavier* for Madame de Saint-Symphorien, and to try to play the gallant with the girl cousins. Indulgent and suddenly pacified, she sat at his bedside until the moment when the dead must leave the living behind and watched over her little one as he snored, worn out with happiness. This vacation at Montebello, meant to last a week, lasted four. At the beginning of the fifth week the hooves of a postman's horse struck sparks from the concrete of the long carriageway lined with coconut palms. A terse note from the father ordered the son home. Sick at heart, Bert took one final tumble with Délices and boarded the last ship sailing for La Pointe. From the small jetty Gilbert waved his handkerchief, its whiteness piercing the descending gloom. At nightfall Bert arrived at Rue du Faubourg-d'Ennery, where the servant girl, who had had to rise at dawn to brew the coffee, was already sleeping soundly on her pallet.

The next morning Bert drank his chocolate and described to Elaïse the pleasures of those recent days already so far away and unreal in that dining room where the pieces of Henri II furniture glared at each other through their slipcovers. Suddenly Albert walked through the room, and without pausing announced he was sending him to study at the trade school in Angers. In his shock Bert found the strength to say:

"I'm not going back to the lycée? Why?"

Albert did not bother to answer.

In the swelling noise of the street outside, the taps on the heels of Albert's boots began clicking. When Bert, for once on the verge of revolt, sought Elaïse's averted eyes, she made a broad gesture of helplessness and ran from the room.

I admit that here we have hit upon a mystery! Why did Albert interrupt his son's studies, which had begun so brilliantly? Who had put that Angers trade school in his head?

All that the family counted of men brave enough to dare look him in the eye paraded through either the store or the Rue du Faubourg-d'Ennery. Camille Désir set aside Marx and Engels and spent entire afternoons explaining that armed with the second part of the baccalaureate degree, Bert could even better serve the race. He might become a doctor, a lawyer, or a civil engineer; he might open wide the doors to the Grandes Ecoles, the leading state universities, and occupy places on their benches presently forbidden to Negroes. Albert, his lids lowered over lusterless eyes, sucked on his pipe and did not answer. But Maroussia, the wife of Marcel, master sailmaker at Port-Louis, would not admit that she was beaten—she who had always had a weakness for her nephew. She went to see Man Mélissa, who had straightened out many of Marcel's tangled affairs. Man Mélissa's room had so many candles burning that it was as bright as day inside; its floor was sprinkled with holy water, and images of the Virgin Mary, Baby Jesus, and Saint Thérèse of Lisieux covered its walls. Hearing Maroussia's tale, Man Mélissa looked worried:

"The boy must not leave! If he leaves, it will all be hurricane and shipwreck for him. . . . "

"What can we do?"

Maroussia's voice was anxious. But Mélissa remained calm:

"That brother of yours, he's no ordinary Negro. He curls up tight in his shell like a conch and you can't do a thing. Nothing at all! What's more, right now he's suspicious and sleeps with his eyes open like a toad! Is there someone he loves?"

Unhesitatingly Maroussia said:

"Elaïse!"

So Elaïse was brought into the picture. From that day on she mixed into each of Albert's meals, snacks, coffee, and tisanes some powdered papaya, chicken hearts, and a hundred other ingredients intended to soften his character. Nothing worked.

On September 3, 1924, Albert informed his son that he had reserved a third-class berth for him on the liner *Cherbourg*, sailing for Le Havre. He was to leave the next day.

That night Liza raised hell.

She perched herself in one of the attic loft windows, and her shrieks cut the air like the loud howling of the wind above the sea. People stirred uneasily in their sleep. Was that a hurricane coming?

Then Liza went downstairs to the floor where the children slept and planted nightmares in their calabash heads, nightmares so horrible that in their turn they took to howling and soaked their beds to the springs. Finally she launched herself against Albert and Elaïse's bedroom. Mad with the injustice done her son, she herself became unjust and struck the innocent Elaïse with the illness that was to carry her off well before her time, diaphanous and emptied of her blood. She did not spare Albert. However, accustomed as he was to nightmares and the sleeplessness in which old fears and endless sufferings were revived, he was not unduly moved.

My grandfather Jacob heard that terrible uproar more than anyone. But he attributed it to Théodora. He who had adored Grandmama had begun to dread her ever since seeing her bloated with rot in her coffin, her chin bound with a strong strip of cotton to keep her jaws from gaping open over her teeth of Guyana gold. He huddled down in his bed, but the urine-soaked sheets clung to his skin and he wound up seeking refuge next to Bert, who himself was soaking his pillow.

18

My grandfather Jacob's memories truly begin with the year 1928. Up until then his life, dreary as a book without pictures, flowed along offering no fare for his memory. At a quarter to seven Elaïse would call to him:

"Ti-Kongo, get up!"

He rose and reassured himself that he had not wet his sheets, for if he had, the servant girl would hang them on a clothesline in the courtyard to humiliate him and he would have a taste of his father's cane. He went downstairs to wash himself in cold water, went back upstairs to pull on the clothes he had placed on a chair the night before, and stuffed his schoolbag with the first books he could find. Then came the ordeal of breakfast. By some daily alchemy his father's glance would change the Ya bon Banania breakfast drink into nauseating bile, the braided bread into a latticework of nettles that stung tongue and palate. At last he took Serge by the hand and left for the school he could hardly bear, but where at least Albert was absent. He adored his mother. Alas! At present he had three rascally brothers! And so the attention he so sorely needed was measured out to him like the slices of marble cake at his afternoon snack. Thus, he rushed to her whenever he could, his eyes filled with tears drawn from he knew not what spring, and he covered her with kisses. At first she returned them. Later she assumed a stern tone and gently pushed him away:

"All right, that's enough now."

Why enough? Why, when he dreamed only of disappearing into her flesh again, of returning to live in it and remaining there, eternal fetus shrinking from life in the world!

In the year 1928, the year of his thirteenth birthday, there occurred three events he was never able to dissociate from each other. For the terror, pain, and anguish caused by each of them mingled within the depths of his heart and insinuated themselves into the innermost recesses of his mind. One morning Albert appeared in the dining room, glared at him as if he were a cockroach on a fruit, and announced that he would not be returning to the lycée.

Like Bert four years earlier, he found the strength to hold his father's eye and ask:

"I'm not going back to lycée? Why?"

Albert, of course, did not answer and continued his progress toward the door, from which Serge was backing away with all the speed of his short legs. Armed with the daring brought on by despair, Jacob went out to try to find an explanation.

Under the low and leaden sky sheets of tin were playing kite, chasing each other and crying: "Yoo-hoo." The low, bedraggled houses were falling off their footings, and the usually slack sea that closed off the end of the street was arching its back like an angry animal that scratches and bites everything around it. A torrential rain was beginning to fall. Frightened, the water already as high as his waist, Jacob went back into the house and shouted:

"Bonnemama!"

The servant girl who was hanging his sheets in the courtyard venomously flung at him:

"*Kiteye trankil!* Leave her alone!"

He took the stairs two at a time and found Elaïse in her room under an open umbrella, water leaking in everywhere, Serge, René, and Jean huddled against her. She wailed:

"He's dead! He's dead! Bert is dead!"

"Bert," he stuttered.

Elaïse sobbed even louder:

"Your father forbade me to tell you! Swear to me, *swear to me*, it will remain a secret between the two of us!"

He broke down in tears:

"How did he die?"

"An accident! A terrible accident!"

At that moment, with a loud, tinny tearing sound, the balcony of the house collapsed and the little ones began to scream.

The next morning (but was it the next morning?) Elaïse came to wake him at five thirty:

"Ti-Kongo, wake up! You have to come with me to Mass, to pray for him!"

The youngster obeyed.

A fine rain was still moistening the street, which was cluttered with sheets of tin, wood planks, and dead animals. An ox lay across the sidewalk, and two men were trying to haul it away by means of a rope attached to its horns.

The hurricane of 1928 and the tidal wave following it left five hundred dead, as many lost, and more than ten thousand injured. In some communities there was no wood for coffins, and the parish priests grew hoarse singing "Dies Irae." On the square in front of Saint Jules's Church, tents were raised and women in drenched rags were doing their best to feed the children. Elaïse went from one to the other, her eyes drowned in tears; but with love's intuition Jacob knew that she was weeping mostly from another wound. Jacob himself spent the time of Mass imagining Bert stiff inside his coffin. Had they tied up his chin, as they had with Grandmama, and put cotton in the holes of his nostrils? Who had kept vigil beside him? How many candles were weeping their tallow into saucers? And where had they found the rum? Elaïse signaled him to follow her to the Communion table, and he dared not refuse, even though the previous nights he had played with his rigid sex for a long while beneath the sheets. The odor of his unworthiness nauseated him, and he began to sob. Misunderstanding, Elaïse clasped him close:

"Don't cry! He has found eternal peace!"

As they left the church, a sky of innocent blue covered La Pointe. Elaïse kissed Jacob's forehead, whispering:

"*Swear* that you won't talk about this to anyone!"

He shook his head and set off for the store. He had taken the place of Julien, the head employee, who had become furious because Albert had refused him a raise after his wife gave birth and in his rage had predicted that Albert would die like a dog.

Jacob had been prepared to hate the hot odorous lair where Albert crouched in the back like some monstrous spider, endlessly verifying his account books. He did not know that it was as well the temple of a god to whom, like Albert, even more than Albert, he also would become a devotee: money! The commerce of cod, of herring, of oil, of lard, of rice, of red beans, and of dried, split green peas was perhaps not glorious, but it brought in money. Bundles and bundles of doubtless stench-ridden money, which was shut up in a bank where it produced more and more bundles of bank notes, just as stench-ridden, but no matter! Soon it was Jacob who was the real boss, the chief, refusing and granting credit, keeping the employees in their place and dismissing them. His authority grew. He became the master of the tenement yard and inaugurated his reign by evicting six families who had lost everything in the hurricane and could not pay their rent.

While his son was changing completely, so was the father. Now it was decrepit old Albert, dressed any which way, beard bristling, shoes muddy! He so neat about his person!

People could not fail to notice the change. When had it begun?

Julien, a former employee, the very one Jacob replaced, said that it had all started with a letter that Albert had received about two years earlier. He had read and reread it in his boxlike office and then rushed outside as if a stinging ant had bit him on the heel! Afterward other letters arrived that he let pile up, unopened, in a drawer.

If anyone had asked the children, they, too, would have had much to tell. One night, after their mother had glanced anxiously and often at the clock, they sat down to dinner without their father. Then Albert had come in, reeling across the dining room like a Tabonuco-wood dugout on the Dominique Channel, rowing with invisible oars. For no reason he banged his cane down on poor Jacob's head and, as Elaïse rose in a strong gesture of protest, clearly shouted:

"I should've killed him! Killed him is what I should've done!"

Then he had headed for the stairs, Elaïse following closely on his heels!

Elaïse did not come down again. The children had finished eating their meat bouillon under the eye of the servant girl and used the occasion to be rowdy and utter a series of swear words in Creole, all except for Jacob, who was weeping and rubbing the bump on his head.

From that day on, the already heavy family atmosphere grew heavier. Albert no longer even grunted. He was a zombie ruin! Elaïse no longer sang as she rubbed their necks with bay rum or combed out their hair. On the contrary, she sighed all the time! She even began to box their ears, which was far more painful to them than their father's regular canings. . . .

It was at this time that Albert purchased an automobile for Elaïse. A brown Citroën C4 trimmed in chrome, with a bank of headlights of various sizes, like a set of pots, on either side of the snub-nosed hood.

Elaïse began by having herself driven to church by a nephew who was clever at mechanical things. Then she judged the array too ostentatious for going to pray to God and started walking again beneath her parasol.

So the C4 grew rusty. Spiders wove their webs in the corners of the seats, whose leather grew green and then whitened with mildew. A bird made its nest in the mouth of the horn, and one day when by chance the rear trunk was opened, a mother cat was found to have installed her litter there!

Myself, I liken this gift, more extravagant than orchids or a wreath of arum, to a clumsy plea. Albert had much to be forgiven.

PART TWO

19

Year by year my grandfather Jacob became the undisputed head of the Louis family.

People said:

"*I pi mové ki papaye!* He's even meaner than his father!"

And that he was! He had plywood partitions installed in the rooms of the tenement yard, dividing them in two and at the same time doubling the number of his tenants. He dismissed the store's three employees and in their place hired one of his Aunt Nirva's sons, a man well past thirty and the father of five children whom Jacob ordered about with all the arrogance of his eighteen years! He bought twelve acres of land near those Albert already owned at Juston and planted market crops on them. He also had rabbit hutches, chicken coops, pigstys, and cattle pens built, which meant that Elaïse no longer needed to buy her provisions elsewhere. The abundant surplus he sold to the peasant women of Juston, who in their turn resold it in the marketplaces of Goyave and Petit-Bourg. Jacob managed to acclimate a variety of juicy and seedless grapefruit that came from Dominica.

Since his son had taken things in hand, Albert had had the time to let himself go completely: back hunched, feet dragging, feathers of white hair growing inside his nostrils and ears. He had always spent the weekends at Juston; now he spent most of the week there, Elaïse coming to join him when she had no classes. She hated the country,

Elaïse did, the endless nights, the racket of rain on tin roofs, the concerts of dog barks, the mosquitoes eager to suck blood—mosquitoes that the smoke of the bonfires did nothing to chase away—the restive, gnawing rats her sons found lurking in every corner. Above all she hated it because there more than anywhere else she sensed the presence of Liza. Her rival, vanquished by day, took her revenge at night. She prowled about at mealtimes. She turned in ever-narrowing circles above the bed, spoiling the pleasure Albert still dispensed so generously. Elaïse awaited the final killing blow and was not surprised when one morning she woke to find blood welling out of her. Up before daybreak as usual, Albert was setting out support stakes for the yams. She raised her voice to call one of her sons, but emitted only a moan before drifting weakly into the ocean of red around her. Surprised because she never slept late, Jacob pushed open her door about nine o'clock and fell to his knees.

That was the first of Elaïse's great hemorrhages.

The family, assailed in what it held dearest, did nothing but moan, sob, pray to God, or consult obeah men. So the nurse, Jeanne Lemercier, took matters into her own hands, carrying out the doctor's orders all the while adding innovations of her own invention, for she came from Marie Galante, the island of healing herbs. In a few weeks Jeanne had Elaïse sitting up, weak but smiling, in a rocking chair beside her bed. This nurse had an only daughter, Ultima, Tima, a beautiful name for someone both first- and last-born, who assisted her in her night vigils and medical care. She was an arrogant and difficult young person who one by one had refused all the honorable Negroes her mother introduced to her, someone who people said had no liking for her own color. One day, at his mother's bedside, Jacob's heart collided with

Tima's beauty. He retreated onto the landing and stood there, panting from the shock of that cruel and wondrous pain. He had never looked at any other woman but his mother and suddenly realized he would die if he did not possess this stranger.

How beautiful my grandmother Tima was! A shining, black complexion, her forest-thick hair fashioned into the heavy plaits known as "vanilla-bean style" and greased with carap oil, her eyes burning with the fires of unscrupulous ambition and sensuality. People say she married my grandfather Jacob without love, because of his bank account, the store, the tenement yard, the two houses, and the acres of yam fields at Juston! And it is true that Jacob had not grown more handsome with the years, dressed as he was like a chicken's backside, sporting old military boots on his feet and an oversized topee that was forever falling down onto his nose.

To please his Tima, this half-ignorant boy who had never done anything but sell at a profit, became a fine judge of carpets, curios, and decorative folding screens. He had the idea of growing dwarf bushes and trees; and so clay pots were planted with bird-of-paradise, everlastings, and a jacaranda with its flamboyant blue flowers, whose seeds had been sold to him by a Negro from Grenada. In the Rue du Faubourg-d'Ennery house he installed the first indoor bathroom, choosing the faucets himself in the shape of sea horses and deciding on the monochrome pottery tiles. It was he, too, who transformed the Juston cabin built of imported lumber into a "change of air" house that had nothing to envy those owned by the rich colonial merchants at Saint-Claude.

One week before his marriage Jacob realized that he was about to pass with Tima out of the stage of those listless conversations beside Jeanne Lemercier as she worked her needle through a table runner—conversations that ended with a chaste kiss on the cheek—and advance to a terrifying intimacy between two sheets. But at the age of nineteen, he had never made love! How to get past this difficulty? He instinctively had such respect for women that the idea of going to glean a little experience from some fallen woman never even crossed his mind. So it was with apprehension that he climbed into a gig to drive Tima to Juston. The horses neighed as they crossed the bridge over the Gabarre, lifting their tails to unload a ton of droppings and swallowing up the seven and a half miles at a gallop. Losing her ladylike air, Tima clung to Jacob, who, controlling the animals and calming the fears of the woman he loved, felt for the first time in his life big, strong, invincible. At Juston, before the huge canopied bed he himself had installed in the best bedroom, that uncharacteristic self-confidence almost deserted him. But a millipede seemed to be wriggling in the mosquito netting, and he took advantage of Tima's next burst of fear to embrace her. After which he wreaked havoc on her virginity. . . .

Immediately after the wedding Elaïse abandoned management of the household to Tima, who became the one and only Madame Louis! With the exception of Elaïse, whom she treated like a mother, she made the household toe the line. The servant girl learned to lower her gaze and not answer back; Jacob's brothers, to make their beds and empty their own chamberpots; relatives and acquaintances, to visit only when invited. The sole rebel, need it be said, was Albert. Walking across the freshly scraped floors in his muddy boots, he spat tobacco juice from his pipe into the corners of the rooms and displayed his well-formed penis while urinating in the courtyard. War immediately broke out between daughter- and father-in-law, but it was the former who was forever suffering defeat.

The marriage of my grandfather Jacob and my grandmother Tima was not happy, for their sexual incompatibility spoiled everything.

No sooner had he tasted of her than Jacob developed such a yearning for Tima that he could not leave her in peace, neither in the blackness of the night nor in the broad daylight of the siesta hour, when the closed shutters never do manage to give shade. He explored every corner of her, penetrated every orifice. When his member, itself weary, refused him its services, he went at it with tongue and fingers, teetering on the crest of a pleasure he was incapable of giving. He could see that he was wearying, pestering Tima, exhausting her, and he scolded himself. Alas, he relapsed into his desire like a sinner into his sin. Taking what revenge it could for those constant assaults, Tima's body expelled a fetus six months after the wedding. Twice more it bled the thick black blood of its belly before there was born into the world that rebellious and exceptionally gifted little girl: my mother. I dare to believe she was conceived in a moment of grace.

One thing strikes me when I think of my grandmother Tima, dead before I could know her: She did not work. Unlike Elaïse, who no doubt, on the stroke of eight, was in the schoolroom, tapping a ruler against her desk to quiet the noisy or wake the sleepers before making them recite: "Our ancestors, the Gauls . . . " or some other cock-and-bull story of the sort. Unlike Elaïse, who would return to Rue du Faubourg-d'Ennery to oversee meals for her rascal sons, go back to school at one o'clock under a parasol, with a student proudly carrying the pile of notebooks she had to correct and not leave Dubouchage until that moment when the small bay turns purple.

Later she would oversee the dinner the servant girl was cooking—for Albert, who did not eat at noon, was hard to please and might well push his plate away after a single bite—and at the same time supervise her lazy sons' homework. No, unlike Elaïse, Tima did not work. Among that class where the women struggled as hard as the men to bring honor to the race, she did nothing but harass her servants, her brothers-in-law, her mother. Then, after battling with her father-in-law, she would sit herself on her balcony, some crewelwork in her hands, and hum:

"Ramona, I hear the mission bells ringing. . . . "

She was a siren with neither tail nor legs. A siren who no longer charmed the passersby. A siren miserably killing time.

20

Albert had always displayed an aversion for Jacob and absolute indifference toward Serge and René. Yet he appeared to be fond of the last boy, Jean, born shortly before the hurricane of 1928.

Jean was handsome; people wondered where he had got that beauty. They exclaimed:

"*Si sété an ti fi!* Oh, if only he was a girl!"

For he had Elaïse's light-brown eyes with their occasional flecks of gold, almond-shaped below such purely arched eyebrows that people thought his mother plucked them! And with that, he displayed a kindness that was quite disconcerting coming from that ungenerous family! Did he not save the small coins Elaïse and even Albert let him have for *sinobol*, the shaved-ice "snowball," or *kilibiki*, powdered cocoa sugar, to give to a lame man who nailed taps on shoes outside the Le Bonheur des Dames ladies' shop? At Juston, instead of chasing rats with his brothers, he would go into the peasants' cabins, wondering at their rags, their premature wrinkles and the callouses on their hands. The peasants hated our family, but they made an exception for this little rascal who tried his skill at speaking Creole with them and ran his hands over their *gwoka* drums. Albert, on the contrary, was extremely angry. Whenever Jean came back from his wanderings, he cuffed him soundly and made him stand in a corner in the midday sun. The child melted with sweat. Sun motes danced before his eyes; then, once Albert had left for his

109

beloved yams, he returned to the village.

Jean was also the pet of Jacob, his elder by a dozen years, as if a special bond had been forged between the one most out of favor and the one who was the luckiest of the brood. It was to Jacob that Jean recounted the pains and glories of his schoolboy life. He also tried to share the books he read with Jacob, for he devoured everything. It was he especially who benefited from the *Complete Works* of Marx and Engels, with annotations in the margins, which Camille Désir had given Bert and which sat gathering dust in a corner. There never was but a single problem between the two brothers: Jacob's choice of Tima, whom Jean instinctively hated to the point of refusing to carry her train at the wedding. Nevertheless the affection between them was such that they never mentioned the subject, skirting the obstacle as able navigators do a reef.

One day Jean came to Jacob and showed him a photograph: "Who is this?"

The question surprised Jacob, who exclaimed:

"But that's Bert. Our brother, Bert."

"Isn't this Bonnemama Elaïse's son?"

More and more surprised, Jacob suddenly realized that all the pictures of Bert had disappeared from their frames and that even his name was no longer mentioned. He mumbled:

"No, he was the son of an English Negro woman Petit Père knew in Panama. He died in an accident."

"What accident?"

At this point the two brothers became conscious of a mystery, a voluntary erasure, a grave purposely buried beneath tons of concrete. They promised each other to speak to their mother about it that same night. It was written that they would do no such thing. For that very day Elaïse was brought home to them on a stretcher. At four in the afternoon she had collapsed in front of her blackboard, a scarlet rivulet snaking between the feet of her terrified students.

This was the second of Elaïse's great hemorrhages. The third, which occurred one year later, was to carry her off.

After the second, executioner-doctors, speaking their jargon among themselves, opened up her belly and cut out some organs that had nothing to do with the matter. After the second, she stubbornly set off to school again. But her days were numbered, and every morning her five men, who were well aware of it, prayed each to his own God that He leave her with them one more day. One day more.

Meanwhile Albert's five sisters, Nirva, Mérita, Sandrine, Gerda, and Maroussia did not waste a minute. Nirva braced herself upon the deck of the *Stella Maris* in order to go consult a famous herbal healer in Cap Haïtien, she who had never crossed the sea, not even to take herself to Marie Galante where one of her daughters was married. She took advantage of the occasion to have herself brought to a voodoo temple, and there made offerings of calabashes full of *manger-loas*, the food offered up in sacrifice to the voodoo spirits. Elaïse docilely allowed herself to be nursed but was not taken in, for Liza's carnivorous smile continuously reigned over the canopied bed and made her defeat clear.

The premature death of Elaïse Louis née Sophocle, deceased at the age of forty-two, was the lowest blow the villainy of life inflicted on our family.

When Albert came out of the stupor into which the disappearance of his wife had plunged him for weeks on end, he granted Jacob power of attorney over all his accounts, his goods and chattels—all this to the son he did not love but whose relentless work had earned his respect. Then he set off on the road to Juston.

His life was over, even though he was to live another ten years.

21

Dead, Elaïse and Liza made peace and came to terms about keeping house for their Albert.

In the morning, the two of them still drowsy—for Albert could not sleep and as early as five would go to piss against the ylang-ylang—took turns stoking the stove he had never learned to master. Then they brewed coffee in the old blue enamel coffeepot, reheated the manioc cakes he kept in a cracker tin, and flaked some salt herring. They did not scold him for sucking at the bottle of Féne-teau Les Grappes Blanches. A little rum never hurt any-one. It's even the best remedy for life. Albert thanked them with one of his grunts, left them to wash the mug and tin dish, and went to join the farm workers already sweating their sweat in the sun. Annoyed, the workers watched him approach. For although he hovered about them, he handled neither hoe nor machete in earnest. Rather, he played with the dirt like a child. He kneaded it, dug holes in it, and let it slip through fingers as black as the dirt itself and ended in nails like shards of flint. Eyes closed, he also liked to feel the mound at the foot of the yam plants, to heft the belly of the tropical pumpkins and suck the purplish jocote fruit or the West Indian plums he gathered beneath the trees. Around midmorning he went down to the Sanguine, entered a small bamboo grove, and stripped himself naked. Then he splashed about in the slow waters, unconcerned by the leeches clustered there.

At times a child wandering in search of a rose-apple

to quiet the hunger in its belly saw him floating like a log of wood and fled, terror-struck.

Refreshed, he went back up to the house. The bread-fruit *migan* mush was already heating in the cookpot along with a piece of salt pork. But Albert turned away from the *coui* his wives had filled for him, took another suck from the mouth of his bottle and went to snore open-mouthed on the porch. He snored for hours on end, waking when the squeaking bats darted from the roof to the kapok tree.

Real life began with the blackness of night.

Albert and his two wives chatted endlessly, admitting things to each other they had never admitted, unwrapping bundles of old dreams grown mildewed from never having taken form. Obviously, of the three it was Albert who talked the most. He had several obsessions:

"I thought I was going to raise gold. But it was my brother's blood that ran. So I no longer wanted to live there where he died and I came back home. Home! To find what? If it hadn't been for Elaïse, I would have crossed the sea again. Maybe in Jamaica or in Cuba niggers ain't as mean."

Sometimes Albert became upset and spoke meaning-less words:

"He, he! What did he do to me? He who was to be the manjack tree of my old age. I should've killed him! On the very day he was born. Anyway, I should've known he'd kill me! He'd already killed his mother!"

Then Elaïse and Liza quickly calmed him with a good-sized swallow of Féneteau Les Grappes Blanches. Each took him by an arm for a little walk, as he lifted his head toward the constellations Canis Major, Canis Minor, Taurus, Grus the Crane, Carina the Keel, the Corona Borealis, Cetus the Whale to help him forget his own earth. He had taken a liking to this, so they pushed on as far as the beach at Viard to watch La Pointe twinkling. The inhabitants of Juston who heard them pass by, laughing and chatting, crossed themselves!

Ah, yes, how they feared the *Soubarou* and how many stories went around about him! Each newborn baby that could not accustom itself to the visible world and went back where it had come from, each careless boy who in falling from a genip tree fractured his skull, each Tabonuco-wood dugout that overturned on the high seas with its fishermen on board—each one was Albert's doing! He himself was in the nocturnal toad, in the dog that bayed at the moon or roamed leashless.

Everywhere, he was everywhere! And to protect themselves, at all four corners of the property, frightened people raised shrines to the Virgin Mary, which they filled with flowers and vials of holy water.

To tell the truth, this bad reputation did not bother the trio. Having disposed of her flesh-and-bone rival, Liza had recaptured her youthful energy. Once she and Elaïse had put their man to sleep by dint of long strolls, shots of rum, and chatting, she set off on lively tales of her life in Panama. Elaïse, the only daughter of a worthy woman, who had passed from her mother's tutelage to that of Albert, lent a somewhat wistful ear. There had not been much laughter in her life!

When Jacob came on Saturdays to dole out the farm workers' pay, he was amazed to feel himself light and airy. He who could not bear the loss of his mother and day after day ruminated notions of rat poison, terebenthine oil, or manioc root, felt almost joyful, as if the dead woman had been restored to him. Ah, yes! She arched her back in the flames of the bonfire. She hung from the ylang-ylang vine. She clamored in the rain on the roof.

She was everywhere. Everywhere.

So he turned toward his father, surprised to no longer feel himself bitter and seething with anger. So he lingered in the ease of Juston, and it was past midnight when he returned to Tima, who was waiting for him with a scowl on her face.

The torrential November rains obliged him to spend two nights in Juston. The water not only inundated the cane fields, carried off banana trees, and overflowed onto the paths and road, but it also severed both ends of the Gabarre bridge, which it then deposited in the mangrove swamp. Father and son sat themselves down to a curry of wild goat and well-cooked rice, whose taste amazed Jacob and—something that had never happened before—they talked. About themselves. No acrimony in the conversation. Albert croaked:

"You think me a Negro with no feelings, a rock where my heart is, don't you? It's because when I was your age, I expected things that that crazy lady, Life, never gave me. You see, she tore the second apple of my eye from me. Luckily, death makes good the loss. . . . "

Jacob mumbled in echo:

"And me, you always walked all over me. You never stopped to wonder if your foot on my body was hurting me. Luckily she was there, she who now is no longer here. . . . "

"You say, 'who is no longer here'? Look beyond death. . . . "

Jacob curled himself up to sleep in a mildewed bed. But his dreams were so sweet that, overwhelmed, he opened his eyes again and distinctly saw the woman for whom he still grieved: Her beauty was restored and she was seated by his bed as when he was six! He stammered:

"Bonnemama, are you back?"

She smiled:

"Ti-Kongo, what are you saying? I was never gone!"

22

When an egg decided to fasten itself inside Tima's belly and, male or female, hatch at its appointed time into the hell of the living, disquieting rumors began circulating in Europe and even made their way through Guadeloupe. Well-informed people, such as Camille Désir, began speaking the word *war* aloud. Hearing all this, Jean tried to bring it to Jacob's attention. But Jacob was interested solely in Tima's belly, which at last, month by month, was growing rounder until it formed a mountain of truth beneath her housedresses. A child! A child! Jacob hoped for a girl. First of all because for so long only boys had been born to the Louises, boys with their future installed as stiff equipment between their legs. And then because a little girl, especially if she resembled Elaïse, would give him the illusion that he was bringing his mother back to life. Father of she who had borne him.

However, the rumors of war grew more distinct and changed into the clanking of boots. Then Jacob was forced to pay attention. He looked to see which way the wind was blowing. His cunning mind understood that if France were invaded by the Germans, the island would have no more source of supply. No more oil, sugar, flour, rice, nor Ya Bon Banania breakfast drink. Immediately he began laying in supplies, buying up the reserves of the naïve smaller companies. At the same time he increased farm production at Juston, especially of manioc, which yields a fine flour; and he added sisal, cotton, and castor-oil plants. From then on, when Friday night came around, he could be seen leaving his pregnant wife and tramping up and down the property with his workers.

All this to explain why his name figures prominently among "God's Own Helpers," as Governor Sorin called them.

"Marshal Pétain holds you, farmers and peasants, in the highest esteem, for he knows it is you who will rebuild a rich France, a rich Guadeloupe.

"He knows, as do we all, that although it is God who makes the plants grow, you, by farming, help God. . . . "

" 'God's Own Helpers.' What more beautiful name could you want?"

The war coming after Elaïse's death began to split our family apart. Up until this point I have said almost nothing of Serge and René. They were youngsters who caused no trouble, neither handsome nor ugly, neither geniuses nor dunces, who went their own way at lycée and in women's beds.

But now wouldn't Serge declare himself a pacifist and rail against that white man's war in which blacks were losing their lives; while René became captivated by the ideas of the Pro Patria Committee and repudiated "the spirit of capitulation." Their quarrels became daily events. The two boys threw themselves at each other, grabbed each other's throats, bit each other like Cuban pit bulls, and at times even tried to plant kitchen knives in each other's back. Tima shouted and threatened to leave the house, taking her belly with her, if the commotion did not cease.

One night René left his room and met behind Lodge Hill with a group of boys his own age, who had decided to go join General de Gaulle. A dinghy was waiting for them at Trois-Rivières and was to take them to Dominica, from where they hoped to gain England. This departure would certainly have broken Jacob's heart if another event had not taken place the same night. Around eleven o'clock, although she was supposed to drag her belly around for another few weeks, Tima's water broke. A frightened Jacob rushed down the stairs to pull the servant from her sleep and send her for Madame Malenfant, the midwife. When he came just as quickly back upstairs, he saw a little girl babbling and playing with her umbilical cord, which was wrapped three times around her neck.

Thécla Elaïse Jeanne Louis, my mother.

The christening resembled a wedding. For the occasion—a girl! a girl!—even Albert, donned the best suit remaining to him, combed his hair, splashed himself with a remnant of Jean-Marie Farina cologne, and came down escorted by his invisible wives.

The christening resembled a wedding. But the family did not know that death was in the midst of all that jubilation, hidden in Tima's belly, which would never bear another child, and in René's departure, which was to become permanent, as he would be killed during a mission with the Special Operations Executive for France. The christening resembled a wedding. Pommery champagne flowed like water. When Thécla returned from church beatifically sucking the salt of wisdom sprinkled on her lips, for the first time Tima gazed at her husband with a look of gratitude.

The christening resembled a wedding. Liters of vanilla cream *chodo* were drunk. Jacob could feel his beloved mother's presence everywhere, as if she instead of Nirva occupied the place of honor at the center of the table; as if she sang through the throat of Létitia (who had a nice little voice).

Three months after the christening Jacob was making himself look ridiculous feeding his daughter her bottles, powdering her bottom, changing her diapers, and watching for her angelic smiles. It was then that he received a registered letter from Governor Sorin. His ingenuity had been noted in high circles. He was invited to join with several county councillors and become a member of an economic mission that was going to New York! Denied the milk of the mother country, the island was searching for other sustenance. Jacob, member of an economic mission! What an honor! Far too much honor! Twenty-four years old and he had never left his country except to go to Dominica; and each time, upon the raging arm of the sea, he had thought he would give up the ghost along with his dinner! Besides, the idea of being away from his Tima and his Thécla in these unsure times filled him with horror. He therefore was preparing to decline the flattering offer, when Tima convinced him otherwise.

Ill-resigned and sick at heart, he came to announce to Albert that he was going to New York, to tell him that he was leaving his most precious possession in the care of Serge, a twenty-two-year-old youngster who was somewhat of a rover and ladies' man. Albert found his tongue again, audibly so, a thing his son had never known.

"You going to New York? Then you'll deliver a letter to Marcus Garvey from me. He has an office there! You know who Marcus Garvey is?"

Jacob, who had never heard the name, kept silent. With the same garrulity, his father exclaimed:

"The greatest Negro of our time! There's not another one, not another two like him!"

After which he hurried to buy writing paper and an

envelope at the Seven Deadly Sins rum shop and bar,
where the peasants almost crossed themselves at the sight
of him. One must admit that Albert had a staunch and
hopeful heart! Still stunned, Jacob watched him trace
great loops of euphoric and incoherent words in the light
of a smoky lamp fed with "West Indian fuel," the oil
extracted from chopped sugarcane.

> *My very dear Marcus Garvey,*
> *I shall never again see you with my own eyes. But*
> *my son will give you this letter and may find profit in*
> *your stirring teachings, better than I was able to. I have*
> *done nothing with my life. And yet like you, I am*
> *proud of my race. I believe in a pure black race as much*
> *as a self-respecting white believes in a pure white race.*
> *Which is why I have been wounded to my very heart.*
> *At present I live like a savage, I am mute, I am deaf.*
> *I have again become the Modongo, the Soubarou she*
> *laughed at. Yet I still believe that our race will avenge*
> *itself for all the humiliations it still suffers every day. I*
> *know that the history we will construct will astound the*
> *world.*

(I do not have the text of this letter in my possession
but can easily imagine its contents.)

Returning to La Pointe, Jacob set Jean on the trail of
Marcus Garvey, of whom the child had never heard despite his erudition. The little snoop did wonders. He
clipped articles from defunct or dying newspapers, questioned knowledgeable people such as Camille Désir, went
and shut himself up in municipal libraries, and was able to
piece together the great man's baroque and tragic course.

"He wanted all the Negroes to return to Africa. . . ."

"To Africa?" Jacob said, horrified.

In a learned manner the youngster said:

"Is it not from there our parents came? The West Indians were very divided about him. Read this extremely laudatory article by a man named Adolphe Maturin! And this one by André Béton, who has been inspired by his ideas! But Candace and Satineau opposed him. And as for the communists!"

All this seemed far too complicated to Jacob, who had other worries on his mind! Whom could he leave in charge of the store, in his absence? Who would collect the tenement-yard rents, which he himself did each week, his face as shut as a prison gate to avoid the lamentations and the attempts to soften his heart? Who would oversee the work of the farm workers at Juston? And what if his little honey-sweetie-sugar fell ill? Jacob could already see the child being butchered by surgeon-executioners. . . . Above all, who would care for Elaïse's grave, which he visited every day, rain or shine, changing the water in the vases, trimming the softened stem ends, seeing to the splendor of the bouquets of tuberoses, frangipani, arums, and lilies?

Situated at the town gates, the graveyards of Guadeloupe are cities of the dead, where the *filau*, the beautiful beefwood tree, keeps weeping watch over the departed. There marble, glass, and carefully whitened concrete strive to outdo each other. Ornamental bowls, flowers, crosses, or crowns of pearls are placed on the graves. Votive lamps are kept lit on each side of a picture of the deceased, their tenacious and fragile flames symbolizing the affection of the living.

Elaïse's tomb was worthy of a queen.

And so Jacob spent the weeks preceding his departure worrying. Yes! Who would take care of it in his absence?

23

"City of contrasts, puritan and libertine, double image of an orderly America and an untamed continent, East and West: a few steps from the luxury of Fifth Avenue is Eighth Avenue, squalid and battered. New York symbolizes America and half its population is foreign. . . . New York is big, it is new, but all America is that. What New York has that is supremely beautiful, is truly unique, is its violence. New York ennobles and excuses it, it makes one forget the vulgarity. For New York is vulgar, is stronger, richer, newer than anything, but it is common. The violence of the city is in its rhythm."

It is certainly not my grandfather Jacob who wrote that. This text is by the French writer Paul Morand, who visited New York in 1930.

Here is Jacob's letter to Tima:

My very dear Tima,

Our delegation is lodged at the Ambassador Hotel on Park Avenue. The food here is very good.

New York is a very large and very clean city. We were taken to visit the central incinerator at the corner of Fifty-seventh Street and Twelfth Avenue that each day burns tons of garbage and even stray dogs. What an appalling sight! Tomorrow we will visit the Police Department. I have been impressed by the height of the skyscrapers. Tell Petit Père that I have not yet delivered

*his letter, but will not fail to do so. . . . I think of Thécla
and you day and night.*
    Your affectionate husband.

Potbellied and bemedaled men of middle age and
light skin, the several county councillors on the trip, let
that puny Jacob Louis, son of Albert that Negro of bad
repute, know he was not one of them. They let him
know it as soon as they had all set foot on the dinghy that
was to take them to Roseau, the capital of Dominica,
from where they were to set sail for America on board the
S.S. *Catalina.* At mealtimes they did not speak to him.
They left him to lap up his soup, eat his asparagus starting
from the root end, and slice his noodles with both hands.
They ignored him whenever he looked as if he was about
to enter the sanctuary of the bar-smoking lounge, where
they sat savoring their port and fingering their Havana
cigars. And unhappy Jacob racked his brains:

"Why? Why do they treat me like an intruder? Is it
because I'm black? Have they forgotten that their mother
or their grandmothers were black? Is it because I'm not
educated? Yet my bank account is as good as theirs!"

Anger and the beginnings of revolt found their way
into his mind. Striding the promenade deck, back
hunched and hands in his pockets, he thought up stinging
rebukes, which, however, he did not voice.

On the morning of the fourth day the ocean bared its
fangs, leaped and thrashed about in every direction, and
Jacob was too occupied with his stomach spasms and
nausea to think of anything else. He arrived, undone, at
Pier 90, at the foot of 50th Street, a stone's throw away
from that monstrous Statue of Liberty he refused to
look at.

In truth, the potbellied and bemedaled county coun-

cillors of the delegation had seen no farther than the end
of their own noses: they were very wrong to slight this
extremely ordinary-looking young Negro. Thanks to his
frequent trips to Dominica, made necessary by his plant-
ings of grapefruit, Jacob spoke English perfectly, and he
was the only one able to get along without an interpreter.
He also had an extraordinary instinct for commercial
dealings. Before His Excellency the Ambassador of
France himself, his awkwardness disappeared when it
came time to demand long-term credit from the American manufacturers and emergency help for the island in
the form of basic necessities. Without his touchiness and
tenacity the mission would have been a failure!

When he was not busy talking business, Jacob literally
lived his stay like a dream. He constantly expected to
open his bewildered eyes and find himself standing next
to Tima, or feeding Thécla her bottle or being beaten at
cards by Jean. Instead of the insipid missives he sent his
family and friends, how he would have loved to have
them share the fascination New York held for him! But
in order to describe New York one must have an artist's
inspiration, and Jacob was only a shopkeeper! How to
describe the long, sinewy legs of skyscrapers striking the
sky with their sabots of stone, the triumphant framework
of the blue metal bridges over tamed rivers, the prancing
horses of the mounted police, the harlequin rags of the
beggars, and that suffocating mass of unfamiliar trees in
the parks. He who had lived nowhere but in a community of ten thousand souls was frightened, overwrought
by this furious flood of men and women flowing, swirling
about him, carrying him, a human straw, in directions he
did not wish to go. The incessant clamor of the city
weighed on him, and he believed himself always deli-
ciously in danger of being robbed, relieved of his valu-

ables, murdered and left weltering in a puddle of melted tar.

One day he strayed through streets lined with wooden houses of red, pink, scarlet, and apple green, whose porches were sheltered beneath elaborately festooned balconies. Men with slanting eyes and long oiled hair smiled mysteriously at him and pointed to displays of herbs and powerfully scented fruits. This reminded him of certain photographs he had furtively seen in his father's office. After an hour of asking questions (in what surprising America had he landed?), he finally approached a little boy. Doffing his cap, he informed Jacob that he was in Chinatown.

He returned several times, attracted, without being aware of it, in the same manner his father had been years earlier under another of the country's skies—it was as if the blood bore atavisms. He drank a cup of tea at the Red Dragon, and squatted on street corners to watch players solemnly move pawns in the form of winged horses across boards of gilded wood.

It was in the middle of the second week of his stay that, at the bottom of his attaché case, his fingers bumped against the letter Albert had given him.

114 West 138th Street. Jacob had never ventured so far uptown. He dove into the subway, stumbled along interminable corridors, climbed up and down stairways, and came to daylight in a threadbare square strewn with greasy paper where destitute people were warming themselves in the sun.

God, in what new America had he landed here?

It was not the filth of the place that took his breath away. Nor the air of poverty and abandonment, thick as factory smoke. It was that every face—men's, women's, old people's, children's—was the same color as his own, as if they had donned the appropriate masks in order to welcome him. But what masks! Ferocious, mocking, grotesque, desperate!

True, the presence of blacks in New York, from the elevator operators to the hotel porters, from the shoeshine men to newspaper vendors, from street peddlers selling ties out of an upturned umbrella to taxi drivers, had struck him from the very first. He was not, however, prepared for the shock he received there, in the heart of Harlem.

He hurried on.

One hundred thirty-eighth Street was a smelly thoroughfare along which skyscrapers of garbage cans stood guard in broad daylight. On the ground floor, at number 114, a brass plate read: U.N.I.A., UNIVERSAL NEGRO IMPROVEMENT ASSOCIATION. Timidly Jacob knocked on the door, which swung open on a tall, gawky man, eyes hidden behind dark glasses and his hair slicked back by a good straightener. He listened to Jacob in silence. Then he burst into tears and gasped:

"Marcus just died, man! In London!"

24

Jacob had never seen farther than the end of his own nose, which he had kept lowered over his cases of salt herring, his barrels of lard, and the uncleared land of his plantations—when, that is, he was not trembling with adoration at the sight of his wife and daughter. Now he discovered that America was peopled by millions of men whose ancestors, like his own, had been torn from Africa to raise gold. He sobbed as he listened to the recitals of torture, lynchings, and segregation, wept as he followed the long march of his newfound brothers from the plantation to the ghetto. All those Negroes burned alive, hung, beheaded, whipped, mutilated, kept him from sleeping, and he woke screaming with pain in the early hours of morning. Brother Ben, the tall, gawky one with the dark glasses and straightened hair, in reality the most tender and brotherly of men, marveled as he wiped away the sweat of Jacob's nightmares:

"What kind of hole is that country of yours, they don't teach you 'bout these things?"

Jacob sighed:

"Believe me, they only tell us of the windings of the Seine, the powdery white snow of the Alps. . . . "

Unlike my forebear Albert my grandfather Jacob never had the least inclination to keep a diary. Nevertheless my investigations have led me to certain discoveries.

Immediately after his visit to 138th Street he moved out of the Ambassador Hotel. The potbellied and bemed-

aled councillors went without him up into the torch of
the Statue of Liberty and to the very top of the Empire
State Building to view a scale-model New York. He
shared a book-filled hovel with Brother Ben and his
younger brother, whose nostrils were white with cocaine;
and Jacob, who had never done more than leaf through
his local daily paper, set himself to deciphering, with the
aid of a dictionary for the hard words, the speeches of
Marcus Garvey. During these arduous reading sessions he
sometimes fell asleep, and Brother Ben would find him
snoring like a saw over an open book. Waking him, he
would scold him roundly:

"You're here sleeping, and meantime the enemies of
our race don't sleep! They killed Marcus, man! We have
to take up the torch! And here you are, sleeping!"

Aside from that, Brother Ben and Jacob got along like
brothers weaned on the same arrowroot. Jacob accompanied Brother Ben to all manner of meetings, demonstrations, marches, and commemorations where the misdeeds
of the white man were interminably discussed.

"When it's a question of defending America—well,
then our blood's red enough! The rest of the time they're
killing us on every street corner."

Jacob learned to relish grits, collard greens, and the
ham hocks, to which Ben was so partial, and he even
injected a touch of American nasality into his English.

Noticing the way Jacob was looking at women, Ben
took him to see Louise, a sister on 147th Street who was
not too choosy when it came to men. When Louise
grumbled that Jacob was pretty black and pretty ugly, Ben
presented this act of fleshly charity as being good for the
race. And Jacob, who had never dared dream that one day
he might cheat on his adored Tima, found himself an

adulterer in the twinkling of an eye. Yes, this visit to New York made a new Negro of Jacob.

As for me I rejoice in this digression in my grandfather's life, in this breath of air in the suffocating prison of his existence. I rejoice in this window opened for an instant onto another place. Alas, it was to close again soon enough. Nevertheless I am certain, without ever having discussed it with anyone, that he preserved the memory of that bit of Heaven he had glimpsed.

The first to notice the change in him were the potbellied and bemedaled county councillors. The day of their departure they saw him reappear from who knows where surrounded by a veritable delegation of Harlem Negroes, who transfixed the distinguished visitors with their contemptuous looks. After embracing Jacob, one of them delivered a homily, which the others didn't understand a word of since during the twelve weeks of their stay they had made absolutely no progress in English. The passenger on board the S.S. *Portsmouth* had nothing in common with the one who had made the voyage aboard the S.S. *Catalina*. He walked past them without offering a good-day or good-evening. He sat himself down alone at a far table and immersed himself in his reading. Even when the ocean started its performance again and bared its fangs, he remained dignified and peacock proud, striding about the promenade deck. The second to notice the change were the Louises. They were all present, standing like a wall at the foot of the gangplank, except for Albert, who had not made the journey to welcome his son. Jacob descended with a martial step that was new for him, crushed Jean's fingers in a boxer's grip, and whispered:

"So much to tell you, little brother!"

As for Tima, who had slept chaste in her embroidered nightgowns, she was again forced to start beseeching God to shorten the nightly torment. However, to compensate for her refusals, her rebuffs, and unwilling surrenders, Jacob took a mistress. She was one Flora Lacour, a beautiful woman with a reddish cast to her black skin, a cashier at the Bonheur des Dames ladies' store, whom Jacob installed amid her own oak furniture on Rue Vatable.

Soon La Pointe and the whole of Guadeloupe could see the transformation. Gossip had it, in effect, that Jacob Louis was founding a political party. The *Nègres Debout*, or Negroes Arise party.

"The Negroes Arise party? *Ka sa yé sa?* What does that mean?"

A person does not simply declare himself a politician. One is born into a family that for generations has dealt in lies and election fraud. That knows how to stuff ballot boxes with the votes of the dead. That knows all the tricks. Who did Jacob Louis think he was?

One must admit, the party's program was rather vague. It could be summed up in Marcus Garvey's splendid phrase: "I shall teach the Black Man to see beauty in himself." In fact Jacob had done nothing more than adopt the slogans of Légitimus's that were used during the founding of the much-feared black people's party, which the whites and mulattoes called the Terrible Third.

When Albert learned his son was contemplating entering politics, he once again came out of retirement to appear at the store, his hair and beard in a state of neglect, his breath stinking of alcohol.

"Don't do it! Don't do it! They hate us! They never forgave us for leaving the cane fields. They'd rather have us on an oxcart, with a whip in our hand. They'll cover you with shit like they did me!"

Jacob shrugged.

Obviously Albert was right. The attack on Jacob was fierce and universal. Every newspaper of every political leaning loosed its rage—for once they were in agreement. But the prize goes to the communists. One Silius Siléus dipped his pen in bile and vitriol. In meticulous detail he described the tenement yard where needy families were exploited and unceremoniously evicted for the slightest lapse. He gave figures for the store employees' wages as well as for the farm workers at Juston. He went so far as to interview a servant Tima had just fired for talking back, and printed her exact words:

"It's only their skin that's black. They're worse than the whites."

To put the finishing touch to his editorial, he pretended to forget that my great-uncle René had gone off to join the Dissidence and that the Louises were paying a "blood debt" to France. Taking as pretext Jacob's membership in the economic mission to New York, he labeled the entire family Vichyites and collaborators.

At the Rialto movie theater, the well-known deputy Saturnin Filcoste cautioned against the "quartermasters of imperialism" and ended his fiery speech:

"Men and women of Guadeloupe, show that you will never swallow an insult nor be led to believe that the moon is made of green cheese. Send this lard smuggler back to his rigged scales."

At first Jacob stood up to it, holding meeting after meeting even when there was no one in the hall but a dozen or so spectators laughing at him. He was not, as one might imagine, a great orator. He did not trust his memory. So he read all his speeches, which he carefully wrote down in violet ink in a school notebook. I have been unable to find any of them.

He did not become discouraged until after the incident at Capesterre. Leaving a hall he had rented for the occasion and that contained hardly more than Jean and a half dozen young hecklers, he found himself face-to-face with a small crowd that began throwing rocks at him. One almost tore out his right eye. Another grazed his right cheek, and blood poured down his detachable collar. A third punctured his abdomen, and he fell facedown in the mud while his assailants bravely fled under the black cover of night.

That time he learned his lesson. He set aside his fine ideas and let Tima lecture him:

"Go on, if you're dying to die! If you want to leave me with a fatherless child!"

In a few months he became as decrepit as Albert, to the point where people mistook the son for the father when they saw Jacob from a distance. Badly dressed in his suits of drill that grew larger and larger on him. His forehead forever covered in sweat beneath his eternal colonial helmet. He cared about nothing now but making money, ever more money, and spoiling his Thécla.

A short time later two boys were born to him by Flora Lacour, but he set so little store by them that the poor mother wailed:

"*A pa té la pen!* It wasn't worth the trouble!"

He never complained. He confided in no one. Nevertheless all those who gazed into his eyes knew that in those waters a great dream had drowned!

25

Jean was suffering as much as Jacob.

Already disheartened by the death of Elaïse and the disappearance of René without even a good-bye, this formerly cheerful person changed completely. Apart from his beloved books, he held no conversations with anyone other than Jacob; and Jacob, for his part, could go for weeks without saying a word out loud. Jean's sole diversion was to walk straight as far as Bas du Fort and swim furiously to the small isle of Gosier, which he reached in twelve minutes and thirteen seconds. At that rate his muscles lengthened, developed: the body of an athlete!

One morning he entered the store and settled himself in the tiny room where Jacob was going over his account books line by line.

"Listen, I want to go to the Normal School. I want to be a schoolteacher."

Looking up, Jacob protested:

"Schoolteacher! But you're at the top of your class! In a few years you'll have your baccalaureate degree and you—"

Jean interrupted him:

"I don't want a baccalaureate degree. I want to be a schoolteacher."

As Jacob stood there open-mouthed, the younger man explained:

"I don't want them doing to me what they did to

135

you! I want to live far, far away from them in a town, a hamlet, a village. . . . "

Wiping the moisture from his eyes, Jacob said nothing more.

So, four years later, the war having ended without bringing René home, Jean headed for Grands-Fonds-les-Mangles, a village on Grande-Terre that was planted in the middle of the sugarcane fields like a rock in the ocean. The peasants had no great love for schoolteachers. However, this one was so young, so handsome, that they adopted him. They helped him to repair the tin of his roof, to scrub out his cistern, and to kill the millipedes teeming in his straw pallet. They even gave him one of their girls, Anaïse, whose breasts had just budded and whose skin smelled of cinammon. Jean, who knew nothing about girls, managed to do what was expected of him. Soon Anaïse's belly was attracting prognoses:

"*Sé an ti fi!* It's a little girl!"

How Jean began to love that countryside, as dry and filled with echoes as a tapped phone! Rain rarely fell there, even in November, when the rest of the country overflows.

On the first day of school he assembled his forty brats, snot hanging from their noses and hair reddened by the sun, and said to them:

"You have to understand, I know nothing. So I have come to learn from you what you learned from those who feed and clothe you! It is they who know. . . . "

What a good joke! Grinning, the children looked at each other. However, it did not take them long to realize that their schoolmaster believed what he was saying. And little by little, they began to tell him everything.

At first material things. How oil and soap are made from coconuts. How one can construct a cool yet rain-proof shack made of poles. How the loofah makes the skin soft. How carap oil untangles the hair, but also gives a smokeless light. How vetiver is braided into baskets. And after that secret things, things scarcely spoken of, which are transmitted primarily by women, mothers, grandmothers, and forebears! How to bandage, to heal, or to strike down with illness! And the mysteries of death too!

Jean wrote it all down, accumulating one long notebook after another. These notes comprise the work *Unknown Guadeloupe*, published by the author himself.

Soon the children were no longer speaking mere hearsay but bringing Jean to the source: to their parents' shacks. Jean sat down on the bare ground, ate *migan* mush from the *coui* and peered into the lined faces, worn by poverty yet so beautiful in his eyes. Each day he wrote letters to Jacob in which he described his happiness, Jacob who was bound to La Pointe by his preoccupation with making money, by his love for Tima and for Thécla.

Peace. Poverty. Poverty. Peace.

One day Jean was returning from Anse Laborde, riding upon the back of Melchior, the sleepy donkey Anaïse's father had given him. He had gone swimming, racing against and beating two fishermen's dinghies before letting them head out to sea. Suddenly, at a crossroads, Melchior began to bray, and with a hard jolt of his hindquarters, threw him to the ground. Furious, Jean rose and was about to beat the animal when he saw a girl kneeling beneath a mango tree. A true *chabine* she was, blond braids dancing beneath her hat and circles of freckles surrounding her rainbow eyes. Now, Jean had been trained to avoid light-skinned people. Yet he was well brought up just the same, and he was about to mumble a brief greeting and climb back on his donkey when something melted inside him, forcing him to look twice at the girl and binding him hand and foot. He heard himself saying:

"Good day, beauty, in which direction are you going? Want me to take you part of the way?"

Icily she answered:

"Go be on your way! I didn't ask you for anything!"

From the moment of this meeting Jean was no longer the same. No more questions for his students nor secret meetings with their parents. No sooner was school over than he would jump on Melchior's back and disappear across the cane fields. He returned in the morning, well after the cocks had crowed in the henhouses, his eyes red from being up all night. Anaïse could no longer recognize her man, wept every tear in her body, and asked the advice of her mother, who counseled patience. Things went on that way for weeks. Then one dry and quiet Saturday afternoon that Anaïse was to remember all her life, Melchior reappeared bearing on his back an enormous Caribbean basket wedged between Jean and a girl who, to Anaïse's amazement, she recognized! Marietta, Mario's daughter!

Mario was a white of whom nothing was known, not whether he was French, Italian, or English! Some people said he had killed someone in his own country, others that he had robbed a bank and was hiding out with Adélia, his mistress, who certainly must have had some Negro blood to judge by the nature of her hair. What did the couple live on? People wondered about that, Mario spending most of his time in a hammock, his two feet higher than his head, Adélia by his side! They had had two children, whom they raised like feral cats: Adélio, a boy who one fine day was nowhere to be found (it was said that Mario had sent him back to his own country);

and Marietta, a girl whom every man from Moule to l'Anse Bertrand dreamed about.

The church wedding, for he married her in church, of my great-uncle Jean and Marietta marks a breach in the wall of color that surrounded our family. One after the other the Louises had come tumbling from their mother's belly sporting every nuance of black. From then on Marietta added reddish skins, frizzy *chabins*, and even one apparent mulatto, who resembled grandfather Mario.

When he learned of his brother's marriage, Jacob hastily lowered the store's steel curtain, sat his Thécla by his side, and had himself driven to Grands-Fonds-les-Mangles (he had just bought a Citroën automobile for the greater glory of his Tima). Following a custom twenty years old, the two brothers took each other by the hand and began wandering at random. Suddenly Jacob broke the silence:

"Don't humiliate Anaïse. If you humiliate her . . . it's as if . . . you were humiliating . . . our mother!"

Jean nodded his head.

In reality Mario had killed no one. One day he had simply looked at the world around him and found its face ugly, pimples dripping pus. So he had bought a boat and brought it to dock at Paramaraibo, where he had rescued Adélia from a brothel. Then together they raised sail and traveled to Guadeloupe. Of course, like Jean, he had read Marx and Engels, but he preferred Rousseau to both of them:

"You take a Guadeloupe peasant or a fisherman! A peasant or a fisherman. He has a soft heart, a head filled with generous ideas. Sit him behind a school desk. Put a collar and tie on him. Teach him French and he becomes a beast, a rock in his heart and fangs made for drawing blood. Negro, mulatto, white, it makes no difference, it's the normal process!"

Jean wanted nothing more than to believe him and in return recounted how his father and then his brother had been destroyed!

On Thursday when there was no school, Jean went down to l'Anse Laborde. There father-in-law and son-in-law talked until Adélia, weary of listening to that endless verbiage, began to shout:

"Come on, you hush your mouths! And you, Jean, you have two wives to keep satisfied, you ought to be with them!"

As for myself, I believe that Mario's influence was decisive and completed the transformation of Jean into a sweetly rebellious dreamer, a cross between a Rousseauist and some fusty residue of Garveyism. . . . My unfortunate great-uncle was not made for the role he was forced to play, and if he died a martyr, it was not his fault.

Casually the inhabitants of Grands-Fonds-les-Mangles would make a detour to see how Jean was getting on with his two wives. It was not the number that intrigued them. Every man has two women, and more! There are even men who have a wife in every village, in every town! No, it was that they drank, ate, and slept beneath the same roof. The townspeople would enter the hut and inspect the three well-kept and leafy-smelling rooms: two bedrooms, one on either side of a thin partition into which had been cut a doorway that was masked by a tinkling curtain of wooden beads. Though at present it was moving inside Anaïse's belly, in one of the bedrooms two iron cots flanked the cradle where the little one would sleep: iron cots as narrow and chaste as those of two sisters or two schoolgirls growing up side by side and straining their eyes in the light of the same candle.

And Anaïse and Marietta in effect appeared to get along with each other, everything seeming to indicate that they equitably shared the work as much as they did the pleasure. . . . barely a shadow in the depths of Anaïse's eyes as she washed her laundry, her hands in the blue water of a basin. As for Marietta, tamed by love, she lost her wildcat ways and sang as she swept the courtyard and tried to make roses grow in the garden. Jean seemed to be in clover. After all, every person has his own idea of what happiness looks like.

26

In the meantime Thécla Elaïse Jeanne Louise, my mother, was heading toward her eighth birthday. She was a little girl who everyone agreed was beautiful but totally lacking in charm. One might have hoped for some defect, a flat nose, thick lips, pink gums (for black gums are a sign of beauty) in order by that very irregularity to give some life to her face. In place of that, an icy perfection. A wide forehead firmly rounded below hair thick like her mother's, and always scrupulously greased with carap oil. Large almond-shaped eyes that stared straight ahead without blinking. An almost straight nose. A wide-lipped mouth, but not excessively so, the lips sometimes parting long enough to display a smile over white, evenly set teeth.

And outrageously spoiled with that. Nothing was ever refused her, neither by Tima nor by Jacob. At enormous expense the latter would buy her French apples or Muscat grapes, so that the little girl remained unaware of the bananas and mangoes that grew on trees to feed the hunger of underprivileged children her own age. Out of fear of losing her, Tima had doomed her to wearing white until the age of twelve; and Thécla went to the private school run by the ladies of the Verteux family in her patent-leather ankle-shoes and her lace-trimmed organza dresses, hand in hand with a servant who also carried her parasol and her book bag. The other children sat next to her only when compelled and forced to do so, and they stared and slandered her in whispers:

"She spit at her maid!"

"She said her papa has enough money to buy La Pointe!"

"She stamped her foot!"

"She said that . . ."

On Sunday she accompanied Tima to High Mass, her hair tortured the night before with hot irons and tissue-paper curlers and now squeezed into a semblance of side-curl ringlets beneath her picture hat. At four o'clock an older cousin, invited to Sunday lunch, escorted her to the La Renaissance movie theater and took more pleasure than she did in the films of Shirley Temple. At six o'clock it was Jacob's turn to hold her by the hand and take her to change the water in the flower vases on Bonnemama Elaïse's grave.

On ordinary days there were lessons in piano, violin, dance, singing, and catechism, as well as mathematics, for she could make no sense of the square of the hypotenuse.

Not surprising that my mother hates her childhood!

27

When it became obvious that war's end would not bring my great-uncle René home, Jacob brought Guidicelli, the Italian photographer on the Rue Frébault, a picture taken at Thécla's christening. Guidicelli did remarkable work, considering the artisanal nature of his equipment. He separated out and then made an enlargement of René's face as he bore the new baby to the baptismal font. This enlargement, although somewhat blurred, restores to us the immature features—angel or devil?—of a tight-lipped young man wearing glasses and a stiff collar. Jacob had it framed in black, and since then it has reigned over the sitting room in the Rue du Faubourg-d'Ennery house. As he was hanging it, Jacob had a strange feeling, that of having forgotten someone else, of denying him the honor of family memory. With a pang in his heart he recollected his half brother, Bert. Under what circumstances did he die? In a tumult of emotion he promised himself to question his father the following Saturday when he went to Juston. However, it was written that he would do no such thing.

On the afternoon of that same day, Tima sent the servant girl to inform him that Anaïse, his brother Jean's wife, had been killed. Killed?

Jacob arrived in a village silent as a petrified forest. Three months earlier Mama Georgina, who delivered all the women of the region, had brought into the visible world a big, fat-cheeked boy not at all frightened by the metamorphosis he had just undergone. Three beaming faces had bent over him, three pairs of eyes had joined in inspecting the plump little body. Nothing to report. Ready for the adventure!

On the day of the christening there was no skimping on rum or *chodo*. And if the Louises, who could hardly bear Jean's way of life, were noticeable by their absence—Jacob excepted—Mario himself was present and sang Corsican songs:

"*Ile d'amour* . . . Isle of love . . ."

After that Anaïse was seen undoing her blouse to nurse her son, Dieudonné. Everyone had listened as the schoolchildren brayed a lesson of Jean's invention:

"In earlier times my country, my island, Guadeloupe, was called Karukéra. Men lived there who knew neither killing nor evil. They ate fish that they took from the sea and from the beautiful waters of the streams. They grew tobacco, manioc, and maize."

(In those days the history of Guadeloupe was not taught in school.)

Marietta was seen coming and going from the lean-to kitchen.

What had happened?

Anaïse lay on the locustwood bed. She had been clad in her mother's shroud, and it contrasted singularly with her face. Young. Defenseless. Jacob sobbed:

"What did you do to her?"

Jean gestured helplessly. Anaïse's body had been found after a search lasting three days and nights. The men had lit torches and divided themselves into several groups. Some had covered the cane fields. Others had knocked at the door of every shack. Others yet had pressed on as far as l'Anse Bertrand, Moule, Saint-

François. No one had thought of the sea, and it was at the bottom of an inlet that fishermen launching their boat had found her, seaweed covering her sex.

At Anaïse's death it poured for seven days and seven nights, a paradoxical sign that the suicide had loved life. Although it was June, the month of twinkling lights above the sulphur-colored cane fields, the month of fire in the waterless outskirts of La Pointe—although it was this month of sovereign heat, it flowed like a broken roof gutter. A flood saturated the land until it thirsted no more. Three days and three nights they kept vigil beside Anaïse, waiting for it to clear. Having lost all hope of seeing the weather lift, the funeral procession started off, wading through mud, splash, splash. Raindrops bounced off the coffin like fountains of tiny stones, and the members of the cortege, heads lowered, took shelter as best they could: some under umbrellas, others beneath broad banana leaves, still others under jute sacks, only to find themselves instantly soaked to the bone. Since Anaïse had taken her own life, she was not entitled to a religious service. For her suicide had greatly angered Father Lebris, who had christened her before giving her Communion and each Thursday confessed her of her insignificant girlish sins. Flowerless and wreathless, her casket, that box of infamy, was to be thrown into the paupers' grave. But those who had loved her did not permit this, and it was the most beautiful funeral anyone had ever seen!

Anaïse's death definitely plunged my great-uncle Jean back into the world of books, of thought, of reflection. Class over, he practically stopped speaking, as his father had, and it was by barely audible grunts that he communicated with Marietta. Refusing all help, with his own hands he raised a pole shack and shut himself inside, on the pretext of needing quiet in order to organize the news and information he received from so many sources. When Marietta, with midnight long past, weary of re-heating his dinner, came, hands on hips, to call him, he rose like a zombie and followed her to the great bed, where he made love to her. (Even so, ten children were born of these wordless embraces.)

The death of Anaïse drew Jacob and Jean even closer. At least once a month Jacob came from La Pointe. He closeted himself with his brother in the pole shack; and, as in the time of their youth, Jean leafed through the pages of his books or read to Jacob the fruit of his personal reflections. (It is to Jacob that the work *Unknown Guade-loupe* is dedicated.)

Often, too, Jacob and Jean conversed, the former articulating words in his croaking voice, the latter manipulating them as a blacksmith does a rarely used metal:

"It's funny, isn't it? Since she's gone, I feel her even closer!"

"It's like me, with Bonnemama Elaïse! There's times, in Juston, I'm sure she's there in the room, that she sees everything I'm doing!"

Sometimes, against Tima's advice, Jacob brought Thécla with him. Paradoxically, although the child hated the life she was forced to live at La Pointe, she hated her visits to Grands-Fonds-les-Mangles even more. She hated the peasants, stinking of sweat and speaking Creole, who kissed her with their greasy lips. And she hated her father lecturing her each time:

"Come on, stop acting so spoiled! Say hello!"

She hated the *coui* out of which she ate, the pallet on the bare floor where she stretched out among her cousins, who did not even brush their teeth after supper. Above all she hated Marietta, blond, barefoot, and casual, so different from Tima, always so spick-and-span, and with her hair neatly combed by seven in the morning. Deep within Marietta's eyes Thécla thought she read a contempt that was perhaps only deep within herself:

"So what if you put on airs! So what if you puff yourself up like the frog in the fairy tale. You'll never be anything but a little nappy-headed black girl. And pretty black at that. . . ."

28

People no doubt remember the year 1953 as the one in which Joseph Stalin died, for that death made headlines in newspapers around the world. However, that particular event was of small importance in the mind of my grandfather Jacob; and even of my great-uncle Jean, once so fervid in his discussions of Marxism, race, and class. If the year 1953 left an indelible mark on them, it is because it was filled with milestones of no importance to anyone but themselves, milestones that changed the direction of their individual history far more than did the death of some Russian dictator. On January 13, 1953, the first volume of my uncle Jean's *Unknown Guadeloupe* appeared. It had taken him seven and a half years to write. By dint of stinting on his salary and refusing Marietta what she needed for resoling the children's shoes, he had managed to put together the sum of money Jean Repentir, the printer, was asking. This work was published in an edition of two hundred copies and is today considered a classic, plagiarized over and over again by students for their master's-project outlines and theses. Somehow Jean, who had come down to La Pointe for the occasion, packed them all into a cardboard valise. Then he went over to the docks to give one to Jacob, who did not understand why his brother was clasping the valise so tightly to himself and had the fulfilled look of someone returning from the Communion table. After his visit to Jacob, Jean went to see Camille Désir, now an influential member of the Communist party, and asked him to mention his book in *La Flamme*. *Unknown Guadeloupe* was, it seemed to Jean, a monument to the creativity of those eternally unappreciated ones, the people. Camille's mind was on other things (on the death of Stalin, after all!) but he promised everything asked of him and suggested that twenty copies or so be placed with the bookseller Hubert Mondésir.

No article appeared in *La Flamme*. But reports in *Le Nouvelliste*, *La Voix du Peuple*, and several others, sneered at the work's style and at its naïveté (ah, those passages on the supernatural!), and the little schoolteacher who took himself for an intellectual was quickly sent packing back to his savanna.

Jacob wept on reading those lines:

"Why, why do they hate us so much? They never let up."

As a consequence the copies entrusted to Mondésir stood yellowing on a shelf before being relegated to a corner. Yet *Unknown Guadeloupe* did not go unnoticed by everyone.

On March 2, 1953, a school inspector named Monsieur Besnard, alerted by the administration, entered the schoolroom at Grands-Fonds-les-Mangles. He seated himself on the rear bench in the classroom and for three hours listened to a French lesson, a lesson in history, and a lesson in general sciences. After which he withdrew to make his report.

The results were immediate. On April 17, 1953, Jean was informed by registered letter that he had been struck from the official roll of licensed teachers. Thus he would have to vacate the house he was occupying and make room for the new teacher.

That very evening Jean and Marietta gathered their

children and possessions. They piled them onto an oxcart lent by a neighbor and, under the saddened gaze of the schoolchildren and their parents (certain of whom were openly weeping), took the road to l'Anse Laborde, where Adélia and Mario lived.

Three days later Jacob learned of the calamity. He came running to l'Anse Laborde and found Mario swinging in his hammock with his two feet higher than his head, Marietta and her mother engaged in one of their daily quarrels, and Jean cutting tree branches to make poles before the fascinated eyes of his sons.

"Come to Juston! I had the house refurnished!"

Jean shook his head.

"You know, I'm only managing our holdings. Do you want your portion of the estate?"

Jean shook his head even more firmly.

"At least let me help you."

Jean looked at Dieudonné, Anaïse's son. Jacob understood and, taking the boy by the hand, returned to La Pointe.

To earn his living, Jean became the public scribe. Armed with an inkpot and a Sergeant-Major pen, he would seat himself at the edge of the marketplaces. There he helped peasants fill out their income tax forms, fiancées write love letters to their soldier-fiancés, and tenants send petitions to their landlords. Social Security caused him the greatest fatigue: No one understood it at all.

However, he often forgot to collect his fee and accepted as gospel any lie designed to melt his heart. In truth all this was of little importance to him. Real life began on the stroke of nine o'clock at night, when, alone in his pole shack, he worked on the sequel to *Unknown Guadeloupe*.

So, after some time had passed, Marietta found herself

forced to step in. Though she had not held a brush since her short stay in school, she took great pains to paint two signs. One was large: POUR SOME MORE. One was small: CREDIT IS DEAD. BAD DEBTORS KILLED IT. She then opened a saloon, recouping in her own establishment what Jean had let slip away.

And wasn't Tima happy to see Dieudonné's muddy feet come land on her floor! Having been warned by the expression on Jacob's face not to protest, she waited for him to leave before placing a basin of water and a stiff brush in the poor boy's hands. When Thécla came home from her piano lesson, she found the intruder on his knees, crying, his cheeks smeared with soap. Without her exactly knowing why, the sight plucked a string in her heart. Previously unheard, the sound grew until it filled her completely. She embraced her little cousin tightly and from then on defended him tooth and nail against her mother's claws.

The children of the Petit-Lycée saw the arrival from Grands-Fonds-les-Mangles of this black, fat-cheeked boy who murdered the French language and studded his note-book with inkblots. In no time at all they had nicknamed him *neg mawon*, "maroon nigger"!

On December 20, 1953, with everyone's mind al-ready on Christmas and children and parents singing the hymns of Advent, Jacob received a visit at his store from a handsome stranger: Monsieur Gilbert de Saint-Symphorien, recently returned from Paris to take over his father's practice. The two men remained closeted to-gether for four hours. Following that, Jacob was seen to come out staggering like a drunken Negro. He seated himself behind the wheel of his automobile and, after two or three Sunday-driver lurches of the car, left the city. People were to remember that day, for on seeing him go racing past, one fanciful individual suggested that the Louis house was on fire, which caused an unholy commotion in La Pointe.

Jacob brought his car to a stop in front of Mario and Adélia's house, scaring a chicken scratching the ground for her chicks, and shouted:

"Jean! Jean!"

The sound of his voice was such that the younger man, who was returning from the market at l'Anse Bertrand, sensed something terrible had happened and came running:

"Did something happen to Petit Père?"

Jacob stuttered:

"He killed him! He killed him! He's the one who killed him!"

GILBERT DE SAINT-SYMPHORIEN'S TALE

When Bert stepped from the boat train at Paris's Gare Saint-Lazare, huddled in a coat his father had purchased years earlier in San Francisco and carrying a cardboard valise, he felt terribly disappointed: His friend, Gilbert de Saint-Symphorien, whom he had written to announce his arrival, was not there. He did not know that of late poor Gilbert had been languishing in a Jesuit boarding school in Le Mans and had been unable to go over the wall. He had been so happy at the thought of seeing Gilbert again! All the same, he was not entirely on his own, since a friend of Camille Désir was waiting for him, holding a small sign in his hand. This was a man named Jean Joseph, a wholesaler of tropical foodstuffs.

It was raining.

The gleaming streets were filled with cars as funereal

as hearses, with women beneath black umbrellas and men in round hats; policemen wrapped in heavy capes were choreographing the dance for all of them. Bert gazed at the great gray city with dread, remembering Gilbert's glowing descriptions and wondering if his friend hadn't been pulling his leg. Then he told himself that cities exist perhaps only in the subjective experiences of those who live in them.

Jean Joseph helped him up into a streetcar. A crowd in clothes the color of dirty water turned their heads to stare at them and openly laughed. Paying them no heed, Jean asked for news of the country he had left almost fifteen years earlier. Before, well before the war!

"Bah," Bert thought, "maybe you get used to it!"

In the meantime the stares humiliated him, tortured him, made him painfully conscious of his black skin, which until then he had worn without too much trouble. A blond woman stretched her hand toward his face and caressed it, exclaiming:

"Ah, that's guaranteed not to run, that is!"

Everyone laughed, even, which shocked Bert, Jean Joseph. Should one laugh at one's own self?

Jean Joseph's business must not have been very prosperous. For he lived on a dreary street (Rue de la Roquette, whose name Bert managed to decipher), lined with sausage shops filled with the heads of dead calves and bistros where men with their caps on boozed, a street where snot-nosed kids with mops of straw-colored hair ran. Bert held back a sob as he thought of Elaïse's parting kiss. Jean Joseph chattered on without stop:

"I've just been named a member of the Committee for the Defense of the Negro Race, and believe me, Monsieur Gratien Candace, that fanatic ideologue of French imperialism, will hear about me! Every Negro, as soon as he arrives here, he only has one thing in mind: to have a white woman! You know the joke? At the moment of orgasm, the Negro yells: 'Long live Schoelcher! Long live the French abolitionist movement!' "

Bert laughed politely. For his part, he found this man who was old enough to be his father quite frivolous!

"Even Lamine Senghor's married to a woman from Picardy! Me, my woman is like you and me: black. That's where our pride begins: with the color of our women."

The street abutted on a huge cemetery, and Bert was horrified by the mournful forest of tombs, as for the first time he contemplated death far from home, a bad death. Who would come to sit beside his grave? Who would place flowers in vases?

After an agonizing six flights of stairs, Jean introduced his black woman inside a very dark apartment. She was in reality a North African, enveloped in the silk shawl of her hair. Bert, who had never seen a mane like that on a woman, stood there looking at her. Jean was still talking:

"Tomorrow I'll take you to meet Monsieur Gothion Lunion. A great man of Guadeloupe."

The North African woman took Bert's face with its tear-filled eyes in her hands and softly kissed him on the mouth.

"Leave the boy alone! And don't start stuffing his head with your nonsense. I'm going to take him to hear Fifi!"

Actually Bert did neither. At dawn he slipped away to search for Gilbert. He was carrying his friend's address over his heart: 51 Rue d'Alger.

His conscience bothering him, for it was a Sunday, he entered the first church he passed. So different were its walls of stone from the Cathedral of Saint Peter and Saint Paul that all desire to pray deserted him. Nevertheless he

fingered every one of the silver beads on his First Communion rosary before again setting out aimlessly through
the streets, doing his best not to hear the catcalls from the
passersby. Without quite knowing how, he found himself
in front of a monument that indeed appeared to be the
Louvre Museum! Gilbert had described the place to him
at length:

"The Place du Carrousel dates from 1692. It owes its
name to the tournament, or *carrousel*, held there by Louis
XIV. In 1600 it was a garden, called the Parterre de
Mademoiselle, built on the ramparts and filled-in moats.
In 1793 it was renamed Place de la Fraternité. A statue,
removed in 1795, was raised there in memory of
Marat. . . ."

He was terribly disappointed. It was all greenish gray,
striated with darker streaks. It felt very old; its history
crystallized out of the depths of the centuries and did not
touch him in any way. Was he going to waste his time in
this museum of horrors? Determinedly, he turned his
back on it and went on his way.

On the Rue Vignon girls walked up and down the
sidewalks swinging their hips and their handbags covered
with rhinestones. Without ever having seen it, Bert recognized the face of vice. When one of the girls cried:

"Oh, the cute Negro! It's half price for you!" he took
to his heels like a coward.

At Rue d'Alger the concierge received him very
rudely and informed him that there was no one home
upstairs.

That whole day Bert walked through a city that
hummed like an Oriental bazaar, his hands in the pockets
of his ridiculous coat, which did not even keep him
warm. In spite of himself, he stopped to stare defiantly at
Asiatics, who repaid him in kind; at veiled women, who

because of him raised their veils; at dwarfs; at giants showing off their muscles, who seemed tickled pink at the sight of him.

Suddenly he realized it was ten o'clock at night, and rushed to Rue de la Roquette. The cold, dark apartment was deserted. In the kitchen some bread and cheese sat on a plate. He did not touch it and spent the night crying.

The next day Jean Joseph put him on the train to Angers.

The city of Angers had inspired Balzac, who wrote of it: "The history of France is there in its entirety."

In the same way it had also inspired numerous etchers and lithographers. In 1826 the famous artist Turner arrived there on foot while on his annual walking tour along the Loire River from Nantes to Orléans. He filled five pages of his sketchbook with pencil drawings and then executed a series of watercolors on blue paper, entitled *Wanderings by the Loire*, based on those sketches.

Angers evoked nothing in Bert. At the station a man dressed all in black was waiting for him: the school's superintendent, Monsieur Piedelu! Coming out of the station, Piedelu opened his umbrella, for there was thunder in the air. That same night Bert, who had nobody else to confide in, wrote to Gilbert:

> *My dear Gilbert,*
> *Where are you? What are you doing? How will we see each other again?*
> *If you only knew how unhappy I am! I who thought I hated my life in La Pointe! If you knew how much I hate this city, this school, these teachers, and these racist students, ignorant of everything that is not their country of the Loire. How much I hate this sky. . . .*

However, after the first weeks of absolute despair had passed Bert noticed the river's splendor, its blond islands, and its bridges with their audacious struts. Above all he made a friend: Xavier de Lannoy, son of an industrialist from Tours.

Xavier explained to his mother that he had a West Indian friend, that is to say black, but someone he adored; and he was granted permission to invite him to lunch one Sunday. Then Madame de Lannoy lectured the household, especially Xavier's younger brothers and sisters, so that no one might deliver himself of an inopportune remark regarding their guest's color.

Bert stepped from the automobile that had come to pick him up at school, before a double row of onlookers. All the servants had come from their pantries, common rooms, and kitchens; the gamekeepers arrived from their forests, the girls from their boudoirs, the children from their nurseries, and the chaplains from their chapels—all to see the Negro and marvel at his unlikely color! Despite maternal explanations and counsel, little Sophie, five years old and the last-born of the De Lannoys, loosed a long howl of terror and, letting go of her nanny's hand, ran to hide behind a piece of furniture.

Aside from that, everything went very well. Bert knew how to use his fish knife and fork, and Monsieur de Lannoy engaged him in a conversation regarding the conquest of Madagascar and a certain Monsieur Gallieni, already made famous by his exploits in Senegal. After the meal Xavier's sisters overcame their intermittent fits of uncontrollable laughter and chatted with him; and they were astonished to find him so courteous and interested in books. After he left, they tried to outdo each other in repeating:

"How well he speaks French!"

And Xavier answered angrily, upheld in this by his father, who had been impressed by Bert, that he was a Frenchman.

Xavier introduced Bert to the public dances!

Once a month students from the various schools in the city went slumming at the public dances. There they found the means to relieve themselves of all the sperm that remained unused despite daily masturbations, and they were abetted in this by the connivance of the little housemaids from the fine houses of the town. Outside of his escapades with Gilbert, Bert had been well behaved as an adolescent and then as a young man. No question of asking Albert for permission to attend dances! In the family that sort of bacchanal was little appreciated. It was, perhaps, Létitia and Camille Désir's wedding that had been the nearest thing to informality. Bert, who thought of himself as awkward, now realized that he had the fire of dance in his veins! Waltzes, Bostons, Charlestons—he was good at all of them! His heels sprouted wings while his great body lost its stiffness and took on the suppleness of the liana. He whirled, spun, leaped and pirouetted, sketching loops in the middle of an enraptured throng. So did he avenge himself for everything. For his father's cruelty. For the loneliness of his days. For the curiosity. For the laughter. For the paternalism.

On the Feast of Saint Rosalia there was a dance in the Moulin du Pendu quarter.

Bert and Xavier arrived at exactly eleven o'clock, after giving the crowd time to warm up!

Bert's arrival in a community hall always produced a flutter, a mixture of amazement, hilarity, and, in those familiar with his talent, a happy anticipation. A Charleston was playing, a dance disastrous for those whose legs are not nimble! Bert, vain and swaggering, his jacket gaping, planted himself before the row of excited girls, who held their breath while he made his choice. Among all those familiar faces—Big Lulu, to whom he had made love in a doorway; Nana, who had let him come up to her attic room; and Fifi, who had imitated Josephine Baker for him—he suddenly found himself attracted to a pair of two pale-gray eyes set in a not particularly pretty, little, milky, round face! The immoderate emotion mirrored there was flattering, and he let drop a princely:

"You want to dance?"

"Oh, yes, Monsieur Albert!"

"How did you know my name was Albert?"

"Because it wasn't the first time I'd seen you, even if it was the first time you paid any attention to me! I tell you, I hate those dances, the young gentlemen who treat us with such contempt! I'd never have gone there if the other girls from the shop hadn't dragged me. I'm from Britanny. I work in the bottle factory. Oh, I'd like to go back to my village, and go back there with you!"

Marie lived in a mansard room not far from the railway loading docks. From then on, instead of going to spend his weekends with his pen pal, Jean Joseph, Bert hid out there from after lunch on Saturday until the early hours of Monday.

The illness Bert was suffering from had a name: Solitude!

He received one letter a month, two at most, from Elaïse, letters that were started, then interrupted to help lower a child's fever, begun again, again interrupted, and finally came accompanied by a money order taken out of her salary as a ninth-grade teacher. For if Albert paid his son's boarding-school fees and sent money for his school supplies, he did not concern himself with his clothing, much less his diversions.

"He was always cold. My mother, who realized he was very sensitive, was afraid to hurt his feelings and could not give him any warm clothing. And, too, never a *sou* in his pocket. At the bistros I was always paying for him!"

This is Xavier de Lannoy speaking.

And along with that, Gilbert locked up in Le Mans!

So the lonely boy swam, dove, wallowed in love soothing as a lotion! He never tired of the mindless litany of tender words:

"You are my Magi king. My big strong Negro, mine!"

On the physical level, however, things did not go too well! Marie's skin was very white, and when Bert saw her offered up to him, spread out like some milky substance, he experienced a profound feeling of nausea and had to whip his lazy horse of a member in order to satisfy her. She was aware of this and complained in a small voice:

"It's because I'm not educated! I'm just a working girl!"

Bert raised his eyes to Heaven and then consoled her as best he could, though avoiding the pallid line of her mouth.

One morning Marie lost her smile. Circles grew dark around her eyes. Her cheeks became hollow. She turned even chalkier. When he entered her mansard room, Bert found her bent in two over the chamberpot. At last she whispered:

"Bert, I'm pregnant!"

Pregnant! Bert faltered. Then he took hold of himself. Weren't there drugs, purgatives, laxatives, vomitives . . . ? Marie shook her head:

"I've tried everything."

Bert's first impulse was to flee. He borrowed money from a surprised Xavier and jumped onto the train for Paris. Jean Joseph saw him appear at suppertime.

"I understand now that he wanted to ask for my help, or at least my advice about this thing that was tormenting him. But at that moment we were all very busy. I had to go to Marseilles to set up a local chapter of the Committee for the Defense of the Negro Race. I didn't have a minute to myself, and the poor boy, he didn't have even a moment alone with me!"

That is Jean Joseph speaking!

Having no one to confide in, Bert got drunk in one of the many cheap bars on the Rue de la Roquette. Absinthe and red wine had him dancing on the tables in the middle of a shouting crowd. One night he climbed up a lamppost while delighted onlookers shouted:

"Hey, Negro, come down from your coconut tree!"

One afternoon he went to a Turkish bath and was thoroughly buggered by some homosexuals! On another, some hoodlums left him for dead on the Pont des Arts.

There were two weeks of uproar and pain, and meanwhile the trade school decided it was time to apprise Albert of his son's truancy.

At Le Mans, Gilbert received a letter that made him go over the wall:

> *My dear Gilbert,*
> *A calamity has befallen me. I am a dead man. My father will kill me if he learns about it. I made her pregnant. She is white and works in the bottle factory.*
> *Your desperate friend.*

When he reached Angers, the banns were posted. Bert married Marie on December 15, 1925, little more than a year after his arrival in France. Xavier and Gilbert had spent the night before the ceremony trying to dissuade him from committing such a folly. Gilbert, one of whose uncles was a magistrate in Tahiti, suggested he flee and take refuge there. Xavier placed the necessary money at his disposal.

Bert wrote Albert only after the calamity was complete. Was he hoping in that way to force his hand? It is more probable that in his terror he postponed that duty, only resigning himself to it when his back was to the wall. Gilbert de Saint-Symphorien has neither the letter the poor boy finally wrote his father nor the answer he received from him. He has only a copy of the letter that the good-hearted Jean Joseph sent Albert in an attempt to move him to mercy.

> *They are living in horrible poverty. Due to her condition, the girl had to leave her job at the plant. As much as you, I am a follower of Marcus Garvey's ideas (who is contemplating coming to Paris to honor us with his presence in spite of the actions taken against his visit). I believe in a pure Negro race as much as a white who respects himself believes in a pure white race. I maintain that our pride begins with the color of our women. But here it is a question of your son, of his life, and of that of the innocent about to be born. Have pity, and forgive! Send them the money order that will save them. . . .*

That letter received no reply!

Bert found work in a bakery. Wearing a white smock, his face and hair covered with flour (here Gilbert passes over the commentaries and endless jokes!). Each morning

Bert donned a cap, knotted a heavy scarf about his neck, picked up a lunch pail, and set off for work with a heavy, automaton step. In addition, as his wife's pregnancy was a harrowing one, he did everything. The cooking. The laundry. The housework. The shopping. The story of his situation had made its way around the city, and with distressed looks on their faces the tradesmen at the Saint-Pierre market slipped him damaged vegetables and spoiled cheeses:

"How's she doing, that Marie of yours?"

Only on Sunday did he enjoy some small respite, when he could be seen walking endlessly along the river until the night and mist forced him back up into his mansard room.

> *My dear Gilbert,*
> *What use is it living as I do? . . .*

Here Gilbert de Saint-Symphorien weeps. Let us respect his tears!

Bert's son, Albert Louis, third of that name, was born on March 3, 1926. Xavier lay siege to his father, a good Christian who never neglected his Easter duty and had a kind heart. He pulled some strings, and Bert was hired on at l'Electricité de France, the national electric company. Electricity was being brought to the countryside. So many electric poles to raise! So many wires to be put up for the birds!

From then on, Bert went by bicycle along with the work crew to the surrounding villages.

One day as he found himself at the top of a pole, his vision must have blurred, for he lost his balance and fell, breaking his neck.

Accident? Suicide?

Suicide! Gilbert de Saint-Symphorien is categorical on that subject.

"I have all his letters here! Imagine that brutish existence, shriveling up a little more each day, that mind, so keen such a short while earlier, dying in mediocrity! Face-to-face every day with that woman who loved him, but . . . !"

29

The two brothers looked at each other:

"What are we going to do?"

Jacob wavered. His terror of his father, the memory of being thrashed with his cane, and, even more bitter, his father's contemptuous looks were weighing heavily on his mind. He gathered together a bit of courage:

"We have to talk to him! Come with me to Juston, on Saturday."

Jean shook his head:

"No. It can't wait until then. It's too late, now, but tomorrow we'll leave at first birdsong!"

He took his older brother by the hand:

"I'll be the one who'll talk to him!"

It was a long night. Born after Bert had gone to Angers and, it would later be learned, to his death, Jean wondered at this lack of memories. What? Not once had that name been mentioned in Jean's presence! Not a joke Bert had made retold! Not a story in which he must have played a part recounted! Jean felt guilty for his family. Jacob was torturing himself, as usual. He had loved Bert, that big brother who had carried him on his shoulders, who had carved oxcarts out of avocado seeds for him and made the ripe mangoes fall with a blow from his tennis racket! And yet Jacob, too, had let him die!

That night the wind raged. It rose above the sea and swelled before blowing with all its strength, flattening cabins and their banana trees. Then it slackened, and a vast silence fell until the rain in its turn made its voice heard, striking the tin roofs with all its might, taking advantage of the smallest crack to seep inside and soak the straw mattresses. Finally, the furious thunder began to pound. Amid that great anger of the elements, Jacob thought of his father's great anger and, like a frightened child, wished tomorrow might never come.

Having fallen prey to the same fear, Jacob and Jean took the bus on a limpidly clear morning under a newly washed blue sky.

However, it was written that they would never confront their father. When they reached Juston, they found him dumb, blind, and deaf on the piece of jute cloth that served as his pallet, lying in his pigsty of a room full of empty bottles and clay chamberpots floating with excrement. His heart was still beating. No one knew when the attack had struck him down. The farm workers had indeed noticed he was no longer harassing them but did not exactly know when that tranquillity had begun. Two days ago? Three days? A week? Relieved at the idea that the much-dreaded explanation might perhaps not take place, Jacob and Jean had a doctor come from Petit-Bourg.

The *Soubarou* survived a few weeks more. One morning his sister Maroussia opened her eyes after a night's vigil had finally made her nod off beside his bed. The *Soubarou* had passed.

People said that death had dealt its justice and that Albert Louis, who had lived like a dog, had died the same way. Without receiving the final sacraments of the Church. Without confessing the abominable sins he must have had on his conscience since the days when he was searching for gold in Panama. And it is true that he looked terrible between the rows of candles, stiff upon his embroidered sheets! The women of the family had done their best, washing the heavy body, shaving the dread-locks from his hair and the bristles from his chin and ears. His boots had had to be cut open so that his feet, like the roots of the *lignum vitae*, could be slid into them; and in places his toes pointed through the leather like a leper's stumps.

In fact the people were wrong. The *Soubarou* was happy at last. Delivered from the gaze of others. Face-to-face for eternity with the two women he had loved—as much as *Soubarou,* a miser, and an autodidact as he was. Knowledgeable in that knowing that comes only after life is done.

The body was removed and buried at La Pointe, and on the following night the people of Juston began to hear bursts of laughter, joyful cries, and murmurs of happiness come rippling from the trees of the property, above which floated something that looked like arabesques of clouds. Then the birds, hummingbirds, and magpies, gathered to join in the concert that ended only with the wan emergence of the sun. The nights when the moon was full were worse. The racket kept children and adults awake. Yet—and this was surprising—no one thought to fear it. For it was as joyous as a *dansé lewoz*, as enticing as the sound of the bamboo flute. Those who heard it had to hold themselves back from jumping over the swamp bloodwood hedges or from pushing open the rusty gate that now guarded nothing.

Of the two sons who followed behind the coffin (my great-uncle Serge was absent, detained in Toulouse by the medical studies that had been delayed by the war), Jean's eyes remained dry, Jacob's were damp for days on end. He was practically incapable of speech. Tears streamed down his cheeks, exasperating Tima. She was of the opinion that a man has better things to do than cry in public! And Jacob could not possibly have been trying to make people think he missed his father? Once again she did not understand. Jacob was weeping precisely because he felt so little grief in his heart. In its place there was a profound relief. The relief one feels at having let a criminal escape when one is incapable of dealing with him as he deserves. What could he have said to Albert so as not to irritate him from the very outset?

"Father, tell us about him. Tell us of his life that was so short. Tell us of his death. We know nothing about him. At most that he was the son of an English Negro woman you knew in Panama. . . ."

Well, now, that fearsome conversation would not take place!

However, despite the tears that were blinding him, Jacob did not lose his bearings. He divided the estate into three equal portions, which he shared out among Serge, Jean, and himself. But Jean shook his head in his stubborn way and said:

"I wouldn't touch it with a ten-foot pole!"

Then he returned to his Grands-Fonds.

One night, in the bed where she could no longer sleep but lay beside him with her back turned, angry from all the pleasure he had taken without having given her any, Tima felt Jacob touch her shoulder:

"We're leaving for the mother country!"

In spite of her way of grumbling whenever Jacob informed her of a decision, Tima was so happy that she rolled over completely, crying out in a voice childish with delight:

"The mother country!"

After which she quickly rose and threw herself into a round of visits to her relatives and friends, in principle to say good-bye to them, in reality to have them weigh the wealth of the Louises. Ah, no, it was not just any old skinflint who was going to Paris like that, paying his own passage on the French Line! Maroussia, whom Tima went to visit at Port-Louis, greatly irritated Tima when she put on her all-knowing air and said:

"Ah, yes, Jacob told me he had business in Angers."

In Angers?

Isn't Paris the only city in France?

30

Mindful of not interrupting the children's school year, Jacob entrusted Thécla and Dieudonné to Camille Désir's care and settled himself with Tima in a second-class cabin aboard the *Colombie*.

The voyage began auspiciously. Twelve days of blue sky. The sea as smooth as silk. Then Jacob and Tima rented a comfortable three-room apartment on Paris's Rue de l'Ancienne-Comédie that had previously been occupied by people from Guadeloupe. Tima delighted in the sales at La Samaritaine department store and found her way to the Marché Saint-Pierre and the Carreau du Temple. Jacob hooked up with a tropical-produce broker named Pierre Perrutin and sold him the sacks of coffee beans—a still-rare commodity—he had brought with him. Alas, in the seventh month everything went wrong! Having gone to visit his brother Serge in Toulouse, Jacob returned quite surly from a mysterious side trip to the provinces, when a registered letter brought him news that a fire had broken out in the tenement yard! In those days fires were a common occurrence in La Pointe. Not a Lent went by without fire breaking out in the working-class districts! So Jacob could have slept easily if that fire had not caused the death of an entire family. Burned to ashes! The father, a good workingman from the Destrellan sugar factory, the mother, and five children!

Once more, the left- and right-wing newspapers joined in an attack on those black Shylocks who were

171

drinking the blood of their brothers and had had the nerve, sometime earlier, to try to pass themselves off as defenders of the race. Jacob's assistant, insulted, threatened, and for days on end forced to keep the dockside store's steel curtain lowered, begged him to come home.

Which he and Tima did!

At the foot of the gangplank Jean welcomed him with a single word: "Well?"

Jacob shrugged his shoulders: "I'll tell you all about it. . . ."

For out of the corner of his eye, he saw the sign-carrying union members who were waiting for him under the tropical almond trees: MURDERER. NO MORE EXPLOITATION OF MAN BY MAN.

The people who saw my grandfather Jacob on his return from France wondered what could have happened to him. Jews coming out of the concentration camps at Auschwitz and Dachau looked far less wretched. Emaciated. Walking with his head so low that his chin lay flat on his chest, his eyes glazed with despair. On the other hand Tima had never appeared so abloom as in her plum-colored dresses with their muttonleg sleeves. Although she worried, Tima did, about her daughter. Her Thécla! She no longer recognized her!

Ah, if she had only known the truth! One weekend Thécla had agreed to accompany her cousin Dieudonné to l'Anse Laborde, for the boy missed his father. In his pole shack Jean was taking notes at Gesner's dictation—Gesner, the master drummer, who was explaining to Jean how to chop down a tree, cut it into sections, and hollow it out before making it beat like a heart. Seated next to Gesner was his son, Gesner Junior.

How I would like to have known such loves, which are wrongly called puppy love, since they contain all the anguish and torments of adult passions!

No sooner did young Gesner and Thécla set eyes on each other than burning floods of lava set them afire. Gesner Junior left his father and his former schoolteacher standing there:

"Let's take a walk!"

When it came to males, Thécla had never spoken to any but her cousins and her father's brothers. She obeyed and soon heard herself being told what a boring life she led.

And so began the love between my mother and Gesner Ambroise. A birdlike love whose wings she mercilessly clipped. Love she locked in a cage. Yet deprived of its song, her mornings were to be forever gloomy.

Was it the same night that their love was consummated? In a shack made of poles? The sea had begun to shriek in the distance, and the rats were galloping across the roof.

"Hold me tight, I'm afraid."

In any case Tima was not fooled by her daughter's sudden infatuation for the countryside. She began inspecting her underwear, relieved when it was spotted with red only to begin fretting again four weeks later. It was Gesner, expelled from school at the age of fourteen, who taught my mother that Guadeloupe is a country. An island. A land surrounded on all sides by water. Until then she had not cared at all!

"See, mangoes grow on mango trees and genip on genip trees. See, after it rains, the land is covered with pink or white datura, and the crabs come out of their holes brandishing their claws like pincers. Don't stare at the yellow-eyed dog: He could have the evil eye."

Jean, too, realized what was happening between his niece and that reputed good-for-nothing Gesner Junior, whom Gesner Senior had finally despaired of making into a schoolteacher. It warmed his heart and seemed to him a vengeance against Tima, a salutary return to the starting point. The Louises had turned their back on the people without, however, managing to have themselves accepted elsewhere. They needed to get back to them. Thus, under cover of Thécla's liaison with Gesner, Jean set himself to stuffing her mind with diatribes on color, race, and class (matters no one had ever talked to her about) and even tried to give her the *Complete Works* of Marx and Engels, which he had inherited from poor Bert. I hold my great-uncle Jean responsible for the confusion that reigns in my mother's head, for those contradictions she was never able to resolve between her disdain for the people, her fierce desire for social advancement, and her dreams of Negro liberation.

I shall try to present an objective picture of my mother, even though in such cases objectivity is almost out of the question. I well know that my feelings will be seen as merely a banal mother-daughter conflict, and that perhaps is true. She loved me far too little for me to forgive her for it.

My mother possessed neither my forebear's helpless desire to serve, nor my grandfather's muddled sensitivity and humility; even less the generous and naïve idealism of my great-uncle Jean. She was arrogant because self-doubting. Pretending to disdain the esteem of the bourgeoisie since she knew she could never earn it. An outsider due to an excess of ambitions impossible to satisfy! For me, my mother was a sham!

As for Gesner, he was in a good position to know what was happening in Thécla's heart. He knew that one fine morning she would turn her back on him without a backward glance. He also knew that such a fine morning would take the shape of a city boy bearing a well-known name and preferably having light skin. In a sense it was to confirm his suspicions that he went to see Sergette, his mother's own sister, who also dealt in unsnarling tangled matters. Having lit her candles, Sergette dipped her fingers in holy water and opened her Old Testament. After reading, she meditated for a while:

"That girl isn't for you. She'll turn you upside down for no reason at all. But someone else'll take revenge for you and get her pregnant."

"What?"

"No, she's not for you. She's going to leave our country and stay away for an eternity. . . ."

"An eternity!"

From that time on Gesner lived his love like a condemned man awaiting execution.

31

One Saturday Jacob showed up at l'Anse Laborde, pretending not to see his daughter stretched out in the shade of a mango tree with Gesner crouched like a dog at her feet. Closeting himself with his brother, he took up the tale where Gilbert de Saint-Symphorien had left off.

A fourth-class hearse had carried Bert's coffin to the cemetery. Neither flowers nor wreaths. Nevertheless that same day a poem appeared in *La Gazette angevine*.

> *Born on a far-off shore*
> *It is among us that you confronted*
> *death!*
> *Albert of an especial color*
> *Alien to our states*
> *Sleep!*
> *Forever sleep!*
> *Strangers loved you.*

Naïve and maladroit perhaps, this, Bert's sole eulogy.

Bert being dead, what remained of him—that is to say, his memory—began to take on a singular life. Though he had been a taciturn husband who had displayed little zeal in bed, his widow, Marie, made a paragon of him, a saint.

"He had the manners of a great lord. He spoke French to perfection. If it wasn't for his color, you'd have taken him for the son of some great family. In any case his family, black as they were, were very fine people! You should have seen the letters his stepmother sent! What beautiful handwriting! And not one spelling error! He kept the silver rosary from his First Communion! Here, here it is! And, always in a good mood! When he laughed, it was like the sky lit up. I met him at a dance. He came right over to me: 'Mademoiselle, would you like to dance?' Ah! Sometimes you wonder if God knows what He's doing: He takes the best away and leaves the others to do their wickedness in the world. When he left us, my little Bert wasn't even two years old!"

Forced to compare himself with that imaginary idealized Bert, small wonder the son turned into a zombie. Little Bert, Bébert, was a stammering child who urinated on himself long past what was normal. At school they laughed at him for his color and his kinky, sulphur-yellow hair. They also laughed at his stammer, little knowing that it was his hatred of his mother that was making him hold onto each syllable for such a long while before bringing it forth like an egg, past pursed lips. Think of it! In the memory of man there had never been but a single Negro in Angers, and his mother had to go have a child by him! Once a month his godfather Gilbert de Saint-Symphorien showed up from Paris. Winter and summer alike he took little Bert to eat ice cream at the Aux Très Riches Heures tearoom and spoke to him of matters he did not understand:

"When you grow up, you'll come live in our country. That's where your true place is. You're a Negro. Never forget it, and be proud to be one!"

Once each month, too, his mother held his hand and made him write to his family in Guadeloupe. Sometimes she would attach a photograph to his letters, painstakingly writing on the back: *Albert Louis. Angers.* I wonder what happened to those photos.

At war's end Bébert, an eighteen-year-old stripling, disappeared.

"Disappeared?"

Jacob wrung his hands in a familiar gesture:

"Yes, he wanted to be a musician and went to Paris. It would have taken me months to carry out my investigation and pick up his trail. I had already discovered that he was admitted to the conservatory, and I had the address of a hotel on Rue des Abbesses . . . then that business about the tenement yard brought me home."

The two brothers set off on one of those long walks through the countryside they liked so well.

The Lenten heat was torrid. In the fields the sugarcane was drying where it stood, and the cattle lowed with hunger, weary of grazing on scorched soil. They seated themselves under a mango tree and wiped the water from their foreheads, and there Jean unburdened himself. The members of an association calling itself the Group for the Organization of the People of Guadeloupe had approached him and offered him the honorary presidency of their movement.

"You?"

The group was convinced that traditional politicians, occupied as they were with their sinecures, could not lift our country out of the rut into which it had been sinking since the war. They were uttering a word that had never been uttered before: *independence.* And they had given themselves a name: the Patriots.

Jacob looked at his brother in horror:

"What are you going to do?"

Jean pretended to stare at the blazing horizon and answered:

"I don't know yet."

However, by the tone of his voice Jacob knew he was lying. That same night Jacob had a dream. He was walking along a trail crowded with giant ferns that scratched at his eyes, when he heard the unmistakable screams of a pig being butchered. Believing himself far from any plantation, he was surprised, yet he hurried on. Then, in a clearing, he saw Jean hanging by his feet with his head in the grass and bleeding away every drop of blood from his body.

So Jacob understood. Death was upon his brother, and he hurriedly returned to La Pointe to discuss this with Bonnemama Elaïse in the cemetery.

Meanwhile love was doing my mother some good. She lost her stiffness, her angular movements. Grace and feline gestures came to her. And with all that, still at the head of her class. When she passed the first part of her baccalaureate with honors, Tima had a thanksgiving Mass said; while Jacob, never having been much given to religiosity, presented her with the small case where he had kept Elaïse's most beautiful jewelry especially for his daughter. Jean elected to lecture her in a few well-chosen words ending:

"Well, now you are well equipped to work for the race. . . ."

Thécla paid attention neither to the joy nor to the emotion or pride of one and all. For on the Place de la Victoire she had come face-to-face with a young man recently arrived from Senegal, where his father was a magistrate. He was a young whippersnapper of a mulatto but fairly handsome, who walked past without seeing her and left a trail of Roger-et-Gallet cologne behind him. Something in his arrogance had stung her, causing her an emotion that resembled love.

My mother had just met Denis Latran, my father!

32

People say that ghosts do not cross water. So one must therefore believe that Bert, poor Bert, began to live his eternal life in the country of the Loire, a place famed in song and story yet lacking all grace in his eyes. The first summer it was the drought. Scalding sandbanks rose from the thirst-maddened river and weakly dragged themselves to the sea. Poplars, acacia trees, and willows wept from the heat, and thousands of insects honed their cries of distress.

The second summer it was the rain. The rutting river took its pleasure in the bodies of careless swimmers and quickly, quickly rolled them toward its mouth. The rock was as grim as the water, as somber as the sky.

The third summer was sumptuous. Lovers lay themselves down to die of love in the high grass of the riverbanks.

As for Bert, he could stand it no longer. He wandered the night and space as far as the coastline, trying to glimpse in the distance that forbidden island sprawled in the middle of the ocean blue.

He wept:

"Dead or alive, will I always have arms too short to reach happiness?"

PART THREE

33

I, Claude Elaïse Louis, was born in secret at a small private hospital in the fifteenth arrondissement of Paris, on the night of April 23, 1960. My mother had just turned eighteen. She had laced herself into a corset until just before giving birth in order to hide her belly from the sons and daughters of the rich she associated with because of Denis; and so I had a face that was completely flat and a head shaped like a loaf of sugar. Those sons and daughters were in any case beginning to suspect her condition and had never deluded themselves as to the couple's future. Within the first week of her pregnancy, Denis had reminded himself that he was engaged to the daughter of his father's best friend, a judge and mulatto like himself. Yet the two young people continued living together until my birth, when Thécla finally understood that Denis would not marry her.

That night, the night of my birth, Tima became aware that her daughter was in great pain. At the exact moment when I pushed my head from my mother's streaming loins, Tima felt as if some savage hand was wrenching at her guts. At the same time she saw a name being written across the black screen of her closed eyelids: Thécla! She hammered at the blissfully sleeping Jacob's shoulder. In his turn he woke the servant girl, who slept on a pallet on the bare cement of the kitchen floor, and sent her to fetch the doctor.

Good Doctor Alcius, who could never see farther

than the end of his own nose, was completely dumb-founded and prescribed rest for this woman who did nothing but oversee others at their work.

Two weeks after my birth my mother took a train to Finistère without the slightest thought for me, a nursling who was just beginning to look human. Breton foster mothers were the least expensive, so the social workers said. Depositing me with Madame Bonoiel, my mother left me there for ten years.

Madame Bonoeil had never taken care of a black child, but did not love me any the less for that.

A small poem especially for Madame Bonoeil. I wrote it when I was five. Please forgive me for it!

> Mama with white hands
> So gentle to the abandoned
> Black child
> Mama with a heart like good
> White bread
> So good to the abandoned
> Black child.

And so I join with Bert and Bébert, and belong as do they to the lineage of those who are never mentioned. From that no doubt comes my instinctive solidarity with them.

In the limbo I was relegated to, I of course knew nothing of what was happening at home. Thus I was not aware that people there were beginning to speak of several Louis families, the l'Anse Laborde Louises, the La Pointe Louises, and the Basse-Terre Louises, forgetting that they all came from the one and only belly of Bonnemama Elaïse.

My great-uncle Serge had come home a gynecolo-

gist. He had wed within the family, in a way, marrying
Céluta, one of Camille Désir's daughters and the granddaughter of his Aunt Nirva. Alas! A little more than a year
later she was to die from eating an apple-banana in the full
heat of the afternoon, even though she was perspiring
heavily. To tell the truth, this was not the opinion of her
doctor of a husband, who talked of a heart attack. It was
that of her maid, Rose, who tried in vain to warn her
when she saw her take the fruit. So Serge found himself
a widower with a three-month-old baby and wept bitterly at the funeral, comforted by Jacob. People noticed
that Jean did not wear mourning in the funeral procession; but they had no time to find fault with that for soon
afterward a blond woman stepped off an Air France plane.
Who was she?

The people of our country have a stereotyped idea of
the white women who marry our men. They believe
them to be low-born and uneducated. They suppose
them to be drawn like flies to the honey of a life surrounded by servants under endlessly clement skies. Colonial lives, as it were!

Nadège, my great-uncle Serge's second wife, in no
way matched that crude and simplistic image. She was the
daughter of a professor of medicine well known for his
work on rickets and was herself a surgeon, who had had
an English governess and always addressed her mother in
the polite *vous* form. So there is no need to describe how
she regarded our family of Negro peasants. Tima especially made her die with laughter, with her leg-of-mutton
sleeves, her far-too-light-colored stockings, and her tooth
of Guyana gold.

Little by little Serge came to view our family through
Nadège's eyes, and to please his wife, he began to distance
himself. When he opened a clinic with her at Basse-Terre

and had a "change of air" house built for himself at
Gourbeyre, he definitively passed into the bourgeois
camp. He now came down to La Pointe only on hurried
visits, and soon stopped coming there at all. It was by
chance that Jacob learned of the birth of Serge's son,
while reading the "society column" of *L'Eveil basse-ter-
rien*. Embittered, he complained to Tima, who shrugged:

"What do you care? You saw he'd changed sides long
ago!"

As for the quarrel between Serge and Jean, it had
begun far earlier.

Shortly after coming home, Serge had gone to visit
Jean at his retreat at l'Anse Laborde. Jean had had him leaf
through the two volumes of the just-published *Unknown
Guadeloupe* and admire his pole shack, which the rains
flowed over without entering. Then he had sat Serge
down among his peasant friends, showed off his remas-
tered Creole, and drunk one straight rum after another.
At first Serge said nothing, and everything appeared to
indicate that he was, and with good reason, impressed.
Suddenly, while Marietta was ladling *Soupe Z'Habitants*
into small *couis*, Serge looked up at his brother with eyes
that sparkled with flashes of irony and mockingly asked:

"What are you playing at?"

Stunned silence from Jean! Then Serge stood up:

"Stop these masquerades of yours! No matter what
you do, you'll always be an ill-at-ease little petty bourgeois who plays at being a man of the people!"

After which, roaring with laughter, he headed for his
car. He was never again seen at l'Anse Laborde!

In its early stages the discord between Serge and Jean
brought great sadness to Jacob. He would so have liked
the sons of Bonnemama Elaïse to remain as united as the

fingers of a hand. Then the worry Tima's health was giving him superseded all else.

Indeed, once Thécla left La Pointe to go study in Paris, she no longer wrote to either her father or her uncle Jean. Nor to the abandoned Gesner. Not even to her mother!

Day after day Tima watched for the postman. Then she began to suspect the Postal Service, according to her a nest of communists, of playing some evil trick on her and wrote a letter to that effect to the ministry in Paris. At last she had to look ingratitude in the eye and understand that her beloved daughter was neglecting her.

From that day on she fell into morosity and resentment.

Every morning she rose dolefully at four and made her way to early Mass along with the overzealous church-going women in black madras. After taking Communion, she retreated from the Communion table with such a languourous look that for a time word spread that she was having holy visions. She no longer abused her servants, and they in turn allowed dust to powder the furniture and shutters—over which the mistress of the house stopped running her finger—and gave up watering the indoor plants. Deprived of water, the potted lataniers began to die, and the whole house took on a slovenly air. Likewise, Tima no longer had the heart to tyrannize Dieudonné, who dared bring his school friends home to smoke and play harmonica in his room. As for the night, she let herself be taken as many times as Jacob wanted, her eyes closed, without a protest or a grimace, and practically unconscious. Jacob did try to convince her to go spend some time in the "change of air" house at Juston he had fitted out for her. But she grimly refused to do so. It was as if she knew that it was forbidden private property where at present her old enemy, the *Soubarou*, despotically ruled.

From then on Tima lived at Thécla's rhythm, despite the distance and silence that had settled between them. She felt her daughter's labor pains, without wanting to understand what they were. During Thécla's miscarriage a blackish blood spurted from Tima's own belly, even though she was no longer subject to menses. When Thécla sank into her nervous depressions, Tima plunged into the purple waters of anxiety, gathering only enough strength to rock back and forth, forth and back, in her rocking chair on the balcony between the potted bougainvilleas. The passersby sadly nodded their heads:

"*A pa jé, non!* If that isn't sad!"

She died one night in her sleep, my grandmother Tima. Without my ever having known her and without my being able to ease the pain in her heart with all of my affection. She died one night when the darkness was black, the weary moon asleep in the folds of clouds behind the Casuarina trees. She died a death that inspired no regrets, no great sorrow in anyone. Except in Jacob, who was inconsolable! When they saw him walking bent in two behind her coffin, no one thought he would ever recover.

However, he was barely fifty years old and had carnal desires to spare. So he brought into his house on the Rue du Faubourg-d'Ennery Flora Lacour, his mistress of many years; and she came along with her two bastard sons, who continued to address him as Friend Louis, as they would an acquaintance. Where Tima was, however, she was not hurt by this, for she had found the serene fulfillment life had long denied her.

34

I would like to know how many men used my mother's sorry body on those foggy London nights and mistook the groans of her wounded pride for moans of pleasure? The list, was the list of them long?

When Denis finally abandoned her with the bastard daughter he would not even acknowledge, she who had received the Prize of Excellence from the sixth grade to the twelfth; who had finished high school, one year of college prep, and one of university; who had earned a certificate in English at the Sorbonne—she, Thécla, thought herself an object of derision in Paris, and even worse, of pity. So she chose a few items of clothing at random and hopped on a train at the Gare du Nord. In the course of her studies she had often gone to London, that sad, rainy city, which she hated yet which suddenly seemed to her to suit the debacle of her youth.

Out of habit she signed up at the university and began research on Joseph Conrad. *Heart of Darkness*. In the bloodred neon hours, when she could no longer bear her shame and sadness, she went to a small club called the Purple Rose of Cairo. There a singer with camellias in her hair sang old Billie Holiday songs. Without fail, 'round midnight found Thécla sobbing into her handkerchief. One evening a man sat down at her table: very short, very handsome, and very black. He said, tenderly:

"What *is* the matter, baby?"

Something in his carbuncle eyes was signifying more than a desire to take her to bed.

Manuel Pastor was the son of a Cuban peasant. His father, tired of wearing himself out in the cane fields, had tossed aside his machete and taken the boat for New York. No sooner had he arrived than he married a black American cleaning woman and gave her four sons. His brothers ended up doing varying amounts of time in State prisons, but unlike them Manuel had gone to school and was working toward a doctorate at Temple University. He had been in London for several months, for he was endeavoring to collect all of Marcus Garvey's correspondence. In fact he had two heroes: Marcus Garvey, who alas had died in poverty amid the arid indifference of Negro hearts, and Malcolm X.

Thécla had often heard talk of Marcus Garvey. Not, however, from her father, who kept his mouth shut about that period of his life. It was from Tima, who liked to recall all the stupid mistakes and dirty tricks Jacob had committed and the way he had left her alone with a young child to seek death in the night. She mocked that famous phrase—"I shall teach the Black Man . . ."—which had been the program of the Negroes Arise party, and commented:

"Try telling me a Negro's beautiful! When there's nothing uglier than him because of all the meanness in his heart. You know what my mother used to say: 'Ooh, a nigger's a hurricane and an earthquake. He leaves nothing but desolation behind him.' "

On the other hand, Thécla had never heard of Malcolm X, and Manuel pounced:

"You don't know who Malcolm is, baby? His words'r going to set America on fire, and in the burnin

ashes of the white man's evil and racism we will plant
Love!"

Rational Thécla wanted to know more about it.
Manuel explained:

"Malcolm's father was a follower of Marcus Garvey.
You see, at the beginning of everything, there's our Father Marcus. But *he* wouldn't listen to nothin. Stealin,
rapin, drugs, jail . . . until the day he came face-to-face
with the black god of Islam. . . ."

"The black god of Islam?"

"Yes. Don't you make fun of it, honey! They told
you all those lies and, in spite of yourself, you wound up
believin. The cursed race of Ham. The truth is we are the
twelfth tribe of Israel and we *shall* see our kingdom
again!"

The first few times Thécla had to hold herself back to
keep from laughing, wondering what kind of half-crazed
man she was dealing with! Then, little by little, the magic
of his dreams and of the words they carried took hold of
her. But most of all, Manuel did not merely manipulate
frenzied phrases. He made love so well! The nights were
never long enough in that suburban brick house he shared
with three musician brothers from Jamaica, that house
where the air shook with the blare of synthesizers. Mornings, a worn-out Thécla plummeted into sleep, waking
again well after the university libraries had closed.

Thécla and Manuel had known each other for a
month when with Latin gallantry he knelt down on one
knee and offered to marry her. She refused, mysteriously
stammering that there was an obstacle to such happiness,
but agreed to accompany him to America.

My mother's first transformation dates from this
meeting with Manuel. She arrived in London a rather

rigid petty bourgeoise with her high heels, her copies of Chanel suits, and her face smeared with blue on the eyelids and red on the lips. She became the wholesome activist with her hair left natural and cut short and her feet shod in black-linen ballerinas (it should be pointed out that she was a good eight inches taller than Manuel!). It is during this period that she set aside Conrad and his *Heart of Darkness* and replaced him with the black American novelist Richard Wright, to whose work Manuel had introduced her. It is during this period, too, it must be said, that she began drinking very hard; like Manuel, and with him.

It is during this period, finally, that another event occurred. My great-uncle Jean had not been seen on the streets of La Pointe for almost two years, so horrified was he by what that city was becoming (and the people on their part found him quite changed, unkempt, he who had been so handsome). One day he came bursting like a madman into the house of his brother Jacob, who sat across from Tima finishing a joyless lunch.

"I have a letter! A letter from Thécla!"

> *My dear Uncle,*
> *You will forgive my silence when you know that I have gone through terrible trials. But they have made a woman of me. My eyes are being opened. Now I see clearly, and I understand the meaning of the lessons you taught me. Yes, you will be able to be proud of me soon. My best regards to Gesner. I kiss you.*
> *Your affectionate niece.*

Jacob replaced the sheet of paper in its envelope. Wordlessly, he handed it to Tima, who had stood up, placing her hand over her heart. She in her turn read it before falling back heavily into her chair and moaning:

"And us! And us! Not a word for her papa! Not a word for her mama! Oh, Jesus and the Virgin Mary! Those people who tell you to have babies never think! Why? Why, I ask you? What can be more ungrateful than a child? More unfeeling? My belly tore open for that girl. The doctors thought I was going to die, but I got better anyway, and now she writes to her uncle, *to her uncle*, and she doesn't even ask if I'm alive or already in my grave!"

Jacob and Jean left her to her lamentations, no less earsplitting for being justified, and closeted themselves in their father's former office. Jacob wept openly for a moment, then hiccuped:

"She says 'trials.' What could that mean?"

Jean shrugged:

"Bah! Some little love affair that went bad! At her age!"

The unhappy father noisily blew his nose as Jean turned to another subject:

"You know what that fool of a Serge has come up with now?"

For at present it was open war between Jean and Serge, even though they were not yet taking potshots at each other in public. Politics! Always politics! Serge had joined the triumphant party of General de Gaulle and, running under its banner, had been elected to the Gourbeyre city council. Since Jean had accepted the honorary presidency of the Patriots' movement, the AOPG, each brother had taken the other as his favorite whipping boy. For Jean, Serge was the symbol of the assimilationist middle class that for three centuries had let down its pants while crying: *"Vive la France!"* For Serge, Jean was worse than a communist! Jacob was careful not to take sides in the quarrel, for he knew from his own experience that politics is a pit into which none but the fiercest, rum-drunk gamecocks must venture!

"He's the one who'll be guiding De Gaulle when the general proposes a special status for Guadeloupe! At the same time, maybe he'll get that Legion of Honor of his!"

Deaf to these words, the unhappy father went on hiccuping, wiping his nose, and torturing himself:

"She says 'trials.' What is she talking about? You see, Jeannot, if some man's fooled around with my daughter, I'll pick up a rifle and I'll kill him with my own two hands, with these hands!"

Jean knew well that his brother couldn't hurt a fly. Not even listening to him, he forged ahead:

"Maybe he'll get it! I bet Serge will wind up a deputy, sitting there doing nothing in the National Assembly. What do you think?"

The unhappy father did not think about it at all.

A week or two later it was Gesner's turn to come bursting like a madman into the pole shack where Jean was frantically scribbling:

"A letter! A letter from Thécla! She's going to New York!"

Jean was taken aback:

"New York? What the hell is she going to do there?"

The letter did not say.

My dear Gesner,

Will you ever forgive my cruelty toward you? My sole excuse is that I was a victim of my upbring-ing. . . . Need I tell you that you taught me everything and that you are the only man I will ever love?

Your poor Thécla.

Poor? The two men looked at each other, and Jean saw, rising wildly in Gesner's fine brown eyes, a desire to sell the piece of land left him by his father and discover America for himself. Youth! Youth!

Jean muttered:

"Don't get all worked up! Don't get on your high horse! She hasn't asked you to come join her, that I know! You'd do better to study for your stretcher-bearer's exam!"

Far more than Dieudonné, Gesner was a son to Jean! For though Dieudonné was flesh of Jean's flesh, he was growing up at La Pointe under Tima's influence and, in spite of his father, taking on her ways, rinsing a goblet twice and pushing away his breadfruit *migan* after only one mouthful. Jean had first seen Gesner when he was very young. The boy's large, knobby head was high as his father's knee, and he moved his small fingers over the taut skin of a drum as he solemnly listened to his teacher's explanations! Dozens of times Jean had stood him in a corner of the school yard for punishment, arms outstretched and a rock in each hand, to make him learn his multiplication tables. Then he had come to understand that he had to let the boy do what he wanted: make music!

What a musician! He had just formed an orchestra made up of, besides himself on tambour drum, a flutist and a *ti-bwa* player! Ah, the wonder of those sounds!

Gesner's group, christened *Kreye*—"Passel," as in "passel of fish"—was a hit at every town festival from Petit-Bourg to Vieux Habitants. It only had to be advertised for the stands to grow black with an eager and spellbound crowd. For Gesner's music did not simply speak to the senses, like the beguine, but to the heart and to the soul. It did not simply make legs wriggle and hips sway. It awakened in each person the mysterious desire to love, to reciprocate, to share; and it was not rare during these concerts for two strangers to cling to each other and kiss. As for the words that accompanied it, they were never vulgar or bawdy, but poetic!

During that period, however, Gesner was still trying to find himself. He had not yet composed the piece he would dedicate to his mother, a song that immediately made its way around the French- and English-speaking Caribbean, not to mention Cuba, Puerto Rico, Aruba, and Bonaire before going on to conquer Africa and Europe: *"Limbé,"* or "Lovesick."

35

When Thécla arrived in New York in the month of August 1963, more than twenty years after her father, she had a good head start on him in the person of Manuel—a guide capable of opening the belly of the city like a moneybox to her. Born and raised on 130th Street, Manuel had shined shoes on every Manhattan street corner and sold drugs in every public toilet to pay for his education and, for entertainment, had screwed in every basement. He moved through the airless hothouse of its streets and avenues holding Thécla by the arm.

"Look at it all, girl! It's the prettiest and most perverse creature in the world! The very image of my feelings for America, this land where I was born. Hate verging on love. Brutality and poetry. It's a whore. Who knows how to be sweet. Sometimes it's poetic and dreamy. But fundamentally it's evil. When it fucks, its shrill yells can bust your eardrums. Can't live without it!"

It's true, Thécla did have this knowledgeable guide at her side. She had known some great cities: Paris, London. One summer she had even ventured as far as Barcelona with Denis and drunk red wine in the barrios. And yet she was not far from feeling the panicky emotions that her simpleton of a father, barely out of his native backwater, had himself felt. Bewildered, taken aback, terrified. For New York is a philter that arouses the sturdiest of natures. And then, Manuel swept Thécla straight into the seventh circle of Hell, there where the odor of vice is no longer foul, where violence rules, and where a man's life is worth almost nothing.

His family was still going to seed on 130th Street. The father, a country boy in his youth who had been converted into a hotel porter, bore the harsh winter of his life with shots of bad Bacardi rum, drinking from morning to night. Lost in his nightmares, he nodded off next to a window that looked out on fire hydrants and the patched shoes of passersby. At times he moaned:

"Life's a bitch! Never saw no sun rise for me! I have crossed the sea, and on both shores it was hunger and desolation. Oh, yes, we are a cursed race!"

Whenever he heard this, Manuel flew into a rage and rained despairing and loving insults on him. Meanwhile Mrs. Pastor, who had been cleaning toilets all day, prepared mounds of food and ruminated on the sins that had led three of her sons to maximum-security prisons in every corner of the land. Thank God, Earl, the favorite, would soon be coming home.

Mr. and Mrs. Baltimore were sermonizing visionaries who lived in the next apartment. At exactly seven o'clock they entered the kitchen, summoned by the aroma, and gobbled down fried chicken legs, jambalaya, shrimp gumbo, and slices of sweet potato pie, all the while reading aloud from the Good Book between bites.

"Cast thy bread upon the waters; for thou shalt find it after many days. Divide it unto seven and even unto eight persons; for you do not know what evil may befall the earth."

Or:

"The wise man's heart is at his right hand, but a fool's heart is at his left. Yea also, when he that is a fool walketh by the way, his wisdom faileth him and he saith to every one that he is a fool."

They had perfected their infallible technique, had Mr. and Mrs. Baltimore, prophesying preachers ever since they had left their cabin in Alabama! Each morning they posted themselves on a street corner, set a bowl between their feet, and foretold the end of the Negro race amid the foul odor of its sins. Mr. Baltimore, the more inspired of the two, clarioned:

"Hurry, hurry. Azrael, the angel of death, be rushing toward us now with his shining scythe in his right hand. Give, give, to hold back his chariot. . . ."

Pennies, dimes, half-dollars rained down on them. When the bowl was full, Mr. and Mrs. Baltimore went and bought a few carefully wrapped bottles that they deposited in their apartment. Then, the day's efforts done, they came to refresh themselves at Mrs. Pastor's. The Baltimores terrified Thécla, especially the preacher-woman, who stared at her out of reddened eyes as if Thécla were some prey. How she would have liked to flee this airless slum and go down, ever downward toward those avenues where dreams are sold, or to take off for the cozy suburbs where trees bedeck themselves in the colors of Indian summer. Alas, it could not be helped. Manuel's parents were the apple of his eye!

In mid-September Earl returned from San Quentin, where he had served his ten-year stretch for armed robbery. Thécla had never met a professional holdup artist. She saw a short man enter, shorter even than Manuel, but with the same carbuncle eyes and a voice sweet as a choirboy's at Mass. He kissed his elderly father's forehead and took his old mother, who was sobbing, into his arms, saying:

"Come on, come on, it's over!"

He did two more important things. He neatly got rid of Mr. and Mrs. Baltimore when they showed up at dinnertime and, when night fell, he slid into the folding bed where Thécla slept with Manuel, the latter explaining:

"We've always shared everything!"

From that period dates my mother's second transformation. I look at the photographs. Gone the unadorned activist! In her stead a glorious female, body hoed and spaded, voice low, cracked, ringing like the saxophone in the after-hours clubs where she spent the nights with her men.

In the intervals between these two risks of an overdose, however, there was no lack of intellectual preoccupation. Earl the holdup man was, paradoxically, a partisan of nonviolence and a devout disciple of Dr. Martin Luther King. He fervently followed his marches on television, commenting:

"There it is! They loosed the dogs! They really mean to finish us off!"

As for Manuel, he continued to venerate Malcolm X. All he could dream of was discussing several points of Islamic theory with him that were still obscure in his mind. Indeed, in the hope of meeting him, Manuel was a regular at Malcolm's 116th Street temple. Unfortunately the great man was either attempting to light the salutary fire in diverse sections of the country or else was visiting Africa or else was too busy. Thécla took no part in the brothers' quarrels. She had abandoned Richard Wright and felt burgeoning within her a more ambitious subject: "On the Condition of Blacks in America." To this end she attempted to interview Mrs. Pastor. Had her parents spoken to her of their life in Virginia? What had they found in the North? Alas, Mrs. Pastor, who blamed this intruder for stealing her two sons, would not open her mouth!

My dear Gesner,
    What I see around me in New York, in this city
dominated by the Statue of Liberty, is unimaginable.
By contrast, how our lives and that of our parents seem
rich and uneventful. . . .

A few months later Thécla's belly began to grow round beneath her flowing dresses.

Thécla, raised by Tima to respect God and the terror of the opinion of mankind, had freed herself from the precepts of her childhood. Not enough, however, to be completely content with the ambiguity over who had fathered the fetus quickening inside her. She fell into a somber humor that a prediction from Mrs. Baltimore, whom she passed in the hallway, made even gloomier:

"The fruit of sin shall not ripen!"

Manuel exulted and danced about:

"One more little Negro! Seems to me I can see him now, with his eyes big and wide with wanting all the things the white man won't let us have because they know if they let us alone, we do everything better than them!"

As for Earl, he was more reserved, at times almost as somber as Thécla. He paced the room:

"It's not the peanuts Manuel's earning at that university of his going to buy our boy the kind of life you need to come out on top in this evil country!"

After which, he set himself to oiling the sawed-off shotgun he had stored atop a piece of furniture and, one night, disappeared.

36

It's always the same thing! If you take any American on the street and ask what struck him most about the year 1965, there is a good chance he'll answer: "The assassination of Malcolm X two years after the assassination of Kennedy in an America gone mad."

Yet despite his admiration for the leader, Manuel was almost indifferent to his death. All that he would remember of it that year was his brother's furtive departure, his return at dawn three days later, his blood-covered clothing, and his last smile as he looked up at Thécla:

"Take care, baby!"

For Manuel, living in the mourning and revolt of his country's black community, the year 1965 was that! And he came to realize with amazement that for others the sojourn on earth of Earl M. Pastor, deceased in the thirty-third year of his life, barely counted.

Earl's death saw the triumph of Mr. and Mrs. Baltimore. Scarcely had the blood-soaked body been removed than they burst into the basement, where Thécla's sobs were echoing those of Mrs. Pastor. This time there was no one to get rid of them. As Mr. Baltimore knelt, Mrs. Baltimore bore down upon her quarry like some carnivorous spider. Quickly abandoning Mrs. Pastor as far too easy a prey, she set her sights on Thécla. To hear her, the signs were clear:

"It's the smell of your sin that's offended the nostrils

of Eternal God. It's sin's blackness that's disgusted his all-loving and easily forgiving heart. You lay yourself down under a sheet between two men, two brothers! What will you call the monster who is to come from your innards?"

Thécla sobbed:

"And you don't know everything! You don't know the extent of my sins. I, Thécla Louis, killed my mother and father. I stuck a knife in their hearts. I made their blood flow. And licked my lips at the sight of it!"

"Why'd you do it?"

"They made me ashamed. I blamed them for being too black. Being uneducated. My mother didn't know anything about anything. She could only talk about her recipes and her dreams. 'To make *dombwé* and peas, you take . . .' And at the same time she thought of herself as sprung from the thigh of Jupiter. Because of her money she had contempt for everyone. As for him, as for him . . ."

"Now, now, calm down!"

"I wished I had other parents, a different family! I wished . . ."

One week after Earl's death Thécla was reading the Good Book: "The fool hath said in his heart: 'There is no God!' They are corrupt, they have done abominable works; there is none that doeth good. The Lord looked down from heaven upon the children of men, to see if there were any that did understand, and seek God. They are all gone aside"—and pains suddenly began belaboring her belly, out of which a dark blood came streaming. She fell over onto her back as Mrs. Baltimore tried to make her join her hands together and repeat after her:

"Hosanna! May Thy justice be done!"

———

At that same moment, in La Pointe, a conference of doctors was gathered about the bed of Tima as she grit her teeth from the effects of a mysterious malady:

"It's the menopause! Women don't take it too well. You ought to take her on a trip to the home country!"

Jacob calculated the cost!

Her child dead and the sin expiated, Thécla was careful not to sin any further.

She left Manuel and 130th Street and rented a room from a respectable Haitian family in Brooklyn.

She went back to her studies.

37

Yes, after having buried so many bodies, it was normal that to go on living, Thécla and Manuel should have separated.

Manuel remained, his feet in the snow of New York. Daytimes he worked on his Ph.D., which for some time now had begun to feel like an obituary notice. Nights he handed out bedpans and kidney basins to old people in a hospital and received their foul breath full in his face whenever they joked with him about his obvious sorrow. He neither heard nor saw them. Thécla was forever blurring his vision.

I find Thécla's trace again in Port-au-Prince, Haiti. It is true, she had fairly well pulled together what was left of herself and signed up at Columbia to do research on "The Influence of the Harlem Renaissance on the Intellectuals of Haiti." She had done this out of a sort of reflex, believing that studying gives sense to a life that has none.

She found herself in the Turgeau quarter, in the Les Poinsettias *pension* run by the Volder ladies.

The mulatto Volder family had suffered much since the advent of the Negro dictator Duvalier. Their men had fled in disorder to Central or North or South America to escape the Tonton Macoutes, and all that remained was this quartet of women. The mother. The aunt. The older daughter. The younger daughter. All four with skin the color of an ivory crucifix and dressed in black; for they were mourning a husband, a fiancé, a father, and a beau who had never declared his intentions but who would have given the family beautiful children. The portion of their time not spent in abusing frightened little downtrodden servants was divided between conversing with visitors and reciting prayers. Prayers for the living. Prayers for the dead. Prayers for the absent. Prayers for those present. Prayers above all for beloved Haiti with its unending suffering. Visits from all their friends and relatives in mourning. A funeral procession that came flocking from everywhere. Widowers. Widows. Fatherless and motherless orphans, mopping up their revolt with holy water.

Thécla was coming out of a library when a veritable ebony statue planted himself before her, a statue that in earlier times would have, no doubt about it, cost a fortune.

"Mademoiselle, pardon my boldness!"

God! She had never seen a man so tall! And broad-shouldered! She whose eyes had for years looked down at Manuel and then at Earl, she who had pressed both of them, scarcely heavier than children, against her breast! She was turning dizzy from all that strength!

"May I introduce myself: Henock Magister!"

Henock Magister was not much, a reporter on *Le Nouvelliste*, but he had great arms that wrapped clear around Thécla, a wide mouth that covered her with kisses, and a large cock that he stuffed passionately between her lips or between her thighs. And with all that, his mother was sweet and tender to the homeless woman from Guadeloupe. She sold bread, Madame Magister did, bread made by her husband, who was named Henock like the oldest son, and she considered the dictatorship philosophically.

"We been suffering for centuries. We fought to make

the French leave and freedom come. The French left, but freedom, she didn't come. Then we fought to make the Americans leave, and make freedom come. Same story. The Americans leave, freedom, she didn't come! We mobilize to drive out the mulatto presidents. The mulatto presidents leave. A Negro come, and it's worse! Me, I tell you our race is the race of the cursed!''

Old Magister could not keep so cool a head and, carried away, was always saying:

"Hand me a rifle! Set that Duvalier in my sights and I'll kill him for you! It's stone dead you be picking him up!''

As for Henock, thanks to the press card that gave him entry to the Presidential Palace, he could put on a knowing air:

"The thing is, he's not what people think, and if you prick him, blood won't come out! Only water mixed in with some pus. It's . . . it's Baron Samedi, and me, I tell you, week in, week out, he needs his fill of new flesh! That's why the Tonton Macoutes kill all those people.''

One fine day Henock, who dreamed of appearing important in his belle's unsmiling eyes, brought her an engraved invitation. In gilded letters Madame and Monsieur le Président invited Mademoiselle Thécla Louis International Researcher (sic) to a garden party on the lawns of the Presidential Palace.

For once I shall be generous toward my mother. There is no doubt: If she had not felt herself so alone, so lost, if she had not felt the weight of all those deaths on her conscience and the anguish of the time she was wasting each day, she would not have accepted that invitation.

But wearied by memories and boredom, she did accept it. She thought it very beautiful, the Presidential Palace, with its goldfish swimming in a basin of bluish marble, its pink flamingos pecking food from the guests' hands, and the green parrots endlessly jabbering in their cages. She danced impassionedly with Henock, who was dressed to the teeth and who introduced her to other men as tall and broad-shouldered as he. Ah, what a beautiful race, that race of Haitian Negroes!

The president was said to be suffering from severe urinary incontinence, due to his prostate, and he was almost unable to stand. Nevertheless he pulled himself to his feet and delivered a very long speech enumerating the blessings of his reign. He was warmly applauded. At a given moment a trio of musicians settled themselves on the platform, and Ottavia was introduced.

Ottavia's great voice had sung the sorrows of the Haitian people on all the stages of the world, and some in the audience expressed astonishment that she could now sing them before the very people who had caused them. For Thécla, schooled in music by Gesner, time stopped as the harmony of those sounds rose upward to the gates of Heaven. Tears streamed down her cheeks as she recalled, pell-mell, her childhood, her first love, the death of one of her men, and the loss of her child (it pleases me to believe that she also thought of me, growing up in my exile in Finistère!), and a bewildered Henock Magister wondered what god had sent this woman to him!

> *Souflé van*
> *Souflé van*
> *Pitit-mwen ka mo*
> *Mari-mwen ja mo*
> *Mwen mem an pa sav*
> *Si sé viv an ka viv . . .*
> *Blow, great wind*
> *Blow, great wind*

My baby be dying
My husband already dead
Me, I don't know
If I be dead or alive.

That night Thécla came home late from the Presidential Palace escorted by one of Henock Magister's friends, who, it turned out, was the minister of something or other. Or a state secretary.

The next day the Volder ladies did not appear at breakfast, always taken in the old dining room with its faded-green walls under the good-natured gaze of Trygve Volder, an ancestor with blond side-whiskers who had come from Norway with a few crowns folded inside his shoe. Neither did they appear at noon; nor at the evening meal, for which a surprised Thécla, already suspecting the calamity, took her place at table. Between the soup and the conch pot pie a servant tremblingly handed her a note from Madame Mother Volder, which ordered her to leave: "We cannot accept under our roof those who treat with our enemies."

Thécla did not even consider trying to exonerate herself. Mournfully she packed her valise and went to the Hotel Ibo-Lélé. Living in the room next to hers was Ottavia.

38

Friendship between women can resemble love. It has the same possessiveness as love, the same jealousies and lack of restraint. But the complicities of friendship are more durable than those of love, for they are not based on the language of the body.

In a certain way Thécla and Ottavia were made for talking to each other, like the bamboo flute and the *ti-bwa* in the music that makes the wooden carousel horses go around. Ottavia's father was an Italian mason. Having come to repair some tiles, he wound up in the bed of Meralda, the youngest and most beautiful daughter of the aristocratic Malden family, who were mulattoes of German origin. The mason was a drunk. After giving Meralda seven children he fell to his death from a roof. Meralda, who had never worked a day in her life, had tearfully thrown herself at the baker, who was allowing her to buy bread on credit. Until the day he died, this superb ebony statue must have wondered if on a certain morning he would not have done better to leave his truck in the garage. Ottavia had therefore grown up among a swarm of brothers and sisters and half brothers and half sisters on an equal footing with the peasant children of Cayes, throwing stones at mangoes for her lunch as they did, yet contemptuous of them and believing herself of a superior species. A conviction fueled by Meralda, who owned several pieces of fine jewelry and a Caribbean basketful of damask table linen. Later she was adopted by

Carlotta, her mother's oldest sister and a spinster. Carlotta emprisoned Ottavia's wild child's body in a uniform of white and blue and enrolled her in a boarding school at Lalue, where the children of the bourgeoisie made fun of her accent and whispered that her mother had been someone's mistress. So Ottavia, like Thécla, hated her childhood, her family, and the land that she believed symbolized them. Luckier than Thécla, however, Ottavia had sublimated her resentments. Verbally attacking the authorities and middle classes, she rid herself of all that temper. So Thécla emptied a multitude of bottles of Barbancourt rum with Ottavia, who was no longer thinking of taking her plane back to New York despite the fact that she was supposed to sing for Haitian refugees; and the two of them lay stretched out side by side. Throughout the night they rambled on about the world, about life and its basic meanness, about Negroes, mulattoes, sexual pleasure, religion, death, politics. The result being that poor Henock Magister could no longer find a way to make love to his Thécla and unflaggingly hung about in the garden, his head and cock low.

I have no exact information at my disposal about the manner in which matters were conceived and carried out, and I have to admit that here I cannot fill in the missing pieces. Had Ottavia actually been charged with a mission by some politically minded friends? In what measure did she exceed her orders? In what measure was she playing sorcerer's apprentice? Is it true that she placed her trust in certain voodoo priests she knew from having studied the music of their rituals? Is it true that at her instigation they ordered the people to take to the streets and march on the palace? Is it true that she likewise had the advantage of collusion among members of Duvalier's entourage? The fact remains that all this led to an event well known to those who take an interest in the history of the Antilles: the savage repression of 1967.

It all began with the burning of the house belonging to the minister of the interior, Luckner Damidas, such a fine dancer and so well liked by women. At midnight orange-colored flames licked the black sky. (Some say it was a signal.) Damidas had only time enough to jump from the window of the attic, where he slept alone. His wife and five children, sleeping on the second floor, were burned alive. Taking advantage of the chaos fire kindles in our lands, innumerable groups rose up out of the shadows, joined together, and surged forward in angry waves, chanting:

"Down with the regime!"

The Tonton Macoutes promptly woke from their sleep and gave no quarter. Five days later, for there were five days of it, five days of riots, the dogs were free to lap up blood from the puddles and to gnaw bones. Mangled bodies were dragged from the gutters and brought to the city gates to be burned. Thus fire ended what fire had begun.

Ottavia was arrested. But her reputation and pressure from Amnesty International brought about her quick release. My mother, a foreigner, was speedily deported to France and would have gotten off altogether cheaply if Henock Magister had not been killed in the affair.

Oh, the befuddlements of love!

Henock Magister, a young man of mediocre education who had never given a thought to man's exploitation of man, so wanted to see himself look noble in the mirror of his beloved's eyes! So he took over leadership of operations in one neighborhood and was in the front lines when the Tonton Macoutes and soldiers charged.

I believe that we may number him among our mar-

tyrs, unless we demand that our martyrs have the baccalaureate.

So my mother renewed her acquaintance with Paris
at the beginning of the year 1968. True, the manner in
which she viewed the city had not changed, and in certain cafés, certain movie houses, certain parks the
scratched record of her memory harked back, harked
back. Yet for its part the city regarded her otherwise. She
had been closely involved in important political events.
Would she expound on them?

"Thécla Louis, what are your thoughts on the American policy of intervention in Haiti?"

"You were also in the United States at the time of the
assassination of Malcolm X. How did the American black
community react?"

Instead of shouting for them to leave her alone, Thécla sat straight up in front of the microphone, leaned
toward it, and talked about the Monroe Doctrine, about
voodoo, about Black Muslims, about Black Power. . . .

It was at this moment that my mother subtly began to
resemble her father. She was said to be beautiful because
no one looked deep into the two black holes of her eyes,
there where fear, anguish, and despair blended; because
no one grasped the incoherence and madness beneath her
soft, stammered words.

Since her photograph appeared in quite a few newspapers, one day my mother received a letter.

Albert Louis
Hotel du Nord
2, Place des Abbesses
Paris XVIII

Mademoiselle,
  I take the liberty of writing to you in hopes that you

might help me resolve a very grave problem. Very grave for me, quite obviously.

A native of Guadeloupe, my patronymic is the same as your own, and I imagine you know the local genealogies better than I ever could. My father's name was Albert Louis too. Born in 1904 (actually he was mistaken: Bert was born in 1905), *he came here to study at the trade school in Angers. Following his marriage to my mother, his family broke off all contact with him and, in despair, he committed suicide. I am trying to trace his people, who are mine, too, not to claim vengeance, rest assured. Simply to know what tree I am part of. One cannot live without knowing where one comes from. I do not know where to begin. Might you know the descendants of a certain Albert Louis, a merchant, he himself long dead I imagine, and whose wife was named Elaïse?*

. . .

If you care to meet me, I am a musician and play at the Cuban Cabin every night. I may also be reached at my hotel. Pardon me again. . . .

My mother never answered that letter.

39

May 1968 shook Paris, and I shall not speak of that far-too-familiar story.

One day Thécla, as she wandered through the streets like a sleepwalker, tripping over barricades and burning herself at the fires, was hit on the forehead by a rock, and thanks to this was placed with other wounded in an ambulance that headed for Val de Grâce Hospital. The intern who set her three stitches had just turned thirty-two and was named Pierre Levasseur.

All her upbringing had led Thécla to believe that whites belonged to a separate species, like cats or bulls, and that there was no way to communicate with them. Yet on June 23, 1968, she married Pierre Levasseur in the church of Saint-Louis-des-Invalides. One week later, after a honeymoon at a property owned by his family, the new couple were on their way to Finistère, in whose depths I was growing up, a skinny soon-to-be-ten-year-old.

However, before commenting on the upheaval that this marriage brought into my life, let us rather speak of its repercussions among our family in Guadeloupe.

For almost ten years my grandfather Jacob had not received a letter from his daughter, and he reacted to this one by weeping all the tears in his body. Then, little by little, happiness spread through him, and he reread it, his nerve-raw intuition surprised to find it sad as a death notice. But no matter! He ran up the stairs two by two to

Tima, who was rocking dolefully in her rocking chair with her *Imitation of Christ* wide open on her lap.

> *Dear Mama, Dear Papa,*
> *In spite of my dreadful silence, you must believe me, I have not stopped thinking about you and loving you for an instant. . . .*

Temporarily restored to health, Tima wept bitter tears and took it upon herself to shout from the rooftops that her daughter was marrying a white doctor in Paris. A white? The family was frantic. This meant that Thécla would be lost to them forever, as Serge of Basse-Terre was lost. No matter how much Jacob protested that it was this very marriage that was bringing news of Thécla, foreheads remained furrowed.

"This means she's going to settle permanently in France."

"You don't mean to tell me her husband is going to come here? Guadeloupe's finished!"

Jean and Gesner were the most affected. They had hoped against hope that once Thécla had committed the inevitable follies of youth, she would return to the straight-and-narrow path of her land, that she would discover what a Kimberly diamond her first love truly was and march down the aisle with him before giving him some healthy children. Crash! This fine edifice of dreams was collapsing. For the first time, Jean flew into a rage against his brother and reproached him for having—on account of an "idiotic" upbringing—made that white man's bed for him. In front of a flabbergasted Jacob, he called Tima a neurotic and stingy petty bourgeoise who had passed her insanity on to her daughter. Poor Jacob again wept and found nothing to say in her defense.

My great-uncle Jean had become an extremely important man. For though the Patriots were allegedly clandestine, in reality they organized the peasants wonderfully and gave them a voice, and it was they who had made a symbol of Jean. A petty-bourgeois who had broken with his class. Misused by the French administrative government. Author of *Unknown Guadeloupe*, a work unique in its genre for its knowledge of folk traditions. Spiritual father to one of the country's greatest musicians, himself heir to the master tambourin drum player, Gesner.

All this had done nothing to improve my great-uncle Jean's disposition, as Marietta complained to anyone who would listen. This man, in earlier times so sweet, so much a dreamer, a man haunted by the feeling of guilt caused him by his first love's suicide, this man had become a pretentious martinet who took himself for a Saint John Chrysostome. He argued about everything: about Cuba and Castro. About Guinea and Sekou Touré. About America and Martin Luther King. He, who, Marietta stressed derisively, had never been any farther than the island of Marie Galante.

With all the arrogance drawn from his status as symbol, Jean sent an epistle to his niece reminding her of the slave trade, the horrors of slavery, the assassinations of Malcolm X and Martin Luther King (among others), the blight of colonization, and the death throes of colonization. It ended with these words: "I cannot believe that you treat with the torturers of our race."

Poor Thécla! Does one blame a skipper whose catamaran has capsized on the arched back of the sea for clinging to a life raft? Around her all was ruin and desolation, failure after failure. Often she had the impression she was making her way alone along the dark paths of a graveyard. But Pierre Levasseur had glasses, and the square, good-natured face of a family doctor. With him she felt so secure that she told him everything. Even about me. And he tried to understand her, while listening without judging, much less condemning her.

My real life begins, therefore, not in that private hospital in the fifteenth arrondissement of Paris where I gave my first cry, but in Mama Bonoeil's small dining room. On its walls hung a reproduction of Millet's *The Angelus*, a large wedding photograph, and a photograph of the husband who had been lost at sea like the good sailor he was. It is there that my mother's water broke before she cast me from her forever. It is there, while gazing at that stranger, that the angry blood flooded my heart and the air made my lungs gasp. She was sobbing, was Mama Bonoeil!

"Kiss your mama, Coco!"

(As if by chance, her affection had transformed one of my names, Claude, into this word, which also designates an exotic fruit.)

I did not move. So Pierre, a polar bear of a man in a fur-collared coat, came toward me, lifted me from the ground, and covered me with kisses.

"How beautiful you are!"

We settled in Paris in an untidy apartment whose windows opened onto the cluster of tombs in the Montparnasse Cemetery. I practically never saw my mother, who slept, rested, ate, read, wrote, and talked on the telephone—all beyond my reach. Pierre bathed me, helped dress me, took me to school, to the movies, to a tearoom, to the Masons' *Fête des Loges*, and to the annual festival given by the communist newspaper *L'Humanité*. While doing so, he explained:

"You mustn't blame her. The truth is, she's not very well. Not well at all. There are some people who are very strong; that's not her case. You understand, don't you?"

Out of respect for his concern, I nodded my head.

I do not know exactly how long this state of affairs lasted. Weeks? Months? Time was as gray as a convict's concrete cell. One morning I opened the door to a telegraph messenger. Ultima Victoire Apolline Louis née Lemercier had just passed away in her fiftieth year.

Thécla's pain was terrifying. She who in the last ten years had not written three letters to her mother downed full tubes of quinine. Falling into a comatose state, she had to be taken to an emergency room in the middle of the night. For months we only saw her in a hospital room, her hands folded in her lap. Finally she recovered, for pain does not kill. Sad but true! The first of the great crimes whose blame I lay on my mother is my grandmother Tima's death. For it occurred without Tima ever being able to hold me in her arms and listen to me recite my lessons, without her ever being able to plait my hair, or rub me with bay rum. Tortured by remorse, Thécla made up her mind to journey to Guadeloupe to at least kneel beside the grave. I don't know why Pierre did not go with her. I alone accompanied her.

40

A man was waiting for us at Raizet airport. A stranger whose face was not strange to me, for it most untidily harbored certain of my mother's features. These I was seeing in the original, as it were, while at the same time suddenly being able to envision them in old age. Not that the man was old, for he gave an impression of timelessness, the impression of always having been there and of having to remain there when the others would be gone and the world would be reduced to a play of light and shadow. Thécla held out her cheek to him and said, as if she had left him only yesterday:

"Hello, papa!"

He kissed her, visibly restraining himself from embracing her fiercely, while his gaze never left me. At last he wiped the moisture from his eyes and asked:

"Whose child is that?"

She raised her chin and said with an air of bravado, though I could read the shame in her eyes:

"It's mine!"

41

Ever since my great-uncle Jean had been raised to the rank of a symbol, the status of l'Anse Laborde had found itself affected. In former times only nature had paid attention to it. Now, all during the week, but especially on weekend Saturdays and Sundays, the young and the not-so-young came to seek an audience with its master or simply came to gaze at the modest house built by Mario (at present dead and buried alongside his Adélia in the l'Anse Bertrand cemetery). L'Anse Laborde was where Mario had taken refuge after his unfortunate dealings with the colonial administration; it was where the pole-shack outbuildings he had raised with his own hands continued to stand and where you could find the saloon in which Marietta, never at a loss for words, still poured. When Gesner left Grands-Fonds-les-Mangles in 1965 to settle near his spiritual father, l'Anse Laborde became a site of pilgrimage, as Mecca is for Moslems and the city of Lourdes for Christians. (This concerned, of course, the nationalists, all the others going out of their way to avoid this den of communists [sic].) As a result, one shrewd individual with a head for business opened a bar and restaurant called the Horn of Plenty, which specialized in traditional dishes that the bourgeoisie would not touch, such as breadfruit *migan*; *bébélé*, a dish of meat, breadfruit, beans, and pork, and *la soupe à Kongo*, a soup of yams, green beans, and pigeon peas. Soon l'Anse Laborde saw two stars appear next to its name in the tourist guide-books.

"Worth the Detour: The Horn of Plenty, for the latest culinary creations of chef Man Tine. If you're lucky, you may attend a rehearsal in the small banquet room adjoining the restaurant of the band led by the great musician Gesner Ambroise, a native of the area."

If Gesner's growing fame made little impression on him and changed nothing of his simplicity and modesty, the same did not hold true, as I have already said, for my great-uncle Jean. Having finished with *Unknown Guadeloupe*, of which after all he had sold two hundred and fifty copies, he had set himself to writing a work he considered more noble: *Revolutionary Movements in the Black World*. Aware that he lacked information, he called upon Thécla for help. Once again, instead of telling the truth about her situation, she sat herself down and pontificated before a Uher tape recorder, telling Jean anything he wanted. To better fulfill this assignment she wound up settling nearby; that is to say, at Gesner's. The truth was also that she had not forgiven her father for having brought Flora Lacour and their two bastard children into the house less than one year after Tima's death! In her revulsion she had indeed tried to go live at Juston. Before her death, in an attempt to distract his Tima from her moroseness and languor, Jacob had in effect transformed the *Soubarou*'s shack, built of imported lumber, into a "change of air" house that had nothing to envy those of the rich merchants at Saint-Claude. An electric water heater dispensed hot water and—luxury of luxuries—the kitchen was equipped with a refrigerator. But the presence of the "invisibles" troubled Thécla's already fevered sleep. Only too happy to see their granddaughter again, after swirling about her the *Soubarou* and Elaïse coiled themselves inside the folds of her mosquito net. Meanwhile Tima, at last reunited with her child, would not move an inch and wound herself about her daughter's neck at the risk of choking her. At times she sang lullabies to her as if to a baby; the sounds mysteriously issued from the walls around her and from the roof above her head, terrifying Thécla, who turned on her bedside lamp to search the darkness. Was it the wood settling? The tin roof cooling after the heat of the day?

Tolerant as they were, the people of l'Anse Laborde liked Thécla no more than I did. First of all, she smoked like a trooper. Whenever she happened to walk through the fields, one could follow her trail like a sugarcane train by its plume of white smoke. On top of that, she was drinking shot after shot of straight rum. It was Marietta, whose stock Thécla was depleting, who took it upon herself to spread the news to those who did not know it. Then, it was as if Creole set her teeth on edge. Always on the straight and narrow of French-French! And, lastly, people did not care for the way she drove Gerty from Gesner's bed, where Gerty had been so comfortable for the last three years. Oh, good God! Sometimes men are so blind! Allowing themselves to be driven crazy by the heartless, they turn around and bring grief to other, loving hearts. Nevertheless what completely disgusted the people of l'Anse Laborde was the way my mother was treating me. I was going around with hair like straw, my arms and legs studded with mosquito bites that quickly turned infected with running sores. Never bathed, rarely changed. There are times that you wonder what God can be thinking of? Some people make the pilgrimage to Lourdes on their knees to have a child, while He impregnates other wombs! He should set a rock inside them, and not the precious gift of a fetus! Moved to pity, the women of the village took me into their homes to do up my hair in "vanilla bean" plaits wrapped round with bits of ribbon like sails around a mizzenmast. Thus adorned, I went to plant myself in front of my mother. But she was busy talking revolution and the development of the black world, and she did not, any more than usual, even glance at me.

Despite my youth, I clearly saw that my great-uncle Jean was taking Thécla in hand again. This marriage to a white? No one wants the death of the sinner. It is enough that he repent and sin no more. Let her leave that white where he was and let her take up the torch again where she had set it down in a moment of discouragement. Let her once again work for the Revolution and the cause of the people.

One will notice that as the years went by, the language had changed somewhat. Where the *Soubarou* would have said "niggers," and Jacob "the Negroes" or "the race," Jean said "the People." (On this point as on so many others my great-uncle's train of thought was not quite clear. He constantly wavered between Negritude, blackness, and a sort of populism with a Marxist ring to it.)

Nevertheless the injunction remained the same:

"Our fathers sought individual success, which is nothing but a betrayal. One does not succeed alone."

Jean did not see the pleading deep in Thécla's eyes:

"I can't stand it anymore. All I want is to live my own life! Not all among us are a royal ceiba tree meant only to provide shade for the others!"

Deaf and blind, Jean went on speechifying!

If there were any people who clearly understood Thécla, however, they were the Patriots.

I shall take no part in the quarrel that raged then, and

still rages, between those who call themselves the Patriots and their enemies. Patriots or not, for me they were above all adults, which is to say strangers to my world! I saw a succession of men who patted me hastily on the cheek, then took me by the shoulders:

"Go play, Coco!"

At every meeting that was held in one of the pole shacks and that lasted well into the night, I listened to Marietta rage and storm about how those men never gave a thought to their women alone at home with the children. She concluded:

"Before changing the country, you have to change yourself. As long as they have no respect for women, far as I'm concerned . . ."

Was she right? I don't know.

All I know is that one afternoon, to please my great-uncle Jean, the Patriots agreed to meet with Thécla. What was to be a simple and courteous preliminary meeting quickly turned sour. Why? Everything leads me to assume that Thécla's inability to express herself in Creole annoyed them. And even worse, there was her inveterate habit of studding her French with short English expressions: "Well," "I mean," "Let's see . . ."

The conversation quickly turned to mixed marriages, that betrayal of betrayals. And then on to Africa, the Patriots admiring it blindly without ever having set foot there and Thécla, influenced by Manuel, criticizing it without knowing it any better than they. Everything went irremediably wrong when the Patriots spoke disparagingly of America. Thécla reminded them of the magnitude of the struggle the blacks were leading there and showed surprise that they knew practically nothing of Malcolm X and Martin Luther King. Back outside again, one of the Patriots asked, as they were climbing into the car, if my mother might not be an agent of the CIA. That cloud of suspicion hung over her head for a long while, and even those who shrugged their shoulders at the enormity of the accusation could not keep themselves from remembering what a sad specimen of humanity the *Soubarou* had been. And how dubious, Jean excepted, his issue. The fruit doesn't fall far from the tree! Exploiter's blood will tell!

42

Poor Jacob! The long-awaited presence of his daughter was bringing him none of the joy he had hoped for. He could not guess what her stiff neck, her about-faces, or her evasions meant, and twilight found him sobbing in Bonnemama Elaïse's ear.

As the knife knows what is hidden in the heart of the fruit it pierces and cuts, only Gesner knew what was happening inside Thécla. He could have told Jacob how much she, too, was suffering. For although throughout the day pride and posturing sealed her lips against the truth, a hint of love unsealed them and she talked and talked. Inexhaustible.

About her mother.

"I thought I hated her and now I realize that without her my life has no more meaning. As empty as crushed cane fiber. In everything I did it was she I was aiming at. It's she I wanted to punish, to shock—or, on the contrary, to amaze. Since she had read nothing except the romantic novels of Delly or Max du Veuzit, I wanted to fill my mind with everything. Because all she knew of painting was Millet's *The Angelus* or *The Gleaners*, I took a course in art history at the Sorbonne. Because her world was so limited, I wanted to soar like a kite in the sky."

About her father.

"He stinted on everything. Lard. Rice. Dried green peas. So I would give him what he did not have: a laurel wreath of diplomas. Poor man who believed that education opens every door for a Negro. Alas!"

Of her husband.

"It's the first time someone didn't ask a thing from me, demand that I be anything other than what I am, play another role than the one I can play. And because of you who expects the impossible of me, I'm supposed to leave him!"

It rained torrents that month of January. The peasants at l'Anse Laborde caped themselves in jute sacks and their feet dug muddy puddles in the fields. The mood of the weather matched that of the country, which was in its death throes. One by one the great mills closed. The sugarcane was dying. Students who worried about the future laid themselves down in a hunger strike. One morning a hired car drew up in front of Gesner's cottage, where, melancholy from all that water, he was feeling a tune as sad as a lovesong growing inside him. A short man topped with a huge Afro stepped from the car. Manuel Pastor. This man stepping out of the taxi in the rain did not resemble the one Thécla had left behind in New York. He had seen the fall, one by one, of all the men white or black, who spoke of justice in America; thus he had become convinced that no fruit fit to eat could grow upon that cursed fig tree of a country. Avoiding Africa, where dictatorships were rising, he had discovered a small island in the sun a few nautical miles off Miami where the advent of a black God was being celebrated. Jamaica! Yes, the name of the Eternal was Jah, and Marcus Garvey was his prophet! Secure in this certitude, Manuel had moved Heaven and earth, and finally found his Thécla.

Compared with Manuel Pastor, Gesner was a lightweight. The former had too much self-assurance and the advantage of speaking three languages. He had seen the world and come from a land that had had its revolution.

Regarding his native land, however, Manuel did not mince words:

"In Cuba, there's no place for the Negro. In Cuba, the Negro's treated like a dog. Like everywhere else, ain't nothing there except for the whites and mulattoes! Communist or not, Cuba is as racist as the United States of America!"

At each of Thécla's objections he shrugged his shoulders, while my great-uncle Jean feverishly wrote down his words. Ignored by all, Gesner strode back and forth in the rain. It was in these circumstances that he wrote his famous song, "Dey-o, Mourning, Oh."

My grandfather Jacob had always considered Thécla the apple of his eye. Yet he was obliged to reprimand her when he learned that she was going from Gesner's arms to Manuel's in one of Jean's far-too-welcoming pole shacks. Perhaps we can grant the affair with Gesner, that almost touching relapse into the puppy love from which no one ever recovers! But where had this second man come from? Jacob had his own opinion, even if he did not agree with the flood of insanities reeled off by Flora Lacour, so secure in her entrenched position in the Rue du Faubourg-d'Ennery house, or with the opinions of all the other women of the family. And so, during a lull in the weather, he appeared somber and tormented at l'Anse Laborde. Controlling the terror that the intensity of his love was causing him, he dared look directly at Thécla and rebuke her:

"You must not leave yourself open to slander. What would your poor mother say if she were alive to see what I see? We belong to a small country where people care more about the color of their neighbor's sheets than the smell of their own. Remember, you are a married woman. Even if your husband is far away. . . ."

Thécla was gathering her thoughts for a sharp retort when Manuel came rushing from the bathroom, one-half of his face shaved, the other half covered in white lather. With his well-known exuberance, he threw his arms around Jacob. In no time at all Manuel turned Jacob's heart around, as had also happened with Jean, who now took everything Manuel said as gospel. That infernal glib tongue of his!

"They say my father's grandfather took to the mountains with a dozen slaves—Joaquim Pastor, an Ibo Negro who had a reputation as a *santero*, a *santería* priest. When they reached the very top, he laid out a clearing and surrounded it with a two-foot-wide moat studded with poison-smeared spikes. So was born the *quilombo* of Camaguey, the kingdom of rebel slaves that for twelve years held out against the whites by the grace of the African gods. In vain they loosed their dogs. The ones who came too near fell, frothing at the nostrils, struck down with an epileptic fit! Papa, we must bring back the *quilombos!*"

In despair Jacob said:

"How? How?"

Manuel was only too ready to explain:

"The spirit of struggle is not dead in us. It's only lying dormant! So, each of us must make himself a rebel in order to carry the others along. . . ."

Jacob burst into bitter laughter. He who never talked about himself because no one ever listened found himself recounting the sad odyssey of the Negroes Arise party and the wreck of his illusions. Oh, yes, he had indeed had his followers! "Killed me, they almost killed me!"

Manuel paid him uncommon attention, then concluded:

"You should've watched out for the communists,

who I'm told are powerful in this country. They're the most dangerous. With their theory that race doesn't exist and only class counts, they'll dig our people's grave. They destroyed Marcus Garvey. They haven't yet finished destroying others."

For three days and three nights without stop Manuel held Jacob under the fire and charm of his voice, extolling the profound unity of all diasporas, a unity that Jacob had only confusedly sensed. In Manuel's eyes the *Soubarou* and his own father were twins. Their gestures of turning their backs on the sugarcane were similar, and so were their leave-takings, one for the gold of California, the other for the skyscrapers of Manhattan. Both born out of the same belly of anguish and denial. But the *Soubarou* had had more luck. At that, thinking of all the bitterness in his father's life, Jacob protested:

"More luck!"

"Yes, because he put an end to the misery of the flesh, for himself and his own! My brothers and I, we always had a sister with us: hunger! In winter, when New York is covered in miles of ermine, we'd be shivering, frosted to the teeth. We had only one pair of shoes for the four of us that made Duke's feet look like Charlie Chaplin, and Earl's like the bound feet of a Chinese woman. At the age of four I myself was selling horse to junkies in Central Park. I was spared, but my little brother died of an overdose after coming out of prison. The cops got my other two brothers. I tell you, Papa, we have to bring back the *quilombos*. I hear tell some are coming up on a small island nearby: Jamaica. Well, I'm going there to have a look!"

43

My grandfather Jacob lowered his eyes in that awkward way he had whenever he was trying to hide his feelings and said:

"I would have so liked for you to stay here with us. But your mother doesn't want you to."

I gasped: "Why? Everyone knows she's not exactly choked up with affection for me!"

He made a small sound of vexation:

"Tut, tut, tut!"

Then he put an old cardboard box in my hands.

"Here, I found these pictures in the attic. How would you like to put them in order?"

He knew it was my favorite pastime.

The truth, always so unpleasant to look at, has a body studded with barbs, sharp points that wind up by tearing the cloths and shrouds in which it is wrapped. In the end it cannot be kept from parading naked through the streets, like the emperor in the children's tale. "Whose child is that?"—my grandfather's first words at the airport did not express an actual question. Rather, they had come bursting forth out of his terrified recognition. For a time a persistent rumor had gone around that the beautiful, the proud Thécla Louis had got herself pregnant like any peasant woman. But nobody ever saw the belly or the child with his own eyes, and then Thécla conveniently disappeared from Paris; so that rumor was no longer kept alive, no longer fanned in those centers where students

234

from Guadeloupe gather to keep themselves informed of the misfortunes of some and the good fortune of others. However, it had not entirely died out and was still hovering about, whispered of on occasion. What had tortured my grandfather's so easily wounded heart when he saw me at Raizet airport had been the confirmation of all his daughter's lonely pain and her humiliation. He had clenched his ineffectual fists, thinking:

"Ah, if I'd been there when that young man toyed with my daughter, I'd have beaten his face to pulp! After my lightninglike attack, his own mother wouldn't have recognized him!"

And so, his eyes avoided me during those first weeks, carefully flitting past me, rarely coming to rest. Until one day, I don't know exactly how, I find myself sitting on his lap, cheek against the white drill of his jacket, listening to a story.

"One morning, a few days after his mother died, and she had a fine funeral, Ti-Jean came out of his house and locked his door. The people were surprised:

" 'Hey, where's he going so early in the morning? The roosters haven't yet crowed in the chicken coops and the fog's still hanging deep in the traces.'

"Man Sonson, who had been midwife to his mother, could not contain herself and cried over the bloodwood hedge:

" 'Where are you going without, I'm sure, even a drop of coffee in your stomach?'

" 'I'm going to look for my father.'

" 'Your father?'

" 'Yes, if I don't find him to tell him what he did to my mother, I want no more of life. . . . ' "

My grandfather well knew that if he did not intervene, one morning, like Ti-Jean, I would set off on some fatal journey. So he tried to hold on to me by seating me in front of a dozen or so heavy cardboard albums. He opened the first of them to the first page, to the face of a man about thirty years old, handsome with his egg-shaped skull, his chin marked by a dimple, and his wide mouth opening over an infinity of teeth meant for devouring the world.

"My father, your forebear, Albert Louis."

Yes, that day my grandfather tried to cover up the infamous line, "Father unknown . . . !" Yes, he tried to give me roots!

Still gasping, I opened the cardboard box. I had come to know them, the faces of all those dead long since returned to dust in the shadows of the family crypt. Théodora. Maroussia. Nirva. Albert the *Soubarou*. Bonnemama Elaïse. René. Camille Désir. And I liked listing, arranging those ever-more-faded images that reduced these lives to a succession of ritual ceremonies—christenings, weddings, First Communions—and to mere entertainments—swimming in the creek, picnics at the seaside. I was going on, barely paying attention, when suddenly for the first time I found myself face-to-face with him who was never to leave me again. A little mulatto boy. Hair parted on the left and carefully slicked down. Sailor-suited. Hoop and stick. High ankle-shoes. Staring un-laughing, unsmiling into the camera lens. On the back of the photograph a hand little used to writing had traced: Albert Louis. Angers. 1934.

"Grandfather, who is this, this one here?"

My grandfather's face tensed with the shame and pain he felt:

"We don't know what became of him."

What! "We don't know"! In that family where the smallest deed was catalogued? Where each one could remember with certainty exactly what day Maroussia—taken from the visible world ten years earlier following a dental abcess—had had one cheek larger than her largest pumpkin? Where everyone knew at what time the labor pains had started for the boys of Bonnemama Elaïse, that woman missed by one and all but still alive in the recesses of the heart of even those who had not known her, Bonnemama Elaïse! "We don't know"!!!

Despair ravaged the features of my grandfather's face:

"Every family hides a crime; he is ours. My half brother, Albert, whom my father had of an English Negro woman he knew in Panama . . ."

And so on!

In truth, Bert and Bébert did not begin to haunt me that afternoon, for my heart was filled with a very selfish sadness. I was going, leaving the island that had already become my own, leaving those who had set me in affectionate ground, covering me with little words of tenderness:

Ti chabine an mwen! Little chabine mine!
Coco doudou! Coco sweetie!
Choubouloute! Sweetie-honey-lovey!
Douchérie! Sweetness!

I was going to wander Thécla's vain wandering.

I do not know at exactly what moment Bert and Bébert took hold of my imagination. But once they had decided to do so, they never let go.

44

My dear Pierre,
　　Everything is so confused! Don't try to reach me,
I'll be in touch with you as soon as I see clearly in
myself. Forgive the disorder I bring to your life. . . :
　　Your poor Thécla.

Poor? Still?

45

The small city of Kingston, like so many cities of the Caribbean, is made up of a juxtaposition of neighborhoods: some blaring poverty in reggae tunes, the others burnishing the greensward of their English lawns. Cricket fields and tennis courts adjoin empty lots studded with the carcasses of cars. Litter and filth stand guard at certain crossroads.

When Thécla and Manuel arrived there with their party, Kingston was barely recovering from a frenzied food riot, and the stores were empty. Rice sent by American relief agencies was being sold on the black market along with powdered milk from the Red Cross. Mustering up their anger, the peasants had come down out of the mountains, and it had taken a slaughter by two regiments of soldiers to send them back again.

Manuel had a room reserved in a house at Red Hill occupied by a Rastafarian community. This community was special in that it included a great number of American blacks. In fact it was one among them, who had come to New York to sell his apartment and bid farewell to his family, who during his stay had "converted" Manuel.

Oh, the sweetness and beauty of the Rasta women. Velma was a Negro woman and smelled of ganja; beneath the large tricolor headscarf that encased the heavy mass of her hair I could see pearls of sweat forever gleaming around her night-black eyes—and her mouth, when in place of Thécla she devoured me with kisses, tasted of the fruit of the wild guava picked before noon.

It was Rasta Roy, Velma's man, who taught me English, he who was so serene in the face of the dozen noisy children the community counted. His tawny hair fell in a lion's mane to his shoulders and his *chabin* skin was spotted with freckles, greenish in the morning and becoming orange as the day progressed. The schoolday finished, he would take up his charcoal pencils and draw. He allowed me to come into the small studio he had arranged for himself in one of the villa's outbuildings, and I pried into everything. Endlessly, I returned to the portrait of a fat, round-cheeked man in a uniform with many buttons and wearing a helmet topped with white-feather plumes, a man whose name was familiar to me from having heard it from my great-uncle Jean or Manuel or Thécla or all three. . . .

"Him? But I already told you, that's our prophet, Marcus Garvey!"

Those familiar with Rasta art should know that it is I who served as model for the portrait called *Little Girl* that toured our islands, and which I saw again in New York in a Haitian bookstore on Amsterdam Avenue. A rebellious little girl, arms folded, defiantly looking straight ahead under her sumptuously tangled head of hair. On the days off Rasta Roy gave us, we went down to the market with Velma and the other women to sell the brooms and vetiver baskets they wove. Before heading back up the road to our hill, they would take us to the beach at Hellshire, where the sand is the color of molten gold. The bourgeois and their children swam in circles around us the better to stare at us and make comments about our ugliness. Then their progeny, already corrupt and aware of their impunity, sneakily tossed sand at us to make our eyes water.

Why did they hate us?

We went along, our eyes fixed on the eyes of Jah, our hands in his great protective hand. We smoked the grass of the field according to his ordinance. We put no impure food in our mouth. We gathered together to read and comment on long passages from the Bible. During the Sunday service, before a huge picture of Haile Selassie swathed in a flag of red, yellow, and green, we sang our hymns.

> *Exiles in Babylon*
> *Where the earth is dry as their hearts*
> *and all the fig trees cursed*
> *We cry out to you. . . .*

I saw little of Manuel and Thécla, who had entry to Bob Marley's community because they had begun to compile a *History of Black Nationalism.* Awful! I would have liked someone to denounce them for the imposters they were! Instead of which, they were treated with the greatest respect, like comrades of some superior species. They brought in no revenue to the community, since they participated in none of its activities, and yet they were waited upon like avatars of Haile Selassie himself. A young sister in a white headscarf was even charged with changing the sperm-stained sheets between which they had wallowed, with emptying their ashtrays stinking of cold ashes, and with washing the filthy glasses out of which they had drunk their strong drink. The day I saw Velma ironing my mother's laundry, I choked with rage. Rasta Roy, who could read me like a father, kept me in after class:

"See, on this earth we're passing through, everyone must express his talents the best he can. The two of them work in another way than I do, or Rasta Jim. It's our duty to support them like we do, for they will bear witness to the visible world that we're not what we're believed to be. We are the true children of Israel!"

I laughed contemptuously:

"The book they're supposed to be writing will never get written! No more than the others were!"

He took my hands and forced them together level with his heart:

"Repeat after me:

'The father of the righteous shall greatly rejoice:
and he that begetteth a wise child
shall have great joy of him.
Thy father and thy mother shall be glad,
and she that bear thee shall rejoice.' "

This rebuke utterly wounded me, and as I always did whenever my heart lay heavy as a rock in my breast, I wrote a letter to my grandfather Jacob. He kept them all, with their scribbled spelling errors, in a champagne cookie tin. Almost fifteen years later I reread them, feeling the pain that filled me in those days reawakening within me.

One afternoon, class over and the aroma of cooking beginning to rise from the kitchens, some bottle-green trucks stopped in front of our house. Dozens of men in dark-blue uniforms got out of them brandishing clubs, truncheons, and automatic rifles. In no time at all they had climbed over the fence and came rushing at us, beating, brutalizing, throwing the weakest or the youngest to the ground. (Happily) Manuel and Thécla were at home that day. Intellectuals or no, they were bludgeoned senseless like the rest and clubbed toward the trucks that waited, jaws gaping, for their prey of men, women, and children. When Manuel, seeing Thécla's blood run, lost his head and shouted that he would inform the French embassy and the U.S. embassy, and would bring about international repercussions, he received a masterly blow to his face that turned it to pulp.

After which the trucks moved off toward the main police station.

46

After the days we spent packed in a jail cell nothing was ever the same. Thécla and Manuel, along with all the other American blacks, were released with apologies, their hair forceably shaved and the skin of their scalp lighter than their faces. But Rasta Roy, Rasta Jim, and the others were charged with breaking and entering, transferred to prison, tried, and found guilty. They did not receive suspended sentences and would not see daylight again until the moment Michael Manley came to power in 1972. Bravely the women went on caring for the children, but grief over their men made their eyelids turn black. Between nightmares I could hear Thécla's sobs. One night I joined Manuel at the foot of the magnolia tree in the garden. Throughout the city the bourgeoisie had padlocked doors and windows while their dogs howled at prowlers and the moon. There was little love lost between Manuel and me. Nevertheless, on that particular night his barely audible words found their way to my ear and, from there, into my heart:

"What a bitter pill the life of a Negro is! Don't know where to find the sugar to sweeten it. U.S.A, Haiti, Jamaica . . . the same thing!"

In a hopeful tone I suggested:

"What if we went back to Guadeloupe? At least there they leave us alone!"

He caressed my hair, which was growing out stiff and straw-yellow:

"Sure! Don't you make any mistake! One of these days that island'll topple over into blood and violence. It won't be good, being there. . . . Listen, I'm going to leave. . . . "

"Leave?"

"Yes, I love this country and I think there're plenty of places we could be happy. I'll come back soon as I've found one. Meantime you take care of your mother. . . . "

Luckily I did not have to carry out that assignment!

Three days after Manuel took the bus for Negril, which he had heard was the best place on earth, a black American carrying a backpack showed up at the house. Well, a sort of black! It took true American perspicacity to track down that fatal drop of blood in him and, as a result, stick him in a ghetto! Terence Cliff-Brownson belonged to one of those Washington, D.C., families who call themselves the first families. For at a time when the majority of their peers were trying, in spite of the obstacles placed in their way, to learn trades other than those that lead to a hunched back, they had already produced a schoolteacher, a nurse, and an insurance salesman. Terence's father was a psychiatrist. His mother was the daughter of a preacher beloved of God for his unctuous sermons. So it was not surprising that he had been unable to hold out past the age of sixteen and had tried his hand at drugs and robbery. Before, that is, he realized the effect he produced on men and women both, and devoted himself to prostitution.

But all that was ancient history. In a pale dawn, returning from some dreary orgy, he had suddenly had enough of the stench of his life and had made the decision to clean out his own Augean stable. He had therefore converted to Rastafarianism.

When Terence was a rich man's son, he had practiced scales and exercises five hours a day, for his parents had dreamed of a concert-pianist son in tails. He had, of course, turned his back on that fine career. Nevertheless he had been unable to destroy the world of sounds inside him and was trying to create a language, part music, part poetry, that critics have since named roots poetry. He had come to Jamaica to do research.

When Terence came into our garden, the sun had gone down to the sea to take its daily swim there, and at last the twilight and the coolness were refreshing us after its excesses. Suddenly it seemed as if the despot had impulsively risen back up to the place it just left: dazzling, regal, irresistible. I was hanging from the branches of the magnolia tree. At the sight my arms grew weak and I found myself on the ground, my breath taken away. Terence ran to me, raised me up, and hugged me tightly:

"Did you hurt yourself, honey?"

My mother, who was lollygagging on the veranda, came over to me in turn:

"If it'd only teach you to keep still!"

But she was not looking at me, and already he was no longer looking at me. I do not know if from that night on Terence slept in Thécla's bed. What is certain is that it did not take long, and soon everyone had to notice that as far as Manuel was concerned, the proverb Out of sight, out of mind was proving true.

In any community there exist rules without which life would spill over into the deep rut of promiscuity. Faithfulness to one's mate is one of them, an essential one. Of course the men did not give up bringing in women from the outside (a Canadian woman from Winnipeg spent six months with us! Another time it was an American from Detroit!), but never would a Rasta have looked at one of his brother's women. No one, however, said one word of censure or exclusion in Manuel's absence, and the couple were able to devote themselves to all the indecencies of passion. To stay in bed amid laughter, sighs, and secrets until well past midday. To go off to swim naked in some deserted stream. To write and read poems together. To pick at their food off of the same plate. To go be rowdy in nightclubs. To come home drunk on music and liquor in the wee hours of the morning.

Velma, who was carrying another little Rasta Roy, beautiful, oh, beautiful in her ever-more-ample dresses, came and went, her forehead creased in a large, worried frown above eyes dark with anxiety. Yet nothing showed in her voice.

"Sister Thécla, I'm going down to town. You want something?"

"Yes, yes! Bring me two small packs of typing paper!"

Me, I was waiting for the violence. The blood. On the front page of the *Daily Gleaner*, the Kingston newspaper: "Horrible murder in a Rasta community at Red Hill. For years the citizens of our city have constantly complained about the misbehavior of the Rastas. Today at dawn it was two American emigrants, drawn to that paradise of drugs and vice, who killed each other over a woman, from Guadeloupe this time. . . . "

And yet it must be said: Of all the men who followed each other into my mother's bed, none took better care of me than Terence. Not out of duty, like Pierre, my legal stepfather. Out of affection. Out of love. For Terence loved me. Each day he wrote a poem for me.

On the green savanna
With its pink guava trees

Go the black cattle.
Between their horns, a white spot
The ox-pecker bird!

(Or this other one:)

Come my pretty gangly girl
Cheeks spotted with sun freckles
Eyes studded with star nails
Your white laughter
In your golden face.

Physically I resembled him. I could have been his own, and when he taught me to dive at Hellshire, no one doubted it.

"Look at the Rasta and his little girl! If that isn't a pity!"

He caught fish with a harpoon and lay them on a bed of embers after brushing them with pepper sauce. It took the roof off your mouth. I would climb up his broad back to reach the forbidden fruit at the side of the road. Alas! He committed two crimes that I can never forgive!

Manuel's absence, which seemed interminable, lasted only a month and two weeks. From time to time he telephoned from various parts of the island. Unexpected, his voice echoed like that of a corpse risen without warning from its tomb, as shocking as that of a widower shouting his joy in the middle of a cemetery.

"Hi, baby. Negril's filled with leftovers from San Francisco, 'Flower People' who've turned their petals into oyster shells. It's not on this land here that we'll build our house. I'm following another lead. Just hold on!"

Finally he returned on a Sunday morning in the middle of a service. Rasta Moses, spared God knows how from jail, was reading the words of the Book: "To every thing there is a season . . . a time to be born and a time to die; a time to plant and a time to pluck up that which is planted; a time to kill and a time to heal; a time to break down and a time to build up; a time to weep and a time to laugh; a time to mourn and a time to jump with joy. . . . "

47

The only violence that accompanied Manuel's return was that of the elements.

That Sunday the sun had refused to rise, and since morning the sky had been the color of lead. Suddenly, shortly before noon (at the moment Manuel set foot in the temple?), it turned ink black. At the same time the winds came hurrying from the four corners of the horizon, while the sea, like a madwoman, screamed in a rage of waves and surges of spray before hurling itself against the rocks. In their enclosures the cattle lowed. Chickens cackled, the hens running in circles with their feathers puffed out. Dogs, tails low, begged whiningly to be let into houses whose residents were hurriedly barricading doors and windows.

In the tumult of children's tears (as well as in their hearts?) Rasta Moses raised a voice he meant to be soothing: "I say unto the Lord: 'You are my refuge and my fortress. . . .' "

Having swept into Kingston Bay, the wind left the town and galloped quickly down the road to Savanna-la-Mar, sending trees and buses flying. After which the rain moved forward, graceful as a horse, seeming not to touch the earth—then more and more furious, smashing, crushing, twisting, grinding beneath its hooves.

The violence of the elements lasted three days. On the fourth morning it ended. This was Hurricane Beverly, one of the worst Jamaica had ever known. Two hundred were numbered as dead, and three thousand as homeless. Bridges were ripped from swollen streams, roads caved in, hectares and hectares of land were gouged into channels. When we had finished clearing the garden, Terence told me we would be leaving for Black River the following day.

The hurricane did not touch Guadeloupe, where it merely rained an unusual amount for the month of April. All the same, Flora Lacour, my grandfather Jacob's woman who for several years now had had visions in her sleep, woke at midnight saying that a great danger hung over Thécla. Of what sort she could not specify. In any case they would have to say many prayers for her. This solicitude was especially surprising since Flora hated Thécla like poison and had taken advantage of the intimacy that comes from sharing someone's pillow to extract a promise from Jacob to have a serious talk with his daughter.

"It's true, you can buy education, but you can't buy breeding. She's already brought shame to your name with that misbegot child. But also, she leaves the one who delivered her, her husband, in France to come here and set up housekeeping with a good-for-nothing Negro like Gesner. Whatever you do, whatever you say, it wasn't for a *gwoka*-drum player that you raised her! And in the bargain she puts horns on him and runs off with an English or Spanish Negro. Sometimes, when I think about it, I wonder if it isn't your brother Jean who's behind all this, trying to hurt you!"

Jacob shrugged his shoulders.

"You're crazy! You lost your mind! Jean and me, same difference."

Nevertheless Flora was a good woman beyond that

outburst and, despite her forty-five years of age, far more talented in bed than Tima—and the vision that had come to her merited consideration. After changing the water in the vases and rekindling the candles that gave off spirals of smoke, Jacob sat himself down on Bonnemama Elaïse's grave:

"What's wrong with her, that child of mine? Why can't she find what she's looking for? And anyway, what's she looking for? My father wanted money. Me, an education. She, she's got one and the other. What's she looking for now, and why can't she get it?"

Wiping away his sweat with her shadowy fingers, Bonnemama Elaïse answered:

"Leave it be, leave it be, Ti-Kongo! Me, I'm telling you, you were the best of fathers."

Just in case, Jacob had a Mass said and asked one of the women in the family to see her *séancier*, her obeah man. Then he started out on the road for l'Anse Laborde, where he had not set foot in months.

For despite Jacob's protestations, Flora's words had touched something within him and he wondered if his brother had not been working to take his daughter from him. Oh, of course, Jacob did not appear to be a very interesting person. Shopkeeper, lard seller! Still, it was thanks to his constant and generous money orders that not only Dieudonné but three of Jean's children were pursuing their education in the mother country. Money is like manure. It's dirty, it stinks. So the trouble of handling it is left to the gardener, to make the flowers grow!

Jacob worked himself up to such a degree that he reached Jean's home in a rage, determined not to mince words with him. Alas, the great man's cabin was empty! Marietta, mournful and red-eyed, suggested Jacob go look around Saint-François to see if his brother was at the home of someone named Fabienne.

"Ah, I tell you, he's no longer the same man! He's running after the young ones now!"

Jacob climbed sadly back into his car. The road ran black through the blackness of the sugarcane fields. Insatiable, the frogs were going hoarse demanding the very water with which they had just been soaked, and the tethered cows lowed miserably.

Suddenly Jacob wished that his life could end right there, on this stretch of asphalt crumbling from the recent rains.

Marietta's jealousy told the truth. Jean was indeed with Fabienne, in a double bed under a wrinkled linen sheet.

Unlike Jacob, who was forever harried by his penis, Jean was in this respect as placid as the Moustique River. Yet at a meeting where future actions by the Sugarcane Workers Union were being discussed, everything had abruptly turned upside down. A young mulatto woman with glowing eyes had reviled the stunned comrades:

"If we go on dragging our feet with you, abstaining from a revolutionary vote, not coming out into the open, in the year 2000 Guadeloupe will still not be independent. What we need is armed struggle."

"Armed struggle you say?"

"Yes, guerrilla war! You bunch of pigheads, don't you read the newspapers to know what dance the world is dancing? No! You sit here comfortably bellowing your slogans: "*Palé kreyol! Dansé gwoka!* Speak Creole! Dance the gwoka!"

It was intolerable for a woman to talk to men that way, and Fabienne was expelled. But they came to realize that her speeches were not just hot air and that young people were collecting them like nuggets of gold from a stream. Soon these very young people would form a Movement for the Immediate Liberation of Guadeloupe, and this was that first great schism in the proindependence camp that our historians speak of.

Jean followed Fabienne around like a leashless dog who surrenders of his own free will. As she was almost twenty years younger, it seemed to him that having given birth to her revolt, he had fashioned it. Fabienne was what Thécla might have been!

It is not seemly for a forty-eight-year-old man to fall in love with a girl not yet thirty! For, doubting himself, he wondered day and night how to dazzle her. In bed Jean was so frightened of not satisfying Fabienne that he became tedious about it! Outside of bed it was the terror of disappointing her intellectually. So he launched into long speeches on revolution, Marxism, getting back to the people, and consciousness-raising that she sneeringly listened to before saying, cuttingly:

"My poor Jeannot, you really don't know what you're talking about. Have you read Gramsci?"

Poor Jeannot had to admit the name was new to him! Add to this that his annoyed former friends regularly heaped abuse on him in their newspaper columns and you will understand: Jean, head bowed, began to shuffle his feet like an old man and jump, torn from some painful inner meditation, whenever anyone said a word to him. Marietta watched him and grumbled to herself:

"It's strange! I never noticed how much he resembles his brother Jacob, after all! Not as black, but almost as ugly! Well, no one stays the same! Luckily we still have the children!"

And she turned to Manuela, her favorite daughter, who was glumly shelling pigeon peas!

People say that those years, the beginning of the seventies, were terrible in our country. The men, weary of mourning the cane, left for elsewhere seeking hope for their lives. Like my forebear, other Alberts went off to sell their sweat in France, tightening and screwing bolts on automobiles.

One story brought tears from Basse-Terre to Grande-Terre. Roselaine, a humble woman from Saint-Sauveur, had five sons in the home country. Because of that she lived alone in a house too big for her, and she went mad from it. One evening before midnight Mass, as she was readying herself to go to sleep without her supper of *boudin* sausage, pork, and pigeon peas, she went out onto her front step and screamed:

"No, it's no life we're living here! No men to hoe our gardens and warm our hearts! That beast of an Emigration Office swallows them up and leaves us nothing but our two eyes to cry with! When, when will the cane bloom again?"

Then she fell stone dead before the neighbors could do a thing.

PART FOUR

48

The Waterloo boardinghouse at Black River that Manuel had just taken over was a Georgian structure built in 1799 for the Barrets, a family of rich English planters. It remained splendid despite its dilapidation and decay and the abuse its various buyer-vandals had inflicted upon it. The roof shingles had been replaced by sheets of tin, the balconies walled over with boards, and the wrought-iron balustrades torn away. To crown its disgrace, someone had broken through the front wall to install a Westinghouse air conditioner. In the hands of its last owners, Americans from Boston, the business had come close to failing; but Manuel was determined to make it profitable again.

Inside the front door a procession of rats scattered wildly, while hairy spiders climbed quickly back up into their webs to watch us with their cold eyes. Manuel, gesturing grandly and still talkative but with his voice hoarse from pent-up sadness, led us on an exploration of both floors, pointing out the repairs and restoration that would be necessary.

"Here, we got to replace the walls because they're being eaten up with worms! Here, we got to add two wood beams! There, we have to stop up the leaks. There . . . "

While waiting to see where the money for all this was coming from, we counted five habitable bedrooms on the second floor. The main-floor dining room, the sitting room next to it, and the kitchen were in almost-good condition. On the other hand, the orchard was a paradise of fine fruit trees. Spanish lime, cherries, litchis, avocado, orange, mango, lemon, apricot, grapefruit . . . everything!

Wasting no time, Thécla, who was enchanted by the place, went back down to the village the afternoon of our arrival to hire herself some servants, but found every door shut in her face. For Black River was a peaceful little community that contained no eccentrics but only fishermen, a few rare farmers, two or three shopkeepers, a doctor, a priest sent there following some mortal sin, and a few white families who ever since Independence and the recent violence lived entrenched behind their shutters. The inhabitants had no great liking for us, and they meant us to know it. Without any doubt possible.

The next morning three toads, legs tied together with red thread and mouths agape, were nailed to the veranda. Two days later a dead dog bared its fangs inside our cistern. Mongoose loosed by day as well as by night slaughtered our chickens, and Thécla almost gave up the ghost when she found a *coui* full of leeches outside her door. Terence took things in hand and in his turn went down to the village. God alone knows what he did there in six hours' time! In any case he brought back two pretty girls, one for the housework and the other to help in the kitchen. But it very quickly became evident that beneath their apparent docility, they were terrible bitches. They pointedly told Thécla that she could do the work herself since, thank God, black slavery was long over, and drowned out her admonishments with a flood of swearing in pidgin. After which, Terence had to shut himself up with them for hours on end in order to pacify them and regirdle them in their aprons. Following that an argu-

ment took place among the four of them in which Thécla's voice for once dominated the others and Manuel for
once remained silent. Finally they left, and Terence
moved himself into a second-floor bedroom whose walls
were covered with mildew. He slept there for more than
a week, deaf to Manuel's pleading:

"Listen, don't be silly! Let's forget about it!"

Much has been said about this ménage à trois, either
in shock or in admiration, according to one's own con-
victions and temperament. Rarely has the opinion of a
fourth person been taken into account, a person who
might find herself involved in it quite against her will: the
child!

The servants Thécla had fired hurried to spread the
news, and at school, a very different one from Rasta
Roy's, the children held their sides with laughter from
the moment I appeared. Questioning:

"How many papas you have?"

Nicknaming me Double-Daddy.

Or holding their noses and singing:

Pass the dutchie by the left-hand side. . . .

Yet, in that hell, friendship flowered. I had a companion, a pariah, ostracized and a scapegoat like myself but
for other reasons. Melissa was a little white Jamaican girl
whose parents had chosen to waste away behind their
shutters rather than go settle in Miami, Florida, like their
other compatriots of the same color. In history class the
teacher made her stand up, diaphanous beside the blackboard, and blamed her pell-mell for white slavery, for the
sadism of the plantation owners, for the execution of
William Gordon, and for a number of other crimes I
forget. She was also blamed for the breakdown of Amer-

ica's relations with Cuba, and for American intervention in Haitian affairs!

Not surprising that Melissa and I ran away, preferring the wild thickets, the sea, and the hillocks to that jail where we were being tortured. How nature becomes love for the loveless child! The mangoes and the fleshy guavas for his hunger, stalks of sugarcane for his thirst, a pillow of Guinea grass for his sleep, and the warm belly of the maternal sea to nestle in! At times we went down along the road to Savanna-la-Mar as far as the house of Patience, who years ago had hired out to Melissa's parents. She showed us pictures of her son, now emigrated to the snowy expanses of Toronto; and in spite of the transistor radio and electric toaster he had sent her, invariably wound up weeping.

"It's not human, all that cold! It's not human, that snow! It's not made for the body or heart of our people, those lands ain't! Sometimes I feel like going to ask the politicians to give me back that boy of mine!"

After which, recovering her good humor, she soaped and scrubbed my entire body and then armed herself with a comb, grumbling:

"Beautiful hair like that! She ought to cut it, your mama ought, if she don't know how to take care of it! Me, I was bald as a coconut till I reached twenty. Then, when my boy was born, oh did my hair come out! Grew so long, I could sit on it! A woman without hair, it's like soup without greens!"

Whenever I reappeared just before the sun went for its swim in the sea, I found Manuel chopping wood in the courtyard. He wiped off his sweat:

"Where you been hanging out now?"

I walked past without even a glance at him and went to seat myself at the feet of Terence, who was typing with

one finger on an old Olympia typewriter up on the third
floor. He typed from morning to night, Terence did, and
sometimes late into the night before going off for a walk
God knows where and coming home whenever he liked.
This infuriated Manuel, who had become, besides the
man who chopped wood, the man to light the fire, go
shopping, wring the chickens' necks, gut fish, scrape root
vegetables, and mow the lawn. Thécla, in a headscarf and
big blue apron, saw to the meals, and I must acknowledge
her imagination and talents as a cook.

For we had guests at the Waterloo boardinghouse!
Young people, Europeans and Americans with a pack on
their backs en route to the paradise of Negril! Travel
agents and environmentalists in Mercedes-Benzes! At
times, lovers on sneak-away weekends! Two French
women of the very chic-and-proper type, Elyane and
Frédérique, remained stranded there for almost six
months, the first adding innovations to our menu such as
duck with turnips, the second making love with Terence
and putting his poems into French. On account of which,
since she was hurting Thécla, we became best friends in
the world, the two of us belittling her as we wandered
through the garden.

"Poor darling, I'd always heard it said black women
had an overabundance of maternal love. That one has
about as much as a fish."

I would go her one better:

"It's a wonder what the two of them see in her. She's
awful-looking, isn't she?"

Frédérique pouted:

"My dear, you're going too far there! You can say
anything you like about her but that. She doesn't even
have Negroid features!"

Poor Thécla! Worry over the infidelity of one of her

men was making her melt away like a candle, tightening the strings of her vast apron about her thinning waist. The sound of her voice was rarely heard now, and since she regularly made errors in her arithmetic, Manuel no longer allowed her to make out the bills. More work for him! Not surprising that he yells while gutting the fish, wringing the chickens' necks, mopping, carrying the garbage cans:

"Shit! Shit! What a bitch of a life! What the fuck am I doing here? Just tell me! Just tell me!!"

After many long weeks during which we welcomed to the dining room only a few "backpacks," as we disparagingly called them, Manuel shut himself up in the sitting room next to it and then came out again, declaring:

"We have to do something. All we have left in the cash register is one hundred and eighty-two dollars. Jamaican."

49

The sun is playing peekaboo with the earth, and our shadows lie circled about our feet like docile dogs. Since there is nothing to eat at my house, neighborly Melissa takes me home with her. She places a finger against lips of so pale a pink. This is the first time I have been inside her house. It is beautiful, her house is, even though it could use a good coat of paint. The second floor, majestic beneath its heavy, faded red roof, slightly overhangs the ground floor and extends into a square veranda filled with rocking chairs, occasional tables, and potted plants. We walk around it, then enter the antiquated kitchen with its brick drainboard and gas refrigerator.

"Because of the blackouts," Melissa explains reasonably.

She opens the oven. Leg of lamb and a chayote gratin. Delicious! I make ready to wolf it down, but well-bred Melissa insists I wash my hands and say grace.

"You want some wine?"

Some wine?

Mischievous Melissa opens the refrigerator, which squeals like a wounded thing, and pulls out a bottle that is already opened. I decipher the label as best I can: Gewurztraminer! Scholarly Melissa comments:

"You're not supposed to drink white wine with leg of lamb."

Why?

Melissa shrugs her shoulders; she doesn't know. I

won that one. I eat, she watches me eat, happiness in the depths of her washed-out eyes. I hold out my glass. She fills one for herself and we clink glasses. God, this wine is good! I have never tasted anything so good! She serves me again. Leg of lamb, and the rest! We laugh. Innocent Melissa asks:

"Why do the children call you Double-Daddy?"

Strange, the question does not bother me! I answer cheerfully:

"Because my mother sleeps with two men!"

Amazement, then wild laughter from Melissa!

"How does she do that?"

I shrug my shoulders:

"I don't know, I never looked."

Melissa laughs even harder. She is literally writhing with laughter:

"I'd like to see my mother . . . "

She hiccups:

"She's the sort who bathes with her nightgown on and covers up her hair to sleep!"

We burst out laughing. The wine flows, sticky and cool.

"I always wondered, always wondered . . . "

"What?"

She is laughing too hard to talk. Suddenly the door opens and a woman enters. The mother, as a matter of fact. White! I have never seen a woman so white, for outside, the sun browns our bodies. Her smooth, black hair is parted in the middle, with touches of white here and there, as I was later to see in pictures of George Sand. She has two green holes in place of eyes. At the sight of us her zombie face comes to life as if she has eaten salt.

Her papier-mâché lips part, and she shouts:

"Melissa! Melissa! Who is that? Get out of here right now, dirty little Negress! Out!"

Did I dream this scene?

50

It was Thécla's idea.

Since music had chosen Jamaica for its kingdom and the people idolized their composers as gods, why not organize some concerts—not reggae this time but another sort of popular music, *gwoka* for example, or carousel music? The boarding house grounds were large enough to hold a thousand people comfortably. At five dollars a head it would be a small fortune. At the same time it would help strengthen the bonds of understanding between the English- and French-speaking peoples of the Caribbean. And so on and so forth . . . Thécla grabbed her pen and addressed a long epistle to Gesner.

Who received it at the very moment that, pacified by paternity, he was hovering over the cradle of the big baby boy Gerty had just given him; and it brought back all the pain he had taken so long to overcome! Ah, the Louises had never brought him luck! Quite aside from Thécla, since woman is born inconstant and cruel! But Jean, his adoptive father! To think that Jean had accepted Manuel with open arms, the very man who had stolen Thécla. The result was that Gesner blindly accepted as true the newspaper *Libèté*'s attacks which portrayed Jean as an insignificant petty bourgeois, a prisoner of his class who was miserly, overly ambitious, and fierce. It must also be added that the affair with Fabienne had sickened Gesner, for he had never been a womanizer. The revolution begins with such self-control. True, Jean was revealing him-

268

self to be the same as the other hacks from the established
political parties who used their position to establish veritable harems for themselves!

So Gesner responded with a terse note in which he
invented a host of engagements for himself. But for days
and nights afterward he fretted about it, walking up and
down his porch like a soul in pain and paying no further
attention to his son. Gerty's eyes grew wet with tears. Ah,
that Thécla! Hadn't she already done him enough harm?
Who, who will save us from female intellectuals? They
have no heart, female intellectuals! They're feather-
brained, and experiment with men's love. They're not
hot-blooded, female intellectuals! Cold as a snake, they
mesmerize their prey. Finally Gesner took hold of himself, and out of the memory of his rekindled pain composed one of his most beautiful tunes: *"Déviré, Turn
Back."*

In her turn, Thécla turned moody at Gesner's refusal.
Summoning up that brightest love of the adolescence she
spent at Grands-Fonds-les-Mangles, she wondered if she
shouldn't simply have drunk deeply of that happiness
instead of going to fish in troubled waters. Nevertheless
she pulled herself together, refused to admit she was
beaten, and turned to Ottavia. Ottavia, her partner in the
earlier disaster! Who, as it happened, was a stone's throw
away in Montreal, where the Haitian community treated
her like a queen, and who made no difficulties about
accepting the invitation.

Ottavia arrived at Black River on the day a hurricane
was due. The hurricane went on to hurl itself against the
coast of Florida, leaving five hundred dead and a dozen
injured. Nonetheless Ottavia caused a stir. People who
usually hid behind their shutters emerged into the glare of
slander and censure to gaze at her two guitars, her Indian

poncho, her black braid that was thick and stiff as a stake, to ogle the warrior-goddess height of her!

I was holding my breath, waiting for the Terence-Ottavia meeting and already enjoying what could not fail to result from it, to Thécla's great discomfiture. What was she thinking of? Apparently, with the advantage of being years ahead of me, she had a better knowledge than I did of the human heart. For the two of them did not even glance at each other and merely exchanged two or three formal phrases.

"I do so admire your work."

"I, too; I've heard you in New York!"

Terence, who through women had entry to any number of houses, was placed in charge of advertising the concert. No one knows how he reached an agreement with the priest, who from his Sunday pulpit mentioned the misfortunes of our brothers, the people of Haiti, and lauded the exceptional talent of the woman who had made herself their spokesperson. Consequently a banner streamed across the pediment of the church:

OTTAVIA DI MAGGIO SINGS HAITI.

Then Terence went to carry the good news for miles around, to the worldly Rasta colonies at Negril, the small shopkeepers at Savanna-la-Mar, and the bureaucrats of Mandeville. He even arranged for an item to appear in the Kingston newspapers. On his own Manuel, armed with an electric chain saw rented in Savanna-la-Mar, cut down two mahogany trees on the grounds, sawed them lengthwise, and set up a podium. After which he installed a sound system and festooned the trees with garlands of multicolored light bulbs. For a finish he twisted his back, which obliged him to remain in bed for a week, moaning in pain.

In the meantime, stretched out belly-flat on air mattresses, Ottavia and Thécla took up their conversation where they had left off. Ottavia lay in the sun smeared with coconut oil while Thécla remained in the shade, both of them equidistant from one of the bottles of Barbancourt rum Ottavia had taken the wise precaution of bringing with her. Ottavia was indignant that Thécla could have married a white (a white!) and pressed her with questions. Thécla, so clever when holding forth on "Race and Class in the Caribbean" or "Music and People Power"—not to mention "Revolutionary Movements in the Black World"—lost her way in the circumvolutions of her own heart and tried to analyze herself:

"To me, Pierre is not a white man. He's . . . Pierre! No one's ever been closer to me, except Gesner maybe, but Gesner and I, we were children. I don't understand why we're so obsessed with race, with color. . . . What do they mean?"

"You're going to get a divorce, I hope?"

"I don't know, I don't know."

Myself, when I was not running around with Melissa or dozing beside her in the back row of the schoolroom, wearied by yesterday's escapades, I killed time wondering which of the two, Ottavia or Thécla, I hated most before giving the edge to the former. I read "Lie" in her velvety Italian eyes. I heard "Lie" in her voice, that voice as compelling as the Artibonite, the great river of her land! "Lie," "Lie," "Lie," everywhere lies. To me, demanding and unjust child that I admit I was, it was all lies; that great concern for the people; that love for the Negroes, as my grandfather Jacob would say; that hatred of the exploitation of man by man, as my great-uncle Jean would say. Nothing but Ottavia's desire to attract attention to herself and her passion for settling private scores.

As noon neared, Manuel, worn out by all that chatter, shouted from his bed of pain:

"Fuck you, women! Go make something to eat!"

So Ottavia and Thécla went down to the kitchen and, amid wild girlish laughter, haphazardly seasoned fish and meat.

The presence of Ottavia attracted a few guests to the boardinghouse, French people or Americans who had heard her in Paris or New York and who surrounded her with their sticky sycophant admiration.

"I saw you at the Olympia Music Hall. You were sublime!"

"I have all your records, you know!"

As a consequence Manuel, who was at the cash register, tripled their bills, charging Norwegian-salmon prices for a slice of overbroiled swordfish.

51

The day of the concert dawned blue above a sea still as a puddle of oil. Ottavia had rehearsed for hours in the depths of the garden, the vigorous echo of her voice reaching us,

> *"Mwen kouché malad*
> *Pa sa lévé. . . . "*

and she had added two of Terence's poems to her repertory (that should have aroused my suspicions, but I was far too busy showing Melissa around the boardinghouse, where she had never dared come before that day).

The concert was set for six o'clock, the hour at which the first stars shine. At a quarter to six two gaudily painted buses unloaded the forty or so Americans and sycophantic French who had already sampled the pleasures of our menu. At six fifteen the kids from Black River took the trees surrounding the grounds by storm, from where they had a clear view of the podium. At six thirty a handful of young people massed themselves about the wide-open gates, as if they feared letting themselves be caught in a trap and were making sure of their getaway. At seven, when it became obvious there would be no more people in the audience and that Manuel's carefully numbered tickets would remain virtually unsold, Ottavia decided to sing.

Melissa and I, we held each other by the hand. Gradually, as Ottavia sang, salt and water blended in the hollows of our wondering eyes and, streaming down our cheeks, traced shiny pathways there. Neither she nor I knew what we were crying about. (Not for our country, whose sorrow and poverty we were not yet aware of.) For our tattered childhoods. For the villainess who lay in wait for us and would not give us a chance, being as we were off to such a bad start. Behind a West Indian almond tree Terence sobbed like a baby and pulled us close to him. About us the night drifted on.

Of the four, Ottavia was the least affected by the failure of the concert. To a Thécla in collapse, a worried Manuel, and a fatalistic Terence she had demonstrated that it was absurd to speak Creole to Jamaicans and simplistic to think of music as a sort of Esperanto comprehensible to all.

"Each sort of music conveys a culture, and each culture is an island."

No doubt for that reason she was in no hurry to put the sea between her and this memory and to rejoin her fans in America, who at least filled her concert halls. On the contrary, she stayed on but turned over a new leaf. No more rising far later than did the sun! No more meandering and garrulous idleness laced with Barbancourt rum! No more wild girlish laughter in aprons tied so tightly they flattened the breasts. No more walks, arm around Thécla's shoulders, among the pear and tulip trees of the grounds! She was up at six while the day still hesitated beyond the shutters, bathed in cold water from the cistern tank, and climbed up to the top-floor room, where she worked. There her crescendo-decrescendo voice made the walls shake, the roof creak, and the insects flee helter-skelter, warning me that it was time to choose between school and playing hooky. Having also turned over a new leaf, Terence went upstairs to join her with a mug of coffee in his hand, for she had decided to set his poems to music after having translated them into French and then into Creole. No small job! Often she leaned over the balustrade and called Thécla to the rescue:

"Say! How would you say in Creole: 'The self-satisfied moon seated on the steps of Heaven . . . '?"

However, Thécla, from the room where she was feverishly scribbling, did not deign to answer. For a silence that I refused to hear had fallen over the house. To protect myself, perhaps, I willed myself deaf, blind, mute. Something was rotten somewhere, and I refused to smell its hateful stench. One night in the sea-and-mildew-odored dining room where for weeks now no guest had come to sit, Terence forced me to tear my eyes from the television set and recited the poem he had written directly in French.

"Listen, sweetie pie!"

Dans la calebasse sans fond de l'eau
J'ai mis du gros bleu d'indigo
Beaucoup, beaucoup
J'ai versé du sel blanc de cuisine
Et j'ai fait naître
La mer. . . .

In the bottomless calabash of the water
I have put coarse indigo blue
Beaucoup, beaucoup
I have poured out white kitchen salt
And brought forth
The sea. . . .

Delighted, I was about to applaud when, with a slap, Thécla changed my impulse for praise to one for tears.

Terence and Ottavia stood up in a simultaneous motion, and everything became chaos; it was like the moment in a cockpit when gamecocks and men drunk on Montebello rum fly at each other in a confusion of wings and voices, steel spurs scraping and warm blood falling drop by drop onto the cemented floor! In his turn Manuel shot up like a spring and, standing small next to the height of Ottavia, banged on the table with all his might. Suddenly Thécla raced into the depths of the garden, and everyone went chasing after her. I was finally forced to admit that something was wrong!

But what? The truth is like a baby in a cradle whose mother refuses to see it is growing up. Or, too, like the bound feet of a Chinese woman that are wrapped in strips of cloth to mutilate them forever.

What was wrong at the Waterloo boardinghouse?

Three Peter Tosh concerts in Kingston brought us their quota of young backpacks trailing their filthy sneakers across the island. Inevitably seized by a passion for Black River, they boarded with us. Thécla and Ottavia, shoulder to shoulder yet no longer speaking a word nor exchanging a glance, blackened fish on the grill before covering it with hot pepper sauce. To his other duties Manuel had added that of waiting tables—which he had already performed in a restaurant on Fifth Avenue—and moved from one table to the other, face impassive. Where was Terence?

I have kept the memory of nothing except Terence's absence throughout those unseeing days, an absence as intrusive, suffocating, and anxiety-producing as some presences can be. He was not there in flesh and bone, but it was obvious that he filled the entire place like those dead who have passed over to the other side of the visible world yet continue to inhabit the places and beings that they loved. Melissa tried to help me resolve this unsolvable equation, but we always came back to the never-ending question:

"If they don't love each other anymore, why do they stay together?"

Really, at the age of going-on-twelve, how can one know that it is harder to let go of than to take each other?

One afternoon, after Melissa had wept through the whole history lesson, we were seeking the shelter of the park in order to prattle on about the unfathomable malice of the adult heart, when our feet stumbled over the knotted and tangled roots of a rubber tree.

The roots of a rubber tree?

And now, touched by the magic wand of one of those wicked witches forever ready to stray where they should not and to cast their evil spells, they took the form of a man and a woman, the very last whom our naïveté would have expected to see in that state of dress. It was a state of dress that left no doubt regarding the act in which they were engaged and which made their faces red and sweaty, an act that made them all the more frighteningly ugly as they were beautiful, that man and that woman, beautiful when the desire the wicked witch had lodged within them was not turning them into swine at our feet.

Someone uttered a cry (I think it was me!) that quivered like an arrow and soared beyond the roof of the village, the fishing boats, and the surge of the sea and struck the bleeding heart of the sun!

Then my heels grew wings, and I flew straight before me, borne along by horror, revulsion, pain!

52

Patience divided my hair into a center part, along which she ran an index finger covered with palma Christi oil. Then she said:

"You really ought to be going home, Coco. Your parents will be worrying."

I burst into tears. She did not insist, confining herself to a deep sigh.

"Do God know what He's doing? I would have so liked a little girl!"

When she had combed my hair into two braids and hung a ribbon on each end, I held out my cheek for her kiss and said to her:

"Thank you, Auntie!"

This was one of the small niceties of manners to which she had accustomed me. There were many others, and I found them all very confusing. For example, in the morning it was absolutely forbidden to speak to her before rinsing out one's mouth. Food was never to be swallowed before a few crumbs of it were tossed to the floor. Bananas were not to be eaten when you were hot, nor *genip*, the West Indian lime when you were cold, nor avocado without cod, nor figs without tripe. The body was to be rubbed all over with bay rum to ward off insect bites, and the legs with carap oil to make them shine. Et cetera. Having never received any lessons from Thécla, I asked nothing better than to learn and was an excellent student.

Patience's shack consisted of three rooms—a bedroom with a big mahogany bed under a mosquito net, a rather empty dining room, and a kitchen with a beautiful Norge refrigerator. There was also a porch where Ben, her husband, a naval carpenter, stored a portion of his timbers and tools. Ben came swaggering down the pathway a little before sundown, a passel of pink-, blue-, and yellow-colored fish in his hand. He tossed out at me, not unkindly:

"Still here!"

Then he went and washed his whole body with Lifebuoy soap and stuck a pipe between his teeth, while he waited for the court bouillon Patience was hurrying to cook. From time to time they gave each other the news of the day:

"Tomatoes are almost a dollar a pound in the market. If you'd listened to me . . . "

"Joe had to change the motor on his dinghy."

"Laureen had twins!"

After eating we listened through the spitting sounds of the radio to news of a war finally over in Vietnam after the total number of dead had exceeded that of the living. At last Patience moistened her index finger and opened her Bible:

> Wilt thou hunt the prey for the lion?
> or fill the appetite of the young lions,
> when they crouch in their dens
> and abide in the covert to lie in wait?

I slept on a camp bed under bedding as stiff and sharp-edged as a sheet of tin.

Oh, image of happiness!

Alas, it lasted barely a week! One morning I heard the

voice of him who I wanted to strike from the map of the living! Of the very man who night after night I dreamed of killing with one of those vicious and vigorous blows Manuel dealt the bonito. He was standing hatless in the halo of the nascent sun, dreadlocks to his shoulders and eyes overflowing with a love I wanted no more of, Melissa standing by his side and traitorous in my eye for doing so.

"Coco, Coco, you have to come home! Something terrible's happened! You have to come back to her!"

53

People say that the death of my great-uncle Jean, which occurred in the wee hours of the morning on March 24, 1971, was a death foretold. People say that one night a comet, lit up like an airplane, crossed the sky above l'Anse Laborde and fell to earth near the island of Antigua. One day at noon half the sun turned the color of ink while a hurricane rain fell beyond a line drawn north of Grands-Fonds-les-Mangles. When the last drop had finished trickling, toads and other water animals were found burned to a crisp, their coal-black mouths in the mud. At l'Anse Bertrand Délices, a forty-year-old Negro woman who had never known a man, was returning from sunrise Mass, where as on every other morning she had taken Holy Communion, when she began speaking in tongues and predicted the sacrifice of a righteous man. As Eastertime was almost upon us, people thought she meant the eternally repeated Passion of Our Lord Jesus Christ, and her prophecy did not receive the attention it deserved.

Following that, Fabienne insisted that Pablo, the son she was carrying and who four months later opened his eyes to weep an orphan's tears in the world of the living, had brutally thrown himself against the wall of her belly three times as if to announce the approaching tragedy.

People also say that the roosters crowed in the black of midnight, that despite kicks and shouting, dogs moaned for hours on end and that for no reason a kapok (the tree of nocturnal spirits) standing atop Zandoli Hill lost its leaves and was left naked as a *filau*.

In the opinion of all, Jean lived his last days like a man who is preparing himself for a difficult passage. He paid a visit to Gesner, and to Marietta, in whose house he had not set foot for months. The former was never to forget how early one morning, while he was feeding Phosphatine breakfast drink to his fat-cheeked son, he saw Jean push open the gate, his face downcast and his clothes wrinkled as if he had slept in them. All Gesner's affection rose up into his mouth in spite of himself, and with a feeling of foreboding he asked:

"Friend Jean, what's wrong? You look like you're worried about something. What is it?"

Jean remained silent for a long moment, rubbing the child's round pebble of a head as the boy tried not to cry, then he made up his mind:

"It's true. First of all, I'm worried about our Thécla. And I'm not the only one. That white husband of hers wrote to Jacob saying she was in a bad way and asking what could be done about it. But what can we do?"

Gesner remained quiet, for hearing about Thécla gave him too much pain, and Jean sighed:

"He's funny, that white man! He seems to love her like the apple of his eye! It's strange! Can a white man love a black woman with his heart? Myself, I thought it was sex, exoticism. . . . "

Decidedly tortured by this conversation, Gesner said nothing, and Jean lit a cigarette:

"Our Thécla's always playing the fool! And then, I'm worried about our country. Fabienne is saying nothing but the sad truth. If the Patriots don't devise some other strategy, in the year 2000 we'll still be at the point of organizing conferences for the last of the colonies."

Gesner finally broke his silence to ask mockingly:

"What are you advocating? Violence? Bombs? You too?"

Jean raised his eyes to where the stars were wheeling:

"Yes, my dear friend! We need martyrs!"

Gesner thought he had heard wrong. What was this already potbellied man talking about? This father of sons? He repeated:

"Martyrs?"

"Yes, some must shed their rich blood so that others may rise up."

Leaving Gesner to his shock, Jean went on to Marietta's.

Ever since Jean had abandoned her with their five youngest children, the last-born of them not even seven years old, Marietta had had no place in her heart for her old companion. At her bar, Pour Some More, she took all her customers as witness:

"What is a man? Oh, no, do not love here on earth. In the flower of my eighteenth year I took my heart and gave it to that ingrate. Mario, my father, a French white man, didn't want me dirtying my sheets with that black Negro. But I said to him: 'You stop right there! None of that nonsense. He's the one I want. No other.' And look at me now! This is my reward! Forty years old in two months, and my bed's cold as an old woman's. My heart's forsaken as a fallow field!"

And then going on about that Fabienne, who, sooner or later, she'd get even with! Tired of listening to this endless refrain, the customers kept their heads lowered over their drinks.

Nevertheless when Marietta saw the father of her children come in with that funereal expression, all her

love flowed back into her heart. She recalled their first
meeting when he went about on mule back and she
snubbed him so badly before nestling in his arms on a bed
of ferns. She asked:

"Jeannot, what's wrong?"

Jeannot said not a word. Knowing what loosens a
man's tongue, she pushed a bottle of fermented rum
toward him, and he drank three straight shots one after
the other, something she had never seen him do in their
twenty years of life together. He said:

"I want to tell you, I have been crazy and prideful. If
anything happens to me, have all the children who are in
France come home. Ask Jacob for my portion of the
estate and buy them a few more acres of land and have
them plant green rice; sweet potatoes; red, juicy
tomatoes. . . . "

By this, Marietta saw that Jean was still completely
irrational, and said irritably:

"You think they're going to stop studying medicine,
studying law, studying pharmacy, to put blisters on their
hands swinging the cutlass?"

"They must! They must!"

Marietta begged God for calmness and patience. Jean
downed another straight shot of rum and repeated:

"They must! That is where our salvation lies! Our
forefathers understood nothing. We must not turn our
back on the land. We just must possess it for our hunger
and our thirst!"

At which Marietta turned ill tempered again, shouting:

"You think you're a priest in church to come preach-
ing that here?"

Which means that once again the spouses parted in
anger and that Marietta would not have time enough in

all the years she had left to live to regret that quarrel.

Then Jean went to rejoin his accomplices.

That is where the injustice is. The death of my great-uncle made headlines in all of the world's newspapers. Even in *The New York Times*, which devoted several lines to him: POLITICAL KILLING ON CARIBBEAN ISLE.

For this petty bourgeois who so badly wanted to write, who had broken with his class, was a windfall for reporters. But hardly a thought was given to the other two, themselves fathers, caring lovers, and loving sons, whose lives ended along with his. Felix Thalassa and Ronny Kandassamy.

The first taught physics and chemistry at l'Anse Bertrand. Son of a plantation manager and a ne'er-do-well since his childhood, he had been irritated at seeing his strict father turn child again, obsequious, as he rolled his straw *bakoua* hat between his fingers and crooned "Yes, boss" to the white man. On his own he had learned to put together small Molotov cocktails that he set off at demonstrations. He had been in his element during the big construction workers' strike, hiding his fiendish devices in mounds of sand so that they would explode under the feet of the Compagnie Républicaine de Sécurité militiamen. As for Ronny Kandassamy, he was an Indian. Born a native of Port-Louis, he had grown up, a model farm worker, on lands belonging to the Darnel Sugar Factory. Then he had grown weary of his own perfection and gone off to Paris just in time for a taste of the student and workers' demonstrations of May 1968. After coming home he had been unemployed for almost four years, for he refused to believe his father, who always said:

"The Indian coolie is made for the cane. The cane is made for the Indian coolie."

Despite my research, I have been unable to discover

how these three men, so different in age, roads traveled, and social class, met and formed a pact of friendship. All I know is that the three of them planned the project together.

That Saturday it was a matter of placing a bomb, built by Felix, inside the car belonging to Prefect Lebreton, at Matouba in the former fiefdom of the ruling whites. Lebreton was marrying off his daughter. Guests had come from Martinique, Saint Martin, and even from France. Decorated with flowers like a carnival float, the wedding car with the joyful father and his daughter aboard was to explode at the precise moment when it turned into the avenue of coconut trees. What finer symbol than this France all bloodied! Exactly what happened? This is still being argued throughout the Caribbean. . . . In any case, at four in the morning an explosion coming from the garage woke Lebreton, his family, and their guests, who found themselves gathered on the veranda in the bewildered poses of men and women brutally torn from their sleep and who saw angry flames rising toward the sky. It took days to identify what remained of the burned bodies.

The Patriots hastened to make a martyr of my great-uncle Jean. They hastened to hollow out a niche for him alongside other Negroes who, in their day, had died amid poverty, worry, and general indifference even when their lives had not been deliberately taken from them. Toussaint Louverture, Dessalines, Marcus Garvey, Amilcar Cabral, Martin Luther King, Malcolm X—the list, the list of them would be a long one. The very people who the day before had denigrated him now showered him with praise, and *Unknown Guadeloupe*, which lay sleeping in the dust of bookshops, was remembered and in a month or two sold one thousand seven hundred and fifty copies.

Worse yet, the communists, who had always considered my great-uncle a laughable though harmless fool, coopted him, realizing the effect of his death on our people, who, it is true, have a need for martyrs. It was thus that the municipality of La Pointe rebaptized our fine old Place de la Victoire "Place Jean-Louis." But the inhabitants paid scant attention to these political changes and continued calling it by the name sanctified by custom! Certain city council men wanted to dedicate a museum to the dead man, going so far as to propose the acquisition of the Fouquier-Barrat house, the city's loveliest, a steel-and-pink-brick structure belonging to former slaveholders that dated back to the end of the eighteenth century. However, what would be exhibited throughout its two floors? A few copies of *Unknown Guadeloupe*? The straw *bakoua* hat under which he liked to shelter? The cane on which he leaned as he walked through the thickets? This all seemed fairly thin, and the idea was finally abandoned. My grandfather Jacob had, for his part, his own point of view on that death. He had never taken his brother's tirades seriously; and from having assiduously kept company with him in those last months, he believed he knew why Jean had gone to his death. In reality it was Anaïse, that spurned fine flower of a woman, who had drawn him to it. The sins of youth are like our volcanoes Soufrière and Pelée. One thinks them extinct. Then one morning, without warning, they wake and cover the banana trees with a shroud of ash that makes life impossible.

The thought of Anaïse had never left Jean. Indeed, how could one forget her beauty at the age of sixteen, her body like the Kongo sugarcane topped by the plume of her flowerlike face. Her lips as mauve and luscious as the jocote! But in Jean's forties she had returned in force, and he had lived solely with her from then on. Before daybreak, when he sugared his coffee, she was there. There when he uncapped his fountain pen to set down his maunderings. There when he conversed with the perceptive peasants, who were so sensitive to the emptiness in his eyes and whispered to each other that something had changed their friend on them. There, above all, when he was readying himself to make love to Fabienne, when upon seeing her neither angry nor resentful but simply attentive and coiled up in the mosquito net, his desire guttered out like a bonfire in the rain. In sleep he saw her again, wiping away the sweat of his bad dreams. Jacob, in whom he confided, made every effort to convince him that there was nothing strange or abnormal about this:

"It's like Bonnemama Elaïse! She's always with me. It's she who counsels me on everything I have to do. If she weren't there, I'd be like a lost soul! And the others are here, too. . . . "

But Jean had not wanted to hear him. He had interpreted that presence in his own fashion and, taking it for a call, had obeyed. Oh, yes, he had planned the deed well! He had not slipped secretly into some swollen stream carrying off calves, cows, and clutches of chicks as it went. He had not furtively chewed the poisonous roots of the manioc nor the apples of the manchineel tree to enter, benumbed and cold, his eternal resting-place. No! He had chosen the spectacular, and with a scarlet brush traced the looping strokes of his death across the luminous island sky! Jacob thought that final extravagance just like him! He had never been able to live like everyone else, that little brother of his, born in the year of a hurricane! In the end too proud, too arrogant in his apparent renunciation! Death could not come to take him from a sickbed and march him, past a widow and grieving children, to an ordinary grave. No! He needed two or three thousand people behind his casket, a Guadeloupe in shock, endlessly asking itself: "Truly, a person can die for Independence?"

54

Thécla stood beside the open crypt as if she wanted to enter its belly, curl up inside it, and die herself. Her unseeing eyes had not read the newspapers that were for once unanimous in emotion and sorrow. Her unhearing ears had not listened to the embarrassed homily by a priest torn between sympathy and his fear of the bishop. Her mouth briny with the salt from her eyes had been unable to kiss the two widows (so to speak!), each of whom could lay claim to a full measure of respect and compassion. I had never noticed how my mother had aged. For it was an old woman who stood in the sun, hatless among the heads covered with picture hats and toques, but stiff and awkward in the full mourning of a dress clumsily sewn by cousin Nirva. Two perpendicular furrows dug their way from the wings of her nose to her chin marked by a dimple that ran sideways. Her cheeks were slack and sunken. Her eyes dull between lashes sticky with mascara, since to repair the irreparable she had smeared herself with Jungle Line makeup ("Especially for Women of Color"). Under that tarry carnival-mask exterior Thécla was in agony. As always, it was at the moment she lost him that she realized how much she had loved her uncle, how ungrateful she had been to him, and how much she had disappointed him. Ah, yes, her life was a rough draft of endless blots, erasures, and scribbled words! What was she doing in Jamaica? What was she looking for there? She no longer knew. In her disarray she leaned her full weight onto her father. He, overwhelmed by the contact, dissolved into tenderness and dreamed of taking her in his arms as he had before, during those few short years when Tima and he had been everything to her. What a hard row to hoe it is, being a parent! Ah, when the death rhythms of the *gwoka* drum stopped beating, they would have a good talk! He would sit himself down in the rocking chair, she would be at his feet, and with Tima invisible between them he would urge her to resign herself, to stop her wandering, to rejoin her husband, white though he was, and take care of her child. To give it all up, as it were. The dreams, the ambitions, the worrying about the Negro, about the people (call it what you want!), since in any case that oblong box with its elaborate gilding stood in the way of all those passions.

Since death has the power temporarily to heal the breaches in a family, my great-uncle Serge had come down from Gourbeyre with Nadège and their youngest children. He wore the Legion of Honor in his lapel and, by dint of swimming the butterfly stroke in his pool, jogging up the flanks of La Soufrière, and taking saunas on the Rue du Sable on Basse-Terre, had become slim; thus he contrasted with, looked out of place in the family, and people wondered where that Louis came from who looked so little like them. Under that alien appearance, however, Serge, too, was suffering from the death, absurd to him, of the little brother born in the year of the hurricane, and he blamed himself for having harshly called him a demagogue and an impostor. After all, it takes courage to live all that time in a pole shack without running water or electricity, alongside peasants who talk in thick Creole about cutting cane, hauling by oxcart to the factory, and scything their market gardens! Perhaps Jean was a saint he had failed to recognize?

As for me, I was the only one to float beaming with joy in that warm bath of mourning in which we were plunged. First of all, I had had little love for my great-uncle, that pretentious martinet who had never said a thing to me but:

"Go play!"

Or:

"Be quiet!"

Above all, I had found myself again. I was healing my wounds.

Flora Lacour, whom I docilely called Friend Flora out of hatred for my mother, had taken to loving me. I went to sleep well washed, decked out in flannel pajamas that had belonged to one of her sons (my uncles actually, but they did not seem born of my grandfather's seed and humbly lowered their eyes when addressing my mother, their sister) and between sheets fragrant as the petals of the ylang-ylang! As far as I was concerned, one Louis a day could have died a violent death if his death had that result!

Slipping away from the wake while the women, rosary in hand, chanted Our Fathers and Hail Marys, and while the men drank white rum and told jokes, I had stolen into my grandfather's office and reopened the family albums. They had not budged. They were all there waiting for me. From the handsome Negro around thirty-two years of age, handsome with his egg-shaped skull, chin marked with a dimple (like my mother's!), and his wide mouth opening onto an infinity of teeth meant for devouring the world . . . to him. To you. Albert, the little boy with his hair parted on the left and carefully plastered down. Sailor suit. Hoop. High ankle-shoes. Staring into the camera lens without a laugh or a smile and of whom no one any longer knew a thing.

"He was the son of a boy your forebear Albert

had with an English Negro woman he knew in Panama. . . . "

I was readying myself to begin without delay my antlike work, gathering up crumbs of information to store them in the safety of my mind.

Soon people would be saying in surprise:

"What a curious little thing she is!"

Protesting:

"What do you care? Your mother herself wasn't even born at the time!"

Frowning:

"Wait, wait! Myself, I was still very little. It's, rather, something I was told. From what I remember it was before the war. Or maybe it was around the time of Sorin? In any case, there were still jujubes on Hospital Hill and tamarind trees. On Thursdays we had no school and we played tag or leapfrog. . . ."

55

My great-uncle Jean was no sooner tucked away for all eternity in the bottom of his grave than he was reborn into another life in the world of the living. Elaïse had given birth to him on the very day of the terrible hurricane of 1928. With the rain raging on the scattering sheets of tin, the wailing baby, a blinding caul enveloping his face to the chin, had been saved from the waters by the midwife, Madame Fidelius, who had waded through in her high rubber boots. Afterward he had greedily nursed for the first time, sheltered beneath an umbrella that a servant girl held with trembling hand as she stood at the head of the bed. For that reason, no doubt, water had always been his favorite element. At the age of four, when children are just finding their balance on their legs, he was swimming straight out to the islet of Gosier. Later, he was to outrace the Tabonuco-wood boats of l'Anse Laborde. And obstinate with that! At the age of six, while reciting that well-known nonsense: "Our ancestors, the Gauls . . . ," he had burst out laughing and arrogantly refused to go on. In the same way, at sixteen he had not wanted to become a farmhand like the others and had set out along the lonely road of The People. And so on and so forth. . . . A rivalry developed between Grands-Fonds-les-Mangles and l'Anse Laborde, each of these localities throwing events from the young boy's life in the other's face. It was at Grands-Fonds-les-Mangles that he had turned his back on the colonial administration. Yes, but it was at l'Anse Laborde that he had written *Unknown Guadeloupe!* His first, fine flower of a woman, Anaïse, came from Grands-Fonds-les-Mangles. Yes, but his wife-in-marriage was a native of l'Anse Laborde! And so forth and so on. . . . Ah, yes, the old men sighed as they puffed on their pipes, he was a great Negro, truly a Maroon, like one of those slaves who escaped to live wild and free in the jungle. Negroes like that hadn't been seen since . . . since Simidor, the overseer, tired of saying "Yes, boss" and had led the farm workers in an attack on the Bertin Desmarais plantation. That was in 1914, the very year the French whites began playing at their favorite little game. And so on and so forth. . . . Even Marietta, who knew better than anyone the true measure of her man, succumbed to the temptation:

"He could go for days without eating or drinking. Not even a drop of coffee in his stomach. Writing, writing. If by mistake I came to bring him a little something, a slice of avocado, some manioc meal, some grilled and flaked salt herring, his eyes would flash:

" 'God's thunder, woman! You think I have eating on my mind!' "

The apotheosis came from Gesner. Forgetting the manner in which Jean had fêted his rival, he composed a concerto in his honor for two flutes, *ti-bwa*, and two *gwoka* drums; it was performed one Sunday at eleven in the morning in the church at l'Anse Bertrand! The audience wept uncontrollably before streaming like a tidal wave toward the Communion table. At "Ite Missa est" a magpie that had inadvertently flown inside soared across the nave, and everyone swore it was the deceased come to take Communion with those who were honoring him.

As soon as the family's mind was disposed to something other than mourning the departed, it became obvious that it was impossible for Flora and Thécla to live together in the same house on Rue du Faubourg-d'Ennery. The former did not understand how someone who respects herself could lead the life of the latter.

"My dear, she's not a woman! She's a fireman forever surrounded by smoke! Whenever she finally makes up her mind to get out of bed, I go into the bedroom to open the windows. Some air, some sunlight! And that hollow leg of hers!"

Loyal to his daughter, my grandfather Jacob was about to order Flora to keep quiet or vacate the house when, stealing a march on him, Thécla left for Juston.

I understand now that in reality she was hiding, catching her breath between two sorrows, two waves of pain like an exhausted, water-tossed swimmer. But at the time I saw only that I was rid of her presence!

Having passed my twelfth birthday, I barely knew how to read and write. I was equally murdering three languages and was about to add a fourth, Creole, which my boy and girl cousins spoke exclusively whenever they found themselves out of earshot of adults. Therefore I was handed over to Madame Lafleur, a retired teacher of exceptional quality who had worked wonders with retarded children.

Thank you, Friend Antonine, as I was ordered to call her! Thank you for so much effort and patience!

1 sunflower + 2 geraniums
3 thistles + 4 daisies
5 cornflowers + 6 jonquils
7 tulips + 8 forget-me-nots
9 red poppies + 10 dwarf dahlias . . .

Alas, to such a point would I lose my way in this bed of flowers never seen and never smelled that Friend Antonine gathered up her courage in both hands, and in her fine, slanting handwriting of a retired teacher of exceptional quality wrote to my grandfather Jacob that I needed the attentions of a specially trained instructor. In France, perhaps? While waiting for my sorely afflicted grandfather to give in to Flora's pressure and make up his mind to have a serious talk with his daughter, I was free to devote time to my passion: the search for Bébert.

Without too much difficulty, I set my feet on the trail left by his father's footsteps. The lycée. The friendship with Gilbert de Saint-Symphorien. The departure for Angers. Having reached that point, however, I came to a dead end and no longer understood a thing. What had happened for him and his soon-to-be-born son to be struck from the list of Louises? Out of loyalty to his father, my grandfather Jacob said to me in his ambiguous way:

"There was an accident!"

Accident? Accident?

If I had the whole day to rack my brains over that enigma, at night it was set aside. At exactly six fifteen my grandfather called to me from the first floor and we left for the cemetery. The short trip to the Saint-Jules district was interrupted by three obligatory stops. At the shop of a shoemaker cousin by the name of Séraphin Chèradieu, who spit nails out of his mouth to ask if I was doing well at school. At the clove-scented *lolo*, the small stall belonging to a cousin named Mérita Blanchedent, who asked the same question. In the living room of a blind, widowed great-aunt, Altagras Sophocle, who asked the same question but in addition ran her bony fingers over my face. After those three stops we entered into the city of the dead. His face transfigured, my grandfather became as agile and nimble as a boy. He changed the water in the vases, trimmed with a delicate knife the stalks of those flowers that were still holding up, replaced those that had faded, relit the lamps that had gone out, swept the crypt with a small leaf broom, and all the while chatted quietly, punctuating his conversation with his invisible ones with sighs and nods of his head. Seated on a stone hot from the noonday sun, I watched him, happy at his happiness without even thinking of my own, and prayed:

"You up there, Gawd or Jah, black or white, make her leave me here!"

Guadeloupe; this was my land!

People do not choose their land. It is handed to them with a mother, a father, brothers, sisters . . . in the dawn of the uterine night. Myself, I had chosen my own in preference to the gray and damp of Brittany, where I had nonetheless spent pleasant days with Mama Bonoeil, in preference to Jamaica, that *quilombo* kingdom founded by rebel slaves kept rebellious by the great sea dogs of the Caribbean!

But what good is it praying to Gawd or Jah? Those two have other things to do than listen to the whinings of humankind. One evening we were returning from the cemetery while I vainly repeated my daily prayer, when instead of Flora, who usually waited for us in the shade of the balcony before going downstairs to reheat and serve the meal, we saw every floor of the house lit up like a cargo ship at night. My grandfather started, then hurried forward:

"Thécla! Thécla!"

Oh, yes, there she was with her sticky mascara and her bushy hair, dragging that no-pride-at-all Gesner behind her. Looking neither left nor right, she said:

"We're leaving tomorrow, Coco and I!"

For a long time I wondered if Thécla knew what awaited her at Black River. I understand now that she was well aware of it and walked, eyes wide open, toward that turmoil of pain as if toward a punishment for a wrong she had not committed, a wrong that had flowed throughout all eternity in the blood of our family. Never content was she, never able to find what she was looking for and to take pleasure in it: money, honor, happiness!

I spent the night in tears and grinding my teeth as I devised a thousand plans. What if I went to hide at Juston? Wouldn't the farm workers be happy to share the fruits of their earth with me and the fishermen returning from Viard gave me some of their *balaou* halfbeak fish? Or what if I went the thirty or forty miles to Gourbeyre to present my case to my great-uncle Serge? The exception not being the rule, he seemed to have settled in nicely where he was and to be doing well. The creatures of the night did not frighten me. I would know how to foil the tricks of the night spirit, Ti-Sapoti. As for the three-legged horse of that other night spirit, Bête à Man Hibè, I would hear him coming from far away and throw myself into a ditch to take cover in the Guinea grass. And what if I ran straight to the sea grotto called Hell's Gate, where for three months the robber, Thesmée, held off the gendarmes come to arrest him?

But the eye of morning opened, blue-gray, to find me nestled in my bed.

Ever since his two bastard sons, Rodrigue and Carmélien, had begun vying to become his right arm at the store, my grandfather Jacob had been allowing himself pleasures he had never before tasted, such as staying in bed mornings until seven, with Flora coming upstairs to serve him good hot coffee along with a braided bread and a piece of soursop. Around eight o'clock he came into my bedroom, his good, mournful face more mournful than ever. He wiped my eyes:

"I tried to talk to her. She won't do it."

"Why? Why?"

He shrugged his shoulders with an air of understanding nothing of what went on in his daughter's head and heart. Then he croaked:

"You'll be back! You'll be back! We'll stay here and wait for you! The dead as well as the living are here!"

56

In the airplane, for the first time in the three years we had lived next to each other, my mother began to speak to me from behind her wall, in that somewhat hoarse yet musical, fluid yet stammering, luminous yet shadowy voice that is hers alone:

"It's true, you are the child of my shame and my sorrow. That I can't forget. When you are with me, it's not you I see, Coco. It's your father, with his fine white-toothed, well-brought-up smile, when the lowest cane cutter has more honesty in him than he did. And it's his mother I see, too, on her high horse, asking me who my family was and sniffing in disgust at the salt-cod smell of our name. For no one ever said a word about my color, which fundamentally was the real problem. They never talk about color, even if it's right there before their eyes: It's not done! It's dirtier, color is, than the green diarrhea of amoebic dysentery or the sulphurous yellow piss of incontinence! When I see you, yes, I can't help it, it's all that I see! Them, him! Filthy stupidity, stubborn arrogance, pettiness, oh, pettiness! Beyond it perhaps there are many other things I myself can't see, which might be beautiful viewed in the light of both our hearts. Alas, that's how it is and neither you nor I can do a thing about it. We are doomed to go on until the end of our lives without ever being able to help each other! Let's hope that in that invisible world that my father, your grandfather, talks about so much it will be different!"

Then she turned her weary head toward the blue oval of the airplane window.

On arriving in Kingston, I was still in tears and had my mind on other things than being surprised at seeing Manuel there alone to welcome Thécla and lead her like someone in the grip of an illness toward a hired Mercedes!

On October 12, 1971, Terence Cliff-Brownson and Ottavia di Maggio were married in the North Shepherd Street Baptist Church in Washington, D.C. Eight hundred and fifty people attended the ceremony. The entire Haitian community in the area was present, including two former Tonton Macoutes, who had recovered their respectability in a New York laundry. Before the Elevation of the Host, Ottavia sang a composition of her husband's that she had put into Creole and set to music. . . .

> . . . Heaven makes its nest and the
> Sun like an ox comes to soothe its tongue.
> Spiders sleep in its inmost recesses. . . .

From that day forward she was never again to appear on stage nor before an audience, but was to dedicate herself to the education of her sons. Four of them, the first of which was born less than five months after those brilliant nuptials.

For years I refused to answer the touching and tender letters Terence sent me. I only decided to do so some three years ago, proof that I reached maturity later than most people. I even went to visit him. The couple lives in a residential suburb of Philadelphia, where Terence, who has published three or four collections of poetry that were highly praised by the critics, teaches at Temple University. He offers a course that attracts many

students and has earned him great popularity on campus:
"Music and People Power in the Caribbean: The Case of
Jamaica and Haiti." He has gone to Jamaica several times,
as well as to Haiti, where Ottavia, for her part, never set
foot again until 1986, when the younger Duvalier's government was overthrown. Breaking her vow, she then
gave a free concert before two thousand people drunk
with freedom. Still handsome, Terence has cut off his
dreadlocks (all that is no more than a childhood memory!). Wearing a jogging suit, he links his arm through
mine and drags me to a park covered with snow that
crunches beneath our boots.

"How's she doing?"

"Fine! Fine!"

Silence. The hoarfrost air burns our lips. Finally he
says:

"I know what you're thinking. I don't deny all responsibility. But you have to try to understand. Thécla
was brought up to think she's entitled. . . ."

I interrupt him:

"That's not what I'm trying to understand. I spend
my time wondering what you were playing at, if you
weren't simply frauds, cheats!"

He thinks about it for a long while:

"No, not frauds or cheats. Naïve, petty bourgeois!
And very pretentious!"

Another silence. Then he looks me in the eye:

"What sort of guy is that husband of hers?"

"A good guy!"

Silence. I sense a host of questions turning round and
round in his head. Nonetheless he does not ask them and
takes my hand:

"Stay with us, Coco! Stay with us! It would make me
so happy!"

I would perhaps have accepted the invitation if it had not been for Ottavia. In her presence my childish moods reappear intact. Like some graceful mother hen, she over-protects her sons. One night Julian, the eldest, is about to go out bundled to the eyebrows to a basketball game with his father. So after Ottavia has sent the other boys to bed, the two of us find ourselves watching a television program. In her turn she tries to exonerate herself:

"I know what you're thinking, but you must try to understand. . . ." And so on. And so forth . . .

A little later, in the bright American night, I wipe away my tears while ideas occur to me. What if I did something evil to them? What if I took my revenge, if I took *her* revenge—for the two of them, although they may deny it, murdered my mother.

57

When Thécla had burned her fingers to the bone, setting
them on the grill instead and in place of the sandfish;
when she had fallen down four times without being able
to get up again, her skirt riding up above her pubis; when
she seemed no longer to see or hear what was happening
around her, Manuel made up his mind to consult the
doctor at Black River. Who declared himself unqualified
and suggested they take themselves to Miami, Florida. A
one-and-a-half-hour flight on Air Jamaica. Manuel refused to do so and took it into his head to treat Thécla in
his own manner. What did she need? Much, much love
and the care of a somewhat Rasta obeah man familiar
with plants and simples.

Thécla began to resemble Tima. From morning to
night, hands folded in her lap as her eyes stared at the
invisible, she rocked herself in a rocking chair: forward
and backward, backward and forward. Manuel fed her
like a baby; seated at her feet, he read the newspapers or
spoke interminable monologues.

"You'll be fine, *querida*. The beauty will glow like a
bonfire in your eyes again. You'll smile once more, and
the people who hurt you will be punished. I know, it's
not only them. It's all of life that ought to be done over.
Be reborn on the morning of a new day. Our people
would be different, satisfied, happy, and we'd no longer
claim that we're bringing them happiness."

As Thécla was nodding her head in rhythm, he

deluded himself that she approved, and fervently kissed her hands.

The obeah man showed up on Thursday, a lucky day for dealing with spirits. He carried an assortment of small gourds and little vials carefully sealed with straw inside his sack. These contained powders, unguents, and lotions; solutions to be swallowed, inhaled, gulped down, and rubbed on the head, the body, the arms and legs. Some were as fragrant as the magnolia or the orange blossom. Others as fetid as toad spittle and goat droppings. And still others as acid as the venom of the *twa-lang* snake that hides itself among the leaves of the Caribbean grape. The obeah man roared back and forth, addressing interlocutors only his eyes could see:

"Back, back! Take your hands off her! Just because her mind is heavy and filled with gloom, don't you be taking advantage of her! Leave her, leave her, I say!"

From the branches of a guava tree Melissa and I watched this barbaric scene, I scoffing, she trembling and telling me:

"Here you are, laughing, making fun! Anyway, this is what saved my papa, who was on the point of death. He was already blue. The obeah man put him back on his two feet again. When he opened his eyes, he couldn't remember a thing. Even now there's a big black hole in his mind. You talk to him about some things, he stands in front of you like a zombie!"

The news of Terence and Ottavia's departure for reasons of love and marriage, and my mother's illness that followed, had gone around like a death announcement edged in black. And with that there was not one more guest in the dining room. Not even a furtive cat on the paths through the grounds, nor a green *anoli* lizard in the roof gutters! As if neither animals nor people like the stale odor of misfortune!

But on another level the fall of the Waterloo boardinghouse produced a complete turnabout in people's minds. From a pariah child, I became everyone's child! Shutters until then kept lowered over the impenetrable privacy of homes rose as if by magic. Doors opened, and a hundred good fairy godmothers took me in to share akee and cod and rice. My scratches were covered with small plasters made of leaves. I was fed bush teas spiked with rum for my cough. Even the schoolmistress, who had kept me in house arrest in the back row of the classroom, took it into her head to have me recite the list of Jamaican national heroes:

Number one: Nanny of the Maroons
Number two: Marcus Garvey
Number three: Paul Bogle
Number four . . . Number four. . . .

Only the schoolchildren refused to bow to fashion and went on ignoring me as before.

Since Melissa was forced to turn herself into a perfect-little-girl every evening before appearing at the family dinner table, I went on without her to Negril, where I found my dear Rastas clustered together like brown algae in the windings of a stream.

Blessed times.

Limitless expanse of the sea beneath the sky.

I came to understand it too late: In place of the love that, by her own admission, she could not give me, my mother tried to give me something all the same. A childhood in complete contrast to her own. Accustomed to

rooting about in arid soil for my survival and to content-
ing myself with crumbs, my heart had grown as hard as
ironwood. As it should be. It is the dreams inside one's
head that kill, the wishful fantasies of changing and of
remaking, of playing a part—the stories of role-model
heroes!

"So Ti-Jean placed a fisherman's harpoon in his sack,
took up his great cutlass, girded up his loins, and started
off: 'I am going off to kill the Beast that swallowed the
sun, and this land, my land, shall have light.' "

Alas, she did not succeed in this aim either! I still
bleed that same blood! However, after some time in Negril, a sharp twinge of remorse at having turned my back
on her in her sad state set me back on the road to Black
River.

Her rocking chair empty and desolote in a corner,
Thécla was standing on the veranda. Emaciated, her arms
and legs like sticks of guava wood and her eyes sunken
and reddened like lava in the depths of a volcano, she was
nevertheless healthy again and perfectly well enough to
shout:

"Where have you been hanging around this time?
Don't you know Manuel wound up going to the police?"

To whom can we attribute Thécla's spectacular recovery? Trimphant, Melissa hastened to ascribe it to the
obeah man. Myself, I have another explanation. The song
says it well: "A fallen woman must never despair. . . ."

Yet we had reached the end of something. For several
months or several weeks I don't remember how, Thécla
and Manuel pretended. The days without guests gave
them time to work on their grand project: *Revolutionary
Movements of the Black World*. Similarly, Thécla was gathering up her memories and wrote to my grandfather
Jacob; for his part he was ecstatic at thus being in corre-

spondence with his daughter. Meanwhile Manuel offered his services as international researcher (*sic*) to the few progressive countries in Africa. But one could sense that it was a last-ditch battle, a final flourish before laying down arms and letting the villainess commit her villainies in peace.

58

On returning from Philadelphia, I had gone to visit Manuel at the second-rate Los Angeles college where he teaches. He lives in a four-room apartment at the edge of the campus, littered with cats, crowded with black students who come to weep over the racism of the white man, and strewn with handwritten copies of Marcus Garvey's letters that he is forever promising himself to have annotated and published. I had no great liking for Manuel; and yet on once again seeing his carbuncle eyes below his dated and graying Afro, all my unhappy childhood slowly rises up into my heart. He stammers:

"How is she?"

"Fine, fine!"

While he suffers, we talk of this and that, of the murals covering Los Angeles, of Alvin Ailey, who is appearing in Pasadena, and of the cactus gardens at the Huntington Library. Then he finally makes up his mind and says:

"In every couple, and everybody knows this, there's always one who loves more than the other. Of the two of us it was me. In my eyes Thécla saw the image of what she wanted to be, an exceptionally gifted activist, when the reality was something else. Her parents made her think she was born to be a queen. When she realized that for most people this was far from being the truth, she couldn't get over it and because of that wanted to turn everything upside down! Myself, I've seen my mother wear her fingers to the bone waxing white people's floors. After he left the cane, I saw my father turn simple from being kicked in the butt and saying 'Yessir.' My brothers; overdose, jail, death. I'm not joking when I say this world is rotten and we ought to blow it away! If I wasn't convinced that one day it'll end up changing, I'd've done myself in long ago!"

I hold back a cynical little comment, though in any case he would not have heard it, looking back as he was into the past:

"She was never really mine, all mine, except when she was getting over one of life's low blows. First it was being abandoned by your father, then my brother's being killed. Then your uncle's bombing coming almost at the same time as Terence leaving. And things I don't want to get into. . . . I was a nurse, a sort of dry nurse, a crutch, until she realized that her great white witch doctor was more powerful than me! When you think about it, the whole thing isn't worth the worry and the gray hairs it put on my head. That Thélca, maybe she's nothing but a bitch!"

Silence. Then he says:

"The obeah man did say it: 'You want me to get her back on her feet? She'll use them to leave you right away.' By dint of churning out articles I finally found work at the university in Dar-es-Salaam. I was beside myself with joy. I was already looking forward to our new life. Uhuru and all the rest . . . I remember it as if it was yesterday or this morning because it's at that moment that my life took on the bitter taste it still has to this very day. We had some guests, two Americans from Chicago with a baby just a few months old. The mother'd come to the kitchen to heat a nursing bottle. When she'd finished going round and round, talking stupid the way Caucasians like to do,

I went out on the veranda waving the letter I'd been hiding to surprise Thécla and I said to her: 'Baby, I think we got something good here! At last we're going to drop anchor in calm seas! There are two heads of countries in Africa who are not like those other bastards. The first one, they already got rid of him. That was Kwame Nkrumah. The other is Julius Nyerere. . . .' She let me get worked up painting word pictures for her of this world we'd be living in, then she said to me: 'I'm not going with you, Manuel. I can't stand it anymore! I'm going back to France. I'm going back to my husband.' I was floored, I yelled at her, I cried, I begged her, and while all this was going on, she stared at me, looking like a horse that's bucked its rider! Then she got up and she went upstairs to one of the bedrooms and locked herself in. After that we had a few real fine days. She had so much to be forgiven for that she no longer refused me the things she'd always refused me before. She slept in my arms like a baby, and the moon, on the seventh step of Heaven, was as oval as a Bourbon orange. And me, I didn't go to Dar-es-Salaam. I didn't go any farther than the ends of my loneliness and sorrow. You see, I haven't given up. At this little college I do what I can, with the help of my old friend Marcus, to heal the wounds of its forty black students. I didn't hear from her for years. I imagined her in the arms of her white man, after all the dreams we'd had, and I had to pinch myself until the blood came to be sure I was awake. Suddenly, last year, I receive a letter from her. You want to see it?''

And he searches for it, unable to find it in drawers overflowing with photocopies of indomitable letters from Marcus Garvey to his wife, Amy, letters to Kojo Tovalou, to Gratien Candace, to Adolphe Maturin. . . . In my turn I look back over this piece of the past.

The Americans from Chicago often entrusted me with Debby, their pallid infant with colorless eyes and tiny teeth like grains of rice. I would take her for a walk around the grounds, trying out on her the stories Friend Flora told me:

"When Mano had been laid out full length, longer than he had ever been, and placed in the earth in his hand-sewn shroud that for years had been kept in a Caribbean basket, his cheeks closley shaved and eyelids carefully closed over his brown eyes . . ." But I was not a good storyteller, and Debbie barely listened to me! She preferred laughing in delight at the golden scarab in the sky. One afternoon, then, as I was coming back toward the boardinghouse with Debbie in my arms, Thécla came out of the kitchen. Still not very steady on her frail legs and wrapped in an apron too large for her, she was none-theless quite capable of ordering me around:

"Stop playing nanny. Put that child down!"

Obviously I did no such thing and glared at her. She stammered, recapturing, as she did whenever she was angry, the West Indian accent buried beneath layers of patient effort:

"Don't you look at me that way!"

Obviously I did no such thing. Resigned to no longer pretending she could order me about, she went on to another subject:

"We're going away. We're leaving Jamaica."

My heart turning over, I whispered:

"For Guadeloupe?"

Triumphant and inflexible, she turned away from me, knowing that on this particular terrain she had won, and headed for the kitchen. There, judging by the aroma, a sandfish was blackening on the grill.

"No. For Paris!"

59

So, in the spring of 1972, when blossoms appeared on the chestnut trees in the Luxembourg Gardens, Pierre Levasseur retook possession of Thécla and her daughter. Although he had love enough stored up for the former, he did not have much of it to give the latter. And furthermore, what was to be done with a girl who barely knew how to read and write, and likewise murdered three languages? After some delay Friend Antonine's advice prevailed. A special-education teacher was found for me.

Reunited with her husband, Thécla in the meantime traveled around the world, for voyages not only form the young but they also cure depressions. While watching the marble façade of the Taj Mahal admire itself in the water, one's heart is less given to quixotic fancies.

This, for Jacob, was another opportunity to taint the blood! What was Thécla looking to find in all those faraway places? Hadn't she rolled about enough without gathering any moss? Lying in the locustwood bed where Albert and Bonnemama Elaïse had slept and where he himself had been conceived, his voice rose, droning, as if he were reciting a litany:

"If someone told me that child would make me suffer like this, I wouldn't have believed him and would've sent him packing!"

Flora, weary of hearing the same lamentations night after night, shrugged her shoulders:

"Go to sleep. You're keeping me from sleeping myself!"

Outside of the worry his daughter caused him, my grandfather Jacob had much on his mind. And now Dieudonné, Jean's oldest son, was back from Clermont-Ferrand, where he had sensibly studied law. It is not easy being the son of a martyr! The father's blood calls out to you and will not be denied. Thus Dieudonné did not quietly remain in the practice Jacob had bought for him. Once quiet and even affected in demeanor, given to reading Proust—whom he had discovered at the age of fourteen while recovering from typhoid fever—he now took it into his head to champion the poor peasants, the despoiled workers, the underdogs as it were so numerous in our land.

That metamorphosis intrigues me. For in his earliest youth Dieudonné had given no hint of this future vocation. I think it was aroused in him by comments from the people of La Pointe. Having watched him grow up in Jacob's household, some quite naturally took him for Jacob's son. While the dabblers in genealogy shook their heads:

"No, he's Jean's son by his first wife. . . ."

Here, they lowered their voices:

"The one who killed herself . . ."

The others were surprised:

"The son of Jean the martyr?"

(Which is how they commonly referred to my great-uncle.) And then commented, in amazement:

"He doesn't take after that side of the family!"

All this wound up rubbing Dieudonné the wrong way, and wanting to show what he could do, he decided that no longer would he have cattle thieves or feuding neighbors drunk on rum as his sole clients.

The Sorlin affair brought him the opportunity he was looking for.

Sorlin sat a few miles away from Sainte-Anne and its sparkling bay, a property of two hundred fifty acres or so that had belonged to the sugar factory. At the time it was still untouched by the tourist trade; at present, however, it had gone to rust, abandoned like a phantom vessel run aground in the dry mangrove scrublands. The peasants, refusing to stand idly by and die of hunger, had decided to take up the challenge and raise rice and pacala and cavenna yams. Their cooperative was prospering, and in the marketplaces of Sainte-Anne the plump pumpkin sat cheek by jowl with the tomato when the corporation that owned Sorlin set aside its anonymity to claim its rights and sue. Ah, he had truly argued well for dismissal, had young Dieudonné Louis, Esq. Since then he was all people talked about, from Grande-Terre to Basse-Terre, while *La Voix du Palais*, the lawyers' journal, reprinted long excerpts from his pleadings.

It was then that Dieudonné took advantage of the talk going around about him and announced he was forming a political party, the NGP, the New Guadeloupe party.

When he got wind of Dieudonné's plans, Jacob sat his nephew down in front of him and croaked:

"Politics has hurt our family too much. Before your father, I myself who you see here in front of your very eyes, in my youth . . ."

His notion had been to recount his disappointments during his attempt to form the Negroes Arise party. But Dieudonné had better things to do than listen to this nonsense, and shrugged his shoulders:

"Uncle Jacob, you were as much made for politics as I am for the lard business. To each his own! In your day you divided up the country into three parts. The whites,

whom you feared, yes, feared. The mulattoes, whom you
envied, yes, yes, you envied them! And yourselves, the
Negroes, who underneath those fine speeches about duty
to the race hated each other. It's not with ideas like
those that you could have made the country move forward. . . ."

Humbly Jacob persisted:

"Let's hear some of your ideas."

But Dieudonné was already gone, out past the door-
step, and Jacob sadly blew his nose.

With the creation of the NGP, there arose an outcry,
a fierce and wide-ranging attack on Dieudonné. It was
understandable that the sudden appearance of this new-
comer in the private arena of their ambitions could cause
such annoyance to the traditional political parties. But on
the part of the Patriots, who might have spared the son of
their ex-symbol, it seems more surprising! I shall try to
make some sense of this. It seems that Dieudonné had
irritated his father's former friends, for by making light of
their effectiveness among the peasants he was harshly
criticizing their slogans: *"Palé kréyol, dansé gwoka."* (He
himself expressed his thoughts solely in flowery French,
adored Proust—as I have already said—and listened only
to the Brandenburg Concertos.)

"And yet I am as much a man of Guadeloupe as you!"

He was in favor of a more enlightened independence,
less sectarian, with, so to speak, a human face!

As for the Patriots of the other sort, he was opposed
to their violence and denounced those who planted
bombs.

"We must open a dialogue with the colonialist
power! Talk with them!"

Myself, I shall take no side in these quarrels. All I
know is that I liked my cousin Dieudonné. During his

stays in Paris he never failed to pay me a visit in those
special-education institutions where I was forgetting how
to smile. He would bring me long letters in violet-
colored ink from my grandfather and sweets that Flora
had lovingly made especially for me. Candied pomelo
rind, sugar-candy *douslets*, grated coconut *sukakoko grajé*.
He spoke to me of certain realities as no one else had ever
done (certainly not my mother, whose duty perhaps it
was, considering her "militant" past):

"Our country has the sea-air tang of a grafted mango.
Why must so many of our people live out their lives in
shabby surroundings and not have a taste of their own
land? Do you know how many people from Guadeloupe
are wasting away in and around Paris?"

Yes, I loved my cousin Dieudonné!

Soon he was coming to see me with someone named
Monique, a young blond girl he addressed as "chérie"
who covered him with adoring glances.

I guessed that once again our family was about to
unite itself with blood of another color.

I was not mistaken. Three months later Dieudonné
married Monique in the cathedral at La Pointe. I was not
present at the wedding, but learned all about it in a
detailed letter from Friend Flora. I learned from which
dressmaker the bridesmaids' dresses came and that the
bride's shoes had had to be ordered from Puerto Rico.

What Friend Flora did not mention was the discord
within the family. The various Louises had hardly di-
gested Serge's marriage and, above all, that of Thécla and
were still wondering about both. How far would it go,
this massive invasion of whites into the heart of the family? So some remained aloof and refused in no uncertain
terms to attend the nuptial ceremony. Others attended,
but once there held themselves stiff and unbending,

barely sipping at the Ayala champagne that Jacob had
bought at a discount. Others, finally, welcomed Monique
and her parents with open arms, delightedly whispering
that these whites were not like the others. This gave rise
to interminable arguments:

"What does that mean?"

"That means that white people, they're like anything
else. There are good ones and bad ones. The ones we had
here were the worst, the *békés*, the rich colonialists!"

"You can say that again! My grandmother used to tell
me how when they wanted to beat a pregnant slave, they
had a big hole dug in the ground to preserve her belly and
whipped her on the back and butt."

At that the old slavery stories rose from the depths of
memory, clouding faces and spoiling the party. Ah, yes,
it was long gone, the time of those festive ceremonies
when the Louises, united as a single trade guild, drank,
ate, and danced to the beguines of Stellio or Mavounzy!

As for Jacob, he found another opportunity here to
weep bitter tears at seeing the descendants of Bonnemama
Elaïse turn over a new color. All the while, Flora lectured
him:

"What do you expect? We have to keep up with the
times. Your stories of Negroes, Negroes don't interest
anyone anymore."

"Stop talking nonsense!"

"It's not nonsense! Soon everybody will be mixing
with everybody. There's already almost no black Negroes
in Gaudeloupe!"

Jacob left the room not to have to listen to her rubbish any longer.

In the cemetery that night he tried to learn his dear
invisible ones' feelings about it, but noticed with surprise
that they had become blind to color. Bonnemama Elaïse

saw only that Monique's heart was warm as good bread
just out of the oven. Jean was of the opinion that she
would be a devoted wife who would never let go of her
husband's arm as he traveled the hard road of politics he
had chosen and that she had adopted her man's country
to the point that some blamed her for "thinking she was
more Guadeloupan than the people of Gaudeloupe"
(people are never happy). As for the *Soubarou*, so intransi-
gent when alive, he shrugged his shoulders and burst out
laughing. No, I was not present at the wedding, but I
dreamed of it. As I dreamed of the island.

Each night I landed at the Pointe des Châteaux. Or
at some other point. The island rose up from the water in
answer to my voice. I mounted its back and soared over
the secret forests of its pubis or the parted thighs of its
beaches before impaling myself alive on the purple shafts
of the sugarcane. My blood dripped onto the rich, veined
earth. I prowled about sugar factories laden with cane
juice.

Sometimes, without warning, the season changed.
We would be in the time of Advent, singing carols. I
remember joining a small crowd on a porch as it beat the
measure for its songs with a triangle and the throbbings of
a *gwoka* drum. It was, I believe, at Saint-Sauveur.

> *Friend, what was that great sound*
> *That waked me in the night*
> *And all who me surr-ou-ound*
> *'Tis true I was greatly wroth.*

In the morning, like a *jan gajé*, a dead spirit returning
to its daytime form, I went back to being an outcast in the
middle of dyslexic, disturbed, retarded, and incontinent
children. Numb from the fears of the black of night, the

memory of my dreams alone helped me to endure.

From how many special schools of that sort was I expelled? We were getting nowhere. My mouth was a vault the key to which had been lost. Not a sound came out of it. More often than not I would lose control and defecate on myself.

My irreproachable stepfather, Pierre Levasseur, had taken matters in hand and was not discouraged. Each week he wrote to my grandfather, Jacob, who tortured himself over these reassuring letters.

I hardly ever saw Thécla, who in any case must have been in a bad way herself. For after having set her heart on changing the face of things, and occasionally inscribing her name on the cover of an illuminating work, such as *Notes of a Native Son* or *The Wretched of the Earth*, she had to content herself with being the wife-from-Martinique-of-Doctor-Levasseur! (What a fine doctor and most of all what a wonderful bedside manner!) I was told that Thécla did not please Pierre Levasseur's relatives, an unbigoted family that had produced an aide to Faidherbe and given a discalced monk, a disciple of Saint Francis of Assisi, to an abbey in Provence. Never speaking. Looking as if she could not keep her eyes open. She came to life only when those subjects so dear to the bourgeoisie were touched upon: coups d'état in Africa, world famine, apartheid. At birthdays and other celebrations the family whispered to each other:

"What does he see in her? What *does* he see in her? You don't marry a woman just because she's beautiful!"

60

It is in dreams that the great events of life are foretold. It is in the secret of the night that one learns, chilled and trembling, of the mother's fated demise, the misfortune of the father, the laughing arrival of the boy-child! Every morning made by God the women of the family furrowed their brows to decipher the messages received in sleep and to elaborate the possible interpretations.

"I dreamed I lost a tooth!"

"A tooth! Was it a front tooth? A premolar? A molar?"

My grandfather Jacob vows that in the weeks preceding Jean's death he had only to lay his head on the embroidered pillowcase and close his eyes to experience the same scene. He was walking along a forest path filled with tree ferns, the canopy of the sky hidden by this canopy of foliage, when he heard the unmistakable squeals of a pig being slaughtered. Surprised, for he knew himself far from any plantation, he entered a trail that had suddenly appeared and emerged into a clearing. There he saw Jean bound and hanging by his feet with his head down in the grass. . . .

"Yes, I knew that a calamity was upon him. But from where would it strike? From where to ward off the blow?"

However, I myself slept a sleep free of premonition that night! Nothing more than the ritual nocturnal wandering at the end of which I found myself, in the morning, back in the troubled adolescent body I had left in my bed. And yet!

We had a new French teacher, terribly young, her eyes filled with missionary zeal, a bit brunette, a bit Arab, undoubtedly a mixed-blood! I barely listened to her and was about to let her blend into that boring cohort of our special-education teachers, when she asked me to stay after class.

"I see your name is Louis and you come from Guadeloupe? I too! Well, almost! It's a very long and painful story that I'll tell you when we become friends. Because we are going to be friends, aren't we? I can feel it."

At first I stared without reacting at this snip of a girl who sought to unlock my heart with her charm and sweetness. That had already been tried on me! But there was something familiar in her unfamiliar light-brown eyes and in the line of her cheekbones, something smiling out at me. So I cleared my throat:

"You say your name is Louis and you come from Guadeloupe? How's that?"

May I be forgiven my blunt insistence! No I did not clearly understand it right away. What with worrying about my own life I had set them aside somewhere, Bert and Bébert. Almost forgotten them. My grandfather Jacob was not there to hand me the family albums and relate, when chancing upon some old photograph, the thrice-lovely tale that begins:

"He was the son of an English Negro woman that my father, Albert, your forebear, knew in Panama. . . ."

It is my unforeseen—yet no doubt foretold somewhere—meeting in a dreary dungeon of a special school with Aurélia Louis that healed me, that unstopped my stopped-up ears, that unsealed my sealed lips and set free, high and clear, the song of my muffled voice. For it took us quite a lot of nerve, and the voicing of it, to merge our knowledge and set it in order, to compare it, to fill in the holes, to deduce, to infer, to understand why two dead men were absent from the roll call of our name. Two dead men. Two suicides.

This is Aurélia's tale.

AURÉLIA'S TALE

When that Albert known as Bébert, the son of Albert known as Bert, arrived in the great city of Paris at the end of World War II with a violin as his sole baggage, poverty did not treat him gently. God! It bared its fangs! He kept his stomach full drinking Viandox beef concentrate, kept himself warm with cheap red wine, and washed his only shirt in the cold water of a hotel-room sink. From where had his taste for music come? He himself did not know. Not from old Marie, certainly, who had spared no effort to thwart his vocation so that she might turn him into a son of whom the dead father could be proud! Whenever he had enough money to pay the admission, he hurried to La Gigale, a nightclub on the Grands Boulevards where West Indians warmed themselves at the fire of their music and their rum. Some of them remember the wordless *chabin*, who spoke only in monosyllables.

"Where you from?"

"Louis? What Louis is that? Because Louises, my friend, there's a pile of them!"

It was an old musician at the club named Bobby Alfred who, having taken a liking to Bébert, started him on alto sax. A remorseless chatterbox, Bobby in fact legitimized Bébert and, all without knowing it, gave him a background by talking about his own.

"Like yourself I started with the violin. My first violin, I carved it myself because my parents made me an apprentice to Monsieur Letellier, violin maker in Capesterre. You wouldn't believe what life at home was like in those days. My folks didn't know how to read or write. All they knew was driving oxcarts to carry the cane to the Marquisat factory. Twelve trips a day. Six in the mornin, six at night. When it wasn't the cane my folks were pushin a plow behind their animals. That was on the Boirin Desrosiers plantation. Sunrise to sunset, the same poverty. That's why one day my papa made me put on my Sunday suit, a little blue serge suit with high ankle-shoes and white socks, and took me around to all the places where they needed apprentices. He didn't want me dyin in the cane like him. Monsieur Letellier was a fine man, even though he was white! (You know, there are good ones and bad ones.) Soon as I turned sixteen, he found me a job at the *Arc en Ciel* movie theater accompanyin silent films. There were three of us. One on piano, another on cello. That's how it all started. . . . The first time I came to France was for the Colonial Exposition and then, well, I stayed. . . . It was Duke, Duke Ellington, who started me on sax when he came to Paris in 1932. One of his musicians got sick. So I sat in. Just like that! Paris in those days, it was nothin but politics! Almost all the people from Guadeloupe were communists! There were some even went to Moscow, in Russia! But me, I'm a musician. I never had nothin to do with those things. You do the same!"

Bébert did not follow this judicious advice. He went to hang around the National Assembly during the stormy debates on Indochina. He was at the Vélodrome d'Hiver to hear Lamine Guèye display his indignation at the massacres in Madagascar. Yet his one true care was for his own little Guadeloupe. Every New Year, as Marie had taught him, he sent his "best wishes for health, prosperity, and success in all your undertakings" to Monsieur Albert Louis and Family, Merchants, La Pointe, and did not grow discouraged at the lack of response.

"Bah, it'll happen next time!"

As he grew progressively more familiar with the circle of West Indian musicians, to the point that they no longer called him anything but *"chabin,"* he took each one of them aside:

"Tell me about it! What's it like, anchored in the middle of the sea? You don't know how much it hurts, not knowing the land you come from! Sometimes my heart's in my mouth and I almost can't breathe. I go galloping around town like a riderless horse!"

In the opinion of Bobby, who loved him like a son, it was after Gilbert de Saint-Symphorien left at the end of 1953 that things began to go seriously wrong, as if, for Bébert, the last glimmer of hope had faded!

"I never liked that tall gentleman who sometimes came to watch us play like we were animals in a zoo and even stooped to lower himself dancin the beguine! In those days I got hired by a countryman of mine to play at the Coutenville casino. Of course I had them hire Bébert, and he asked his godfather, who came up with some of his friends! You should have seen them shake their butts! Mercy!"

(Why, upon his return home, did Gilbert de Saint-Symphorien break off all contact with his godson? That remains a mystery.)

Once Gilbert de Saint-Symphorien disappeared from his life leaving no more trace than a dream, Bert's downfall began. He who a few months earlier had tears flooding his eyes after one measly drink of straight rum became such a devotee of it that Bobby had to scold him!

"You don't know rum, boy! You think it's light, huh? Just a little stronger than the others? But let me tell you, when the rum takes over your head, it takes it over. It won't let go of you, and you're finished."

Bébert did not listen to this judicious advice, either, and no one could slow his fall. He began reeling and rolling in at all hours of the day and night; so often and to such a point did he arrive at the club late or not come in at all that finally he was fired. When one morning he was picked up at dawn out of a pool of piss on the Boulevard de Bonne-Nouvelle, Bobby lost his temper and forbade him entry to his house at Aubervilliers.

"In the beginning we forgave him everythin. He was such a fine musician! Me, I'm tellin you on alto sax he was worth a thousand Charlie Parkers! If he'd listened to the offers they made him and gone to America, his name would've been remembered until Judgment Day! Only you see, he stayed here fillin up his belly with rum and whinin about his family! People got tired of it."

Where and how did Bébert, derelict musician, meet and sire a daughter with Lucette Legendre, seamstress at a high fashion house? It does not appear that this meeting counted for much in his life, nor that he often came to stand at the foot of his child's cradle! Less than two years after Aurélia's birth Lucette married a Corsican, François Paoli, a semiskilled worker at the Peugeot automobile plant who, according to the well-known expression, treated-the-child-like-his-own-daughter! To this very day Aurélia hurts:

"How, how do we survive our childhood? On my birthday my mother would dress me in my best clothes and take me by the hand: 'He has to see you! He has to be ashamed someone else is taking care of you!' So we

tracked that beat-up man from one cheap hotel to another. He would stammer: 'You doin well at school?' and
sometimes slip some money to my mother, who would
be sitting rigid as righteousness on her chair. In fact I
never saw my father alone and only years later learned
how he put an end to his life. At first I knew that one day
my mother received a telephone call and that she cried a
lot because she had loved my father very much. (Only he
was a good-for-nothing!) My peerless stepfather kept saying: 'Come on, Lucette, it's better this way!' Until I was
ten none of that meant very much. At school, sometimes
the children would make a circle around me and sing:

> 'A Negro girl was drinking milk
> Ah, she thought, if only I could
> Soak my face in this bowl of milk
> I'd be whiter than all the Freh-heh-hench!'

"So I knew I was different from the others, from my
little blond brothers and sisters, but it was all fairly vague.
Then one day my mother received a letter from my
grandmother in Angers, whom we had lost sight of completely, begging them to send me to spend a few days
with her. My perfect stepfather did not want to. But my
mother stood firm. It's from that time on that the island
began to set its mark on me. Marie, who had never
known anything about it, had a few yellowed photographs. The ones that interested me were not those of her
family, of her wedding, nor even those of my father at
various ages up until the last, before his total debility,
stern-faced in the middle of a group of West Indian
musicians smiling their white-toothed grins beneath their
straw hats in their flowered shirts. No, the ones I liked
best were those of the island. Two or three of them."

A skinny teenager standing on some steps, a part forced through his kinky hair and a book in his hand: "Your grandfather Albert, but everybody called him Bert, at the Carnot Lycée in La Pointe."

A house with a veranda around it and on the veranda, in a rocking chair, a woman whose face could not be made out clearly, a baby in her arms: "Your grandfather's mother, Elaïse."

Two fairly ugly little boys in schoolboy smocks, one of them sucking his thumb: "Your father's half brothers, I don't know their names.

"Nothing has ever been the same since! But where, and how to begin? How was I to go about it? My mother was always saying:

" 'Those people didn't want anything to do with your father. In a way they were the ones who killed him. Out of respect for him you must not try to meet them.'

"And in any case how would I manage it?

"So what I had left was dreams! And these gave me a fierce desire to turn my back on the public housing where we lived. My mother wept: 'She's got no heart. She's nothing but a head.' Because to flee them, to not hear them, to not see them, I studied and I studied. Head of my class in everything. Amazing the teachers, who knew that not one piece of printed matter ever entered our three-room apartment, outside of the gossip sheets! And finally, when I might have become a doctor, a lawyer . . . and covered the Paoli name with glory, I chose this thankless career in education because I could not forget my childhood, my troubled adolescence, wordless, speechless, sightless and unsmiling, shut away behind its wall of solitude. And here in my first teaching post, I run across you! It's almost enough to make me forget all those years!"

After that I became imbued with a mission and was tempted to exaggerate my descriptions, knowing as I did that reality is never stranger than fiction. Aurélia listened to me with delight. To my surprise she was more interested in the country than in the people, and interrupted me with questions I found naïve:

"Tell me, is it true that when marrying off his daughter the devil can make sunshine with one eye and rain with the other?"

"Tell me, is it true that the sea is as warm as a pocket of uterine fluids?"

In fact of all the gallery of portraits I painted for her, one alone attracted Aurélia's attention—she who, for example, did not blink an eye at the tale of the tragic and foreordained death of my great-uncle Jean—precisely the one I bitterly skipped over, the story of Thécla:

"How she has suffered!"

I scoffed:

"Her men found ways to comfort her!"

Aurélia looked at me reproachfully:

"I think it's just the opposite! Will you take me to see her?"

I said not a word, and while waiting for an affirmative response, Aurélia, on her part, took me to see the Paolis.

It's unfair! One should be able to choose one's relatives! In the great invisibility where little girls and boys are made one should have something to say about it:

"Oh, no, I don't want those two there!"

"I don't like the way they look!"

Lucette Legendre now Paoli still harbored about her beautiful, pale, mint-colored eyes a hint of that desire to escape that had thrown her into the arms of her mulatto musician. Immediately after her wedding she had left the House of Jacques Fath; since then, she no longer pedaled the Singer she had bought on twelve monthly payments anywhere but in the corner of her living room. She made everything: coats, capes, pants, underwear . . . receiving nothing in the way of compliments but sweetly acid comments:

"It's a little tight under the arm!"

"It's not long enough!"

On the other side of the room, François Paoli took refuge behind his newspaper and commented on the horse races.

The two Paoli children, who were still filling the role of being last at school, were huddled in front of the television set watching a game show.

I thought of sweet Aurélia growing up within those walls and wanted to throw myself at her feet to beg forgiveness for all the wrong our family had done her!

For all of this could be traced back to us, to our initial cruelty! Aurélia deprived of sun and warmth, her mind and heart being whittled away!

I owe it to the truth to say that the Paolis were kind to me and that I was almost sorry for having judged them by their uneducated, proletarian look. Kindness is often to be found hidden in those classes; later I learned to discover it there. François Paoli had had his share of exoticism during his military service in Madagascar, and he described at length the beauty of the women, the kindness of the inhabitants, and the splendor of the countryside. Lucette prepared her special flan for me and whispered:

"Are they giving you a hard time at school because of your color?"

At my negative reply her eyes filled with the salty water of a very old, unhealed pain:

"Times change! They gave my Aurélia such a hard time!"

Then the Paolis gathered around me:

"Tell us about your country!"

My country? Now they were giving me the island! In gratitude I gave them dreams. We climbed up along the sides of a volcano whose gaping mouth swallowed clouds. We bathed in a too-blue sea that hid its icy heart, and netted giant crayfish in the crystal of its streams.

After that visit Aurélia took me to see Marie, her grandmother in Angers. My heart was beating a tattoo as I set out. How would she react, this woman who had suffered so much because of us? Aurélia took it upon herself to soothe my fears:

"Granny is kindness itself. It's her kindness that brightened my childhood, and she never said a word against your people. She preferred to describe her beloved Bert: 'When he came into the ballroom, all the other men turned into ashy-skinned, bad-skinned whippersnappers, and it was me his eyes chose: "Mademoiselle, will you do me the honor of dancing with me?" 'Mademoiselle'— can you imagine! Me, who nobody ever called anything but Marie!' "

However, on one essential point I was not prepared for what awaited me.

A person should never arrive at an elderly age if the ship of the body is taking on water everywhere. Well before then merciful death should have sent it to the bottom.

In fact I knew no old people. My grandfather Jacob, a robust old codger in spite of all his troubles, who bent but did not break, had barely begun to go gray. Pierre

Levasseur's father shot doves with a hand steadier than his son's.

At the end of a trip that seemed interminable to me on account of an uneasy anxiety that multiplied the miles, we arrived on a market morning in Angers, whose streets were filled with crowds. Peddlers were hawking their junk, and a long line was waiting to sample a sparkling wine of the region. Marie lived in a neighborhood that was for ages marked for demolition. I saw, seated in an easy chair, a livid doll bundled up like an infant or a mummy and staring straight ahead into the dark confines of her memories. A rubber tube ran from some part of her body to a slop jar, its cover closed over the unspeakable. Aurélia kissed this heap of rotting flesh and motioned me to do the same, which I could not bring myself to accomplish. Then she unwrapped a package of sweets that the old mouth began gumming with a hideous sucking sound. At last the old eyes, faded from tears and great age, settled on me, and an antediluvian voice rose up, quickly proving to me that the mind survives the decrepitude of the body.

"I don't know what Aurélia's thinking of, bringing you here to show you to me. You, the daughter of those who killed my men. First, my poor Bert. Then my boy, my Bébert. Ah, I wasn't good enough for you, huh? Did you forget what you are? Niggers, niggers! Without us, you went around with your private parts showing! You ate each other raw. Cannibals! It's because of you my Bert threw himself off his electric pole. He told me: 'Mama, don't worry. We'll go start a new life on the blessed island of Madagascar. You see, I've put in a request. . . .' The answer to the request came three days after his death. So my Bébert grew up without a father, like a plant without the sun. All stunted and shrunk. All sickly. It didn't matter how much cod-liver oil I poured into him, the doctor kept telling me his heart was too weak. When he was little, my Bébert, he was God's own angel, and then, when he grew up, he started to change! He turned against me. He took their side. He was ashamed of me, it seems. I was a 'working girl,' me who'd sacrificed myself, wearing out my hands at the bottle factory. Until the day he left without even saying good-bye. One morning I went up to his room to make his bed, and it was empty. Empty. Not even a note like in the movies. For years I stayed alone eating my heart out. One day someone brought me his picture he'd found in a newspaper. And then, nothing more. Until they brought me his body. He'd thrown himself under a commuter train. At Massy-Palaiseau. My Bébert. All because of you. Dirty niggers! Murderers! Murderers!"

Followed by her cries, I fled down the stairs and found myself in the sunlight, on the smiling street.

61

"Why are you telling me this story? What does it have to do with me? I have other crimes on my conscience, for which I take full responsibility. Not those! Not those!"

I stood firm:

"Will you agree to see her?"

Thécla shrugged her shoulders:

"To do what? To change her childhood for her? If that were possible, I'd gladly change my own!"

Ah, yes, she was beautiful, Doctor-Levasseur's-wife-from-Martinique! Jules-Juliette, the fashionable West Indian hairdresser on the Rue des Mathurins, had rid her of her bushy Afro and helmeted her in short and shiny locks. The artful blue on her eyelids made the opacity of her eyes, at present streaked with flashes of anger, unsettling.

"What do you want? With your childish hands you expect to abolish hatreds, avenge deaths, even though the world itself can't be changed! Others before you have failed at it. The world is terrible! Ruined!"

Suddenly, in one of those abrupt about-faces so usual with her, she softened:

"It's true, I do remember now! A guy who must have been her father wrote to me. It was . . . it was, I don't know when it was! But at the time, believe me, I had other fish to fry!"

At those words the cry, "Murderer" again rang in my ears. Insisting no further (to what end? Bastards wind up

335

in Hell!) I was headed toward the door when she stopped
me:

"Coco, your grandfather's very sick."

I faltered, convinced that the villainess was dealing
me one of her blows, but Thécla shook her head:

"He's no longer in any danger. Flora says so in a letter
to Pierre, which aside from that is full of sneaky, spiteful
comments about me. . . . He's asking for you as a get-well
present! You could leave in a few weeks, as soon as school
is over!"

I burst into shocked tears:

"Why? Why grant me what you've always refused?"

She did not answer my question:

"You might at least say thank you. As they say at
home, someone could go bring you the moon with his
teeth, you still wouldn't be satisfied!"

As I myself grew up, I came to realize how small
Thécla was. In her childhood photographs it seemed otherwise, for she had grown up all of a sudden, reaching her
adult height at the age of fourteen. But at present her eyes
were almost on a level with my own, and on that day I
had a desire to tear down the wall that separated us, to hug
myself close to her, rumple her hair, wash the rouge from
her cheeks with salt and water! How painful to be forever
keeping each other at a distance! Especially when I hurt
so much! "Murderer, murderer!" Hands red with blood,
I had taken the train back without waiting for Aurélia,
whom I had only seen next day at school, sweet-
tempered and ever the same, working at untangling our
knotted selves.

"Don't even think about it," she said. "She's had
such a rough time of it that sometimes she loses her head.
Believe me, she cried a lot and was sorry for what she'd
said. But you'd already gone!"

Yes, despite what I believed was my lack of love, at that moment I would have liked to hug myself close to Thécla. I would have wanted to awaken for once some glint of affection in her eyes that—above my head—were reserving their affection for Pierre Levasseur, and to whisper as I nestled in the inaccessible hollow of her neck:

"Teach me about your life! Tell me your crimes great and small! Your sins of commission or omission! Your weaknesses, your betrayals, your major and minor cruelties! The traps into which you fell! The mountains you could not move! The beasts who swallowed up your sun! So that at the same age I may not be defeated like you!"

Instead of which, Pierre Levasseur came home from a full day's work, poured himself a glass of whiskey while pleasantly telling us about two or three of his patients, and, to finish it off, invited us to go see *Easy Rider* again, his favorite film!

The announcement of my departure plunged Aurélia into the utmost agitation, to such a point that she no longer paid attention to our pitiful analyses of texts:

"One may say that in this poem Lamartine shows us that Nature can provide consolation for pain."

She reminded me of points in our [historical] reconstruction that still remained obscure, and for which I was to obtain explanations.

"My mother swears that once she so despaired of my behavior at home, and of the battle between my stepfather and me, that she wrote to La Pointe and even sent a picture of me in my Communion dress. That had to be in 1960 or 1961. Did that photo ever arrive? What happened to it?

"You must absolutely learn the exact name of my grandfather's mother. You say simply, an English Negro woman he knew in Panama! Does that mean I have relatives in Panama? On an English island somewhere? It's important to me to know!"

And finally it took Aurélia, so kind, so sweet and as good as she was beautiful, it took this woman who so faithfully practiced the forgiveness of trespasses three tries to write an extremely long letter to my grandfather Jacob, which she also stuffed with photographs! Then, after all that effort, she broke down in tears:

"I'll be going back home there, to Guadeloupe. Soon, soon!"

62

The old people who remembered that Jacob and Jean both came from the belly of Bonnemama Elaïse could not get over their astonishment:

"Does a tree bear two different kinds of fruit? Are a breadfruit and a chestnut to be found side by side on the same branch?"

How could Jean be the brother of Jacob the unfeeling shopkeeper, Jean the martyr whom even those who hated the word *independence* had begun to venerate, placing him on the same footing with Salvador Allende and Walter Rodney? Following the troubles it had caused him and also because, as Flora said, one has to keep up with the times, Jacob had wound up by selling the tenement yard to the city, which was setting out to acquire certain pieces of property for its town-planning projects. Instead and in place of those demeaning dwellings, the city had therefore built those rabbit hutches of reinforced concrete known as public housing. When these first opened, everyone who could pay the monthly rent had made a rush for the new buildings. After all, one had only to press a button for the miracle of electricity suddenly to appear, pull a chain to be rid of what a man was used to carrying on his back to the sewage pit, or turn a faucet tap for a cool spring to flow. Fairly quickly, however, they were singing a different tune. For soon the good old candle that had been too hastily relegated to a subordinate role was restored to its place of honor by endless power outages;

soon the toilets stopped up, befouling the air; soon the faucets refused to run before the dark of midnight. Oh, for the good, imported-wood shacks of yesteryear!

Despite the criticism that rose on all sides, from the patriots, the socialists, the Gaullists, and the centrists (not the communists, of course! They had taken over control of the town twenty-five years earlier!), Jacob quietly bought back Block C of the La Mangrove Residence, which stood right next to the new La Gabarre bridge. Then he proceeded to sublet it, apartment by apartment, at the highest price possible. No matter how the newspapers denounced the dealings of this Shylock (again!), he pocketed a considerable sum of money every month!

People say it is a group of angry tenants who were looking for revenge. However, that has never been proved!

In any case it happened one Saturday afternoon, in the hour when Jacob was taking the air on his balcony and reading an old issue of *Présence africaine* Thécla had left lying around during her stay some years earlier. On a pretty tray covered with an embroidered teacloth, he was brought some coconut flan and a large slice of marble cake sent by one of his customers. Surprised, for not many people displayed friendship for him, though suspecting nothing, Jacob wolfed down both flan and marble cake. Two hours later he was overcome by vomiting, diarrhea, and such violent pain that they feared for his life and sent for a priest at the same time as the doctor. The former arrived before the latter. Though Jacob did not hear him, the priest described the fires of Hell that await adulterers and then officially married him to Flora. Which meant that the bastards Rodrigue and Carmélien, having reached their twenty-seventh and twenty-fourth birthdays, respectively, had to change their surnames and take the name Louis. The change even affected the baby just born to Rodrigue; for he had taken for wife a very pretty girl from Marie-Galante named Elisa Bikok, who was also vaguely related to my grandmother Tima.

All police efforts to track down those who had played this vicious joke that could have caused a man's death were in vain, according to the time-honored expression.

So, when I arrived at La Pointe, my grandfather Jacob was swimming in pajamas far too large for him, a smear of sulfur spread curiously across his black skin, but was quite able to sit up in his bed, leaning against a mountain of pillows. Flora Lacour, excuse me, Flora Louis, to whom the title of legitimate spouse had brought a radiant glow, was at his bedside. In her fingers she was rolling the beads of a rosary, as she had not yet finished thanking God for having spared the husband whom she loved the way he was.

I was given the smallest details and particulars of this event that was going to be filed away in our memories and occupy an important place in our family history. How such an innocent-looking tray had appeared, presented by a skinny more-or-less-Indian in a yellow dress who spoke very good French. How she had politely held out her cheek to be kissed before explaining that this was the saint's day of M.'s child . . . an incomprehensible mutter at this point . . . and that she had been told to bring this to Monsieur Louis. Flora was inconsolable:

"My dear, I don't know what was wrong with me that day. Not once did my heart skip a beat to make me suspicious! She had such a sweet and honest face, that child did. Butter wouldn't melt in her mouth. And all the while it was the exact name of the person who sent her I should have asked her for. And then, you see, when God makes up His mind about a thing, He makes up his mind! Jacob never liked sweets! *Suk à koko, douslets, shad-docks*—that's not for him! He puts barely a teaspoon of sugar in his coffee. But this time he threw himself at his flan and cake! Before I even had time to say 'Oops,' he'd finished. All gone! But who could believe there were people in La Pointe to think such thoughts! Myself, I wonder if it wasn't really meant for Dieudonné! His wife, Monique, is big-as-a-house pregnant. So he eats with us at noon. He doesn't go home to Bergette, where they live. He lets her rest a little. And sometimes, especially when it's Saturday like that and he has no business to do, he stays until four or five o'clock talking things over with his uncle. Don't forget, it was Jacob who brought him up. Dieudonné! Jean, his father, was too busy with his politics and his books! Jacob brought up all his brother's children, one after the other! Every month, it's money orders going out, going out to this one or that! There's even one who's studying in . . . well, in America. So, my dear, if anyone comes and tells me that man isn't good, I know what to say to him, you hear! Jacob's not handsome; no, he's not: handsome seems to have passed him by; but he's good. Good as good bread."

Here Flora wiped away a tear, caught her breath, and plunged ahead:

"Yes, the more I think about it, the more I see it was meant for Dieudonné, that tray was! When it comes to politics, people turn into mad dogs. Ready to bite until the blood comes, ready to kill each other! It's surely some people bothered by that Independence business of his. My dear, this business of Independence has already caused us enough trouble! And it's only just beginning! I've already told Dieudonné: 'Listen, when you're ready, warn me so I can pack my bags!' I have a sister living in Macon, in France, I'll go stay with her!"

Then her large eyes, so glowing and affectionate whenever they fell on me, grew dark with shadows of maliciousness, while her voice turned bitterly insinuating:

"How is your mama?"

"Fine! Fine!"

"And her husband?"

"Fine! Fine!"

Patronizingly:

"Let's hope it lasts!"

Flora, who hated Thécla the way salt hates water, still could not denigrate a mother in front of her child and limited herself to meaningful sighs.

And I myself, sure of finding her attentive and quick to agree, I said nothing, gripped as I was by a vague and new sense of duty.

The entire house on the Rue du Faubourg-d'Ennery smelled of asafetida, terebenthine, and tincture of benzoin along with hundreds of leaves and roots. For Flora had no faith in doctors and nursed my grandfather Jacob in her own manner, rubbing him down, smearing him all over, covering him with leeches, poultices, and compresses.

Besides Flora, all the women of the family brought out their medicinal recipes. Exactly at noon every Sunday Cousin Ti-Maroussia arrived with some miracle remedy hidden in her basket. Although twice a grandmother, she was still called Ti-Maroussia, "Little" Maroussia, because she had the same first name as her mother, who for years now had been resting next to her master-sailmaker husband in the sailor's cemetery at Port-Louis. After closeting herself with Flora in order to describe its properties to her, Ti-Maroussia went upstairs to my grandfather's bedroom and only came down again an hour later to reheat the clam pie she was always bragging about and sadly watch me eat it.

"That child has seen things my own eyes haven't seen. But she doesn't know how to behave at the table!"

"And with good reason my dear!"

A sigh from Flora.

We were just emerging from the worry over my grandfather's health when another crisis came to torment the family. Some bombs exploded (Alas! this was becoming more and more frequent in our country; you would have thought my great-uncle Jean's blood had borne fruit!) and wounded (slightly, thank God!) two Italian tourists who had strayed into the Café Richepanse. And then Dieudonné refused to stop at a police roadblock and drove off without even a fare-thee-well to the CRS militiamen! That is all they needed, when they caught up with him near Trois Chemins Abymes, to throw him into prison!

(In fact Dieudonné did not find the opportunity he perhaps was looking for there, and he was quickly released. Nonetheless for several hours feelings ran high, the family already seeing him laid out next to his father and sleeping the same sleep!)

All this could not fail to have a considerable effect on my grandfather's humor, combined as it was with the idea that some people hated him to the point of wanting to hasten his end, and with the weakness of his severely shaken constitution. Head wobbling, his cheeks glistening with tears, he harked back to his never-ending litany:

"In this country they don't want the Negroes to succeed! Up until this very day it's in the cane they want to see them, the straw *bakoua* hat on their heads!"

I dared to suggest:

"Maybe they can't accept Negroes doing what the others do, walking all over their fellow man to succeed?"

At which his mouth fell open, and then he groaned:

"Where did you get that nonsense? Coco, you've really changed! Have you, too, started in to reading that Marx?"

While waiting for his recovery, I was finding it hard to hold back the news that I had succeeded where he had failed; that is, to not tell him about Aurélia. But I was determined to savor it, to relish it with him. Not hand her over to a mind that was still as weak as his body, nourished on the white meat of chicken washed down with bush tea! Anxious as the mother of a half-wit child, I watched him, measured his progress, and worried when on some days he remained curled up like a fetus beneath the sheets. The afternoon he came down to the dining room, supported on his right by Flora and on his left by Carmélien, I knew the time for confession was drawing near. I, who through love and intuition understood him; I know that this illness, despite its happy outcome, marked the beginning of the end for my grandfather. It was then that he lost interest in his store, in his rental apartments, in his businesses . . . which had held such a great place in his life. He unburdened himself of all the bother they gave him onto the shoulders of Rodrigue and Carmélien, who little by little he came to think of as his "sons" and no longer as his "bastards." And finally he forsook La Pointe, where the increasing number of automobiles were belching too much carbon monoxide for his taste. Like his father, the *Soubarou*, he retired to his "change of air" house at Juston. There he no longer bothered the farm workers and straightened the yam plant stakes himself, pruned his vines, and picked his pigeon peas alongside a bright-eyed and bushy-tailed Flora, who carried on about his chickens' droppings.

Of course my grandfather was in the daily and constant company of Bonnemama Elaïse and his beloved

brother Jean. Of course he had rejoined his satin-smooth
Tima. Of course he felt prowling about him the penitent
presence of his father, he who was ashamed of his harshness when alive and who at times attempted to strike up
a conversation. But two things saddened Jacob, ate at
him, making his old age gloomy.

First, the absence of his Thécla. Ten times a day he
groaned:

"Why, why did that child cast Guadeloupe from her
heart?"

Each time, Flora fell into a rage:

"Enough of that! Are you going to eat away your soul
over that ungrateful girl?"

And there was also the end of the family. Where were
the times when Albert's sisters, along with their husbands,
their husbands' relations and their children gathered on
Sunday to do honor to Théodora's cooking, then that of
Bonnemama Elaïse? When births and marriages were an
excuse for feasting? Deaths an excuse for staying up all
night? Excepting Dieudonné, who came without
Monique and the children, few were those who took the
road to Juston and sat themselves down on the porch long
enough for a good talk. New babies came to brave the
light without Jacob's knowing about it. Likewise, exhausted bodies slipped into the shadow of death, and
often he only learned of it when listening to the obituary
notices at the end of news programs. Then he would
groan:

"And here I am just like a he-crab in its hole!"

At the end of his life he began to babble about his trip
to New York, a moment of respite in the toil of his life.
To speak of Marcus Garvey, whom he had never met, as
of an old acquaintance:

"He's the one said to me: 'Go home and make my

name shine.' That is why I wanted to found the New Negro party. 'I shall teach the Negroes to see the beauty in themselves.' Ohh, ohh, ohh!"

When death came to claim him, Thécla was in Bangkok, where Pierre Levasseur was attending a medical conference. And so the coffin had to wait four days and nights, cleverly kept cold amid the odor of melted candles and wilted flowers thanks to a system perfected by Hercule and Sons Undertakers. She walked dry-eyed behind the hearse and got back onto her airplane, not wishing to discuss the dividing up of the estate with Flora. Nonetheless she did manage to spend several days on Saint Martin with Gesner, scandalizing everyone!

Serge, who no longer spent time with Jacob, came down from Goubeyre, where he was still a municipal councilman connected to the Gaullists. His face as filled with grief as Flora's mourning crepe, he accompanied him to the cemetery. By way of condolences he kissed her and sobbed:

"If he'd been a different color and if he'd been born in another country, he'd have gone far!"

A strange funeral tribute for a man who in a single heart had combined naïve goodness and sordid avarice, idealism and pettiness, a love for his own people and a ferocious talent for exploitation!

63

For a long, long time my grandfather Jacob's eyes remained fixed on a point in space, then they turned to rest on me:

"It was 'Murderer' she said? Is that it?"

I sought to deflect the sadness I saw ready to overflow onto his cheeks:

"Why don't you read Aurélia's letter?"

But he went on muttering as if savoring the cruelty of the word and the pain it gave him:

"Murderer. Murderer. That's it, exactly!"

Then his head fell forward and he burst into tears. Uneasy at that heavy, grown-up sobbing, I beat a retreat. Anyway, Dieudonné was waiting to take me home with him to Bergette.

Dieudonné hated what had been done to La Pointe, the public housing with its barred windows and all the rest of it, and he wished to remain in the Petit-Bourg area, where he had spent his childhood vacations. Thus he had bought up a former plantation and restored it to its original splendor by dint of English-style lawns, jackdaws and peacocks, stone statues, topiary trees, and German shepherds. People riding past it in swift buses nodded their heads:

"Will you look at that? The day the Patriots live in shacks, that's the day I'll take them seriously!"

Dieudonné was one of the few members of the family to love Thécla dearly. He never wearied of telling me how she had protected him in his childhood from Tima, from Tima's servants, from the children at the lycée who had nicknamed him *"Maroon,"* or rebellious slave and from evil stepmother Marietta, who was always handing him the scrub brush, and ending with:

"Thécla's an extraordinary person! If only she could have written us about all her experiences!"

I snickered quietly! My mother, a writer! God save us from that!

There was much commotion at Dieudonné's house. For Monique had just given birth to a new Jean Louis, indifferent to the weight of the martyr's name he bore and wailing in his cradle just like anyone else. At the same time the grandparents had arrived from Clermont-Ferrand, France, and I wondered what sort of face fore-bear Albert would have made, he who had in no uncer-tain terms excluded Bert for a sin similar to Dieudonné's and . . . Thécla's! When I confided my (naïve) thoughts to Dieudonné, he launched into a peroration, since owing to his trade he had a somewhat tedious taste for lofty language:

"Scientists say there is no such thing as race. There are only cultures. Our parents and our grandparents mobi-lized themselves around an erroneous idea that will die out of its own accord. But in the present case I believe our forebear, pariah and outcast that he was in the eyes of the established bourgeosie, exhibited class prejudices! If Marie had not been a factory worker, the world as we know it would have been different!"

True or false? At fourteen and a half I was in no position to make up my mind on that!

Yes, it is Dieudonné who put a love for the Petit-Bourg region in my heart. No spectacular sites. No breathtaking beauty. A vague charm. The traveler hurrying to reach Basse-Terre can cross it without being aware of it. There, cane is not king. It shares its realm with yams huddled about their stakes and banana trees with their lacquered leaves. A stream or two drowsing between the fields. If someday I come back to live "at home," I told myself, it is there that I shall plant my roots!

When I strolled along the paths of Bergette, the peasants stared hard at me, the women leaving their irons on the glowing embers and the men forgetting to lay down their playing cards. I read the same question in their eyes.

"*A ki ta la enko?* And where does this one come from?"

For just as the peasants of Juston had not liked the *Soubarou*, who had no hesitation about exploiting them, the peasants of Bergette did not like Dieudonné, who claimed he had only their welfare at heart. It's not easy, winning over the peasants! Traditionally suspicious when it comes to gentlemen-from-the-city, Negroes, or mulattoes—for them it's all the same! Those oh-so-proper gentlemen! Even if they take off their jackets and listen to tales being told in the night! Dieudonné was suspected of having no great thirst for the rum after rum he drank, and he was found wanting for not speaking Creole. Some went far enough to insinuate that he had defended the people of Sorlin so that he might be as famous as his father! A true patriot, that one! (As if the only true patriot were a dead one!)

Madame Nirmal was a retired school principal quietly living out the end of her life alongside her tax-collector husband in the house they had built with their savings; their children had gone to do their military service in Africa and had deserted them. One day she could no longer restrain herself and called out to me over the bougainvillea hedge:

"Whose child are you?"

In earlier times, questioning me that way was tantamount to torturing me, since my answer revealed the dark and untenanted half of my origins. Father Unknown. Absent. Gone away. On the run. Indifferent. Unsuitable. At present it was all the same to me, that gap in my flank! My grandfather Jacob, Flora, Dieudonné, and the others had filled it in with shovelfuls of love! So I brazenly enumerated:

"I am the illegitimate daughter of Thécla, herself the legitimate and much-desired daughter of Tima and Jacob, Jacob himself the favorite son on the one side, unloved on the other, of Bonnemama Elaïse, known as God's Own Child, and of Albert, called the *Soubarou*, who went off to sweat away his sweat and toil his toil in Panama in order to earn some gold and learn that when it comes right down to it, it buys nothing!"

And I left her lost in speculation. I, I was no longer ashamed. I had planted my flag on the island.

Having come to Bergette for the weekend, I stayed there a week and remained with Monique, whom her mother managed neither to console nor interest in her new son's first smiles and early signs of intelligence. The new mother did nothing but moan:

"It's not a man I married, Coco, it's a puff of air! Do you know that he forgets our wedding anniversaries? That he wasn't there when the labor pains started and I had to ask Ferrant, the auto mechanic, for help? I don't see him all day long. When he's here, it's with a dozen men for some so-called endless meetings. . . ."

I said (without much conviction):

"What do you expect? The cares of the nation . . ."

She shrugged her shoulders:

"What are you talking about, Coco? Isn't it we

women who make and unmake the nation? As long as they keep us in the background, they'll never accomplish a thing! And Guadeloupe will remain the last colony for a long, long time!"

At the end of two weeks—and it is true, I had hardly seen Dieudonné—the Citroën DS19, soaped down, rinsed, and waxed every Sunday afternoon by the children of the family, drew up before the gate and the poor cousin who acted as chauffeur announced that my grandfather was asking to see me. Urgently.

64

He was watching for me. Standing at the entrance to the living room, he was dressed in one of his best suits, black pin-striped with white, and shod in black ankle-boots that gave him an undertaker elegance. His cheeks were close-shaved but still scratchy beneath a wide-brimmed felt hat that shaded his shadowy eyes. I rejoiced at seeing him in such good shape, for the last time he had looked skeletal in his striped pajamas. He said to me with a touch of anger, unusual for him:

"Why did you stay so long at Dieudonné's? You know very well there were things to be done!"

With no more delay he set out, me at his heels, on the oft-traveled road to the cemetery with its obligatory stops along the way. At Séraphin Chèradieu's. At Mérita Blanchedent's, and finally at Altagras Sophocle's, who this time sank her bony fingers into my burgeoning breasts, exclaiming:

"Well, my dear girl, I can feel the buds. How soon until they flower?"

As we left the latter's house, in the middle of the street where swarms of little girls with butterfly bows in their braids and scuffling little boys crossed directly under the noses of cars, trucks fitted with benches, and speeding buses, for the Saint-Jules School was letting out and a nun was leading the children, good as gold, up to the freshly painted green gate, my grandfather began to speak in his rusty voice:

"I asked Bonnemama Elaïse. She's the one who told me not to worry. That what counts is the forgiveness of the dead. If they pardon us, that's the essential. She can call us whatever she likes! 'Murderer' or whatever. I know what you're thinking. You think she's right and that my father, your forebear, was a terrible Negro, heart-less and with no feelings! That's what all the people of La Pointe thought, even the family! When he died, I don't know if there was even one person who shed a tear! On the contrary, people said: 'Ah, the devil's gone back to his Hell!' Myself, for a while I thought that way when all I knew was the feel of his cane on my back! One time he almost put my eye out. See that mark there; he's the one did it to me! And then I understood what happened in his heart to make him bitter as bile, hard as stone! I didn't know that one day, myself talking to you here, I'd be exactly like him! Because I, too, in my own time, I dreamed some dreams! My head was filled with them. When I was awake, they darkened my days. At night they kept me up, turning over and over until four in the morning. The roosters would start to crow and I'd still be wallowing in those dreams! And then, and then . . . When I understood that I'd have no other life than the life I was living, then I dreamed my dreams for Thécla. And that, well, never mind about that! You think she's happy the way she is with her white man? Like they say, I haven't a clue. Ah, life! Let me tell you, when I feel what I'm feeling, I understand my father, your forebear. You, you're still too young. He told himself: 'My child will do what I didn't do, will go to where I didn't go! His star will shine. . . .' And then, and then. What I'm telling you now, it's Bonnemama Elaïse who made me understand it. Because I, too, was sick when I thought about those two deaths! Dying far from home. Maybe because she always loved her Albert, she always understood him. Because that's what love is, understanding! To understand what makes a person evil, a liar, and love him just the same. Yes, it's Bonnemama Elaïse who explained to me that what counts is their forgiveness. Theirs. Theirs alone! I got down on my two knees to ask them for it. I lit candles. I poured holy water and then I had this idea. You'll see. . . ."

We were there.

A funeral party was leaving the cemetery. Musicians from the brass band were milling about and rushing off, rushing after their speedy buses; friends were dispersing, for it was getting late, and leaving the widow in full mourning dress and the orphans to go their lonely way. As at each time he entered the city of the dead, Jacob grew younger, his hunched back losing its hump and his step becoming lighter, winged. He hurried along like a child impatient to rejoin its mother and the sweet scent of her kiss. Myself, I followed at my own speed, as always somewhat frightened by the high funereal façades below the black arching of the beefwood trees.

The Louis family crypt stood at the corner of alleyway number four. For his Elaïse, the companion to whom he had never been able to express his love, Albert had built a Taj Mahal of marble brought from Italy at great expense; it rose massive behind a fence worthy of the Louvre and was guarded by two greyhounds in stone. Théodora, who at first had slept in a fairly modest grave, had been moved next to her daughter-in-law before being rejoined by her son. Since then all of the Louises had taken the same road, and lain themselves down under the same marble slab for their eternity.

As usual my grandfather hunted through his pocket in search of his key ring, trying a half dozen of them with an impatient hand before the gates slid open gently, gently! Crossing himself, he knelt. But this time he did not remain kneeling for long and, after nimbly rising, said to me:

"You see? You see?"

What?

Blindly, I looked around me. Then he pointed to the pediment of the crypt, across which stretched the procession of our dead. To me, the letters on it appeared recently repainted. Black on immaculate white. As I still saw nothing more, my grandfather took my hand and, squeezing it at each name, began to read out loud:

Théodora Bonaventure Louis née Brasdor—
    1856–1925
Elaïse Marie Apolline Louis née Sophocle—
    1895–1937
Albert Quentin Louis—1875–1948
Ultima Marie Madeleine Louis née Lemercier—
    1917–1969
Albert known as Bert Fortuné Louis—
    1905–1925
Albert known as Bébert Jacques Louis—
    1926–1970
Jean Ismael Théodore Louis—1928–1971

"You see, they're all here. I asked their forgiveness. I asked them for permission to put their names there. With those of the others. All the others. With us. Our home."

We stayed in the cemetery a long, long while that night!

Aside from the squeaking and the rustling wings of

bats flying from the graves to the beefwood trees, there was nothing to be heard above the loud murmur of the sea below us but my grandfather's sobs. Myself, I did not cry. I was reliving my chance (chance?) encounter with Bébert through the pages of a family album. And from there, the entire course traveled to this final meeting, at this memorial monument.

How far a distance had been traveled since that first meeting. How many questions asked. Questions avoided. Questions unanswered. Shadows lifted. Clear obscurities. Indistinct clarities. Underbrush cleared. Bonfires burned. Pails of water carted. Until the truth showed its scarred and wounded face. My grandfather, who believed that life counts less than death, thought he had paid his debt. Just as he believed that with his love for me, he could heal the injuries inflicted by others. Reseal the gaping mouths of wounds. Reduce the fractures. Illusory hope! But here, instead of laughing at this eternal innocent, in my turn I began to be won over by his faith.

Would I perhaps have to recount this story? At the risk of displeasing and shocking, would I in my turn, perhaps, have to pay my debt? It would be a story of very ordinary people who in their very ordinary way had nonetheless made blood flow. (Murderer, she had said!) I would have to tell it and it would be a memorial monument of my own. A book quite different from those ambitious ones my mother had dreamed of writing: *Revolutionary Movements of the Black World* and all the rest. A book with neither great torturers nor lavish martyrdoms. But one that would still be heavy with its weight of flesh and blood. The story of my people.

At last my grandfather rose, blacker than the night

around us. He crossed himself, carefully brushed his knees, and said:

"Let's go home, Coco. You know Flora. She must be worried by now."

65

Vacation time did not end without an incident worthy of note. On Sunday, August 15, Marietta married off Manuela, her favorite daughter. Favorite not because she had shone at school or exhibited a dauntless spirit. No! Favorite, by her mother's own admission, because she had set aside the blackness and baseness of the Louises to recall only the maternal side of the family. For she went about, that succulent golden *chabine*, with her face russet-dotted as if she had gazed up at the sun too long through the holes of a strainer, and her blond braid floating in the wind. That blondness had also captivated Ephrem Robert, a young doctor from Port-Louis, who had wound up formally asking for her hand in marriage at Pour Some More. And now Marietta was more puffed up than the frog in that fable about ambition. She reminded anyone who would listen how she had toiled, and sweated blood and water to raise her children while Jean planned fantastical projects before dying the death he deserved late one early morning, and declared that at last she was seeing her reward. These words, amplified and carried by the murmur of the cane, reached La Pointe, Bergette, Port-Louis, Abymes . . . everywhere the Louises lived, causing them much grief. Nevertheless that feeling they had of no longer forming a homogeneous group, a group fed by a single blood and united under a single skin, made them remain silent. Oh, no, they were not going to stir up the fire again and strain already strained ties! Let Marietta talk her nonsense!

On Sunday, August 15, therefore, one could see, dressed up in their Sunday best and deeply moved, all that remained of our family—with the exception of course of those from Basse-Terre, who really no longer counted. A last cluster of sheep under the crook of shepherd Jacob, dressed in light colors for the occasion next to Flora in a hat of Italian straw.

For me this was an opportunity to see Gesner Amboise again, who had just been awarded a gold record for a satirical Carnival dance tune: *"Dévelopé péyi-là, Develop the Country."* Of all my mother's men Gesner was perhaps the one I had hated most. Because he had been so enslaved by her that he had never paid attention to me, except very obviously to regret my presence on this earth. And then, influenced by the family and above all by Friend Flora, I considered him awkward, gauche, and sheepish, and at a loss for words.

"What does Thécla see in him?"

For the first time I was aware of the intense and secret charm of this giant tamer of sounds! Of what use were words to him? Did he have no need of them since he was master of another language? I cannot compare Gesner's popularity in our country to that of a Bob Dylan in the America of the sixties, or to that of a Bruce Springsteen now. Nevertheless he was there, modest and self-confident, familiar and remote, his feet rooted in the soil of the people, taking nourishment from them. His little girl in his arms, he blinked his eyes and said in a tone that hid a very old pain:

"How's your mother?"

"Fine! Fine!"

He wanted nothing more from me and went to sit

down by himself under a mango tree.

The wedding lunch began fairly well. A bit stiff per-haps! One sensed that, beneath the appearance of unity, tensions and differences were only waiting to break out into the light of day. Jacob, seated at the very foot of the table when as brother of the deceased father of the bride he should have been at its head, Jacob was being poorly treated.

It was at the moment when the sandfish was served, grilled over charcoal embers and lying on a bed of yam puree, that it all went wrong. Up until that point people had been talking about this and that. The women ex-changing recipes for conch pie. One of the men recount-ing how a swarm of wasps had almost torn away his face while he worked his field. Who mentioned the name of the Darnel factory? No doubt Ephrem's father, who was working there after his own father and grandfather and rightly feared the loss of his livelihood. It was then that Dieudonné, until that moment silent and as ill at ease as ever in his stepmother's presence, launched into a diatribe against the plant owners and the French. For the owners were closing the plants one by one, and the French colo-nial power wanted to transform the country into a field of hands for its industries.

This speech was not to everyone's taste. In particular Ephrem, who in his turn launched into a diatribe against all the so-called Patriots who did nothing but talk in slogans and, if they were allowed to do so, would unerr-ingly land the country in the hospital. Someone flew to his aid by invoking the example of Haiti, that unfortunate independent neighbor whose refugees by the hundreds were to be seen toiling in our gardens.

Independence, that dangerous word was loosed, and the table was set ablaze!

The cacophony reached its height when the women shouted louder than their men to blame politics, more dangerous than a double-edged knife separating families.

Just the same, with the stuffed suckling pig a lull set in, so greatly did the animal filled with chili peppers, chives, and bay-rum leaves make mouths water.

Nisida, daughter of an auto-mechanic cousin from Abymes, had for four full days lent Marietta a helping hand, and she explained that she had found the recipe while leafing through a notebook that had belonged to her grandmother. Everyone agreed:

"Nobody knows how to cook the way they used to!"

How did the argument start up again?

Ephrem and Dieudonné had calmed down and had even toasted each other, when someone pronounced the word *sugarcane*. Ephrem immediately became enraged again, maintaining that it was a shameful heritage of the past, a relic barely fit to be relegated to a museum along with the garrote and the branding irons of the good old days.

"Sugarcane, it's the death of the Negro!"

At which Dieudonné exclaimed that one really ought to know what one was talking about and cited the case of Australia, where the sugarcane industry was flourishing. Someone rushed to his aid by recalling the example of neighboring Cuba, which drew its principal revenue from sugar.

"Cuba, sí! Cuba, no!"

(Myself, I was still unaware to what extent that island is a bone of contention, a firebrand upon the Caribbean Sea!)

Since there was no way to quiet them, Marietta stood straight up to her full height and cursed the Louises, who always spoiled everything. Ah, yes, they'd had enough of them! Of their avarice, of their self-importance, of their opportunism. My grandfather Jacob kept his calm by reminding himself that this was the widow of his beloved brother! But when she went too far in her anger and dared shout that this Thécla everyone carried on about so much was in reality an unwed mother, the biggest whore she'd ever known who had only been able to find some poor French white man to rid her of her shame, that was too much! Jacob started forward, but at the same moment Dieudonné and Gesner threw themselves ahead of him at Marietta, whose blood flowed bright red!

This lavish red blood put the final finish to our disunity. Poor grandfather Jacob, who had worked so hard to repatriate the two dead bodies when the living were fleeing him!

Of course there was a great hullabaloo of apologies, forgiveness, regrets, tears, and oaths that it would not happen again. Of course the wedding party set off at the appointed hour in the direction of the church at l'Anse Bertrand; and in a car bedecked with flowers as at Carnival, Manuela, crowned with orange blossoms, sat to the right of her father's brother. But it was only a plastering-over, a whitewash on an edifice ready to collapse. From that day on, neither Jacob nor Dieudonné ever again set foot in l'Anse Laborde. As for Jean's children, they agreed with their mother with a single voice. Those who did not settle down as doctors and pharmacists and dentists in Amiens, Clermont, Sucy-en-Brie, or other desolate regions of their mother country returned to bid a hasty farewell to their uncle before keeping far away from him forever.

The time was coming when none would be able to recount the family's past for lack of knowledge. When the living would no longer issue forth endowed with an ancient genetic heritage after interminable pregnancies in one belly or another. When the present would be nothing but the present. And the individual nothing but the individual!

I ended my vacation in a fairly melancholy mood. I did, however, fulfill the task I had set myself and that I would have to report to Aurélia, that of making a collection of all there was to collect.

At times I grew impatient:

"You mean to tell me you don't know how long Albert stayed in San Francisco?"

I persisted:

"What do you know about his English Negro woman?"

And slowly, slowly the memories woke from their sleep, and tongues began to loosen.

It was very hot that summer. Near the Gabarre bridge a fetid odor rose from the mangrove swamp where crabs came out to die belly-up. The cattle panted in the fields, their long, purple, slobbering tongues hanging out. The dogs showed their fangs and, mad with the heat, bit the children on the heel. The streams ran dry. The sea itself receded at the horizon.

An old woman named Espérance burned to death beneath the tin roof of her cabin.

66

The morning of my departure my grandfather gave me a letter for Aurélia that he had spent the night writing. Flora placed in the bottom of my suitcases carefully wrapped and labeled jars of *pisquettes*—those small fish that resemble whitebait—banana marmalade, pomelos, and her specialty, conch conserve, no doubt forgetting that I was going straight to a boarding school, where all these suspect foods would be banned by zealous housemothers. That morning I received an unexpected visit. From Gesner, his ill-behaved and busybody little boy holding his hand. Flora, who did not like him at all, nonetheless opened the doors of the sitting room to him; and he sat down in an armchair, its arms covered with the crocheted isosceles triangles she placed almost everywhere—on the piano, on the backs of chairs, and on the pedestal side tables. For a long while he remained silent, staring at the tips of his tennis shoes that were painstakingly coated with Spanish white. Then he made up his mind, and began, very quietly:

"When I see you, it's your mother I see in front of my eyes. Lighter-skinned, of course. Thécla, she's as blue as an icaco plum, and her mouth, mauve pink as the seagrape! But all the features of your face are the same. Her smile. Her stubborn look when you're not doing what you want to. Knowing her as I do, I wonder if she ever talked to you about me. Myself, I'm not ashamed to say it: I loved her when I was twelve years old, and that love will only end with my living life, to be reborn in my hereafter. When she left me, I kept on going, twisted, limping along the rutted road of my life. Luckily I had my music. Do you know how music came to man?"

I looked at him. Did he take me for a child to whom one tells tall tales? He was smiling with all the naïve goodness of his heart:

"In those days, when the earth was flat as a rock and when only the tall candle-cactus grew, each being had its own language. For man and woman, words and tears. For the cow, lowing. For the frog, croaking. For the bird, singing! Not one of them could understand the others, and death quickly came to shorten those uncommunicating lives. At Grands-Fonds-Cacao there lived Nora, a pretty Negro woman who, despite the fact that her life was hard, laughed from morning to night in her shack. A kiskadee flycatcher that perched in her *julie* mango tree was mad with desire and love for her. One night, unable to bear it any longer, he flew down from his branch, preened his feathers, and hid himself in Nora's bed. When she in turn had gone to bed, he silently drew near and sank his beak into her sex, as if into the pistil of a flower. For several nights he repeated this little game, so much so that he wound up dying of happiness, and a surprised Nora found a little warm still ball between her sheets. To everyone's surprise, several months later her belly began to swell. You know how the people of our country are? 'What's this, a belly? Who gave it to her?' . . . Nine months later Nora's son was born in a burst of trills. . . ."

Suddenly Gesner realized the effect his silly story was having on me and broke off awkwardly:

"Your mother loved that story, she whose mother

never told her any! Your mother! Not a day goes by I don't pray God that she might at least be happy amid all this sorrow surrounding us! Happy with her white man. White though he is. She has suffered so many blows in life, her life, that she deserves it, deserves happiness! At last! Well, what I wanted to tell you is that you, you are the child of our tomorrows. Look at this country, ours, yours, being sold off to the highest bidder. Soon perhaps it will be no more than a memory, little by little growing dim in our minds. Me, what I'm trying to do is save its voice for it. And you, too, you can, you must do something. You don't know it yet, and I can't show you the way, I who haven't gone to all those schools. Your great-uncle Jean's work isn't finished. I'd say it's hardly begun. The entire field remains to be deciphered, with its weeds, its Guinea grass and its touch-me-nots clawing at the ankles. We, we're weary. The villainess has beat us. But you, you are the child of our tomorrows. Think about it!"

I found nothing to say, inwardly rebellious and fearful at the promise he was attempting to wrest from me. The role he meant to burden me with. The task he meant to assign me. Sensing nevertheless in the secret of my heart that my soon-to-be adult age, once the tribute to my dead was paid, would be unable to escape it.

And anyway, how could I deny the blood of my entire ancestry—and this is the other aspect of this story, my story—beginning with my forebear Albert with his fine teeth made for devouring the world, he who left to sweat out his sweat in Panama and raise gold only to realize when all is said and done that gold buys nothing. From Albert up to my mother, yes, even she, especially she, who bled from all her failures and was consumed by all her disillusions before taking refuge on the far side of the world. And not forgetting my poor grandfather Jacob, bound to the floor of his shop. And my great-uncle, my great-uncle Jean patriot hero martyr, whose bounteous blood had permeated our land . . . ?

GLOSSARY

BAKOUA HAT: a straw hat whose form is indigenous to the French West Indies.

BÉKÉ: a rich colonial planter.

BOUDIN: sausage.

CHABIN (m.), CHABINE (f.): a person of black ancestry with light, highly freckled skin and blond or light brown hair.

CHODO: a vanilla cream drink the consistency of melted ice cream.

COUI: a kitchen utensil made of a calabash cut in half and cured.

DANSÉ LEWOZ: *the* dance of the French West Indies, incorporating both African and European forms.

DOMBWÉ (var. DOMBRÉ): small dumplings which look like unstuffed ravioli.

DOUCELET: sugar candy.

FILAU: the filau or Casuarina tree.

THE GWOKA DRUM: the tambour: a deep bass drum.

HABITATION: a family holding: an estate or plantation.

JAN GAJÉ: a night spirit.

KIKI: penis (slang) usually when referring to a child. English equivalent: weewee, peepee.

kilibiki: a sweet made with powdered cocoa and sugar.

KIMBWA: magic, obeah, calling up spirits.

LAKOU: a tenement; also, a tenement courtyard. Cf. Bob Marley: "Tenement Yard."

LIANA: a tropical vine.

LOLO: small shop selling notions and foodstuffs, usually

installed in the front room of a private house.

LYCÉE: high school.

MANGEÉ-LOAS: food offered to the spirits during vaudou or obeah ceremonies.

MAPOU: a name used to refer to several related species of trees, including the Corcho blanco or water mampoo, the light colored *poirier d'Antilles*. Locally, the *fromager mapou* refers to the balsa or Kapok tree, the *mapou royal* to the Ceiba or silk-cotton tree, and the *grand mapou* to the white manjack tree.

MATADOR: a Creole dress style combining African and European elements. Cf. Hawaiian "Mother Hubbard."

MIGANS: breadfruit hash or mush, staple of the West Indian diet, made of breadfruit, onion, bacon, pig's tails, cloves, garlic, ham, parsley, chili pepper and aromatics.

MODONGA: an African tribal group who in slavery were known for their dour and taciturn ways.

NORMAL SCHOOL: a school of higher education, usually in the humanities and for training teachers.

OBEAH MAN: a man who practices obeah, lays blessings and curses, summons and beseeches spirits, and concocts charms.

PISQUETTES: a small fish resembling whitebait.

QUERIDA: darling, dear one.

QUILOMBO: a fortress/kingdom formed by escaped or rebel slaves.

SANTERÍA: a religion combining African animist and Roman Catholic elements practiced in Cuba. Santería is present in the U.S. wherever there is a concentration of population from the Caribbean and northern South America.

SANTERO: a santería priest.

SEANCIER: an obeah man or woman. See above.

SINOBOL: shaved ice with flavoring: "snowcones."

SOU: a small coin.

SOUBAROU: a wild, unapproachable man.

SUKAKOKO GRAJÉ: a candy made of grated coconut.

TI-BWA: a small percussion instrument made of wood.

TONG TOY PARLOR: Chinese pleasure house and opium
   den.

ABOUT THE AUTHOR

Maryse Condé is the author of *Segu* (a bestseller in France), *The Children of Segu,* and several other novels. A native of Guadeloupe, she lived for many years in Paris, where she taught West Indian literature at the Sorbonne. She is the recipient of the prestigious French award Le Grand Prix Litteraire de la Femme, was a Guggenheim Fellow in 1987–88, and in 1993 was the first woman to be honored as a Puterbaugh Fellow by the University of Oklahoma. Ms. Condé lectures widely in the United States and currently teaches at the University of Virginia. She divides her time between the United States and Guadeloupe.

About the Translator

Victoria Reiter, translator of *Tree of Life*, of *Nana, Luna, Lola*, and *Vida* by the Swiss Next Wave writer Delacorta, as well as all the works of the French mystery/fantasy author Michel Borgia that have appeared in English, is a novelist and screenwriter. She currently resides in New York where she is at work on her next novel.

NON-FICTION

__ **ALEX HALEY: THE PLAYBOY INTERVIEWS**, Alex Haley	38300	$12.00
THE AUTOBIOGRAPHY OF MALCOLM X, As Told to Alex Haley		
___ *paperback*	37671	$12.00
___ *hardcover*	37975	$20.00
__ **BLOODS: An Oral History of the Vietnam War by Black Veterans**, Wallace Terry	37666	$10.00
__ **COURT OF APPEAL: The Black Community Speaks Out on the Racial and Sexual Politics of Thomas vs. Hill**, The Black Scholar	38136	$9.00
__ **THE HABIT OF SURVIVING**, Kesho Yvonne Scott	37676	$9.00
__ **INTERESTING ATHLETES: Black American Sports Heroes**, George L. Lee	38220	$5.99
__ **INTERESTING PEOPLE: Black American History Makers**, George L. Lee	37677	$5.99
__ **LATIN AMERICAN HEROES**, Jerome R. Adams	38384	$8.00
__ **SWEET SUMMER**, Bebe Moore Campbell	36694	$10.00
__ **VIBRATION COOKING: Or, the Travel Notes of a Geechee Girl**, Vertamae Smart-Grosvenor	37667	$8.00

FICTION

__ **CANTORA**, Slyvia López-Medina	38166	$10.00
__ **DAUGHTERS OF THE HOUSE**, Indrani Aikath-Gyaltsen *(hardcover)*	38073	$18.00
__ **DREAMING IN CUBAN**, Cristina Garcia	38143	$10.00
__ **THE FLOATING WORLD**, Cynthia Kadohata	38162	$10.00
__ **LONG DISTANCE LIFE,** Marita Golden	37616	$10.00
__ **MUSE-ECHO BLUES**, Xam Cartiér	37762	$9.00
__ **NO MAN IN THE HOUSE**, Cecil Foster *(hardcover)*	38067	$17.00
__ **TREE OF LIFE**, Maryse Condé	38469	$10.00
__ **WHEN ROCKS DANCE**, Elizabeth Nunez-Harrell	38068	$10.00
__ **YOUR BLUES AIN'T LIKE MINE**, Bebe Moore Campbell	38395	$12.00

Name_____

Address_____

City_____ State_____ Zip_____

Please send me the BALLANTINE BOOKS I have checked above. I am enclosing $_____.
(Please add $3.00 for the first book and $.50 for each additional book for postage and handling and include the appropriate sales tax.) Send check or money order (no cash or C.O.D.s) to Ballantine Mail Sales, Dept. OW (8–4), 201 E. 50th St., NY, NY 10022.

To order by phone, call 1-800-733-3000 and use your major credit card